# HIGH INFIDELITY

# HIGH INFIDELITY

*24 Great Short Stories About Adultery*
*by Some of Our Best Contemporary Authors*

EDITED BY JOHN MCNALLY

*William Morrow and Company, Inc.* • *New York*

Copyright © 1997 by John McNally

Additional copyright notices appear on pages 345–347, which serve as an extension of this copyright page.

All rights reserved. No part of this book may be reproduced or utilized in any form or by any means, electronic or mechanical, including photocopying, recording, or by any information storage or retrieval system, without permission in writing from the Publisher. Inquiries should be addressed to Permissions Department, William Morrow and Company, Inc., 1350 Avenue of the Americas, New York, N.Y. 10019.

It is the policy of William Morrow and Company, Inc., and its imprints and affiliates, recognizing the importance of preserving what has been written, to print the books we publish on acid-free paper, and we exert our best efforts to that end.

Library of Congress Cataloging-in-Publication Data

High infidelity : 24 great short stories about adultery by some of our best
  contemporary authors / edited by John McNally. — 1st ed.
      p.   cm.
    ISBN 0-688-15174-4
    1. Adultery—Fiction.   2. Short stories, American.   3. American
fiction—20th century.   I. McNally, John, 1965–   .
PS648.A35H54   1997
813'.0108353—dc21
                                                                                    96-37842
                                                                                         CIP

Printed in the United States of America

First Edition

1   2   3   4   5   6   7   8   9   10

FOR MY FATHER,
*Robert McNally*


AND IN MEMORY OF MY MOTHER,
*Margie McNally*

# ACKNOWLEDGMENTS

I WOULD LIKE to thank the following people: Joe Caccamisi, Bob Cowser, Tami Davidson, Dale Jacobs, Heidi Jacobs, Eric T. Lindvall, K. J. Peters, Scott Smith, and Brent Spencer. Thanks to Tom Beller for twice allowing me to crash at his apartment while visiting New York. Also, thanks to the proprietors of Lincoln's fine used-book stores: Scott and Pat Wendt of Bluestem Books, and Cinnamon Dokken of A Novel Idea. Thanks to my editor, Zach Schisgal, at Morrow for his optimism and encouragement. Also, thanks to my agent and friend Kip Kotzen of the Ned Leavitt Agency for helping out at every stage of this project.

# CONTENTS

INTRODUCTION    *xi*

ADULTERY    *Russell Banks 1*

THE WILD    *Sara Powers 25*

WHEN DOGS BARK    *Charles W. Harvey 44*

SECRET    *Ivy Goodman 57*

GOODNESS    *David Huddle 69*

MY WILD LIFE    *Abby Bardi 82*

FLIPFLOPS    *Robert Boswell 111*

A HOLE IN THE LANGUAGE    *Marly Swick 122*

IKE AND NINA    *T. Coraghessan Boyle 142*

BITTER LOVE    *Lynne McFall 154*

NO PAIN WHATSOEVER    *Richard Yates 165*

BUOYANCY    *Richard Russo 177*

CLEANING HOUSE    *Alyce Miller 201*

THE MIDDLEMAN    *Bharati Mukherjee 206*

HAIRBALL    *Margaret Atwood 224*

PIE DANCE    *Molly Giles 238*

THE FIRST SNOW    *Daniel Lyons 246*

SILENT PARTNERS    *Robley Wilson 259*

DICK YORK    *Max Garland 266*

SPATS    *Valerie Martin 284*

WHEN LOVE IN AUTUMN BLOOMS    *Gregg Palmer 294*

THE YEAR OF GETTING TO KNOW US
*Ethan Canin 304*

RAY SIPS A LOW QUITTER    *Amy Knox Brown 324*

THE LOVELY TROUBLED DAUGHTERS OF
OUR OLD CROWD    *John Updike 339*

# INTRODUCTION

ADULTERY, I SUSPECT, has been with us since the dawn of man. I wouldn't be at all surprised to learn of hieroglyphics on cave walls documenting infidelities and indiscretions, sketched by some woebegone or cuckolded Cro-Magnon. Apparently, adultery was a problem 3,200 years ago, when Moses stood atop the mountain and God proclaimed the seventh commandment: "Thou shalt not commit adultery." And how many people standing at the nether part of the mount must have quaked in their sandals at hearing such a proclamation? Not only could they not commit adultery, they could no longer covet their neighbors' wives . . . a victimless crime, one might think.

Nonetheless, God had spoken and laws were made. In Leviticus 20:10, the punishment was made perfectly clear: "And the man that committeth adultery with another man's wife, even he that committeth adultery with his neighbour's wife, the adulterer and the adulteress shall surely be put to death."

Harsh? Certainly. But the doling out of punishment in matters of sex and impropriety has always concerned people. For many, culpability is a black-and-white issue. One side is clearly right, while the other side is clearly wrong. Until recently, few have been able to acknowledge that a gray area might exist.

In Annette Lawson's comprehensive book *Adultery,* she cites Saint Augustine (A.D. 354–430) as one of the early theologians to recognize that gray area, and to acknowledge the ambiguity of adultery. In a scenario presented to Saint Augustine—a scenario that sounds very much like the plot of a recent movie—a woman accepts the terms of a "bargain" to sleep with a wealthy man who, in turn, has agreed to pay the woman's husband's back taxes, thereby saving his life. When asked if this incident constituted adultery, Saint Augustine claimed that it was a matter for the conscience of the individual. For Augustine, there were two separate issues, that of a person's "will" and that of a person's "lust"—a division that makes a distinction between *rational* and *irrational* behavior. In this instance, the couple was seen as rational, having thought through their actions, and were therefore far less culpable than the couple who simply engaged in an irrational lust-driven affair.

In 1516, Sir Thomas More published *Utopia,* his political romance about an imaginary island, and in Book 2, he outlines the laws of the island.

"[The new government will] punish adulterers with the strictest form of slavery," More states. "If both parties were married, both are divorced, and the injured parties may marry one another if they want . . ."

Imagine: the aggrieved spouses, victims of the same infidelity, actually marrying each other. Surely their conversations, their endless litanies of grievances would send guests running for cover. Fortunately, marriage between the injured parties is not a requirement. More offers it only as an option.

More continues: "But if one of the injured parties continues to love such an undeserving spouse, the marriage may go on, provided the innocent person chooses to share in the labor to which every slave is condemned. And sometimes it happens that the repentance of the guilty and the devotion of the innocent party so move the prince to pity that he restores both to freedom. But a second act of adultery is punished by death."

And so in Sir Thomas More's imaginary world, the laws are less severe than those found in Leviticus. At least in Utopia, you can screw up once before they put the ax to your head.

Skipping ahead four hundred years doesn't do much to diminish the stigma of infidelity. Maxine Hong Kingston's autobiographical "No Name Woman" examines an adulterous affair in China in the 1920s. In the adulteress's final months of pregnancy—a pregnancy that came about while her husband was away—the villagers, wearing masks, arrived at her residence and proceeded to slaughter her animals, ransack her house, and steal her food. That night, the woman gave birth. The next day, both she and her baby were discovered in the well, where, apparently, she had jumped.

Today—3,200 years removed from Moses—the laws and overt retaliation may have slackened a bit, yet an unspoken moral code still exists, and the lovers in an adulterous relationship often find themselves ostracized from the microcosm of friends and acquaintances in their day-to-day lives. We are a duplicitous people, though. On the one hand, we are quick to judge the sinners of indiscretion. On the other hand, we are attracted to the sin itself, and vicariously—through soap operas, sit-coms, novels, and short stories—we live our own lives chock-full of sexual impropriety.

Not surprisingly, great writers have always been drawn to adultery. Shakespeare returned to this theme again and again. In *Hamlet* the ghost of Hamlet's father, the king of Denmark, appears to his son, revealing the facts of his own death: how his brother had seduced his wife, the queen, before a vial of poison was poured into his ear. He says the following of his brother:

> Ay, that incestuous, that adulterate beast,
> With witchcraft of his wit, with traitorous gifts—
> O wicked wit and gifts that have the power
> So to seduce!—won to his shameful lust
> The will of my most seeming-virtuous queen.

Thus, with this revelation, the action of the play is set into motion.

If it's sheer volume of adultery that you want, read Shakespeare's *Antony and Cleopatra,* based on the real-life love affair of Marcus Antonius and Cleopatra, one of history's most famous adulterous couples. When it comes to dysfunctional relationships, Antony and Cleopatra set the standard. At one point, feeling he has been betrayed by Cleopatra, Antony calls her a "triple-turned whore," a reference to her adulterous romances with Julius Caesar, Gnaeus Pompey, and Antony himself, all while she was married to Ptolemy. The irony is that Antony spews this insult after he himself has cheated on two wives, Fulvia and Octavia. In fact, Cleopatra gave birth to Antony's twin children the same year his first wife died and he married his second wife.

None of Shakespeare's plays, though, explore the detrimental ramifications of adultery more powerfully than *Othello.* Othello, a Moorish general, is led to believe by his ensign, Iago, that his new bride, Desdemona, is having an illicit relationship with Cassio, the very man Othello promoted over Iago. There is never any tangible proof of Desdemona's infidelities—only a missing handkerchief—but it is *this,* Othello's not-knowing, that finally unravels him. *Othello* is a chilling play to watch or read—the nearly pure evil of Iago, the insecurities of Othello, and the innocence of Desdemona—a lethal triangle of characters, doomed from the very start of the play.

In American literature, the history of adultery has been rich, from Nathaniel Hawthorne's *The Scarlet Letter* (perhaps the first American novel of adultery) to the very stories in this anthology. As evidenced in the twenty-four stories here, adultery lends itself to a variety of themes and tones.

If revenge is what you're looking for, read Margaret Atwood's "Hairball," a startlingly original story that revolves around a spurned lover, a dinner party, and a cystic tumor. It is a contemporary Edgar Allan Poe tale of sorts, uncomfortably funny and eerie at the same time, yet by the end the reader can't help but think, *Of course she would do that. Perfect.* (I can't tell you *what* she does; you'll have to read it for yourself.)

Guilt and grief are characteristics of Marly Swick's "A Hole in the Language," the story of a woman who, after a child drowns in her swimming pool, falls into a relationship with the child's mother. Their relationship defies language—there is no word for what it is—and yet it is powerful enough for her to make a decision, choosing this woman, the child's mother, over her husband.

You may recognize a touch of Nabokov and Humbert Humbert's lasciviousness in David Huddle's "Goodness," the story of a sixty-year-old man who reminisces about the love affair he had, while in his forties, with a fourteen-year-old girl. (As a side note, if you want to read the same story told from the fourteen-year-old girl's point of view, check out David Huddle's "Past My Future" in *The Best American Short Stories, 1996.*)

In "Secret" Ivy Goodman explores the fantasy world of a woman who merely daydreams about a possible affair between herself and the man whose child she baby-sits, and though the affair takes place only in her mind, the weight of what she summons up seems, in many ways, no less powerful than if it were real.

Russell Banks returns us once again to Moses in "Adultery," which begins, "By the time I was nineteen years old I had broken all but three of the Ten Commandments. I'd made no graven image, had killed no one and had not committed adultery." Banks sets up for the reader a perfect beginning, immediately infusing the story with momentum, the necessary forward tilt of plot. Given the story's title, we know what's going to happen. What we don't know is how it's going to happen, or what the result will be.

Though adultery lends itself more easily to darker themes, some of the stories here are quite funny, as T. Coraghessan Boyle proves in "Ike and Nina," the "true" account, as told by Eisenhower's personal translator, of what really happened between Eisenhower and Nina Khrushcheva during the Khrushchevs' famous 1959 visit to the United States.

Some of the stories involve lovers who have either temporarily or permanently escaped their spouses to start homosexual relationships. In Robley Wilson's "Silent Partners," the narrator's wife has left him for another woman. In Daniel Lyons's "The First Snow," a son learns of his father's secret rendezvous with other men when the local newspaper prints his father's name. You'll meet Jethro—the outspoken narrator of Charles W. Harvey's "When Dogs Bark"— who goes well out of his way to deny to everyone around him, as well as to himself, that he's gay, though he takes up with a transvestite named Toni while on a trip to New York with his wife, Eartha Pearl.

Adultery is not central to every story. In some instances, it lingers on the periphery, as in Richard Russo's previously unpublished story "Buoyancy," which is more about the delayed effects of adultery and deception than it is about the adultery itself. In "Dick York," Max Garland's main focus is on the end of a long-term relationship, though at various points throughout the story, the narrator begins to imagine his lover having an affair, a convenient way of justifying why the relationship is coming to an end.

No adultery anthology would be complete without a story by John Updike. "The Lovely Troubled Daughters of Our Old Crowd" is a brief but chilling look at a man who has somehow missed the cause-and-effect relationship of his own actions as well as those of his "old crowd."

You will find here stories by many up-and-coming writers, including Abby Bardi, Daniel Lyons, Gregg Palmer, Charles W. Harvey, and Amy Knox Brown. Keep an eye out for their work. I am sure you will be seeing more from them soon.

In her introduction to *The Best American Short Stories, 1989,* Margaret Atwood writes that the ending of a good story should be inevitable, yet surprising. These stories succeed on that level, often giving the reader that chill of recognition at the end, when the story suddenly pieces itself together, perfectly and naturally, in the last paragraph or last line. And so I invite you into the underbelly of marriage, the dark side of love. If what people are writing about is any indication of what people are doing, everyone is either cheating on someone or being cheated on. The way I see it, they should have a good book on their bedside table.

BRABANTIO: Look to her, Moor, have a quick eye to see:
She has deceive'd her father, may do thee.

OTHELLO: My life upon her faith . . .

—Shakespeare, *Othello*

# HIGH INFIDELITY

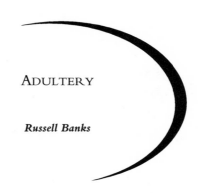

ADULTERY

*Russell Banks*

**RUSSELL BANKS** is the author of twelve works of fiction, including the novels *Continental Drift, Affliction, The Sweet Hereafter,* and *Rule of the Bone.* He has won numerous awards, including the O. Henry and Best American Short Stories awards, the John Dos Passos Prize, and the Literature Award from the American Academy of Arts and Letters. He lives in upstate New York and Princeton, New Jersey.

BY THE TIME I was nineteen years old I had broken all but three of the Ten Commandments. I'd made no graven image, had killed no one and had not committed adultery. On the other hand, I lied, did not keep the Sabbath holy, did not honor my mother and father, especially my father, and I stole—not much, but enough to count as a violation. I'd done it as recently as last week, skimming a few bucks from the night's take at the Thom McAn's out at the Pinellas Shopping Mall, where I worked nights. Selling shoes was a second job—I was saving a thousand dollars for my forthcoming marriage to Eleanor Hastings, an event I'd begun to imagine as capable somehow of washing me clean, like a baptism.

My marriage was going to be a Fresh Start. The new life would cancel the old life and create a new me, a youth who no longer coveted, like the old me, his neighbor's split-level house, his perky, dark wife who looked like Teresa Brewer, new Dodge car, boat, summer vacation, great angular height, Georgia accent. My neighbor was in fact my boss, Art, in the display department at Maas Brothers, where I worked days, a kindly, witty man who now rented the small, damp basement in his house to me. I coveted everything of his.

I could see, however, that my neighbor, despite his wit, was a depressed man, a man who was unhappy being who he was; thus I wanted to be him and yet somehow still hold on to the pleasure of being me, too. Perhaps that was the main attraction of the upcoming marriage. By starting my life over four months from now, I wouldn't have to give up my old life; whereas by continuing to covet another man's life, if I ever actually got what I wanted, I'd lose what I liked. Such was my morality, then, that I opposed, and preferred, early marriage to covetousness.

All this anxiety made me feel weak and stupid (which in turn made me feel something like guilt), but otherwise my having broken and continuing to break seven of the Ten Commandments did not especially trouble me. Not deeply. I'd been unchurched since before my mother stopped making me go to mass, and promises of eternal damnation were no more able to affect my behavior than were promises of eternal life. Eternal damnation and life were too hard to picture, like starvation in Africa or Nazi concentration camps, to make me afraid. This was America in 1959, and most of us were still dreaming versions of our parents' fading memories—the Depression, War Two, as my father and his friends called it, and the dying Roosevelt. Instead of fear, I felt incipient guilt.

The idea of breaking the three remaining commandments, however, I treated the way God must have intended I treat all ten, and I believed that surely, no matter what, those last three would go unbroken for the rest of my life. I knew that I would never, under any circumstances, construct a golden calf and fall down before it and offer bloody sacrifice, acts that seemed somehow sexual and, worse, perverse. And I could not imagine killing another human being. I'd tried to imagine it, killing was a big part of our childhood games, but my mind always snapped off, changed reels altogether, just as it came to my turn to kill the Oriental guy charging over the top of Pork Chop Hill swinging a huge Gurkha knife or machete at my throat, bowels, genitals and screaming Chinese Communist obscenities at my Caucasian manhood, mother and homeland. I always dropped my rifle and blacked out and woke up in another movie, a Preston Sturges comedy starring Rex Harrison as conductor of the New York Philharmonic.

As for adultery, my mother some years back, right after the divorce, had broadly hinted that my father had done it. But I never believed her. Not that I thought my father was an especially upright man; he just struck me as sexually unattractive, an ordinary man, like me, and, therefore, not available to women, except to my mother, whom I thought sexually attractive, certainly, but foolish. In my own mildly Oedipal way, I regarded my father as fortunate to have held my mother's sexual interest all those years before the divorce, and his marriage later to a woman who I felt was extremely unattractive proved it.

As for me, when I married, or so I believed, adultery simply could not occur, any more than murder. Though I was a virgin, I was otherwise a healthy adult male, and the idea of making love to one woman whenever I wanted (which was all the time, twenty-four hours a day) was almost too rich a possibility to bear, so that the idea of making love to *more* than one woman was sheer madness, and I avoided thinking it with appropriate diligence.

I was sophisticated enough, however, to know that one could also commit adultery while still single. One could make love to a married woman, for instance, some other man's wife. But this entailed my placing my penis where another man's penis had been, and that, too, seemed a kind of madness or, worse, perverse, like worshiping Jeroboam's golden calf. Perhaps it was our secret reason for wanting virgins for wives: to avoid sexual contact with other men. Regardless, I had never met a married woman to whom I felt sufficiently attracted that I'd risk enraging a husband, a man presumably older than I, since I was only nineteen, which I knew was young to be married, even in Florida. I might indeed covet my neighbor's wife—it was in fact one of the reasons I myself was getting married—but I would not allow myself to be attracted to her.

It was September, hot, sticky, thick with insects the size of bats, and always about to rain or else just drying off from rain, broad leaves dripping and shining in late-afternoon sunlight. We'd scheduled the wedding for January, to let Eleanor turn eighteen—not because we needed to meet the legal requirements (her parents were delighted to see her married, even to someone as young and unaccomplished and adrift as I), but because seventeen seemed too young to *me*. No matter that Eleanor had graduated from high school and was working full time as a salesgirl and bathing suit model in swimwear at Maas Brothers, where in the basement shop I made backdrops for window displays; no matter that for over four years now she'd been physically capable of bearing a child and was as healthy and attractive as a midcentury American female could get; no matter that she loved me deeply, wildly, absolutely, and would never love another; and no matter that I believed I loved her the same way. Somehow, despite all this social, biological and emotional readiness, the mere idea of regular sexual intercourse with a seventeen-year-old girl frightened me. No, I'd wait until she was eighteen; then I'd do it. Marrying and sleeping with a teenager (which, strangely, an eighteen-year-old woman was not) was something rock 'n' rollers like Jerry Lee Lewis and many black people did. Young white working-class males, struggling to move up by dint of hard work, pluck, luck and force of personality, waited.

By waiting, one honored a kind of taboo. One made a virtue of it. It was a way of getting ahead, like taking a correspondence course in accounting or TV repair. One felt virtuous. So that it never occurred to me that I just wanted to get into bed with Eleanor Hastings, that I wanted only to make love to her mindlessly for hours, then to fall asleep exhausted and wake and do it again and then again and not go into work the next day but stay in bed and sweat and stink and dry out and sweat some more, to empty myself out, over and over, for as long as it took to turn me into a husk, and then shower, dress, smoke a cigarette and move on down the road, maybe try Miami next, Key West, then the Caribbean.

No, I believed that I wanted a loyal and pretty wife, a lifelong companion, a woman to mother my children, and I thought that's what Eleanor Hastings wanted too, because if she didn't, if all that pretty girl wanted was to make love with me, then, by God, she was not fit to be my wife! And, naturally, there was no way I would make love to a woman who was not fit to be my wife. That was *not* how one got ahead in America. Look at my father, a carpenter in a New Hampshire mill town living with someone other than my mother, whom he did not deserve anyhow and therefore did not have. Life was hard and unequally so, but just.

Then one night late in September I drove my beat-up gray Studebaker out to the tract house in North St. Petersburg—a barren flatlands then, of shallow swamps, canals and cheap housing developments—where Eleanor lived with her parents and two younger sisters and brother. Eleanor's father installed ceramic tile for a living. He had been seventeen and Eleanor's mother sixteen when Eleanor was born, which made them thirty-four and thirty-three now—to me, practically middle-aged. They were Pentecostal Christians, deep believers. To my relief, Eleanor was not.

Their daughter's apostasy and my having been raised Catholic didn't trouble them, as it might have worried northern and more liberal Protestants. "The Lord will bring you to Him in His own time and way, children," her mother declared, beaming. "Meanwhile, we'll pray for you. Won't we, Dad?" she said to her tall, bony, grim husband. He smiled with only his teeth, small and yellow, the rest of his face remaining expressionless, and then they left us alone in the living room.

We were on the couch, side by side, feet planted squarely on the shag-carpeted floor. Eleanor's left hand was wrapped in my right, generating heat, but we got to the subject quickly, because time alone was rare and brief and had to be used efficiently. The sisters were at a church meeting for adolescents, and little brother was confined to his bedroom for having said "You shit!" to his bicycle when it fell over on him in the driveway and scraped his leg.

The subject was Eleanor's virginity, not a subject that I was in the habit of discussing, but all day and now well into the evening my thoughts had been looping toward the subject in an erratic, anxious way, as if it were a persistent back itch just beyond my contorted reach. It may have had to do with the late-summer heat, which reminded me of drive-in movies back home on Route 3 in Hooksett and Bow, New Hampshire, and dozens of high school summertime backseat thrashings, grunts and squirts and the crazed, self-loathing envy born of ignorance and male adolescent brag. Or it simply may have had to do with my growing awareness that I knew as little about Eleanor's past as she did of mine.

"All I know about you," I said, almost a lament, "is what I see and what you've told me."

"That's all anyone knows about anyone, honey. It's all I know about *you,*" she said in an accent that Gulf Coast Florida had laid down on her mother's Mississippi drawl, quickening Eleanor's speech without losing the dark, loamy vowels and soft, slurred consonants. My talk was merely that, talk, or so it seemed to me—ideas made over into sounds, feelings translated into symbols and emblems. Hers, though, was the thing itself—food and sunlight and rest. Thus we rarely had actual conversations: I talked, but she spoke, and I heard things, but she listened to them.

"For instance," I said, and cleared my throat, "I know you told me you're still a . . . still a virgin and all, and I believe you, of course. But there's something keeps nagging at me, a sort of intuition or something, and I can't seem to let it go, you know?"

"No, Lovey. What're you tryin' to get to?" I loved it when she called me Lovey. She smiled—large, green, deep-set eyes, long, narrow nose, wide mouth filled with perfect teeth. How could such a goddess love a human boy like me? Unless she was not a virgin.

Of course, I was right: she was not a virgin. She wept, amazed by my powers of perception. "How did you know? How?"

"I just knew you weren't," I told her, a great sadness in my voice. "I don't know how I knew it, but I did, all along. It's in your eyes, somehow, or your mouth. Something. But I couldn't deny it, I knew you weren't a virgin, no matter what you told me, no matter what I wanted to believe. And eventually"—I drawled it out—"eventually I would have found out the truth. It's not a secret a woman can keep forever. Once we were married . . ." I said, and I looked down mournfully at my hands, crossed over one another and open in my lap, as if waiting for a communion wafer.

I felt like a bag of water, but I held myself rigidly in place, kept my voice low and controlled, and when she tearfully asked if this meant that the marriage was off, I assured her that we would still be married, as planned, in January. "Nothing truly important is changed," I said. "I would like to know the details, though."

"Details? What do you mean, Earl?"

"Well, it does make a difference, you know . . . how you lost it, I mean."

"It does?"

"Well . . . yeah, of course."

"I don't understand," she said. "I'm very embarrassed, Earl. The whole thing is just . . . well, it's humiliating! It was so stupid, you know? It wasn't even any fun."

"I suppose if it had been fun, then everything would be okay now."

"No, of course not. Oh, God, I'm so ashamed! Don't make me tell you about it."

"Well, I really do need to know the details. It's important."

"How? Important to what? What possible difference can knowing the details make?"

I took a deep breath. "Well, I need to know, for example, how many times, how often you did it. I guess I need to know a little about the man . . . or men."

"Oh, God, it can't make any difference! Earl, I love you, that's all that counts!" she cried, tears streaming over her cheeks.

"No," I said. "That's not all that counts. There's other things that count too." I examined the palms of my hands.

"Oh." She thought for a moment, then shook her head, and fresh tears sprang from her eyes. "No, I *can't!* I just *can't* tell you! I can barely even admit it to myself!"

I was horrified. I imagined sexual acts so sordid and degrading that, for a brief moment, I forgot about myself and instead felt a flash of sorrow for her. But then, as she managed somehow to face down her memories and told me the story of her first love, a boy she went to high school with and who, on the night of the senior prom, got her drunk on screwdrivers and had his fumbling way with her in the back seat of his dad's car—as she told me this sad, sweet, guilty secret, I felt my sorrow and protectiveness gush from me, leaving me dry and empty and cold, a place where a night wind blew across a desert.

At the end of her confession, I stood. "Well, I have to leave now. It's . . . it's late, and I have to get up early for work."

She looked up at me, her expression a curious mixture of sadness and anger. "It's all over between us now, isn't it?"

"No! No, no, it's . . . *changed,*" I said. "But not over. We'll just have to talk some more, I guess. Not now, though. I . . . I have to think things over first," I explained, and I made for the door, before I fell down crying or threw up or broke my hand punching the wall.

She waved from the door as I staggered to my gray car, wrenched open the door and tossed myself inside. I looked back at the front door of the house, and there they were, Mr. and Mrs. Hastings, standing behind their eldest daughter, waving at me, up and down, sadly, slowly, as if they, too, knew Eleanor's secret, had known it all along and knew now that I had found it out and was in flight, the first of a long line of potential husbands to flee in the night, angry, betrayed, hurt and almost swindled by his own desire.

The problem, of course, lay in the incoherence of my desire. It was too tangled in chains of insecurity, pride, fear, anger and mother love to move responsibly through the lives of decent people. It was desire that was barely conscious of itself; consequently, I was able frequently to deny its existence altogether, which, at such times, made me wonder why I wanted to marry Eleanor in the first place.

I especially wondered it when in the presence of the wife of my neighbor, boss and landlord, Art Pitman. His wife was small, what we used to call petite, round-faced, with large, dark eyes and a bright, quick smile. Her name was Donna, and when I was in her presence, brushing past her in the hallway as I left for work in the morning, she, in cotton housecoat and fuzzy slippers, re-trieving the morning paper from the front steps for Art, who was in the bath-room shaving, I'd catch her smell, a spoor of bed and sweat and sex, and I'd feel myself go weak in the legs, grow cold and then hot, flush red across my face and ears and flood with desire as clear, undeniable and coherent as my desire for Eleanor was muddy, deniable and incoherent. I knew for certain that I wanted to make love to Donna, that and nothing else. I did not want to talk to her, tell her my troubles or secret fears or ambitions, I did not want to brag to her, I did not want to do anything except tear off clothing, draw back the covers of whatever bed was handy and have at it.

Who can say what prompts sexual desire of this sort? Eleanor, by any standard, was more conventionally attractive than Donna, and besides, she was my age, which Donna, in her early thirties, was not. If anything, the quality of my attraction to the two women should have been reversed—neurotic and subterranean for Donna, healthy and straightforward for Eleanor. But we dis-cover ourselves as we can, taking everything that's given us and knowing that it's still only a part of the whole, the tail of the elephant or the trunk or the wide, rounded side. We name the beast as precisely as we can, ass or serpent or whale, name it and move quickly sideways or back, so as not to get kicked by the ass, bit by the serpent, swallowed whole by the whale.

I seem to have spent a great deal of time that year in basements—all day long six days a week in the display shop at Maas Brothers Department Store downtown, and nights, when I was not with Eleanor or at the Pinellas Shopping Mall selling shoes for Thom McAn's, in my apartment in the basement of Art Pitman's new split-level house in West St. Petersburg. Real life seemed always to be going on someplace above me, while I toiled, mumbled, listened to the radio, worked, ate, masturbated, read, slept and dreamed below in my damp, dark quarters.

My apartment was a one-room efficiency with access through a common hallway and a first-floor exit, so I could not come and go without letting the Pitmans know, for I rarely came home after midnight, thanks to Eleanor's parents' rules, and I usually left for work in the morning a few minutes before Art. It was the kind of orderly, predictable, serious life that I believed was required of a person who wished to get ahead, and since I so desperately wanted to get ahead, wanted, as it were, to become Art, I did not find that life boring or particularly inhibiting.

Things were coming unraveled, however. I had just discovered that the girl I planned to marry was not a virgin. This did not surprise me, but it hurt and horrified me. I did not know, of course, that my hurt and horror were connected intricately to my abandoned mother in New Hampshire, to my father with his new wife, to the heat I felt in my loins as I lay in my bed in the basement and heard Donna Pitman cross the kitchen floor above me, her high heels clicking against the tile floor.

The loss of Eleanor Hastings's virginity meant that I could no longer idealize her, could not deal with her as an abstraction. It removed her, and therefore me, from ritualized sex, which was the only kind of sex that did not terrify me. But now there was a smoldering in the basement, a bubbling up of adolescent lust, a superheated midden heap of flammable materials wanting only a spark to ignite it. Trouble, terrible trouble, was coming, and I knew it better than anyone.

In my Studebaker that night, I was a madman, foot pressed flat to the floor, swerving from curb to curb as I cut across intersections, downshifting the clumsy, tired car, squealing the tires and racing on, through darkened downtown St. Petersburg and west, past Webb's City and the railroad yards and on out toward the beach and home. My eyes surely bulged, and my teeth probably gnashed, and my fingers clutched the wheel as if trying to strangle it, while my thoughts raved and roared, terror-struck at what now seemed inevitable, enraged at the girl who seemed responsible for having broken the dike, sabotaged the dam, loosed the flood. That *fool*! I thought. How could she have been so stupid! Didn't she realize, that hot, drunken night in May, that she would be responsible a few months later for keeping a wild man under control? Didn't she know that her virginity would be essential to his ability to function rationally in the world? How could she have been so *irresponsible*? It's over, I thought. Oh, boy, is it ever over now. Like Niagara Falls, it's over.

I yanked the wheel to the right and came to a bumpy halt at the curb in front of the house. Art's new green-and-black Dodge was gone from the carport, and the lights in the house were out. I got out my key and stumbled, as if drunk, to the steps and fumbled at the door, when suddenly it opened in as if on its own, and there was Donna, holding open the door for me and wearing, yes, unbelievably, but wearing it nonetheless, what appeared to be no more than a pink dressing gown tied at the throat with a pink ribbon, at the waist with a silken sash, and she was barefoot, I noticed at once, for I looked down as soon as I saw her there, and then I looked up and saw that her short, dark hair was tousled, tossed as if someone's passionate hands had held her head while he stared intently into her pouting, full-lipped face, her eyes half-closed, her nostrils flared, skin drawn tightly back over cheekbones. And, yes, reader, I committed adultery that night. I passed through the door and into the dark hallway, and took the hand of the woman who was married to my boss, a man who had kept me from being fired when everyone at Maas Brothers, it seemed, wanted me fired and had taken me into his home so as to facilitate my entry into adult life, a noble man, an honest man, and compared to me, an innocent man. That man's wife led me to her bed and kept me there for the entire night, until the sun rose, when I, too, rose and then descended to my basement room, where, for about an hour, I pondered the meaning of this event, while I showered, dressed and went whistling off to work.

\*   \*   \*

Throughout that long first night of rising and falling passion, we spoke almost not at all. At first, in the hallway, I asked in a high, windy voice, "Where's Art?" and she said, "Gone to Miami for three days . . . for the store." "Oh," I said.

A little later, she asked me if this was the first time I'd ever made love to a woman, and I said, "No, not really," and she gave a pleasant little laugh and started kissing me all over my hairless chest again.

When at last I left her bed, she said in a sleepy voice, "Earl, honey, you are the sweetest thing. I got to be careful you don't get to be a habit."

I nodded, as if understanding everything, but I understood nothing. I did *know* certain things, however. I knew, for instance, that in one night Donna had become a habit for me. At least, making love to her had. I still had no interest in becoming her friend, however. What I wanted near me, next to me, around me, was her femaleness, her smooth skin, breasts, nipples, dark thatch of pubic hair, hips, mouth, eyes, ears—I wanted to dive into her as if into a warm, enveloping body of water, to roll, curl and swirl there, floating free of time, fear, greed and dread, never coming up for air to the cold world of men and boys and futures that may or may not turn out well.

Dreams, fantasies, drooling, lascivious wishes, were all amazingly coming true. I rushed straight home from work the next day, and instead of going downstairs to my cellar to change clothes and eat and leave for Thom McAn's, I strolled casually back to the kitchen of Art and Donna's part of the house, and sure enough, there was Donna in a watermelon-pink bikini, smelling of coconut tanning lotion, her hair tied off her slender neck with a black ribbon. She stood at the kitchen counter painting her fingernails to match the bikini, her elbows resting against the Formica, hands like birds touching bills, lovely, small breasts hanging down like soft fruit, plums or tangerines. She turned and cocked her head when I came into the kitchen, smiled, then went quickly back to her nails, while I watched in stunned, admiring silence.

"What you staring at?" she asked without looking up.

I made an uncontrollable noise, "Uh-*huck*!" like Mortimer Snerd, put my hands in my trousers pockets, felt my thighs, and instantly took them out again and started cracking my knuckles like a gangster in a movie about to beat someone to death.

Donna stood back a second, admired her pink fingernails, and suddenly lifted one leg like a dancer and placed the heel of her foot on the counter and began to paint the toenails. I was tumescent. "You want a beer?" she asked. "There's some in the fridge. Get me one, too, will you?"

I grabbed a pair of cans of Colt 45, thrust one at her and wrenched mine open and gulped it down. She turned and watched me, caught me with my eyes filling from the effort of swallowing so much beer so fast and said, "You must be awful thirsty, honey."

"Yeah!"

She smiled benignly and took a ladylike sip from her can. "You got to work at that shoe store t'night?"

"Yeah!" I finished off the beer and crushed the can.

"Too bad," she said, going back to her toenails.

"Yeah! Yeah, it is!"

"You'd probably want to spend the evening out there with your sweetie, anyhow. Whatzername? Eleanor?"

"Yeah, Eleanor. But we . . . had a fight, sort of, so, no . . . no, I wouldn't be going out there tonight, if I didn't have to work. I'd just be hanging around here, prob'ly."

"Keeping me company?" She looked over and winked.

I made that noise again, "Uh-*huck*!" and grinned.

"Well, maybe I'll still be up when you get home," she said, and went back to her nails. "Art's coming home tomorrow," she added, throwing it in as an afterthought.

I swallowed and said nothing.

"You worried about Art?" she asked. "Finding out, I mean."

"*Me?* Hell, no!" I said, my voice rising. "I mean, he'll never find out. Will he?"

She laughed. "Light me a cigarette," she said, pointing with her chin to a pack of Chesterfield Kings on the table in the breakfast nook. I obeyed and placed the lighted cigarette between her lips, while she worked on her toes with both hands. "No, he'll never find out. You don't have to worry," she said, the cigarette bobbing as she spoke.

From a distance of about a yard, I examined her rounded, barely covered butt, her long, tensed flank, her calf muscle, and longed to run my hands along the length of her extended leg, making it quiver beneath my touch.

"But listen, honey," she said, bringing her foot down and turning to face me, hands on hips. "I got to warn you, Art's got one hell of a crazy temper, so we *both* better hope he never finds out. He may *seem* real quiet and all, but he'd shoot you, and then he'd beat the bejesus out of me."

"How . . . how could he find out?"

"Easy," she said. "If you told someone, down there at the store, say, Maas Brothers, and it got back to Art." She sipped at her beer and regarded me over the top of the can.

"Oh, I'd never do that."

"Okay, but let's say you got to feeling guilty about your sweetie, Eleanor, about being with another woman and all? When you're supposed to be engaged to her? So you get to feeling like you ought to be honest with her and clear the air, you know, like people do sometimes? So you tell her about me and you, and then she gets mad at me for taking her boyfriend, which I'm not doing, of course, but she wouldn't see it that way. So she goes and tells Art, sends him an anonymous letter or phone call, say? It happens, honey. Lots. You wouldn't believe what some women do."

"I'd never tell Eleanor, anyhow!" I said. "Are you kidding? Boy, tell Eleanor. Wow."

"Well, you better not, honey. It's got to be our little secret." She smiled, winked again, and as she eased past me toward the hall, leaned up and kissed me on the lips, quickly, but erotically, a brush, a pink flick of the tongue, and then she was past. "See you tonight?" she asked from the hall.

"Yeah! I . . . I'll be back around ten. Little after."

"That's real good. See you then," she sang, and disappeared around the corner and up the stairs.

I went to the refrigerator and pulled out another can of Art's beer and poured it down my throat. Then I headed downstairs to my basement to change clothes, pummeled, as I descended, by images of Art Pitman, huge, towering with rage, kicking in the door of the bedroom he shares with his wife, flicking on the light, me naked rising on my elbows, as if from the bottom of the sea, Donna rising naked below me, then both of us screaming, as Art pulls out his revolver and starts firing.

Ghastly visions did not keep me from committing adultery, however. Not that night after work at Thom McAn's and not one night a week later, when Art had to attend a convention of department store display directors in Atlanta, and not one Sunday afternoon a few days after that, when Art went fishing in his twenty-foot Boston Whaler with forty-horsepower Evinrude that I coveted. I avoided Eleanor at the store, but several times during that period she called my apartment, and we talked on the telephone, shyly, elusively, briefly. And then one Friday evening we agreed to meet, and the next day after work we met on the street outside the store and walked beneath live oak trees to the park by the library and sat down on the very bench where barely six months before we had pledged undying love to one another.

We observed that things had changed. "Do you still love me, Earl?" she asked, not looking at me. She wore a lemon-yellow blouse with a low, scalloped neckline that revealed her creamy throat in a way that made me catch my breath.

"Yes!" I said. "Yes, I still love you. That's not changed. As a fact, I mean."

"What do you mean?"

"Well, I guess that, while I still love you, I don't believe I love you in quite the same way, with quite the same . . . innocence."

"It's not you," she said, "who went and lost his innocence."

"Well, yeah, I guess you could say that. But anyhow, I do love you as much as ever. Just . . . differently, that's all." I tried to explain that since there'd been no quantitative change in my love, there'd been no essential qualitative change, either, but she started to cry.

"It's all my fault!" she said.

I put my arms around her and drew her to me. "No, no, Ellie, it's not. And there's nothing truly important that's different now. It's just that I'm a little confused about . . . about what to *do* now. I mean, here I've been holding back, you know, from making love with you, all these months of waiting and being frustrated and waiting some more, thinking it's all worth it because you're still a virgin and all, which is something a man's got to respect, if only because you're always saying, 'No,' and 'That's far enough,' and 'Wait till we're married.' Only now it turns out that there's no real reason to wait till we're married. I mean, with your virginity gone, what's the big deal? It's confusing. All of a sudden it doesn't make sense anymore to wait like we've been doing. Only I still don't feel right about *not* waiting till we're married. Know what I mean?"

"Yes," she said. "You're right." She had stopped crying and was kneading my back with her hands.

"I mean, what the hell? Right?"

"Yes. Right."

"I mean, why keep waiting? Right?"

"Right," she said. "I love you," she murmured into my shirt.

"I mean, why go on dealing with all this frustration?"

"Yes. You're right, Lovey. I agree."

"Yeah. I mean, it seems so . . . dumb. You know?"

"Yes. I agree with you, Earl."

"You do? We'll still get married, of course. That's got nothing to do with this, I mean. Right?"

"Right. Yes."

"Okay, then," I said. "Tomorrow's Sunday. Maybe I'll . . . maybe I'll drive by and pick you up while everyone's at church. Tell them, you tell them, tell them we're going to the beach or something. Okay? And we can come back to my apartment instead."

"Your apartment?"

"Well, yeah. I mean, it's where we can be sure no one will, you know, come in on us or anything. It's what we both want, isn't it?"

"Yes," she said, kneading my back furiously. "I'll make you happy, Lovey. I promise," she said.

"I'll make you happy too," I said.

\*    \*    \*

I didn't drive straight home, as usual, for food and to change shirts; instead, I went out to Thom McAn's early. Having rededicated myself to my plan to save a thousand dollars before Eleanor and I got married, I put in an extra hour, so we could that much more easily set up housekeeping in January in what I regarded as high style, a cinder-block bungalow in a new development by the Gulf—ten percent down, one hundred dollars a month, a carport for my Studebaker, a treeless backyard, sort of a front yard, asbestos tile floors, tiny metal-framed windows already rusting from the sea air.

While I drove and during the four hours at the store when I seemed to be selling shoes, I promised myself that I would never, ever, commit adultery again. I decided to announce this to Donna tonight, if possible, and though she might protest, though she might weep, though she might feel misled, betrayed and rejected by me, I would not relent. I imagined her beating on my chest, a part of my body she seemed particularly attracted to. I would hold her by the wrists, bring them slowly down to her sides, let go and say, "It can't go on any longer. I don't love you, I love Eleanor Hastings and will marry her." Donna, I had come to believe, did not love her husband. She loved me. That's what she had been telling me for several weeks now, over and over in my ear as she writhed beneath me, then in a lilting whisper as I rose from her bed to go, then with a little laugh as I stopped at the door and blew her a kiss. "I surely do love you, Earl," she kept saying. Her husband she referred to only now and then, but always with a sneer, as "that cold fish," implying impotence, and me she referred to frequently as "my little firecracker," implying, I reasoned, the opposite.

In any event, I arrived home from the shoe store fully prepared, rehearsed, even, to say goodbye to Donna and adultery and consequently was disappointed to see the living room lights on and Art's car parked in the driveway, bright green tail fins reflecting moonlight. I opened the front door and made straight for the hallway and the stairs down to my warren, when I heard Art call out from the kitchen. "Earl, will you come in here a moment?"

Must be something about work, I thought, something coming up unexpectedly at the store tomorrow. A fashion show, maybe. Happens all the time.

But when I rounded the corner and entered the kitchen and saw Art alone in the room, standing by the sink and facing me, his arms crossed limply over his narrow chest, his legs spread as if he would otherwise fall, saw the half-empty bottle of Jim Beam on the counter next to him, I knew what Art had called me in for.

I retreated to the doorway, and he studied me there as if I were of a species other than human, a creature oddly, inexplicably, dressed in human clothes, not a primate, even, and not comical, pathetic—a donkey with trousers. For a long time he examined me, neither of us saying a word, not even swallowing. I knew that I had turned white, and I was suddenly cold, as if an Arctic breeze had blown through the room.

"Do you want a drink of my whiskey?" Art said, his voice low and old, exhausted, depressed, resigned. His face seemed to have collapsed into itself, like a long-abandoned house into its cellar hole, and his hand, when he reached for the bottle, was trembling, an aged hand, I suddenly noticed, with large brown freckles, bulky knuckles and yellowed fingernails. He was a skinny man, and he'd always seemed dangerously sinewy to me, tall and angular and tough, but now he seemed fragile, off-balance, brittle and moving very carefully, like an old man. I could barely see in him the same man I had cheerfully waved goodbye to four hours earlier at the store, a man who had seemed like an older brother to me, or maybe a young father. This man was ancient, an ancestor, and here he was face to face with his descendant, a fresh-faced boy, healthy, strong, full of blood and muscle—and unutterably callow, a creature so unlike his ancestor that it was as if evolution had reversed itself.

To his offer of whiskey I shook my head no, like a child.

"You sure?"

I nodded.

"Well, that's too bad," he said. "That's a real shame. 'Cause I been waiting here for you, thinking we could have us a little whiskey and a little talk, you an' me. Know what I mean, son?" He sounded real Georgian, more so than usual, a country man keeping his thoughts to himself, a trickster. Except that the sadness that covered him like a shroud made him seem frightening. And frightened of him, instead of ashamed of myself, I did not know what to say, so I said nothing at all.

"Here, c'mon over here," he said, and he grabbed up the bottle and pointed with it toward the breakfast nook. "You slide yourself in there opposite me, Earl, so's I can take a good look at you. I want to see you up close for a change. Here I been working and living alongside you for close to a year now, and I ain't had me a good look at you."

I obeyed and slid into the booth and placed my hands on the table.

Art moved in across from me, set the bottle and a glass down before him and said, "How old're you, Earl?"

"Nineteen."

"Nineteen years old. That's about what I thought." He poured an inch of bourbon into his glass and drank half. "Know how old I am?"

"No. Not exactly."

"Not exactly, eh?" Art nipped at his whiskey as if it were hot, and he seemed to be thinking suddenly of something new, a lost memory unexpectedly retrieved. He furrowed his narrow, high brow and said, "I'm almost forty, Earl. Thirty-eight. That's exactly twice as old as you. I got bad knees from basketball and an ulcer since when I was practically your age, back up in Macon, but I expect I can still rip your lungs out, if I want to. You care to contest that, Earl?" he asked delicately.

I wobbled my head back and forth. "No. No, I . . . I don't."

"How old you think Donna is, Earl? Not that it makes one damn bit of difference."

"Look, Art," I said, and I opened my hands as if to reveal a message that would save me. "Look, I . . ."

"You shut up, son," Art said in a low voice. "You shut your goddamned mouth, and if I ask you a question, you just answer it to the best of your little ability, and that's all. You understand, boy?"

I nodded up and down. Not since my father left had anyone spoken to me that way.

"I asked you a question."

"Yes. Yes, I understand."

"Fine." He seemed to smile, like a snake, quickly, and then it was gone. He poured himself another inch of bourbon, and when he lighted a Chesterfield, I noticed, his hands shook. I looked down at my own hands. They seemed asleep or dead, dogs lying by a fire. A great peace had settled over me, unexplainable, necessary, healing, like a warm and soothing light after long, turbulent darkness. I could not understand it or name its source, but felt under no obligation to do so. That was its nature.

Art's mouth trembled, and he brought his face forward toward mine. "Boy," he said to me, "you have done got yourself caught messin' around where you don't belong. An old, old story, ain't it?"

"Yes."

"Not to you, though. It's a new story to you. Right?"

"Yes. Right."

He looked at me as if my face caused him physical pain. "Well, it's an old story to me," he said. "That's why I'm not mad at you. I should be, but I'm not."

"You're not?" I felt my chest tighten with anxiety.

"No. You're too young and too stupid, I guess. Too trivial, and you don't even know it. You're just an interchangeable part, Earl, that's all. I'm not even mad at Donna. She can't help anything. She's just who she is, that's all, and I know who she is. Always have. So it's *me* who makes me want to puke. For putting up with it. Well," he said, and he sighed and grimaced. "It's all over now, ain't it?"

"Jeez, Art, don't talk that way. I mean . . ."

"Just shut the hell up, will you, Earl?"

"Sorry."

"You're lucky, you know. At first, when she told me she'd been screwing you, I guess I wanted to blow your brains out, all right, which is pretty much what she wanted me to do, or she wouldn't have volunteered the information. That's how she does it, tells me about somebody she's been screwing behind my back and then sits back and watches me come apart. Puts a little spice in her life, I guess. But it don't work anymore. Even that don't work anymore." He was silent for a moment. Then he said, looking straight at me, "My daddy would've shot you and cut off your dick. And he would've shot the woman too. Donna. But he was a better man than I am," he said. He poured himself another shot and studied the glass for a few seconds. "No, that's not true, I'm just feeling sorry for myself. Truth is, I don't really care. About any of it."

"You don't?"

"Yeah. Haven't cared for years. Maybe never. She was always a bitch, and I was always scared of her. It was an ugly marriage from the start. No kids, even. Kids would've made a difference. I would've cared then. But she never wanted none, kept putting it off, kept saying she was too young, which in a sense is true. Anyhow, fact is, she's gone, and I don't give a damn."

"Hell, Art, maybe . . ."

"Earl? Are you listening to me? I'm telling you something here, something I want you to remember tomorrow and next year and on down the line. I'm not telling you because I happen to like you, understand. The opposite, in fact. I just want you to *know* that you ain't the cause of anything, boy. In my life, you're an interchangeable part. In Donna's life, you're an interchangeable part. So whatever happened, whatever happens from here on out, it ain't because of you. You're too puny," he said, pushing his index finger against my chest, "to make a man miserable or ruin a damned marriage that was already ruined anyhow. It was ruined at the start, like most bad marriages. You're too puny. Memorize it, son."

"Where's . . . where's Donna now?"

"Gone. She done flew the coop. Took off for her ma's up in Jacksonville, once she had her fun. Told me what she thought of me, which included telling me about you, since that's a big part of what she thinks of me, and I told her the same as I'm telling you. That I don't care about any of it. Never did. I been just going through the motions all these years. So if you forget about how unimportant you are in the big scheme of things, as you might, since you're a decent kid, you just ask Donna. You might someday want to think you mattered here, but Donna will tell you different."

We were both silent for a moment. Art drank, I clasped and unclasped my hands, swallowed, opened my mouth to ask the questions I needed answered but couldn't quite form, questions such as "What kind of person does what I have done?"

Instead, I said, "I'm really glad you're not upset . . . about me and Donna and all. I really am in love with Eleanor Hastings, see—"

"Jesus Christ!" he cried. "Will you get the hell away from me! I never should've called you in here. I got nothing to say to you. Nothing." He waved me away with his large, trembling hand. "Go on," he said. *"Git!"*

I got up from the table, and he repeated his command, as if I were an unpleasant dog. *"Git!"*

"I . . . I don't know what to say, Art. Except I'm sorry. I really am sorry."

"No. You ain't sorry one tiny bit. Except for getting caught. And that ain't sorry. But I don't care. So don't even bother saying it. You'll only grow up believing it, and that'll make you worse than a liar. Just shut your damned puny mouth and go on to someplace else real quick. Find yourself a new place to live tomorrow. And on Monday, start looking for a new job. You hear me?" He stared up at me, a sea beast surfacing, tears streaming over his long face, mouth gaping, eyes wild and suffering from a pain I was not even able to be frightened of. Though I could open my eyes and see it, I could not imagine it. And I could not imagine his pain because I refused to know what I had done to him.

It was twelve hours later, nearly midday, when, driving north toward Tampa in my shuddering old Studebaker on my way out to pick up Eleanor, as we'd planned, I was at last able to ask my question and answer it. Not fully, of course, and not even very clearly—I heard both question and answer as if through a wall, a muffled and ambiguous message from the lives of strangers.

I was coming up on a stop sign and glanced into the rearview mirror and saw my own eyes looking back, only, for the first time, they weren't my eyes, they were my father's, an adult male's blue eyes, scared and secretive, angry and guilt-ridden, eyes utterly without innocence. And instantly, they became the eyes of the whole species, belonging as much to Art and Donna as to my father and mother, and to Eleanor Hastings's father and mother as well, and even, in the end, to me and to the woman I planned to marry. I saw in that moment that every terrible wound they had suffered I could inflict, and every terrible wound they could inflict I could suffer—abandonment, betrayal, deceit, all of them. Our sins describe us, and our prohibitions describe our sins. I had broken them all, I knew, every one. I was a human being, too, at last, and not a very good one, either, weaker, dumber, less imaginative than the good ones.

The breath went out of me and then returned, and immediately my mind filled with images of flight. That's the kind of man I was. I would return to the apartment, toss the few boxes I'd already packed and my duffel into my car, cash a bad check at the corner grocery store and head north into Georgia and the Carolinas, or better, west, toward places like Arkansas and Oklahoma, places where American killers had been disappearing for centuries, fleeing not so much the law as themselves.

I drew the shaky car off the road to the right and shut off the motor and listened to it tick as it cooled. On both sides of the road was a marshland, treeless with clumps of palmettos growing alongside the ditches. The sun beat down on the car, and a slow, hot breeze cut through the open window, while I sat, hands in my lap, sweating and wondering what to do. I had no idea what to do with myself now, for I had never before regarded myself as a bad man, and now I did. Merely to feel guilty, I knew, was so insufficient a response to my new knowledge as to be practically a denial of the facts. I should have understood everything before last night, I thought. For the first time, I was afraid of the consequences of my acts in the right way, beyond guilt, but it was too late. I'd already become the person I should have been afraid of becoming.

Barely a mile away, Eleanor Hastings awaited me. I'd called her first thing that morning and told her only that I'd quarreled with Art over money and was going to move out of his house and would have to find a new job right away, so our plans to spend the afternoon at my place would have to be canceled. "But only temporary, honey," I assured her.

How would *she* respond to the facts? I wondered—for I knew I would tell her everything, about my committing adultery and about my talk with Art last night. I'd tell her about all the other laws I'd broken too, all the lying, stealing, and cheating I'd done, all the envy and covetousness, all the dishonor. I'd say to her, "Here! *This* is what's been hidden from you, this is what I've hidden from myself." I would show her who I was, and then I would ask her if she still wanted to marry me. And if she was foolish and desperate enough to say yes, I was ready to reward her by blinding myself to the most important fact of all, for I also knew at that moment in my car by the side of the road in North St. Petersburg, knew it on a Sunday afternoon in September of 1959 as well as I know it now a quarter century later, that I did not love Eleanor Hastings then, or before, and would not love her after we were married in January.

I turned the key in the ignition, and the old Studebaker coughed and caught, and a few moments later I pulled into the driveway of the home of the parents of my bride-to-be. She ran out the door, smiling, arms open, to greet me.

The WILD

*Sara Powers*

SARA POWERS received an M.F.A. from Columbia University, where she was a graduate fellow. Her stories have appeared in *The Voice Literary Supplement* and *Story*. She lives in New York.

FROM WHAT PHOEBE could see, which was the corner of the Econo Lodge building itself, the strip headed east. Its red illumined path led to the hospital and then to the hills humped on the edge of the town. They were just slightly darker than the sky, waiting at the perimeter of the valley like something just beyond the grasp of her mind. She was drunk enough to have pushed most everything out to that point. Her husband was asleep halfway to those hills, in the hospital, buoyed by layers of white gauze, opiated, floating just above the reach of the bear that mauled him.

The flat palm of the valley cradled her and the pool and the lights of the town. At the edge of the pool a couple was talking softly at a table. Its umbrella was folded and like a finger it pointed at the stars. Phoebe followed it up with her eyes and the water cushioned the back of her head. She smelled the rummy scent of her own breath as she exhaled; she gloated, she was alive.

Her plane had touched down in Missoula the day before just at the beginning of dusk, when the shadows crawl out of themselves, stretching from under bushes and the bases of trees. The air loosened the chill of the airplane from her clothes. She'd read a book about bears on the plane; this was the time that they emerged from the undergrowth to roam the darkness as it deepened, foraging the twilight. And later, after she'd driven her rental car to the Forest Service headquarters, the ranger told her that it was just at that time, the day before, that her husband and his girlfriend ("ladyfriend," the ranger put it, his weight resting on his hands as he leaned stiffly across the desk) had come around a corner on a trail that passed through a thicket of thimbleberry and had surprised a large, blond grizzly. He had pointed to a place on the wall map to show her where it happened.

It was on "blond" that Phoebe got stuck, as if the bear were a bimbo, were somehow the mistress in the situation. It made her drop her shoulder bag, and the manuscript of the knitting book fell out, and the bottle of Xanax that her friend Jane had given her that morning after she got the phone call. The ranger stepped out from behind his desk and picked up the bag and the bottle and the bundle of typed pages.

"I'm an editor," she said. It came out as some kind of apology.

The ranger sat back down at his desk. The grizzly, he said, had been feeding on what may have been her very favorite patch. They didn't have a chance. No trees nearby and nothing to do but watch the seven hundred pounds barreling toward them.

"Your husband's alive because when that sow reached him, and apparently she did clutch at him with one of her paws, he dropped and played dead. Just like we suggest in our brochure." His fingers tapped at a pamphlet on the desk.

She could make out the red letters upside down: GRIZZLY COUNTRY. Of course John had read it—he was scrupulous, overeducated. The back of her neck was aching and she had begun to sense that the ranger took a certain pleasure in the telling of the details.

"The bear took a swipe or two at him and jawed at his head a little but then she dropped him like she wasn't interested and turned her attention to his ladyfriend. We don't know what she did but apparently it wasn't the right thing."

Later, with her head cradled in the chlorinated bathwater of the pool, her toes just scraping the bottom, Phoebe closed her eyes and imagined the end of it, this crazy story that the ranger had been telling her.

Phoebe knew what the girlfriend looked like, because at the hospital in Missoula, the same one where she looked through a small rectangle of glass to view her husband wrapped in gauze and breathing placidly, that same tall ranger with his Yes Ma'ams and No Ma'ams brought her down to a small morgue to see if she could identify the body. Which she couldn't because she had never seen the girl before. The ranger hadn't understood all the complications then, but he grasped them soon enough when Phoebe insisted she did not know, had never known, the face above the turned-down sheet.

From what Phoebe saw (the face was strangely untouched; the eyes were closed yet the face wore an expression of faint surprise) she could picture the scene: John dropping into the fetal position, hands clasped behind his neck, elbows protecting his face, his skull exposed through his thinning fair curls.

The bear turning, almost in disgust, for the woman who was running, or standing and screaming, or shrinking in silence. And as he lay there he must have heard the dreadful crunches, the snuffling, the cries as his lover was killed. Though it was probably over, the ranger said, in two or three minutes, when John was found fifteen minutes later by hikers who'd followed them over the pass, he was still in his fetal tuck, afraid to move.

The hospital waiting room was decorated with only a large, plain cross. The nurse seated behind the Plexiglas had said, when Phoebe arrived, "I'm going to warn you, your husband is on a morphine drip for the pain, so he may not be too aware of your presence."

When she opened the door to his room he was staring right at her. The blueness of his eyes startled her as they did every time she had not seen him for more than a weekend. She was amazed at what she could forget about him.

Hello, wife, he said without moving. His head was still bound in white gauze, and tubes trailed down into his arms from a couple of IV bags. She couldn't see any of his wounds.

Hello, she said. How's the morphine?

Mmm, he said. He stared at her. She knew he was examining her, looking for some difference, the difference that he imagined must be there.

How do you feel? he asked her.

I don't know, she said. Displaced.

He lifted the IV tubing a little with one hand. Would you like some of my morphine?

She pulled a chair closer to the bed and leaned over him. She wanted to catch his smell, to remember him with her body.

Does it hurt a lot? she asked.

What? he asked.

They stared at one another. She wondered which way to take it. How did he want her to? He looked like a boy, she thought, vulnerable, harmless. As she watched him look at her, she felt, with a little surprise, how much she had missed him.

Thank you for coming here, he said. You could have left me.

She took his hand and twisted his hospital bracelet with two fingers. She'd never quite believed that he was her husband. He was more like, to her, the latest and the best in a series of best friends she'd always had.

You had to go and act just like a husband, she said. I suppose I should act like a wife now. I'm not sure I even know how.

No, he said, I don't think you do. It might be much simpler if you did. He spoke slowly, without moving much of his face—the morphine.

She sat for a while without saying anything. Something between them was out of balance.

She said, I thought that everything would be up to me to decide now, but seeing you I don't feel that.

That you would have the righteous position, he said for her.

Yes, she said. But I don't, do I?

It's the tragedy, he said, beginning to fade out. I walked through the fire. He managed a tiny, ironic smile before his eyes closed.

She stood up. I'm really pissed about that, John.

I know, he said with his eyes shut.

She went back downstairs and asked the nurse how long he usually slept.

The nurse put a finger to her pink lips, and then between her teeth. "I guess around dinnertime. That's when we wake them up."

Phoebe just stared at her. Outside the sliding doors the concrete gleamed. Everything was so bright here. The West in general hurt her eyes. She found her car and leaned against the hot door, resting her head on her arms on its roof. Her head felt hollow, scraped out.

"My husband," she said out loud. "My husband was eaten by a bear. And his girlfriend too."

It was no use. That word—husband—didn't mean anything to her. It was only John, her friend, whom she could reckon with. She realized, as her elbows burned on the hot metal of the roof, that John had things bound with him inside the morphine, secrets. He had the bear, would always have it, would know every instant of fear, each odor, of himself and then of the bear. She wondered if he had loved the girl. These two things that he knew, they would make all the difference.

*       *       *

She drove to the old part of town and parked. The streets were wide and nearly empty in midday, the buildings plain-fronted and low. On the corner there was a bar with the door open, and, next to a pair of moldy antlers, a menu in the window advertising corned beef and cabbage. She went in and sat near the far end of a section of vacant barstools. A man with longish, graying hair sat at a table in the back writing furiously into a notebook. Old men drank their beers and looked at her dumbly.

Phoebe ordered a hamburger and a beer, and sat looking at the collection of dusty bottles over the bar. Her hands rested in front of her, and as she glanced down at them she had the sense that they belonged to someone else.

She thought of calling Jane but realized it was impossible. What could she say? *I don't know whether to go shoot that bear or shake its hand. . . .* Around her the bar began to fill up for lunch. Someone put a song on the jukebox. She found the buzz and clatter of the place soothing, and when her food arrived it gave her something to do with her hands, which were still disturbing her, betraying her. I have to be careful, she thought, not to just sit here and get completely fucked up.

Someone sat down to her right and started talking to the bartender, who was roaming back and forth pouring beers. She looked up from her food. The guy next to her was young, with stiff, strawlike hair, and, she noticed, a tattoo on the muscular curve of his upper arm. It showed a heart with a belt pulled tight around it, squeezing it almost in half. A couple of drops of blood fell in an arc. How appropriate, she thought. A week ago she would not have understood it, would have, in fact, thought it ugly. Now she thought, a tattoo is like a scar that tells a story.

He caught her staring. "You like it?" His eyes were dark, almost black.

She nodded and turned slightly away from him toward her plate. She wanted him to know they weren't obligated to discuss it.

"I got it in Coney Island, New York City," he said.

"Really?" she said. "Coney Island." The noise, the heat, the smell of Nathan's, corn on a stick . . .

"You've been there?" he asked, turning on his stool to face her. There was something hard about his face.

"I'm from New York," Phoebe said. She began to eat her French fries, giving each one great attention.

"So what, are you out here on vacation?"

She looked over, a French fry halfway to her mouth. "No, not really . . . business, kind of." His face was acne-scarred but, she thought, handsome.

"Business, kind of. Well, that's intriguing."

"Not really," she said quickly.

Dishes clattered; dust rose and fell in the places where sunlight leaked in the windows.

"Are you from around here?" she asked, to get rid of the silence.

"You bet," he said. "I'm no New Yorker that's for sure. Montana born and bred."

"What do you do here?"

"Fishing guide, hunting guide, pack trips in the Bob Marshall Wilderness . . . Do you want another beer?"

She nodded.

". . . wildlife viewing, raft trips . . . whatever people are willing to pay for is what it comes down to."

"Wow," she said. "A real Montana type."

He narrowed his eyes a little. "I guess so. And are you a real New York type?"

"No. I guess. I don't know." She laughed. "What is a real New York type? Like Woody Allen?"

His smile was sudden; it warmed the hard lines of his face. "Are you a hard-boiled, executive-type woman?"

"No. I am an editor. I edit, like . . . knitting books."

"Pretty hard-boiled."

She felt him looking at her, and became aware that her hair was coming undone from the clip that held it back.

"Do you see a lot of bears when you're out leading trips?" she asked.

He shrugged. "Once in a while."

"What about bear attacks? You must know about them."

"City people are obsessed with bears," he said, leaning on his elbow on the bar. "And bear attacks. The more gruesome the better."

"No," she said. "I never was until I got here a couple of days ago."

"Old *Ursus horribilis,*" he said. "All tourists get the fever."

"About attacks . . ." she said.

"There's not much to tell—they're not that common. Bears are shy and just want to be left alone. I see them out in the Bob sometimes, from horseback usually, and they move away. They won't bother horses."

She drank. "When they kill someone," she said. "Do they eat them?"

"Anthropophagy," he said. "That's the technical term for it."

"How do you know that?"

"Newspaper term." He signaled the bartender to refill their mugs. Phoebe raised an eyebrow at that, but there were things she wanted to know.

"Sometimes they devour part of the corpse," he said. "But it seems that it's an afterthought, like, 'While it's dead I might as well eat it.' "

She thought of the girl. She hadn't seen much of her, only her face.

Across town, John was turning in his bed, troubling the sheets, his lips jerking.

"Somebody I know was just killed by a bear," she said, speaking toward the gold circle of beer in her mug.

He was surprised. "Out in the Preserve? You knew that girl?"

"Well, my husband did."

He was looking at her. *Sizing me up.*

"Is he the guy over there at the hospital?"

She nodded, feeling the tears come, the first.

"You didn't know her?"

"No."

"Did you know he knew her?"

She shook her head back and forth very slowly, no.

He was quiet a moment. "Wow."

She lifted her hands suddenly, and her knuckle caught under the handle of her empty mug, tipping it and skidding it across the bar. She set it upright and pressed her hands into her lap. She didn't know where to look.

He asked the bartender for a Jack, straight, and when the whiskey came he pushed it along the bar to her.

"I thought you needed this," he said.

She didn't like the idea of this guy buying her drinks. He was just trying to get her drunk.

"By the way," he said. "I'm Roger."

She looked away from the whiskey glass to him, and pushed a strand of hair out of her eyes. "Phoebe," she said.

"Go ahead," he said.

"I hate whiskey."

"It helps," he said. "I'll have one with you if you want." He got another.

Maybe he's all right, Phoebe thought. He was someone to talk to in these bad afternoon hours.

"Ready?" he asked, and they drank their whiskeys.

First the odor gagged her, and then immediately the fluid burned her throat.

"That's what it's good for," he said.

"What?"

"The pain it causes gets your mind off whatever else is bothering you."

The whiskey was already easing across her mind, smoothing it, warming her stomach, numbing her toes.

"What does that stand for?" she asked, pointing at Roger's tattoo.

"Well, it's a reminder of a girlfriend who almost killed me."

"How?" Phoebe asked.

"Well, you could say by proxy."

"By proxy?" *Like a bear.*

"Yeah. I was living with her in North Carolina and I found out some things about her, shit she'd been doing, and I just threw all my stuff in my old Honda and drove all night to New York City. Halfway there I lost the brakes on the car and had to drive the rest of the way downshifting at every exit ramp and stoplight. It was raining too, almost the whole way. I practically died a couple of times."

"So that's when you were in Coney Island."

"Yeah." He shrugged. "I only stayed a week in New York. I had no money."

"When was that?"

"About five years ago."

"That's when I got married," she said. "Five years ago." A simple thing, the word *married,* but it set a pain loose.

He looked uncomfortable. "Jesus, Phoebe," he said finally.

It startled her to hear him use her name. Without wanting to, she imagined them in bed together. She looked down at her legs in their black jeans, at their slimness. She couldn't remember the last time she'd been to bed with someone other than John.

And John, he was inside that concrete building with morphine dreams of his lover, of the sides of mountains, of the twig, the dirt that was all he could see with his face turned to the ground while the bear shook his girlfriend like a broken doll.

The place had emptied around them as the lunch rush ended, and Phoebe watched the bartender dipping glasses first in soapy and then clear water, his rhythm unchanging.

Roger played with his empty mug. "Good marriage, bad marriage? Do you mind my asking?"

"No," Phoebe said. "I mean, I don't mind."

Roger ordered them each another beer.

"I thought it was good. Now I'm not so sure."

"A lot of people cheat," he said. "That's why I don't want to get married. I don't want to be a cheater."

"Would you be?" she asked.

"Yes," he said. "I think I would."

Phoebe was drunk. She looked sideways at him. "Are there bears around here?" she asked. "I'd like to see one."

"Out in the Bob there are," he said.

"The Bob?"

"The Bob Marshall Wilderness. If you walk out of this bar and turn left you're facing it. Lots of bears in there."

"Grizzlies?"

"Grizzlies."

"Do they mate for life, bears?"

"I don't believe anything mates for life. I think bears have the same mate for several years anyway. Like people."

"Geese," she said.

"What?"

"Geese mate for life."

"Wild geese or domestic?"

"I don't know. I'd like to see a bear. Could I hire you to take me to see a bear?"

"Seventy-five for the day; I'll provide lunch. You want to see a bear," he said. "I'll take you to the Bob."

"How far is it?" she asked.

"A couple of hours. We can go tomorrow."

"I don't know," she said. "I should go to the hospital."

"It's up to you," he said. "And there's no guarantee you'll see one."

"I would like to see where one lives, at least. Spy on it."

"Read its mail," he said.

"Well, my husband's not exactly waiting up for me."

"Then bear a-huntin' we will go."


Later, steadied somewhat by a shower and the air-conditioning in her room, she lay on her bed.

What the fuck am I doing? She tried to focus on the larger situation. It kept coming back to one thing. She labored over it, as if it were some complicated sum she had to figure. I'm alive and she's dead. I'm alive and she's dead. It was like a scoreboard. *One, nothing.*

Unless of course he loved her. Then it's one, one. She gets a point for having his love, I get a point for being alive.

But what about the bear? When John's in there sleeping, who is in there with him? Is he dreaming about her, or about the bear coming back at him again and again?

"I know it matters," she said.
*"While it's dead, I might as well eat it."*

An hour outside of Missoula the land looked different. Darker; rougher. The air was a little cooler. Thick-trunked pines crowded the road. It hugged a lake, dipped and swooped along the shore; she could see mountains in glimpses on the other side. He turned off to the right, and the pavement soon turned to dirt. He didn't slow down and the truck bounced and lurched along the center of the narrow road. She felt a little sick from yesterday's drinks and the coffee he'd bought them and the driving. She had her window rolled down and air, heavy with unfamiliar smells, kept washing the mantle of damp heat from her skin. She rode like that, half hanging out the window, watching the trees march backward in the side mirror. Somehow it steadied her. She watched for flashes of brown fur between the trees, but the tree trunks themselves kept deceiving her, and it was difficult to focus while moving so fast. Her companion didn't say anything; he seemed content just to be driving, humming, slapping the steering wheel to keep time.

This was completely, totally reckless, she knew. She was looking for trouble. She wanted to be face to face with it. She turned from the window.

A deer stood in the road in front of them, its head turned toward the oncoming truck. Roger braked and slowed, and the deer leapt once and was out of sight in the bushes.

"Wildlife," he said.

The road they were on ended in a dirt parking area, where they stopped the truck and got out. Phoebe felt better when her feet were on the ground. Roger was pulling stuff out of the back of the truck.

Phoebe walked over to a trail that led across a small bridge and up a steep incline into the woods. A sign said: YOU ARE ENTERING BEAR COUNTRY. TAKE PROPER PRECAUTIONS. DO NOT CARRY ODOROUS FOODS. ALWAYS KEEP A CLEAN CAMP. STORE FOOD AT LEAST 15' ABOVE GROUND. AVOID SEXUAL AC-TIVITY IN THE BACKCOUNTRY. MAKE NOISE ON THE TRAIL. It terrified her. She thought of the tubes trailing from her husband's arm, the woman that lay in the hospital's makeshift morgue, and she felt herself losing her balance, listing, a dizziness swarming over her. She sat, where she was, in front of the sign. From the ground, everything seemed to loom over her in some gigantic, inhuman scale. Above the trees, which were not like the trees in the East, but were impossibly, ridiculously tall, she could see the peaks of the mountains. None of this was part of her life, she thought. *What am I doing here?* Everything she had done—getting in the truck with this guy, driving to this place that now seemed so sinister—all of it was so dangerous and stupid that, sitting there, she just gave herself up to it. She was tired, and she was frightened, and she missed her husband so fiercely that it felt like a knocking in her throat. She put her head on her arms and cried; over the sound of her own choppy breathing she could hear him slamming the doors, the tailgate, and the wind skittering across the treetops, making the trees gasp and rustle. There were grizzlies up there on the high slopes, nosing around the lakes, pawing at roots. She lifted her head and stopped crying. For a moment she felt them, a presence, almost an odor that was carried down to her on the wind. They were waiting. She didn't move, her whole body was straining toward it. Her heart pumped blood out the arteries to her extremities, and out again and back, and the blood that came back was different, was both exhilarated and terrified. Her body had caught the scent of something it knew in its deepest corners, like the memory of a shape contained in its own flesh.

He came up the path to where she was sitting and put a small backpack on the ground next to her. He carried a larger one.

"Ready?" he asked. He must have seen her red eyes, but if he did, he didn't say anything.

No Name Lake was about two and a half miles from the parking area. Roger said they would have a pretty good chance of seeing a bear there at a distance, maybe across the lake. The trail they were on climbed steeply through a forest of huge, ancient trees. Cedar and hemlock, he said. Even in the mid-afternoon it was like dusk in there, and cool, though they got hot from the climbing.

"I put a water bottle in your pack," he said. "Remember to drink, you're probably a little dehydrated."

He had told her that they wouldn't be likely to run into any bears in this part of the forest, at least not grizzlies. She thought he was lying, but it calmed her anyway. The trail followed a stream which was tumbling down in the direction they'd come. When the path swerved close to its edge, all other noises were drowned out by the roar. They didn't try to talk above it. They passed through swarms of tiny bugs like misty clouds in the muted light, and Phoebe began to wish for a break in the forest, for a vista. She wanted to place herself.

After half an hour they took a break. Phoebe sat on the mossy trunk of a fallen tree and drank greedily. The metallic, coin smell of alcohol leaked from her pores.

"It's not far," he said. Islands of sweat had spread across the front of his T-shirt. "It's beautiful. You're going to be amazed. It's a lake fed directly from the ice and snow on the peaks, they're all around, the peaks, and you can see the water running down into the lake."

"Why do the bears like it so much?" she asked.

"It's a source of water. Also the grizzlies feed on the berries near the edge of the lake, and they also dig bulbs on the slopes above it."

"What would it be like?" she asked, pressing the cool water container against her chest. "To be really close to a bear?"

"We might find out," he said, and then, seeing her alarm, he laughed. "Don't worry. We won't."

"I bet they smell," she said. "When they're that close."

"*That* close. Yes. And they have stinking, rotten breath."

They walked on. The trail got easier. A light-headedness, almost an elation, had entered her.

Was this how John and his girl had felt? Had they been companions? Did she walk behind him, feeling the sun on her back, watching the muscles of his calves lock and soften with each stride he took up the trail in front of her? How did all this fit into that word *affair*?

They were moving into a lower forest, pines, and the sun was more direct, hotter, but the air had a coldness. Roger stopped.

"See," he said. "These berry bushes are all stripped. Somebody's been here and eaten them."

She stared at the bushes empty of fruit. They were terrifying.

*Her favorite, her very favorite, patch of berries.*

The path was level, and they moved quickly. They could talk now.

"Have you ever had an affair?" she asked him.

He didn't answer right away, and from the back, and with his pack hiding him, she couldn't tell whether he was thinking about it or ignoring her. They'd somehow gotten used to each other though.

"I have," he said finally.

"Why did you?" The forest had opened up to brush on either side, and unfamiliar birds swooped in and out of the bushes.

"There are as many answers to that question as there are people," he said.

"I guess I mean why did he?" she said softly.

"You thought he was happy, the two of you were happy?"

"I guess I didn't think about it that much," she said. "Day to day."

They walked on.

"I'm stupid that way. Or stubborn."

"Most people only see what they want to see," he said.

"My husband told me he was going on a wilderness expedition. You know, adventure camp for boys."

"Well, I guess he did."

They had a laugh. "He did, he did," she said.

He pointed out a hawk, or an eagle, spiraling, carving a great cone of sky, high above them. She could see the steep slope of another mountain off to the side where the stream had been. It was now a blue-white ribbon at the bottom of the ravine between the slopes.

They entered again into a stand of trees and then she glimpsed water. They came out onto a rocky beach.

They'd stepped into a bowl the sides of which were mountains. Snow flashed on the tops, and white threads cut the green sides and fell until they disappeared into the trees. It was all perfectly still.

"Come on," he said, and they walked down the beach a little to some rocks.

They sat, and he pulled a couple of Hershey's bars from his pack.

"I always carry these," he said.

She bathed her feet. The water was numbing.

He put a hand on her thigh, and turned his head toward her.

She didn't move, looked straight ahead. She wasn't offended; strangely, she didn't feel much about it one way or the other. "No," she said.

He took it off a moment later and unscrewed the top of his water bottle. "It might make you feel better," he said.

*He could kill me. Right here on the edge of this beautiful lake. And then the bears could eat my body.*

He brushed the hair from her face.

*So be it.* "No," she said. "Please. It's all too much."

He turned away and put the wrappers and water in his pack.

"That would be too easy for you, wouldn't it?" he said. "Tit for tat."

"Yes," she said.

"Still, I'm very attracted to you."

"Please," she said. "My husband was just killed."

They both froze.

"What?" he said.

"I can't believe I said that." She put her head down in her hands. "Oh God."

"I'm not going to touch that," he said.

"Neither am I," she said, lifting her head. "Let's get going. I think I need to keep moving."

"All right. Let's find us a bear." He put out his hand and pulled her to her feet.

They left the shore of the lake and climbed partway up a steep, meadowed slope. There were colonies of tiny flowers everywhere. He stopped at a flat rock and took off his pack.

"Here," he said. "Sit."

He took an oval case out of his backpack and began to screw together a telescope. She lay back on the rock and looked up. The sky was a blue she hadn't seen before.

*No wonder John came out here.*

"It's funny," she said, toward the sky. "I think I'm finally beginning to understand my husband. I mean, the new husband, the one I didn't know."

Roger had the scope put together and he was slowly scanning the meadows above them, and the valley which held the lake below them.

"I have a good feeling about this," he said. "I think we're going to see one today."

"Do you?" She sat up. "I'm scared to see one. Even at a distance."

"I know," he said. "It's something else."

She stayed sitting, frowning at a strange, buttercup-like flower she had picked.

*It's the tragedy, he had said.*

They sat for a long time, an hour at least.

"Nothing," he said.

And, "I see deer, a big buck mule deer. Want to see?"

And there it was, a huge rack of antlers on its small head, just lying in the shade of a rock ledge, high on the slope of the mountain.

"I don't know what he's doing all the way up there," Roger said.

"He looks peaceful." She was tired; she lay back in the grass again.

Maybe it had been just a fling. Had her death changed that? Maybe he was thinking about her, but dreaming about the bear.

"Oh, Lord," Roger said. "Beautiful. Beautiful."

"What? What?" she said, sitting up.

"Two big beautiful grizzlies, a huge silvertip and a blond."

"Where?" She was yelling, squinting in the direction the scope was pointing.

"Wait, let me get them again. There they are, they're running together."

He moved over, and she bent her head, then hesitated.

"Go on," he said. "Before we lose them."

She put her eye down to the scope. It took a moment for her to see them. They ran into the center of the frame from a patch of trees. They were running almost side by side, unbelievably huge, and fast, their frames rocking, their big legs eating up the distances.

"Oh my God," she whispered.

They were running with an urgency that suggested a chase, but she could see no other animal, and she knew somehow that they were simply running— maybe to feel their own strength, the power of their great limbs. She jerked her head back from the eyepiece.

"Gone?" Roger asked. He was grinning crazily.

"Uh, no. I don't know. I lost them. It . . . they weren't what I expected. They were so huge."

"Bigger than you thought, right? Aren't they incredible?"

"Closer," she said. "They felt closer, like they could've turned, and come right at me."

"They're half a mile away at least," he said. "Let me see if I can find them again."

He went back to scanning the slopes below.

They were running up the mountain. For no reason, she thought. That's the thing, there's no reason. They were so much wilder than she'd expected.

Phoebe thought about the girl and about her husband, wondered what had passed between them as the bear dropped into her first charge. Whatever it had been, after the bear had turned from him, John had lain on the ground a few feet away, unmoving, beyond the frenzy. As she died he lay in his urine. Where would that knowledge leave him stranded? Phoebe thought, as below her in the green scar of the valley her own bears raced. Was it somewhere she could reach him?


The hospital was quiet and they felt like fugitives. In the elevator she squeezed Roger's arm through the sleeve of his jean jacket; he put his hand against her back. Outside the door to John's room, in the hallway thick with the smell of hospital food, they stopped. Roger put his hand on her elbow.

"This is as far as I go," he said. "You take care of yourself." He kissed her on the cheek.

"Good-bye," she said. For a moment she wanted to clutch at him.

He disappeared around the corner into the elevator bay. She opened the door to her husband's room.

The room was dim; it was evening. Her husband lay with his head turned to the side away from her, and she could not see if his eyes were open. She didn't know what to do for a minute. She put her bag on the floor and tiptoed forward. His lips made a sticky sound. His smell coated the sheets, the bed. Under his bandages he was unwashed and the sour musk of his fear was in the sweat on his skin. She pulled back the covers and sat on the edge of the bed. As it sank he moved a little.

"Hey." He didn't wake up.

"Hey, tell me about the bear. I want to know about the bear."

She needed to see what he was seeing in his sleep: the bushes bent with berries and haloed by a haze of pollen and sun, above that the green slope of mountain, the trail turning ahead. She thought the bear would be always just beyond the next corner, as if it were waiting for them.

She climbed into the bed next to him, gingerly holding herself close. Gauze covered part of his back. Putting her ear against his spine, she heard his heart. He let out a broken sound but didn't move. She worked the tape holding the bandage off his skin with her fingernail. The tape peeled easily away; underneath, the claw marks grew downward from his shoulder blades like bloody tendrils. Lying with her head an inch away from the gouged skin, she felt for his arm with her hand. Her fingers traveled down the smooth bunched muscle of his forearm until she felt the IV and the tape holding it in place. She peeled off the tape and slipped the plastic tubing from the flesh of his arm in one motion. Minutes passed; below the needle a shiny pool of liquid appeared. As each drop of the morphine joined it, it quivered, then broadened slightly on the polished floor.

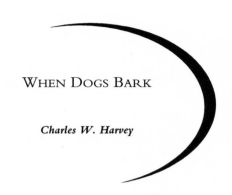

# WHEN DOGS BARK

*Charles W. Harvey*

**CHARLES W. HARVEY** has published stories in *The Ontario Review* and *Story,* and some have been included in several recent anthologies (*Go the Way Your Blood Beats, Soul Fires: Young Black Men on Love and Violence,* and *Shade: An Anthology of Short Fiction by Gay Men of African Descent*). He lives in Houston, Texas, and is finishing a novel, *The Road to Astroland.*

NEW YORK'S GOT two bad bad habits—she'll trip your ass up and she's one long stinking fart. I've been here three days and this place never stops belching and farting—buses, sirens, taxis, trucks, subways, jackhammers, mouths yelling "fuck yoooou!" New York sounds like it's been eating beans all its life.

I'm here with Eartha Pearl visiting one of her relatives, the cousin with the buck teeth. She wants to be an actress. But between me, you, and the woods I think she's only cut out for playing Bullwinkle's sidekick Rocky. I mean that girl can stand toe-to-toe with any beaver who decides some damn forest is in its way.

Eartha and this cousin get on my nerves after a few days of sitting in this tiny apartment—they doing that girl talk about men and me in particular—dishing up men's shortcomings. Stuff like, "I don't know which is uglier, a naked man or a baboon turned inside out."

Eartha Pearl: Some days I think I married a baboon . . .
Cousin: One man can outstink a whole herd of goats . . .
Eartha Pearl: I know one who can outsink two herds . . .
Cousin: And honey, not a brain in their heads . . .
Eartha Pearl: Lord, the biggest muscle *some* folks got is in their heads . . .

I growl softly at Eartha. She looks at me and hushes. Her cousin keeps jabbering away—those big teeth sawing the air as if it's wood. I begin barking.

"Oh Diane, I picked up a cute Butterick pattern for a pantsuit. It's virgin leather or something. I wish I could sew," says Eartha Pearl to change the subject. Eartha's cousin looks at me like I'm queer.

"It's just his nerves when he gets cross," Eartha says smiling as if she's explaining a puppy's bad habit. I get up and put on my shoes to go out. Eartha Pearl tries to establish her ownership rights to me.

"Who you know here? Where are you going?"

I say, "I got eight million friends here and ain't a damn one in this room!" I slam the door behind me.

Now by the time I get from the eleventh floor to the first, my mind kicks in. It must have been the blood on the wall on the fifth floor. My mind says, "Now Jethro, this is a crazy city. All of these eight million people ain't your friends. One of them will kill you if you let him. Go back!"

Naw. I ain't going back. Eartha Pearl and her cousin will just laugh at me. And I'd have to kill them to prove I was a man. I peep out the door and it looks innocent enough outside. Men and women passing by. Trash blowing in a circle. The sky looking like faded blue drawers. So I go out and sit on the stoop. I look east and I look west. Then I look west and I look east.

I say, "Now wait a minute, Jethro, you ain't gonna have no cultural experiences stuck scared here on this stoop. Suppose Columbus had just sat on a stoop all his life. Just suppose. Shit. A man must take action!" While I sit debating, this big white dude in chains and leather walks toward me. Now these chains ain't dainty little things you get from Spiegel's catalog. These chains come from the navy yard. I mean these chains can lift submarines. He wears three around his neck, five on each wrist, and two on each ankle. Now the chains do not bother me. The fact that he has on funky raw uncured leather does not bother me. Even the glass eye—I hope it's glass—dangling from his left earlobe on a chain does not bother me. What bothers me is when he turns in my direction and grabs his grapefruit-sized crotch and smiles—that's what bothers ol' Jethro here. I say, "Uh-oh Jethro, somebody wants you to swing a certain way. And I don't swing that way." I wonder why he pick on me? So what if I do have on these black high-top sneakers, shorts with Texas bluebonnets all over them, and a pink T-shirt that says, I BRAKE FOR MOONERS— that don't mean I'm gay. Shit. I'm just a colorful dude. Well okay if you want to count that time when I was in the eighth grade and me and Johnny Scardino grabbed each other's rods behind the gym bleachers. I wouldn't have gone back there with him, but he told me he had *two* and he would show me if I showed him mine. Okay it tickled and I got a hard-on when he grabbed me and I grabbed him out of reflexes, but I haven't *seen* Johnny since the eighth grade. I dreamed about him once, since I been married to Eartha Pearl. But I woke up and made love to Eartha real quick.

So anyway I hang my head and growl softly at the man in leather. He must think I'm calling him to dinner 'cause he moves a little closer. When I see him step, I bark louder. And not yap yap like a poodle either. I'm Doberman and Great Dane combined. I rattle nearby windows. New York people stare at me as they walk by. And they tell me you're doing something when you can get a New Yorker to stare at you eye-level on the street. The dude slinks away like he's carrying a tail between his legs.

I say to myself, "Damn, Jethro, my barking stuff is right on time. Damn if I'll ever let a head doctor take it from me. Fuck Eartha Pearl's suggestion." I get off the stoop and walk down the street barking my ass off. Nobody messes with me. Not even that gang on the corner with bones sewed to their leather jackets. I'm free as a pigeon. Do *I* stand up on the subway? Hell no! I have a whole car of seats to myself.

Eartha Pearl and her man-hating cousin never want to go nowhere. When it's daytime, they say it's too hot. When it's evening, they say they don't want to get caught out at night. And when it's night, Eartha and her cousin share the bed and give me a rug on the floor with my feet in the bathroom and my head in the kitchen. So I spend most of my time riding the subways and checking out the humanity that rides with me: Brothers singing opera or preaching Malcolm X; cripples on crutches hustling dollars—throw a dime right back at your ass; folks changing clothes—stripping down to their Swiss cheese drawers and looking indignant at you for looking at them.

The most excitement for Eartha Pearl was the suicide that jumped out the window of her cousin's building. Of course that was something to see. We hear this screaming in broad open daylight and look out the window. There's something spread out like a bloody chicken on a car's roof. Downstairs in the middle of a circle of people, a young white boy lies naked on the roof of a black Cadillac with cow horns on the hood. His legs are spread as if he's relaxing on a bed instead of frying in his own hot blood. The car's owner stands with his arms folded across his chest. Every now and then he kicks a tire or fender and yells, "Goddamn!" In a window above us, an old woman waves and screams like a hawk.

"Goddamn! What she want me to do? Throw him back up to her? Who's gonna pay for my car?" the car owner asks as he kicks a fender. Eartha Pearl has to have two Valiums and a bottle of beer to make her eyes stop bugging out and her hands stop shaking. So maybe that's enough for her. But I have to have something else. Something to make the blood rush through my heart like fire.

One day I'm sitting on the subway barking softly, but loud enough for people ten feet away to hear. I look up and see this sweet white chick in a pink leather miniskirt so high up her thighs she has to cross her muscular legs three times to keep out any drafts. So I stop barking and growl softly at her. I had heard that New York girls are the freest, and I love free samples. My friend C.C. said all you have to do to get a New York girl is to say, "Hello, I'm straight and AIDS free." I growl at her again. She looks at me. I see her glance down at my legs and look off, slightly cutting her eyes at me. She plays with a lock of blond hair that's curled behind her ear. I look down at my legs and have to admire them myself. I mean I'm no freak who stands in the mirror looking at my buck naked self and saying, "Oh daddy-o what a sweet daddy you are." But these legs always catch women. (They caught Eartha Pearl, who when she isn't mad at me, and when we're in the bed, runs her hand up and down my smooth brown thighs calling me "doll legs.") I ask the chick what time was it. "Tony," she says in a husky voice.

"Tony?" I ask.

"T-o-n-i," she spells out slowly.

"Well hey, forget about the time. All I got is time. I'm Jethro from Houston."

"I went to Texas once. Nothing was happening. Everything was flat and brown as a mud cake."

"Well you see, you hadn't met me . . ."

"I've met every man, Mister Dogman."

My brain searches for something clever to say, but my eyes stay on her smooth white legs twisted around each other—two long loaves of sweetness. I can see my legs twisted with hers—locked like a pair of brown and white fingers, soft, warm, and sensual. "What part of Texas was a chick like you roosting?" I ask her.

"Dalhart."

"Dalhart? Where in the hell is that?"

"You're from Texas. You ought to know, Mister Dogman." She flutters her lashes.

"What were you doing in Dalhart?"

"I was stationed there in the army."

"Baby, you don't look like any kind of army girl I ever seen."

"I'm not." Her answer is sour as a lemon. Something tells me I have parted my lips before I listened to my brain. Damn, Jethro be yourself cool, man. You don't want the pussy to turn cold before you even get to the front door. What would C.C. say? Shit he even gave you some of his glow-in-the-dark rubbers that he uses for special occasions like birthdays and Christmases. Can't let C.C. down.

"You look like a nice man." Toni's voice brings our eyes together.

There's a flutter in her lashes as if she's lying or has specks in her eyes. Her teeth are too big and her chin is too square for a woman's, I think.

"Ohh, so this is what's going down. You can dig this, Jethro," a voice says to me. "Don't look a gift horse in his big mouth. Guy or girl, a mouth is a mouth is a mouth." "Close your eyes and you'll like it better," Johnny Scardino told me once as he tugged my pants down in his warm oily garage.

"Well, I think I am. I mean I am nice. God knows I'm nice," I say. The sweat of my thighs glues me to the subway seat.

A young woman the color of ebony sitting in front of us glares at me. She has been reading a book, but the nervousness in my voice makes her look up. Her gold earrings shaped like Africa tremble. She looks at Toni and goes back to her reading. Suddenly she slams her book shut and folds her arms across her chest. When she gets off the train I see her look into the window at us and shake her head like we are to be pitied. She makes an ugly sign at me with her forefinger. Before I can make one back the crowd swallows her.

"Don't you scare off my cat, Mister Dogman," Toni says as she opens the door to her apartment. She led me to her place—inviting me to smoke some herb and have a little drink.

I step into a pink zoo. Pink stuffed animals are all over the couch and chairs—elephants, turtles, bears, lions. Two pink alligators perch on her bed, mouths open waiting to bite my buck naked ass when I drop my pants and Toni gets down to business, I think.

"You sure have lots of animals, baby," I say stroking her for-real white cat with pink ears.

"I like all kinds of animals."

"I see," I say looking at myself in the huge gold-framed mirror on the ceiling above the bed.

"Pull your shoes off and relax. I'll get us a little smoke."

"I'm cool as a cat," I say clearing my throat. For a moment I think I see Eartha Pearl staring at me from the ceiling. I bend over to pull off my shoes and my eyes fall on a small photograph in a gold frame. A square-faced white boy in an army suit smiles a toothy grin at me. My head starts to spin. I'm shaking all over as if an ice storm just blew into Toni's window. I stand up, but my feet are stuck to the floor.

Toni comes back and hands me a bubble-shaped glass of amber liquid.

"Sit, Mister Dogman," Toni says calmly. "Nobody's going to take you on a trip that you haven't made a reservation for." She sits a flattened-beetle ashtray on the table and lights the twisted end of a cigarette. She puffs, holds her breath, and hands the cigarette to me. While I'm hitting it, she gets up and puts a Jimmy Smith CD on the box. "This baby knows what's happening," I think to myself. A white girl in Houston had tried to entice C.C. with some country music guy singing "Them Ol' High Alabama Trees." C.C. said he couldn't make nothing happen.

Toni takes a hit from the cigarette. She smiles and asks me to dance. I take her hand and put my other one around her waist. Her back feels tight and muscled, not fleshy like Eartha's. We rock back and forth like a pair of old people. Jimmy Smith's "Midnight Special" and Toni's weed put me in a traveling mood. We start to glide all over the room. The organ's rhythm pulsates through me and moves down my thighs. Toni puts her face next to my cheek and cries softly.

"My whole family is gone away. I'm all alone, Jethro. What can a nice man like you do for a lonely one like me. Can you hold me? Can you squeeze the loneliness out of me?"

"Yes, baby, I can hold you," I say quietly.

We sit down and she sits on my lap. She feels heavy. Her wrists are thick, not thin and feathery like a woman's. Her lips are rough as work gloves. The whiskey and the weed soon lighten and smooth all of Toni's rough edges. Her skirt and legs have the same velvety tickle. She brushes my hand away from her crotch. I pull down Toni's bra and caress her small breasts.

"I'm so lonely. Are you a nice man?"

"Yes, baby, yes. Let me show you how nice I am. I'll take you to Kilimanjaro and we'll smoothly ride down the Nile. Just let me get on the train, baby. Just let me ride." That Nile and Kilimanjaro works with Eartha Pearl, unless she's in her hurry-up-and-get-it-over mood.

Toni reaches up and pulls a cord. The lights go out. "Can you put on a condom in the dark?" she asks.

"Baby, better than the queen can put on her gloves. I got my own." In the dark, my rod glows like a bright yellow banana. Toni's deep laughter fills the room. I curse C.C. under my breath. The cat's bright green eyes move side to side as he follows my swaying rod. Toni and I bray like mules. Then I smother Toni's laughter with kisses. I take another hit off the weed and the wheels of the train start to turn. I'm Casey Jones and I make train noises in Toni's ear. She throws her arms around my neck and kisses me. "Just drive your train, daddy. Just drive it. Just drive, daddy. Ooh daddy, just drive. Lord have mercy. Drive me, sweet daddy," Toni screams in my ear.

When I wake up, Toni stands over me with a bunch of cherries taped above each of his nipples. The cherries dangle juicy and red from their stems. He straddles my body. I pucker my lips around one of the cherries and pull it. Toni giggles like a young girl.

"Oh you're so much fun, baby. You're so much fun." I pull another cherry off Toni and eat it. I spit the pit toward the ceiling. It clatters to the floor.

"Ooh you animal," Toni softly scolds me. I pull a handful of cherries from Toni and stuff them in my mouth. "Ooh you big bad baby," Toni croons to me. "Give me the pits." Toni holds his hand under my mouth. I grab his fingers and put them in my mouth. Toni squeals and I pull him down next to me. We kiss.

"What do you want to eat?" Toni asks slipping into his short silk kimono.

"Pancakes and eggs," I answer.

"Again?"

"I like the way you lick the syrup off my chest."

"I like the way you like me to." Toni giggles and bounces off to the kitchen.

I look up at the ceiling at me staring at myself in the mirror. You don't look like no punk, I say to myself. You don't wear lipstick and false eyelashes like Eartha's "Aunt Don"—that fat sissy with his big feet jammed in pink high-heeled slippers. I spread my legs and look at the outline of my sex under the covers. Shit, I'm a man, am a man, am a man! I fuck. I like the Celtics. I work my ass off. I made a baby once. So what if Eartha Pearl lost it in an aisle of plastic flowers in the middle of Woolworth's? I still made it. She the one who couldn't keep him. Toni Toni Boboni! Why didn't I knock the hell out of you? Got a rod bigger than mine. And I can't leave. Why can't I leave? I'm not a punk. I don't walk funny. Johnny Scardino walked funny. Johnny Scardino kissed my thigh after he blew me. I just stood there. Just stood there like a statue. I'm not a punk. Lots of men take a side trip now and then. I can leave. Just get up and toss Toni a dollar or two and say later alligator. . . .

"Sweet, sweet honeydew," Toni sings from the kitchen. "I can't get over this pageboy haircut you gave me. Are you sure you're not a hairdresser? The girls at the ball tonight are gonna flip when they see me dressed like a man."

"I don't know about that bullshit," I answer.

"Are you still sore about the leash I wanted you to wear? I told you it wasn't racial."

"Always a nigguh got to have a chain around his neck," I answer.

"I wasn't thinking anything racial at all. I was thinking of your barking dog routine. We could really work those girls' nerves!"

"Well you're not putting a chain around my neck. You don't have to remind me I'm a nigguh."

"Oh Jethro, for the last time! That's not what I meant! If you hadn't given me such a hairdo, I'd shoot you!" I can see Toni staring at his hair in the reflection of his coffeepot. I look at the nightstand littered with marijuana roaches and condoms. I look at the gray tube of K-Y jelly squeezed violently by my own hands. I hate Toni and I want to beat him lifeless.

Toni brings the breakfast tray to bed. The fat pancakes are as smooth and brown as Eartha Pearl. "I can't wait to go shopping for our tuxes," he says. "Imagine me buying a tux! Me in pants. Girl, my friends . . ." I spit a mouthful of pancakes at Toni.

"I told you not to call me that." I grab Toni's arm and twist his wrist.

"Oww, baby! I'm sorry. I just forgot."

"Just don't forget again." Toni wipes the pancake from his cheek. He tries to kiss me.

"Let me eat."

"But you've got syrup all over you."

"And you've got shit all over you. So beat it!"

Toni bursts into tears. "Oh Jethro! Jethro, don't be so mean to me."

"Shut up acting like a sissy!" I shout at him. Toni stops crying. A tear rolls down his cheek. He sits with his cat in his lap. They both stare at me as I eat—Toni as if I'm a god. The cat looks at me as if I'm a piece of shit. "Sit with your legs apart!" I bark at Toni. "Men sit with their legs apart!" Toni parts his knees as if I've tossed hot coals between his legs. The cat falls to the floor, clawing Toni's thigh as he tries to hang on. It looks up at Toni and hisses before walking away. Toni shivers in the chair with his knees apart. I brush past him on my way to the kitchen. I stand for a moment at the sink and listen to him whimper and sniffle. A wave of sorrow washes over me. I want to hold him. (I'm the same with Eartha Pearl. When I hurt her and make her cry, love and remorse come up from the pit of my stomach. I get on my knees and beg her to forgive me. I kiss her thighs and hands until she rubs the back of my neck softly.) I walk over to Toni and put my hand on his shoulder. He stiffens his body at my touch. I gently soothe him.

"I'm sorry, baby," I say. "I'm so sorry." I wipe away the blood from his thigh with my fingers. He leans his head on my shoulder. His tears flow down my arm. I kiss him and coax him back to bed.

*     *     *

"Jethro, you've got to hurry! Will you come on! It's four o'clock and the stores close at five!" Toni races ahead of me wearing a pair of red platform shoes. His bell-bottomed pants hug his ass and dangle like loose pajamas around his ankles. His shirt with red and pink roses squeezes his body like a sausage casing. His steps are short and prissy as if he's stepping on spit. People raise their eyebrows at us. I try to walk far behind Toni, but he turns around and pulls me next to him. My head swims. All I see are flowers and eyes circling me—frowning eyes, arched judging eyes, eyes burning us like hot coals.

"C'mon, Jethro, c'mon," Toni sings to me over his shoulder.

Three young men dressed in gold chains and baseball caps pass me and Toni. I hear them snicker like mice. "C'mon, Jethro, c'mon," one mimics Toni's singsong voice. I look around at them. The darkest one tugs at his crotch. I start toward him. Toni grabs my arm. "No, baby, you'll get us killed!" Toni pulls me away. "Ignore them, baby. Ignore them. . . ."

I snatch my arm from Toni. "Stop walking so womanish and don't lean on me! Don't even talk to me." We walk on. Toni's shoulders are bowed. I've hurt him again. But all of this shame I feel. I'm hurting too. All of these eyes on me. "I'm hurting too, bitch," I shout at Toni. "Look what you're doing to me—dragging me through your fucking gutter! I don't want to go to some punks' ball. I don't want to bark my ass off for a bunch of queers. I want to go home, watch the Celtics, and play with my wife. She's got real knockers. She can't have a baby, but she's got real knockers!" I can see Toni shuddering like it's zero degrees. I feel a sharp pain in my tailbone. I grab my back.

"Hey faggot, that's how my ten-inch dick will feel up your ass!" I look around and a hurricane of bottles and rocks blow toward me and Toni. We turn and run. I feel the needle pricks of glass pierce my legs. I run fast and hard until I feel I'm reaching the edge of the world. It's not the bottles I'm running from. I hear a voice screeching like a wounded animal. "Pleeease stop, Jethro! Don't leave me, baby! Pleease! Pleeease!"

Honking horns drown the voice and I stop running. My legs feel as if they're wrapped in thorns. Every building is the same—tall, gray, and ugly. I imagine there are spirits flying out the windows and bumping into me on the sidewalk. I walk in circles and zigzags until I see the horned Cadillac. I look up into the faces of Eartha Pearl and her cousin looking down at me—mouths open like two screaming cats.

"And you just walk in from nowhere and don't say a word about where you've been. Just walk in like King Jethro and don't have to give nobody an explanation. Ha! We owes *you* an explanation about why we standing there with our mouths open. Lord have mercy," Eartha Pearl yelled at me all the way to the airport in the taxicab. "Legs all bloody. And then insulting my cousin the way you did. Lord have mercy. I know it'll rain ice cubes in hell before she invites us up here again. 'Did you screw my wife while I was gone?' What kind of question was that to ask my cousin?"

"All of y'all know she's a dyke," I say smugly.

"It's nobody's business what she is. And how dare a fool like you call her names. She was the one on the phone all day and into the night calling hospitals, morgues, city police, transit police in every county in New York."

"Boroughs. New York has boroughs."

"Bastard, don't you dare correct me! Girl crying herself to fits being put on hold, hung up on, and screaming into that damn phone and here a son of a bitch like you call her a dyke and try to talk back to *me*! If I had half the guts of Momma's Aunt Carrie, I'd gut you like a pig. Just like she did that husband of hers. Cut his roots off too! That's what a nigguh like you needs!"

The cabdriver laughs. I know what he's laughing at. Some vision of me running down the street without my "roots," blood running from a hole beneath my belly. I try to kiss Eartha Pearl. But she's on fire with anger.

"How can you kiss me after what you've done to me and my cousin? When I let you kiss me again you'll be so old and senile, you'll think I'm a man," she says with a sharp jab in my ribs.

Back in Houston a few months and the dust has settled, almost. I've gone back to work. The pain from the rocks and broken glass is gone out of my back and legs. Eartha Pearl has let me make love to her once. I've worn out my tongue telling C.C. about the hot chick I met on the subway, how she made me buck like a wild horse, and her fairy brother.

"Yeah man, her brother wanted to give me a blow job—but I drew the line there."

"Shit nigguh, uh-huh, I bet you did," C.C. says back to me. "I'da took him on and I know I ain't no punk, but turn down a blow job? Shit . . ."

Yeah I'm almost back to normal. If C.C. had said those words to me a month ago, I would have barked at him. But those words don't trouble me now. It's just, it's just that damn piece of paper that troubles me. I wish C.C. had thrown it in the trash instead of hollering out, "Well looky who's got them a letter from New York! Mister Jethro Green, Manager, Exxon, Baytown, Texas, United States of America—Lord have mercy! Manager? Nigguh, what you tell them folks in New York you a manager of? You manages that shovel all right though!"

I snatched the letter from C.C. The first word I saw on the envelope was TONY. I jammed it in my back pocket. "It's just that chick's nutty brother," I said to all the laughing faces around me.

"Ha! I knowed you was lying about that blow job," C.C. bellowed.

That damn piece of paper—I crumble and toss it in the trash, then sneak into the kitchen late at night and wipe the coffee grounds from it. I place it next to my heart.

Dear Jethro:

Please baby, Jethro, please call me. I love you. Here is some of my hair that you asked me to cut. Remember? I made it into a little bracelet for you. Don't that prove I love you? I thought you were going to be my life. You mean so much to me. Can you see the red tearstains on the letter? My heart is so broken my tears are red. I thought you were going to be my life. You loved me and made me love myself. Why did you run away? Please, please call me. 718-622-2169.

Love,
Toni
your love

Some nights after I read that letter, I go out on the back porch and I bark and bark until the far-off sky turns red like Toni's tear-filled eyes. And Johnny Scardino's phone number rumbles through my head—all sevens and a zero.

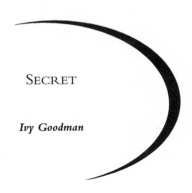

# SECRET

*Ivy Goodman*

I V Y  G O O D M A N's short stories have appeared in many literary magazines and anthologies. A collection of her short stories, *Heart Failure,* was published by the University of Iowa Press as part of the Iowa Award Series. She is currently completing a second collection and working on a novel.

"COLLEEN?"

She walked through the shallow water toward the dark-haired man who'd called her name. She held the sleeping baby in her arms. Afternoons, she took the baby to the town pool so her older two could swim and he fell asleep cradled against her with the water lapping at him.

"Hi, I'm Eric Falk."

"Colleen Howard."

"Yes, I thought so."

She could sense Eric Falk look her over with a downward glance, and she felt oddly innocent, even in a bathing suit. Her belly, like her four-year-old daughter's, swelled and sloped starting high up, with the added curve of her bosom just above. But her breasts were for the baby. When he woke from his nap, she would nurse him on the grass, under the cover of a towel.

"Colleen, the Canavans gave me your name, they said you baby-sit."

"I did, but I haven't for a while."

"We have a four-year-old son, Jamie, and I'm only asking for backup, a day or two a week. . . ." He looked at her as he spoke, not glancing off at the water or the sky, as she would have, nervously, if she were telling such a complicated story. He was a pharmacist at County Hospital, and he worked at night, but his schedule could be erratic sometimes, and on those days he needed help with his son. Their current baby-sitter was moving. His wife worked normal hours in an office downtown. Colleen listened on and unconsciously, behind her sunglasses, took the staring liberties that people took with one another's bodies at the pool. ". . . I'd leave Jamie in the morning, and my wife would pick him up by five or six."

"I don't know," she said. "Maybe I should think about it."

"You'll think about it? That's great, that's a start. Could we talk tomorrow? Will you be here?"

"If the weather's good."

"Then I'll look for you, Colleen."

Before he swam off underwater to the lanes at five feet, her memory seized on details that troubled her long afterwards, the sexy, toothy smile, the ripple of skin at his waist, the gray hairs on his chest among the mass of dark.

After Mike, her first child, Colleen, too, had gone back to work, but then she stayed home with both of them once Julia was born. Mike was three by then. When money got tight she began to baby-sit, and she kept on until her doctor told her to stop, halfway through her pregnancy with Josh. Actually, she asked him to tell her.

Only a day or two a week. Or three. Or five. And overnights. They needed you, they didn't know what they would do without you, and in gratitude they bestowed their child, who was all yours on your time.

Colleen waded back now toward Julia, who was splashing with friends in the shallows at the steps. Mike and another boy his age played nearby, at the side of the pool, endlessly hauling themselves out and jumping back in.

She liked summer and these suspended afternoons. She liked her preeminence in her children's world. With one asleep in her arms and the other two safe and lively, this was the joyous time before it ended in adolescence and beyond, before they grew up and blamed her, perhaps, for who she was and everything she was doing now.

There were good days and bad. On bad days she recalled what seemed the miraculous privilege, from long ago, of having lived the life of another person, a young woman who went to college, took a job, fell in love, got married, and then began those domestic rounds soon to be as ceaseless as the ant life her children exposed by overturning rocks in the yard.

But Tom, her husband, also worked long hours. At home he often answered her with annoyance and walked away from the older children's spats. And yet he'd been able from the start to endure a baby's crying when Colleen couldn't any longer, and soon the little one against his shoulder would be serene, beautiful, and vaguely amphibious, in infancy, with his eyelids closed. That night in bed, when Colleen asked about the Falks, her husband said of course they could use the money. He was a muscular man with a chest almost too thick to get her arms around. He hugged her close; his mouth touched her neck. Then he was breathing in rhythm with sleep, and she had to rouse him momentarily because her full breasts hurt in his embrace.

The next afternoon, she looked for Eric Falk.

It was an old pool, and every week or two, one of the lifeguards would squat at the rim with a bristle brush and a bottle of solution, brushing at a rubbery seal that was mildewed in spots, like the caulk used to fill the gap between tub and tile in people's homes. A number of tiles were broken at the edges. On the hottest days there was a smell of sewer gas from the drains. But to Colleen, who walked there with the children under huge leafy summer trees, past forty-year-old houses that offered variations on the same five or six, the pool was paradise when she came to it.

Inside the grounds, she spoke to Eric Falk on a steep, terraced hill where one could lie on a flattened lounge chair and yet be propped up by the slope. He was reclining with a towel over his belly. She sat on the footrest of another chair with the baby in her arms. Jamie, his son, and Julia, her daughter, her middle child, were running up and sliding down the turf on their bottoms. Now and then she glanced away to check on Mike, below her in the water.

She and Eric Falk made an arrangement, and through the summer Jamie came to her infrequently enough that he remained shy about her house, even about the toys. Colleen was happy to take him as compensation for other little ones she'd cared for in the past, boys who'd never obeyed without a threat, who went amok from the first, racing upstairs and down, emptying drawers and shelves, aiming to make a mess.

But Jamie was a good boy, as Colleen told his mother. The mother, Ellen, arrived straight from work, between 5:30 and 6:00. She opened her arms to Jamie, and Jamie, who was small for his age, would often jump up, wrapping his legs about her waist. She would run out carrying him, their faces gleeful together, as though she had stolen him back, not from Colleen, but from the hours of the day that had kept them apart. Colleen remembered that feeling herself, of having gotten away with something that nonetheless was hers by right. Years ago, she'd reunited every day with Michael, her first-born and a difficult, colicky infant whom she'd left at home with a baby-sitter so she could return to a job she didn't particularly like.

She was a big woman with long, blond, wavy hair, big hips, big breasts. Ellen was small and delicate and so artfully groomed that when Colleen saw her one weekend at the pool with her face bare, her lipstick rubbed off, she didn't know at first who Ellen was. She wore her short brown hair tapered in back and high and curly at the crown. Through long hours at her office desk and then a hot commute home in the car, she creased deep asymmetric wrinkles into her silk and linen skirts. But Ellen brought home a salary, while Colleen earned pin money at most.

"You remind me of Ellen," Eric told her sometimes, "that's how Ellen would think." He would lean back on his lounge chair, on the hillside at the pool, and Colleen would continue to perch for a bit. All summer, in good weather, they talked. At first, Colleen had wanted to stop by for Jamie's sake, to get to know him better. And also, like Ellen, apparently, she was motivated and troubled by social forms. After she'd agreed to watch the child, wasn't hello inadequate when she saw Eric Falk? And so she stopped at his chair.

He had the art of presenting his opinions as though she were on his mind, not so much whether he liked it—book, movie, or restaurant—but whether she would like it. "You should try it . . . you would enjoy it . . . it would be good for you," he said.

His skin was dark from the sun. His trunks were flamboyant and green, much greener than the grass. One front tooth glistened whiter than the others in his smile, and though he smiled at her, she wondered if he wasn't also smiling at his indolence and pleasure, reclining in that chair. But he moved and spoke more purposefully when he stood up. With his folded arms against his bare chest, he was defiant and self-protective at once. Walking, he brought his heels down hard on the grass and the deck around the pool. Who was he? How could she know him? She would need years and years, and then daily life could create the reverse effect of simplifying his character, as it had simplified her husband's, and hers, too, she would guess, in her husband's mind.

At night, in bed with her husband, she sometimes dreamed of Eric Falk. At the pool she went on watching and listening, balancing on her chair and tensing her legs to defeat the surface of warm plastic strips beneath her, designed, purposely or not, to entrap the flesh of a woman's thighs. Her few words to him had the quality of more careful balancing.

She was not a flirt. Sex was never something with whose secondary usages she was ever comfortable. When she was young, she'd been pretty enough, and yet she hadn't gotten ahead in life as a pretty girl. In the disillusioned aftermath of her first son's birth, she had come to look on sex with a kind of biological determinism. Desire prolonged the day when most nights she, and her husband, too, preferred to get in bed and go quickly to sleep.

But some new feeling was working on her, something abasing, unbidden, immoral, primitive, and almost comic, a constriction in her throat, a pounding in her chest, an anxiety that compelled its victim not to flee or fight, but to flee or copulate, to flee or at the very least touch Eric Falk, though she did not.

Did he know the effect of his kindness on her, even the kindness with which he said her name over the telephone, after his initial cantankerous hello? A few times she had to call about their baby-sitting schedule. Late one afternoon, she put the children in the car and actually drove to his house with a forgotten toy of Jamie's as her excuse. When Eric saw her through the screen, he said her name gently, with surprise, in that way he had, and opened the door.

So these were the Falks' things; this was how the Falks lived. Her own house held at least an equal weight of furniture, objects, and detritus that she often surveyed brutally and wished completely gone. But she was awed and rebuked by the ordinary mess at the Falks'. In time even a stranger like herself might learn where things properly belonged, but she would always be excluded from the way that things were left here, like relics in a reliquary, open junk mail, a heap of books, a dirty coffee cup, and a dirty paper napkin abandoned not by chance but with mysterious precision.

"Sit down, Colleen."

"No, thanks. We have to go. It's almost dinner time."

The forgotten toy was lost anew, back among the heap on the floor, where Jamie and Colleen's older children had begun to play, bumping cars and plastic figures with explosive sounds. But Colleen didn't ask Mike and Julia to get up. Josh, the baby, squirmed in her arms, but Colleen didn't move.

She looked at Eric, he looked at her, and her happiness seemed remarkable to her, apart from the happiness of her life. As usual, she wanted to touch him, his wrist, his shoulder, the spiky hair cut close above his ears, gray sprouting among the black. But she couldn't touch him, and by now she'd accepted her frustration as a force complementary to desire and akin somehow to gravity in space, keeping her and Eric together, at this exact distance apart.

He smiled at her, a sexy smile. But then she saw in his eyes that recurring, troubling hint of indelicacy, or irony, or conceit, the conceit of a flattered man. Had he intended nothing but playfulness all along? Had she fallen for a man who was only making eyes? Thank God she hadn't done anything, hadn't even said a word. Words were madness to a woman humbled again by sanity and relieved to have left no proof behind.

She held the baby tighter against her hip. She knew her desires were just illusions of self, self-fulfillment, or rather self-indulgence, tricking her for re-productive purposes. Early on, she'd had the feeling, illusory or real, that she couldn't help herself. That was the marvel; arousal had come over her like a blush. But then she began summoning it intentionally for the thrill, in public, in private, anytime, even now, a secret zinging of a body within her own, which she experienced especially in her breasts.

"Colleen, your shirt . . . your tee shirt is wet."

"Oh my God, my milk."

"It was amazing, the way the stain spread."

"Julia. Michael. Get up. Please. Now."

"Colleen, it's okay. I mean, Ellen nursed Jamie."

She couldn't look at him. His fingers, curled and compact, with black threads of hair below the joint, reached toward her arm, in comfort or restraint. But she felt only the momentousness; she was numb to his touch. Her face went hot. Her stinging nipple gave off the sensation of bearing thorns. On her hip, Josh grabbed her wet, ruined shirt with all the unexpected strength in a baby's fist. Another rivulet of milk ran down her ribs, and the thick elastic waist of her shorts soaked it in.

"Julia and Michael, right now. I'm leaving."

Behind her she heard the sound of a key in the door, and then the front door swung open as a voice, Ellen's voice, called out, "Hello? Anybody? Colleen, how nice!"

"Ellen. We're on our way. Jamie left a toy at our house." She shrank from the touch of wetness inside her clothes. All she wanted was to reach the door, but Ellen, smiling, blocked the way.

"What toy was that? Could he possibly have missed it?" Ellen held out a finger to the baby, dipped her knees to bring her face to his level, and then looked up, still smiling, at Colleen. "You mustn't leave yet. See how nicely Jamie's playing with the kids? You know, it's been a great summer because you're really good for him, Colleen."

"He's just a good boy."

"Then I'll take credit," Eric said, "if no one else will."

At the sound of her husband's voice, Ellen met his glance. They didn't speak, they didn't touch, they'd waited minutes even to acknowledge one another, but there was intimacy in their neglect. He asked, "How are you?" She answered, "Tired," in a lively voice. Her makeup still was bright, her perfume sweet and potent. If she attracted men at work, or felt attracted, wouldn't it be natural for Ellen—not difficult at all—and even good for business, camaraderie, and confidence? Ellen understood sex as a power that women have. But Ellen had done nothing wrong. Colleen was wronging her, if thoughts were wrong, and yet, if Ellen were to find out, the only real threat would be to Ellen's opinion of Colleen.

Eric stood beside Ellen with his arms folded across his chest, his legs apart, at ease, his mouth open slightly, expectant in the silence preliminary to goodbye. He'd been friendly to Colleen because he was a friendly man. But Colleen was irrelevant to his life, and she felt right then as if she had nothing of her own, no children, no husband whom she loved and with whom she was no less happy than she would be married to Eric Falk or any other husband. She did not want another woman's husband. It was over, it was wrong, it was all delusion, and the next time she saw Eric Falk, it would reawaken again.

She said, "Mike and Julia, we're going home."

She turned to Ellen, who just then blinked, looking around the room. Ellen's easy smile fell in what Colleen recognized, from often feeling it herself, as an expression of dismay, eyes widening, head slowly shaking, and then the furious scowl so misproportioned to any likely stimulus that it had to have been compounded from many similar furies in the past, brought on in the same manner and familiar enough only to be met again with ever greater disbelief.

"For God's sake, Eric, what have you been doing in here all afternoon?"

"What do you mean, what have I been doing?"

"I mean this mess, that's what I mean! And with company, too!"

Colleen said, "Please, not on our account, I didn't even call first."

Eric grinned, clapped one hand on Ellen's shoulders and once more filled Colleen with jealousy. "Ellen, we've been playing."

"Playing?" Ellen said. "And when do you clean up?"

Colleen bent to Mike and Julia on the floor. "If you don't come this instant, I mean right now, when we get home you can't watch television."

At home, she sat with the baby on the rocking chair near his crib, with the shades drawn against the sun. Dramatic talk and laughter came muted through the plaster and the intervening space between the baby's room and the den, where Mike and Julia watched cartoons. But even with the baby's mouth on her breast, she felt that she'd arranged for the children's care while she was gone, down into a dark narrow space like the crevice between a bed and wall.

This afternoon she'd lost her lover, but if he smiled at her tomorrow, she would have him back again, and neither love nor loss was real except as the irrational is real before it's judged neurotic or immoral or a waste of time in an ordered life that had been happy and still was now.

But if she kissed Eric Falk in hiding, behind a closed door, unattended children would break their arms and legs, tumbling downstairs. If her wishes became real and let themselves be known, she would bring on the end of her little world.

But of course she didn't really want him, and of course he didn't want her. Eric Falk? And herself? Ridiculous, like a fantasy confessed out loud, which nonetheless was taken with utmost seriousness, in secrecy, at the moment when it worked.

In her arms, the baby dozed, his lips parting, his tongue slowly pushing forward, until her nipple slipped free all at once and that tiny mouth set her whole breast swaying. Before the mirror, she was pitiless about herself, but a man's scrutiny, which she imagined as severe as her own, made her shy and self-protective of her flesh. And yet, she, too, was as cold as any staring man, though unlike him she could hardly make her appraisal in advance.

She felt she needed days alone with Eric Falk, not minutes in her own rumpled bed before the older children came in thirsty from the yard and the baby, in his crib, awoke from a nap. In her fantasies, the repeated motions of a single imaginary act, the soft bombardment of bodies against the bed, had blurred into the illusion, or the necessity, of the two of them endlessly making love.

She would prove insatiable; he would prove inept; no, she would prove inept. She feared her loving repertoire had become eccentric, refined through years of marriage to a man who'd learned, on his part, how best to please her. With another body in her arms, she would be lost, like a traveler awaking lost in bed, her internal compass spun round. She would feel somehow not herself, a lingering physical complaint that might lead her to the doctor, whose list of diagnostic questions was unlikely to include: Are you now having, have you had, or have you considered having an affair in the last six months?

God, no! With three children and a perfectly good husband? When would she have time?

She set out dinner in the August heat, salad, bread, and cold roast turkey sliced for sandwiches. It was leftover turkey for the third dinner in a row, but her husband did not complain. He came home from work almost directly to the table, with a pause to wash his hands. Julia's sandwich fell apart because she couldn't or wouldn't properly take hold, and as he helped her, she began to cry, while Mike interrupted with shouts of "Daddy, Daddy!" for attention and the baby threw squeeze toys from the tray of his wind-up swing, which ticked to-and-fro like a giant pendulum in a corner of the dining room where they ate their meals, now that there were five of them and the kitchen was too small.

That night, after the children were asleep, she got in bed to read. Her husband stood at the bureau, his head bent, a lock of sandy hair falling to his brow as he sorted odd crumpled bits of paper that he'd gathered in the course of the day—phone message notes, an office memo, cash register receipts stuffed in his pockets along with the change from the purchase of something like a cup of coffee or a chocolate bar. Tomorrow morning he would leave these scraps behind, for her to discard, when he once again took up wallet, keys, and coins.

He was a good man, she loved him, she felt she couldn't know him any better than she did, but maybe she didn't really want to know him better, and in this way she slighted his essentially unknowable human core. And he, on his side, treated her similarly with a warm disregard that offered her a privacy she was grateful for.

She lowered her magazine and laid it down beside her on the bed. "Tom, I have a question for you. I just was curious."

Distractedly, he went on studying the piece of paper in his hands. "Shoot. I'm listening."

"I wondered, have you ever thought, in daydreams, you know, nothing serious, of having sex with other women?"

"Thousands of times. What have you been reading over there?"

"And have you ever thought of someone else while making love to me?"

"Colleen," he said, almost angry in the suddenness with which he raised his head, "I would never do such a thing."

She stared back, and neither of them said any more. But later on, remembering that night, she wondered if her husband's severity hadn't hid a normal sense of shame, like hers, the shame of being found out.

Years ago, a man she'd known in college had asked about her fantasies, but she'd had none to tell; she was too excited by what actually transpired. She'd had lovers then, in college. She'd conformed in an era when lots of young men and women fell recklessly into bed. After marriage, surely after childbirth, she recalled her past adventures as thrilling mistakes she was glad to have made, back before she knew better, before it was too late.

Now she gave herself this questionable advice: wishing did not make it so; as long as no one else got hurt, you might pretend anything almost.

Eric's smile, Eric's glance, her name in Eric's mouth: vaporous signs excited her, as in girlhood when she stood in the presence of certain little boys. But she had a woman's foreknowledge now. Her husband touched her in the darkness, and she understood the source of her desires. A man with a soft hairy stomach was her Eros, her pornography, and she willed herself helplessly aroused. But she could not forget who was loving her, with his skilled, husband's touch, and in the daylight at the pool, in Eric's presence, she felt, more and more, a disparity between this man, an ordinary man, nearly a stranger, and those secret pairings of images and sensations in the dark.

The swim club closed in September, Jamie started school, and Colleen had no reason to see Eric Falk. At night, if his image answered her summons, there was added work ahead; they didn't please each other so quickly anymore. And gradually, like an ordinary affair, it faded away, nonexistent though it was. Once something unexpected had happened in her life without happening at all.

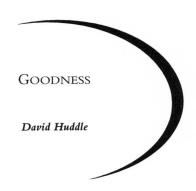

GOODNESS

*David Huddle*

D A V I D  H U D D L E's books include *Paper Boy, Only the Little Bone, The Writing Habit,* and *Tenorman.* He teaches at the University of Vermont and the Bread Loaf School of English.

WHEN I WAS forty-one, I had a fourteen-year-old lover who made me extremely happy. After some months she took an interest in someone her own age. I'm sixty now. The loss keeps coming back to me. Almost every afternoon, I find myself standing at my office window, hands behind my back and gazing out over the lake, so pierced by Marcy's absence that I envision myself bursting through the glass and sailing down into the traffic ten floors below.

Should I ever do such a thing, the sole person on the planet who would understand it is Marcy Bunkleman. She no longer lives in this city, but of course her mother would tell her about it within a day or so. Some comfort comes to me from knowing Marcy would be informed of my suicide. She would understand it, and she would be sympathetic. At fourteen, she felt things very deeply; she cannot have changed so much in that regard.

The person I miss was—technically at least—a child, and that person no longer exists. I suppose it must be that way with any former relationship—the people are not the same—but when your former lover has actually grown into adulthood, the change is drastic. I counsel myself that Marcy might as well be dead. Should I encounter her again (which is not out of the question since I am still on friendly terms with her mother), she would only vaguely resemble the person with whom I spent those enchanted afternoons in bed.

A jury of my peers would sentence me to prison. The prosecuting attorney would argue—successfully—that I had seduced the child. *Seduce,* however, is not the accurate term. I invited Marcy to have "an adventure" with me; she accepted. She was a highly intelligent person in full possession of her mental and emotional faculties. She made a rational decision. One may find the contract odious, but it was a contract nevertheless. It was made on a Saturday afternoon by her parents' swimming pool. My wife and her mother—who were close friends in those days—were sitting some distance away, chatting and tanning their legs. Her father—who is dead now—had made his usual excuse to remain indoors. Marcy and I sat side by side at the pool's edge, lazily splashing our feet in the water. Without thinking, I launched those words out into the sunlight, "Marcy, would you like to have an adventure with me?"

There was no premeditation in what I did or said. Ten seconds before I spoke, I had no notion I was about to utter words that would soon lead to Marcy and me regularly coupling. The adventure I had in mind was one of intimacy, but my conception was actually quite boyish. I wanted to be alone with her and to have physical contact with her, but until then—until I spoke those words—I had not even dared a sexual fantasy about Marcy.

I was, however, in the spell of her. I had witnessed her growing up. I had known her as a little girl playing with dolls and stuffed animals. Very early in her—what should I say?—evolution into humanness, I had come to know her. I've read the Nabokov book, which of course I found enlightening. I was relieved to discern that my attraction to Marcy was unlike Humbert's to Lolita. That man was generally drawn to young girls. I was specifically drawn to Marcy Bunkleman. Other girls her age were of no interest to me. What little contact I had with them led me to consider them insipid.

Marcy, on the other hand, from infancy on, possessed a lively intelligence that increased its brilliance as she grew older. She was exceptionally alert, and what set her apart was her calm attentiveness. Whenever I walked into a room with her, even before she could talk, her eyes focused on my face. She waited to see what I would do, what I would say. She watched me. It was eerie, actually, when she was very young, because I could tell in an instant when I had lost her attention. Her father had noted that quality in her, too. "She'll keep you honest, Robert," he told me once, when Marcy was around eight. She had been studying my face. When I fatuously asked her how she liked school, she simply turned her back on me and walked away. Her father shook his head. "She has very high standards for conversation," he said.

In the early part of my career, I did a good deal of traveling in the Far East. The presents I brought Marcy from Japan and India and Thailand appealed to her. She especially liked me to tell her "stories" from my travels, stories with children in them if possible. It started with my telling her about a Korean country boy, new to the city and lost on an elevator and trying each floor in the building until he came to the one where his parents stood waiting for him.

This anecdote had been conveyed to me by a man with whom I negotiated a number of transactions—as a story from his own childhood. Ordinarily when I traveled, I didn't see many children, and so for Marcy's sake I began asking the businessmen I met about their children. I watched families in hotels and on the street. I tried to engage waitresses and cab drivers and hotel maids in conversation so that they would tell me about their children. I confess that after I learned something I knew Marcy would like to hear, I jotted down notes so that I could remember it for her.

What I sought was Marcy's face turned directly to me; Marcy's eyes slightly widened and moving to catch every nuance of my voice, my expression, and my gestures; Marcy's pupils dilated—as if she wished to take my story bodily into herself. What I sought was Marcy listening to me—completely giving herself over—because there was such intensity in her attention. When it was a good story and I had reached a certain point in telling it, I could feel the air crackling between us.

I can't deny that her beauty, when she matured, had an effect on me. Even in my early forties, however, I'd had enough of feminine beauty. In her time, my mother was considered a great beauty. In high school and college I'd dated beautiful women. I'd married a beautiful woman. I did business with beautiful women. And so on. I don't mean to sound jaded, but I wasn't vulnerable to that aspect of Marcy Bunkleman. She was blond and lithe and graceful—a strong athlete in her school. She had high cheekbones and full lips and her nose took on a few freckles in the summer. If you dressed her in a cocktail dress with high heels and did up her hair, you'd have a stunning creature before your eyes. And even in her plain navy blue bathing suit, she was a girl who'd catch any man's eye. It wasn't her appearance, however, that drew me to her. It was that inner intensity, that power of apprehending me. With her face turned toward me, I felt like a god.

Recently watching an ice-skating competition on television, I saw the performance of a fourteen-year-old girl paired with a twenty-year-old man. The girl's body moved with poise and subtlety. When the performance was over and the pair sat waiting to receive their scores, the camera moved in for a close-up that revealed the girl to be fidgety and self-conscious. She didn't know what to do with her hands. Flitting across her face was one expression after another. Marcy had been far more refined than this child. Yet as I watched that young skater twitching and grimacing and half-smiling under the scrutiny of the camera, I experienced a slight memory of how I felt—as a whiff of a certain fragrance can transport one back in time—around Marcy. I'd never gotten enough of her. In my basement recreation room, by myself, watching a costumed girl on a television screen, I felt my neck burning with shame. It came sharply home to me that I had no right even to the few months of her life that Marcy gave me. Propped up on pillows and gazing at that girl lying beside me, unclothed, in a room full of sunlight, I was committing an act of thievery.

I am, as I say, sixty years old. It has been many years since I experienced anything approaching a godlike feeling. A certain objectivity sets in at sixty. Because time has revealed its shape, one is more and more inclined to look back on one's life. One's rise and fall are evident. In the London Gallery of Art there is a painting called "Time Orders Old Age to Destroy Beauty." That destruction is what I lived through in losing Marcy.

My wife, Suzanne, and I are soon to celebrate our thirty-fifth wedding anniversary. Many years ago we chose not to have children; therefore, as always, we will celebrate this September 30 by ourselves. Traditionally we spend the evening at the Lakeside Inn near Fairport Harbor. We have a meal that is very much to our liking. Afterward, if the weather is kind, we stroll through the Inn's beautifully landscaped English garden. We take our usual places on a bench that awaits us at a secluded overlook above the lake. Here we have what we jokingly call "our annual conversation."

Like many married couples Suzanne and I have fitted our lives together in such a way as to produce psychological comfort. We speak and act so as not to disturb each other. Sometimes at a party, I see Suzanne conversing animatedly with one of our friends, and I am astonished at what a lively person my wife is. I suspect it is the same for her—I've seen her eyes on me at cocktail gatherings. At such moments, imagining how I must appear to her, I've been surprised at my own gestures and speech. With each other at home, however, our voices and our personalities are habitually muted. So it isn't surprising that, once a year, when we are outdoors in the evening after an elegant meal, we find ourselves with significant matters to discuss. It was in this circumstance that we decided to put Suzanne's mother in a nursing home. Another year we committed ourselves to moving to a different section of Shaker Heights. And most recently we persuaded ourselves to review and update our wills. Rigorous as these conversations are, they nevertheless make us feel better about ourselves and each other.

Suzanne's and my seventeenth year of marriage was the year of my involvement with Marcy Bunkleman. I made discreet arrangements for an apartment where Marcy and I could meet when she was out of school. Afternoons when I was with her, a serenity and generosity came into my heart. I felt as I imagined saints must feel—transported, radiant, empowered. I aspired to serve Marcy with higher and higher levels of devotion. I began planning to take her with me to Hong Kong, where I thought it would be possible for us to live together openly. It was a mad notion, really, but just possible enough to entice my imagination. Over there I was very well connected; in that economy my skills and my reputation were highly marketable. I could make an extravagant "gift" of that city to Marcy. I even spoke to her, casually, of the two of us moving to Hong Kong and was pleased when her response was a high-spirited laugh. She took me to be merely entertaining a pipe dream, but I saw how easily I could persuade her to consider the idea seriously. So much seemed possible to me during the hours we spent together.

When I was at home, however, a malaise came over me. For this I blamed Suzanne. I couldn't avoid seeing how she exploited me day in and day out. Through my talent and energy, we were able to live in a luxurious manner; my wife was required to do nothing more than provide companionship to me. Yet when I returned home in the evenings, often exhausted, she would be on the phone with a friend, the living room would be unkempt, and she would not even have begun thinking of what to cook for our dinner.

Suzanne's background includes an education in Fine Arts at Oberlin. Her mind is excellent; her taste is highly developed; she is articulate and personable. Not exactly beautiful now, she was once thought to be so, and she has always been considered an attractive woman. She is considerate. She has a kind heart. She has devoted friends of both sexes. Never losing sight of all her positive qualities, I began that year to resent her so deeply that in her presence I often felt about to fly into a rage.

Suzanne seemed to notice no change in me. I kept myself under remarkable control—for several reasons, not the least of which was that I did not wish to arouse her suspicion. I also realized that she herself had not changed her personality or her habits. It was merely that with my mind and my heart full of Marcy, my eyes could only find fault with Suzanne. Marcy's taut lankiness was a harsh criticism of Suzanne's sagging amplitude. Marcy's energy mocked Suzanne's lethargy. And so on. In spite of how badly she came to appear to me, I was bound by an ethical awareness. Suzanne had become who she was—a placid, overly refined, physically slack, middle-aged, childless woman—in large part, because she had married me. If I hadn't actually made her into who she was, I had nevertheless given her license to become that person.

Such an awareness ought to have produced a higher sense of compassion in me. In fact it had the opposite effect. It deepened my resentment. I felt trapped in a way that I couldn't even protest or complain about. I became more and more divided. With Marcy I lived in springtime. With Suzanne winter seemed endless and inescapable.

I am an intuitively practical man. My business associates credit me with having a superior understanding of international markets—as if I devoted long hours to studying and analyzing the available data. I don't disabuse them, but the fact is I let myself be guided by instinct. If I have a difficult decision to make, I sleep on it, and when I wake up the next morning, I know what to do. Almost always I make intelligent decisions; often I make brilliant ones. I recognize that there is an unconscious part of me that solves the problems I face. I suppose I should give myself credit for being in touch with my intuition and using it. In my year with Marcy Bunkleman, however, I learned to fear that part of myself.

On September 30 of that year, Suzanne and I drove out to the Lakeside Inn as usual. For the past week I had been darkly moody around my wife, but this particular evening we were both in good spirits. On our drive out of the city, Suzanne related a telephone conversation she had recently had with Marcy's mother. Francine Bunkleman had confided that she thought Marcy was working too hard in school; she seemed to have no social life, and the only thing she did besides study was stay after school for soccer practice. "I told her that Marcy must be at the stage when there just aren't any interesting boys her own age," Suzanne said.

I glanced over at her, but she kept her face turned away, looking at something out her side window. Nevertheless, I couldn't avoid asking myself if she meant to inform me that she knew what Marcy and I were up to. Was she telling me that she knew and she wouldn't interfere? I tested that notion against my memory of Marcy's first visit to the apartment I had secured for us. Marcy had inspected the bedrooms, the bath, and the kitchen; she had called out a list of what sorts of snacks and beverages I should stock in the refrigerator. Then she had come over to the living room sofa where I sat waiting for her. Sitting down, she curled herself around to face me, laughed in the familiar way of our teasing, and asked if I wanted to make out. She intended to be mocking my nervous stiffness as well as my suit and tie, but that was the moment I discovered that I did indeed want to make out with her; that was exactly what I wanted. Remembering that first embrace and kiss with Marcy instructed me that the experience wasn't something to which Suzanne was giving her approval. She might have been warning me that I'd better not be up to anything with Marcy. But I decided she meant nothing; she was merely aware of how I had doted on Marcy for years and knew that I would be interested in news of the Bunkleman household.

As was our custom on our anniversary, we ate slowly, consciously savoring and commenting on our food and wine, but I was aware of wanting quickly to get through this part of our anniversary celebration. I wanted to move outside. Suzanne was attuned to my mood; she sensed my eagerness. All day the weather had been warm and clear. We knew the garden would be pleasant and fragrant. Indeed it was so. There was no breeze that evening, which meant that the scents of the garden's herbs and flowers hovered in the air as we strolled toward our bench. When Suzanne took my arm, I surprised myself by pressing my fingers over hers. Instead of sitting down immediately, I guided the two of us down the little path to a ledge above the cliffside that looked out over the lake. This, too, was a familiar spot to us. It wasn't much of a cliff, really, a drop of maybe thirty or forty yards down to a rocky little cove. But on that windless night, the expanse of water below had settled into a smooth glassiness that brightly reflected the moon. Immense space seemed to open up all around us; this larger dimension of the natural world was revealed to us without any of the usual haze or mist. I felt almost supernaturally powerful.

When Suzanne turned to me, I was in the throes of such excitement that I mistook what I felt for desire. I locked my arms around her and began to nuzzle at her neck—in my lovemaking with Marcy this was something that aroused her. When I did this—when I put my face right up against Suzanne's flesh—I experienced a brutal short-circuiting of my emotions. The woman I had locked my arms around instantly became repugnant to me.

I looked Suzanne straight in the face. "Robert," she managed to rasp out, "don't."

Her single word *don't* showed me what I was up to, what I had apparently been up to for the entire evening. We stood directly beside a knee-high stone wall that marked the edge of the cliff—what was probably the only cliff in the whole state of Ohio high enough to kill a person who fell over it. My arms were locked around Suzanne. At the moment, sufficient adrenaline had entered my system that I could easily pick up my wife and fling her over the edge. So the part of myself that had brought such success in my career had rather neatly solved the problem of what to do about the aging woman who stood between me and my young lover. I saw it—I witnessed that monstrosity within myself. "Don't . . . Robert . . ." Suzanne barely had breath within her to whisper because of how tightly I held her. She was begging.

God forgive me, I nearly did it anyway.

I didn't, of course.

I would like to say that some better part of me won out over the hateful schemer that had planned to dispatch Suzanne down to the rocks. In the immediate circumstance, I believed I was being merciful. I realize now that, even as I released Suzanne and helped her walk back up the path to our bench, my monster was still at work. For two afternoons in sequence, Marcy had mentioned the name of a boy at school. Her conversation had been so casual that I had taken little conscious notice of what she was saying. But my intuition had been alert. It had begun to discern that she was taking an interest in someone else—the boy whose name she had begun saying aloud. If I spared Suzanne's life, it was to avoid being alone in the heartbreak that was about to come to me.

"I'm sorry, darling, I had this sudden image of the two of us plunging over that cliff. That's why I caught you up like that. I hope I didn't hurt you." Those were things I said to Suzanne when I released her. "Let's go sit down. I feel dizzy," I said. And with elaborate care, I led her back up the path. "I might have had a little too much of that wine," I said as we took our places on the bench.

Once more we looked directly at each other. Across Suzanne's nose and cheekbones was a glistening of perspiration. With the evening's cool air on my face, I realized I must have been sweating a bit, too. Suzanne's eyeliner, eye shadow, and lipstick were in need of repair; her hair needed brushing. A scent emanated from her. In her face I saw that she knew. She knew how close to death she had been. She was taking stock. As she examined my face, she was carrying out a calculation.

"Golly," I said, shaking my head. "Wasn't that something?"

Suzanne took a deep breath as she sat there studying me, as if she were weighing what to say. Finally she spoke. "Yes, it was, darling. It certainly was." Her voice found its natural register. "What got into you?"

"I think it was the port." I used my droll tone—the one she would recognize as my effort to be witty.

We laughed. And we went back to our old selves. My wife and I sat on the bench in the moonlight, talking about one thing and another for quite some time before we rose and walked slowly back to the Inn to take our suite upstairs. As was our custom on our anniversary night, we made love.

There was a dark thing, though, that came to Suzanne and me in our moment by the cliff, that was with us in our lovemaking later on, and that has remained with us to this very day. How to say what it was, what it is? Something like a spirit or a ghost? Or perhaps a small, invisible, and deeply malicious child? It is not an entirely unpleasant companion for us. I relished its presence during the month that followed, when it became obvious that Marcy no longer enjoyed my company and that I had to release her from our intimacy.

Sitting on the bench with each other that evening, Suzanne and I realized we were going to spend the rest of our lives together knowing that I had nearly murdered her. She contracted to go on. I contracted to go on. That much I understood at the time. What I have come to discern over the years is that the terms were equal. If I had it in me to murder Suzanne, well so be it. She had it in her to murder me, too—or so I have come to believe.

It was never conveyed openly. Our invisible little companion has helped me to the understanding—my first suspicion came one evening when I was washing dishes and something prompted me to glance over at Suzanne drying the carving knife. Her hand seemed to clasp the handle in an odd way. Our eyes locked, and Suzanne's mouth took on the slyest grin, as if I had caught her in some mischief. She set the knife in its rack with a flourish. "There," she said. "All clean and dry." I heard the music of her voice informing me that she didn't care what I thought of her behavior. Also, I have become aware that late at night when I am almost asleep and she comes in to change into her night-gown in the dark, Suzanne often stands beside our bed, hovering over me for some moments.

As I say, at sixty a certain objectivity sets in. In the late afternoon in my office, I stand at my window, gazing down at the traffic and receiving into my heart these less-than-beloved insights. More and more twilight hours I wish I could just turn the machinery off. Nothing bloody or dramatic. Just switch off the old self like the car or the air-conditioning or the television.

The question that comes to me in these dimming hours is, where is good-ness? One of my first answers is that goodness is elsewhere, because it is cer-tainly not in me. Only the most deluded religious idiot would claim that to be so. And if not in me, then is it in other human creatures? Mother Teresa? Billy Graham? The tall Haitian lady who cleans my office and whispers, "God bless you, sir," when I leave the building each evening? It is very hard for me to believe that anywhere in the whole range of human activity there are acts of disinterested goodness. As I suspect myself—the man who chose not to murder his wife—so do I suspect my brother and sister creatures—my gracefully aging wife, for instance, who became more attentive to her domestic duties and who even now is preparing a dinner for me that may or may not contain a dose of poison.

It is all right with me for us to understand that either we kill each other or we don't—just as we either have sex with each other or don't. The reasons for committing or not committing the unacceptable act have very little to do with love or decency. I accept that circumstance. It helps me appreciate the blood coursing through my veins. Over the years, however, seeing things as I do has worn me down. My weariness relentlessly drives me back to the question: If goodness is not where it is usually thought to be, where might it be located?

It has been my privilege or my punishment to live among well-to-do people. Self-interest and deviousness are so starkly visible among my kind that it's a miracle we can stand to be around each other. At our social gatherings I half expect us to turn on our weaker ones, say, some bejeweled fleshy old dowager who's abused her power and demanded flattery for years but who is now failing. In someone's living room one evening, we'll simply rip this woman's body into bloody pieces. Savagery like that would make more sense to me than what actually does happen, that we tolerate grossly hypocritical and harmful behavior—not to mention the atrocities of our stupid, simpering conversations—for hour after hour, day after day, year after year. An acquaintance of mine—a former CEO of Euclid Steel who has devoted his life to exploiting hard-working people, cheating the poor, and degrading the environment—has a building named after him over at Case Western. Another fellow, a friend of Suzanne's family and a very civilized mobster, has recently received a liver transplant that will extend his life another half-dozen years; everyone in Cleveland knows this man should have been executed many times over for the pain and suffering he personally has brought into the city. These are my brothers; acceptable evil is our truth. It is the truth of me.

When the cars below my office window switch from parking lights to headlights, I know I have reached the hour of *l'addition, s'il vous plaît*. I must reckon with the bill. If things are as bad as I tell myself they are, then what else should I do but take a running start at the window and give myself over to the flying glass and the noxious air above St. Clair Avenue? If they're not so bad, then I might as well prepare the crisp five-dollar bill I have ready to hand the cleaning lady, get my coat and hat, and head for the elevator.

So what's it going to be tonight, Robert?

My answer is the usual one. *Home. I'm going home. I'm going home to my wife.*

As to the question of goodness—it isn't anywhere around this office, and it won't be waiting for me at my house—though likely an excellent meal will soon be set on the table before me. But I'll tell you where it was once. It was in the curious heart of a fourteen-year-old girl on a sunny day beside her parents' swimming pool, when she looked across her shoulder at me, wrinkled her nose, squinted her eyes, and said, "Yes." It was right there about half a hand's length away from me. Goodness was there—and I was clasping after it—when Marcy Bunkleman looked me straight in the face and said, "Yes, Robert, I'd like that very much."

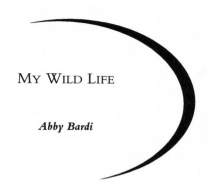

# MY WILD LIFE

*Abby Bardi*

**ABBY BARDI** spent almost a decade in Okinawa and England, and now lives in Maryland, where she is an associate professor of writing at Prince Georges Community College. She is a founding member of the Baltimore-Washington Songwriters' Guild, and contributed two songs to its recent CD, *Little Visions*. "My Wild Life" won an AWP Intro Award for fiction in 1995.

IT DIDN'T TAKE me long to find out that he had a wife. That first night, he came alone, and again on the next. I could see him at the side of the ring. All of that second night, I watched him out of the corner of my eye, and even when I went into the lion's cage, he never stopped smiling.

It was the third night that he brought her, and by that time we had already been everything a man and a woman could be to each other. The wife sat beside him, and even though she didn't know me, when I put my head into Trixie's mouth, I think she fainted. I saw her slumped beside him when I took my head out again. Of course, many women did faint in those days, before the War, and we used to have a laugh about it. How were they to know Trixie had scarcely any teeth?

I never knew her name. I never asked, and he never told me—never mentioned her at all, in fact. We were there four nights—they loved us in Colchester—and on the fourth night, she came again, and this time she didn't faint, or if she did, I didn't see it. You can't take your eyes off a lion, you know. Even Trixie, whom I'd known since she was a cub. I'm missing a quarter of the forefinger on my right hand to prove it.

She was a thin woman, too thin, really. I'm small, even now, but then I was all muscle. This woman was thin as thin, with a pinched, hungry-looking mouth. As the years went by, I began to understand what she was hungry for, but I was young then—just fourteen—and I didn't care. She was nothing to me. Whatever went on between them was their own concern. When she came in that first night, she was wearing a red felt hat, and it didn't suit her. I gave him a look when I saw them, as if I pitied him. He laughed right back at me as if it was our joke. Her eyes were a little too close together, and her brown hair was done in what I reckon were meant to be marcel waves, but they had gone a bit funny so they looked like wrinkles, and the hat was probably meant to hide them. Of course it didn't hide them at all. She had a flowered dress that belted at the waist, and it had not a scrap of red in it. That made the hat look even more ridiculous.

He walked in with her, bold as brass, and when he caught me looking at them, he smiled. He just smiled, and that's what he was like. When people found out about it later—and they all found out—they asked me, what was he like, then, I told them, he was a smiler. He smiled all the while, I said, and of course they knew what I meant and they left it alone.

You would think I would have minded her, you see, but you don't know what I was like then. I knew that I had a body that made men sweat. When I stood on the back of my pony and let her run, then flipped over onto my hands and spread my legs, I'd come back round and see them all staring at me, their tongues hanging out, their foreheads covered with beads of perspiration. Of course it was hot in that tent—those paraffin lamps, we used to brew tea on them—but I know it was because of what they saw in me, what they didn't see in their wives, these mousy women next to them, their skin gone gray from bad food, their clothes drab and worn, while there I was in my frills and spangles, my white tutus, tights, and feathers, riding around on Magic, my white pony, as if I was part of someone's dream.

That day in town, when I ran into him in the market, I knew that's what he was thinking. I could see his eyes change, widen, as if part of his dream had just come alive and walked up to him. I was wearing a man's shirt—one of the clowns had left it lying about, and I had nicked it—and I had my hair down, not pulled tight in the little bun that Mum made for me every evening. Still, he recognized me instantly and his smile focused on me like a spotlight and made me feel like I felt in the ring, as if all eyes were on me and I was lit up from inside.

I was by the cheese stall, trying to cadge some lunch from the boy, who had seen me last night—of course, everyone had seen me, I knew that. I would come flying into town after a performance and the crowds would part like the Red Sea, like I was some supernatural being. I could see that the boy was already half in love with me, so I was playing with it, the way I used to play with Trixie, who is long since dead. You let the lion think that she is in control, see. But the truth was if she made one move towards me, my papa would have shot her. Still, sometimes the lion does win, and that's part of the game. I was so young when I started working with lions that I was never afraid.

"Are you coming again tonight, then?" I asked the cheese boy, fluttering my eyelashes at him. I knew he'd be coming again that night—everyone did. It didn't cost much, and in those days before the war we thought we were doing well if we made ten quid in a day. "I might," he said, flirting, as if I gave a toss whether he came back or not—I just wanted a piece of cheese. "Let us have a bit of that Double Gloucester," I said, pointing with my forefinger, or what there was of it. "I'll dedicate my act to you."

"Mum would have me guts for garters," he said, but as I wrapped my hand around the hunk of cheese and stuck it into my pocket, he didn't stop me.

"I'll see you, then," I said, turning around to leave without so much as a thank you. That's how I was. Of course that's when I nearly smashed into him—him, the smiler, whose name, I found out later, was really John, but everyone called him Jack. "What's your hurry?" he said, putting his hands on my arms to stop me. I could tell that he recognized me and that he had been watching me with the cheese boy.

"Mum will be wondering where I am," I said, but I didn't try to break away, just stood there with the weight of his hands on my arms. My arms were very strong and muscular—well, you have to be, don't you—but I could feel that his hands were strong too, and they felt good on my arms. That's all— they felt good, so I left them there, and maybe that was my first mistake, if it was a mistake at all, if anything is ever truly a mistake. Because of course in the end, it seems when you look back that none of it could ever have been any different, really.

"Stop a bit," he said, "I want to ask you something." He took his hands away and put them in his pockets. I had noticed him the night before because he was wearing a black suit, with a bow tie and perfectly pressed trousers, and I would have thought he was a toff except that it was a shiny suit, and his shoes were poor and dirty. I had seen him looking at the elephants, and I had taken note of him because the suit said something to me—that we were alike, somehow, that this was a man who was in the center of the ring.

I had not been the least bit interested in him when I'd seen him down by the elephants—I was too young to be seriously interested in boys, let alone men, or so I thought, and besides, he was old—at the time I thought thirty was as old as Methuselah. But there in the marketplace, I didn't notice his age, and when he took his hands off my arms, I minded. I felt a little butterfly's wing twitch inside me, a shimmer of fabric as fragile as the skirt on my tutu, and I felt like he had left marks on my arms where his hands had been, like stains of gold.

"What do you want to ask me, then?" I said like I really didn't have time for him at all. But I found I was looking at him carefully. His face in the daylight was red and rough, as if too much sun had started to wear it out, and his nose listed slightly to the left. His little blue eyes had squint lines around them, and his teeth looked fake (which I later found out they were). He was wearing rough farm clothes, and I could tell that he must work on the land somewhere.

He leaned over and put his face just a bit too close to mine. He must have been testing to see if I'd move away. I didn't—I stayed right where I was, and he leaned over to me and as he spoke I could smell his breath on me. It smelled of cigarettes, and I suppose I might have found it unpleasant, but there was something else in it too, as if this was the way a man was supposed to smell. Of course, working with animals, I know how important this is—scent, I mean. You must never go into a lion's cage if you've had a drink, for example, because they can smell it straightaway. That's what happened to my uncle George, who was killed by our old lion, the one we had before Trixie, before I was born. So I suppose it was something in his breath, some chemical perhaps, that grabbed hold of me and made me want to draw nearer, that's all, just to draw nearer.

"What's it like?" he said.

"What do you mean?" I asked, suddenly bored, because everyone always asks what it's like to put your head into the mouth of a lion, and the truth is that after a while, it's just smelly and horrid and even a bit dull, but I'm used to it and it's my job. I always want to ask, what's it like mucking out stables? but I don't.

"I mean, what's it like being up there in front of all those men and knowing that all of them want to make love to you."

"What are you on about?" I asked, grinning a little, not even blushing.

"I saw them last night. When you were up there on that pony—cor, they just wanted to eat you up, all of them. Just take all your clothes off and eat you right up."

"And how do you know that?" I asked, sort of laughing because I knew he was right, and I hadn't known that anybody knew this but me.

He threw back his head and laughed. "What a silly question, darlin'. Because I sat there, and all I could think about was—" He stopped, leaned over and put his head next to my ear, and now I could smell him even better. His skin smelt of shaving soap, and his cheek was smooth as it brushed up right next to mine. His hair was brown and a bit too long, and it had an oily smell, like it wanted washing.

We stood there like that, him silent, me wanting, suddenly, to hear the rest of his sentence but not wanting to ask, like it was some kind of game. Finally I said, "What, then? What were you thinking?"

"That I just had to have you somehow," he said into my ear. Then he did something no one had ever done to me before, and at first I had no idea what it was. My ear felt warm and wet suddenly, and then I realized that he had put his tongue in it.

He took me over behind the old Roman wall on the edge of town. We walked slowly, as if we were taking a stroll and had no idea of our destination. If anyone from the show had seen us, it would have been all over, I would have been rushed home and locked in our trailer—but no one saw us. As we walked, we talked about the show. He said his favorite parts had been mine, of course, but next to that he had liked the ringmaster best. "That's my papa," I told him, and for a second he looked a bit nervous, as if he wanted to ask how old I was but was afraid of the answer. I looked older than fourteen, but not much.

"Is it rough work, being a ringmaster?" he asked.

"It's all rough work," I said, and for a moment I remembered that I was supposed to be helping Mama with the animals just now.

"All work is rough," he said, but in such a lazy voice that I could scarcely imagine that he worked at all. "It's all beneath us, really, you and I. We were meant for finer things."

I felt slightly offended. At the time, I thought of myself as nobility, sort of like the pop stars today—I thought what I did was a finer thing. Wherever I went, people were all over me, looking at me with such naked envy that I often pitied them. "What do you do, then?" I asked.

"This and that," he said. "It doesn't matter. Do you ever feel that you aren't living your real life?"

"No," I said, though later, when I was older, I often felt that way. "But I feel that my real life begins when the show starts each night, and when the lights are up, and Papa comes out and the clowns come running in and then everybody always makes this sound, this sucking sound, like the very breath has been taken out of them."

"Yes," he said, "I heard just that. Well, here we are." We had rounded the back of the Roman wall and reached what looked like a tiny wooden cottage, though it was really a toolshed. He took out a large key ring and opened the padlock on the door. There was no light inside, and all I could see was a wall of garden tools and a thin bare mattress on the floor.

I must say that the whole while, as he took all my clothes off, beginning with the clown's shirt and ending with my old cotton knickers, I had no idea exactly what he was going to do to me. He was staring into my eyes, smiling the whole time. Afterwards, when it was all over and we made our way silently back into town, I still was not entirely sure exactly what it was he had done.

That night, I looked for him in the stands, and there he was, still smiling.

The next day in town, he was at the cheese stand, as if he was waiting for me. At first I wondered if he wasn't supposed to be working, but later I realized that the toolshed was part of his job on the estate he worked on, that he was some sort of gardener or handyman for the posh people who lived there, the sort of people who never came to our shows, though much later, when we became really successful, Papa was often photographed with them.

I've often asked myself why I went back to the toolshed with him that second day. It wasn't as if the experience itself had been entirely enjoyable. Parts had been painful, but even more, it had seemed so strange to me, as if we'd been doing something truly odd that no one had ever thought of before. It wasn't that part of it that I was anxious to repeat. Mostly—I'm not sure—

I think I just wished to smell him again, to be that close to his scents, these male scents I had never smelled so closely before. He wore a kind of cologne, too, and that first night I was a bit nervous with Trixie because I knew she didn't like strange smells, but I couldn't quite wash it off. It was as if I had come so close to maleness that now I stank of it and could never wash it away, and in a way that turned out to be true, I never did wash it away.

The second day, he'd brought a torch with him—not an electric one, but a flame on the end of a stick. He stuck it in the wall and moved me this way and that, so that he could see me—parts of me that no one had ever seen. He studied me. I think now that that is what all the men in the audience wished to do—to hold me still, to stop me spinning and glittering round the room on the pony, doing handstands and backflips—they wanted to stop me and just look at me, still, the way a butterfly is when it's been stabbed with a pin. I was afraid the shed would burn down at first—and then, after a while, I no longer cared.

That night, when I looked for him in the stands, I saw that he'd brought her with him. When I saw her next to him, I felt absolutely nothing toward her because I knew that I was part of his real life, and that she never could be.

The next day, I met him by the Roman wall. There was no longer any pretense at accident, and there was no doubt in my mind about why I was there. Something about that torch had stayed with me, and in a way it's never left me. It's the same kind of light I felt in the ring, and it all blurs together in my mind, the torch and the light from the paraffin lamps and the way I began to feel with him, as if I had discovered a parallel world beside ours and had slipped into it through a hole in the earth.

That last night, he brought his wife again, and this time she didn't faint when I went in with Trixie. It was as if she was learning just how much in life she could bear. She was still wearing the red hat, and her hair looked even worse than before, and for a second I found myself wondering if he had touched her hair, if he had touched her the way he had touched me, but then I heard Papa call out my cue, and I had to leap on Magic's back and whirl around the ring so fast that the two of them were only a blur.

*        *        *

The last day, I waited for two hours by the Roman wall. He never came. When I got back to the fields we were camped in, everyone was nearly finished packing up. "Where on God's green earth have you been?" Mama yelled in Danish when she saw me. She always spoke Danish when she was agitated, which meant that she spoke Danish rather a lot. I made some excuse to her that she didn't even seem to hear. It was only a short run to the next town, and we were there by evening. It was always such a thrill to come into a new town, the horses running before us, the tigers (when we had them) roaring in their cages, and all the townspeople with looks on their faces like it was the second coming, like all the light of heaven was reflected on them. But that day, I remember, I didn't give a toss where we were or who saw us.

Autumn came. We made our way across the downs, to the south coast and then back east again to our winter quarters in Kent. I went every day to the village school and stared out the window at the new snow in the fields while I was supposed to be learning math. In the evenings, Mum and I worked with the animals, and sometimes when I was practicing a new routine with Magic, I could feel a warmth begin to spread within me, and I could almost smell him—Jack, I mean, though it felt a bit funny to call him by name. I did not reckon that this was love, but whatever it was, it flowed through me like a liquid.

Winter seemed endless. By the time it finally did end, I had not forgotten about Jack, but he had begun to seem unreal, the way things seem unreal over time. One day in February I exchanged a few kisses with the son of a local farmer. While we were kissing, I tried to summon up the image of what I had done with Jack. It seemed impossible that it had ever happened.

Finally, the snowdrops came up, then the daffodils, and then, the tulips, and then we were back on the road. We traveled in a great arc to the north, then dropped down again, working our way into the countryside further west of London. Our path varied a bit each year so we never gave people a chance to tire of us. We passed through Oxford this time, where a gypsy, some friend of Mama's, read my cards and told me I would meet a man in the west country who would love me. Everyone laughed when she said this, and Mama scowled at her as if it had been quite inappropriate.

We went west. It was strange—the closer we got to Jack, the more vivid my memory of him became, as if the landscape itself, the road rimmed with fields and hedgerows, were animating it. It was a Tuesday when we got to Colchester. The rose-gold stone houses of the town looked odd, too bright somehow, as if I had dreamed them into being. I had an urge to go to the marketplace straightaway, but Mum insisted I help with the animals. I had worked up an act with Steffi, our bear. I was dressed as a ballerina—I had taught myself to dance on toe. We put a little frock on Steffi, and she and I danced together in the ring while Daniel, one of the clowns, played the violin. The act had gone over well so far. After the show, I could hear the people say, "Did you see that slip of a girl with that clumsy great bear? Cor, I wasn't half afraid for her." Of course, Steffi was gentle as a lamb, at least in spring and summer, though she was a bit irritable during the winter months.

I was practicing with Steffi before the show when I saw him. He walked right into our tent, and then pretended he'd lost his way. "I beg your pardon," he said to Daniel, who had stopped playing and was standing there brandishing the violin and the bow like weapons. "I was looking for the box office." He barely looked at me, but I knew he'd seen me—he could hardly miss me, standing there with an enormous bear, both of us in tutus like she was my ugly sister.

When I saw him, I opened my mouth to say something, but suddenly I remembered how I had felt that last day, standing at the Roman wall and waiting for him when he never came.

"We got no fucking box office," Daniel said. "You buy your tickets tonight like everyone else."

"Go on, Daniel," I called as Jack left the tent. "Play some more. Don't stop."

Of course he was at the show that night—alone, without the wife. He was wearing the same suit he'd had on last year, and perhaps the same shoes. My part in this year's show was a bit larger than it had been. My sister, Mary, had got married and was six months pregnant, so I was doing all her acts. Besides, I was one year older and that much more substantial. I barely looked at him all night. I was still angry with him, and I was a bit disturbed by his intrusion into our tent, as if he'd gone behind the lines somehow, beyond where the townsfolk were allowed. I hadn't thought before of the tent as a border, but suddenly I was aware that it was what separated us from the rest of the world, and the thought of losing that boundary suddenly made me afraid. Perhaps it was because Mama kept me awfully busy minding the animals, but I didn't go into town the next day.

On the third day, Mama asked me to go into town and find some meat for the tigers. It was a tradition with the local shopkeepers to give us scraps when we passed. I was in the marketplace, holding a bag of lamb shanks, when I saw him hurrying over to me. He was wearing an old white shirt and black trousers that were smeared with earth, as if he'd been kneeling on the ground. He stopped right in front of me and smiled, but it was not the same smile I had seen before. It looked a bit unsure, and something in me felt smug, as if I had triumphed somehow. This was probably my second mistake. I should have known that I could not triumph. "I wanted to see you," he said after a moment of silence. "I was there last night."

"I saw you," I said in a flat voice. I balanced the bag of lamb on my hip as if holding a child.

"You were so lovely, you didn't half take my breath away."

"Yes," I said.

"You've grown a bit," he said, smiling a bit wider and reaching for my shoulder. I stepped back.

"Ah," he said. "We're standoffish, are we?" He studied my face for a minute, then, to my annoyance, he laughed. "So that's all it is. I thought sure it was another man. Maybe that bloke with the fiddle."

"You weren't there," I found myself saying without really wanting to. "That day. I waited for you at the wall, but you never came."

"My darling," he said, looking into my eyes as if he wanted to grab me and have me right there in the middle of the marketplace. "I'm so sorry. There was a problem with one of the ewes, and by the time I got there, you'd gone. Can you ever forgive me?"

It wasn't until much later that night, after the show, as I lay in bed alone, that I realized that I had waited at the wall for two hours that day, which was an awfully long time for someone to have problems with a ewe. And then I realized that I had left the bag of lamb bones in the toolshed.

As I lay there, touching myself, feeling where he had been, I found that something had changed—suddenly I didn't care if he had been lying about the ewe, about anything. And at that night's show, when I saw his wife sitting next to him, wearing a blue hat with a feather that made her look as if she was trying very hard, I wanted to leap at her and tear her to shreds with my claws.

The next afternoon as we lay there, he said, "I love you," casually, without looking at me. I was lying on my back and staring upward. Shovels and hammers hung all around me. I felt something tickle my arm, and I turned to look. A large brown spider crawled up the side of the mattress, and I brushed it away. Juices were running out of me and whirling around in my veins.

"A gypsy woman told me a man would love me," I said, still without looking at him.

"That was me," he said. I could tell from his voice that he was smiling at me, and that his teeth, which I now knew for certain were false, were gleaming. "I love every inch of you."

"I reckon you must," I said. "You've seen every inch of me, haven't you? You've kissed every inch of me. I wonder if you don't find it a bit—"

"No," he said. "You're lovely. All of you. Every inch."

The next winter went by even more slowly. By now, it was clear to me that I was simply getting through it, waiting for summer to come so I could see him again. I thought of him so often, and as I sat in the schoolroom, staring at words on a page and watching them blur and disappear, I tried to conjure him up with the power of my mind. I wanted to write him a letter, but I knew I could never mail it. I wouldn't have wanted his wife to read it, and besides, I didn't have his address, though I reckoned he must live on the estate just beyond the Roman wall.

Nothing in the circus ever seemed to change, really. My sister had her baby, and some of the clowns came and went, but apart from that it was all the same—hours of practice with Trixie and Steffi (I wouldn't go near the tigers), hours in the ring with Magic, a few small shows up in London. Day after day helping to serve the same food, hearing the same conversations, it seemed to me, about whether to buy some elephants and if so, how many we could afford, and who was going to go to Ceylon to fetch them (I volunteered, but my offer was laughed off by everyone). Mama said something one day during dinner about how soon I would be grown up and married. "I'll never marry," I said in a voice that was a bit too loud.

"I swore I'd never marry," she said, "and look at what happened to me. And then children." Mama's accent grew more pronounced, and for a moment I thought she was going to fall into Danish. She had been in this country for donkeys' years, but she never seemed comfortable with the language. She came from an old circus family that Papa's family had teamed up with for a while, and none of them spoke good English.

"I won't have children, either," I said in a voice that sounded childish even to me.

"She's at that age," Mama said to no one in particular. She often talked about me as if I wasn't there. "She can't help being disagreeable."

"She's getting older," said my sister Mary, who was sitting in a chair not far from us, breast-feeding her baby. "Soon you'll have a boyfriend, Rosie."

"Not me," I said, unable to find my way out of the conversation. "I'm going to travel the world. Not just these stupid little towns we go to. I'm going to go everywhere. I'll never marry."

"Come on, precious," Mary said to the baby. She put the baby up to her shoulder and began to rub her on the back.

"Not like that, Mary, harder," Mama said, walking over to Mary and taking the baby from her. Mama pounded the baby on the back. The baby let out a resounding burp. Mama handed her back to Mary without a word, and Mary went back to breast-feeding. "It ruins your figure," Mama said, turning and walking away.

Summer, at last, and we were back in his town again. I ran to the marketplace straightaway, but I didn't see him. The same boy was at the cheese stand, and I could tell time had passed because he'd got big and handsome. I tried to get some cheese off him and found that instead of looking at me with shyness, he was looking at me with the same look men always gave me. "How about some Red Leicester, then?" I asked.

"I'll give you Red Leicester," he said.

"There you are," a voice said behind me, and before I knew it, I was back in the toolshed.

During each performance those four evenings, I felt exhausted. At one point, I stood on the back of Magic and nearly fell over. I felt so weak, as if all the life had been sucked out of me. On the third and fourth evenings, he brought his wife, as always, and I watched her from the side of the ring. She laughed at the clowns, and when she laughed, her thin lips pulled on the sides of her face and made her ugly, and she clung to Jack's arm like a monkey. As they were leaving the tent on the final night, she with her arm linked in his, I pushed past them, hard, so that I knocked into her. "Sorry," I said, looking at him. He, of course, was smiling, but his eyes were a bit hard.

"Oh look, Jack, it's the circus girl," she said, as if I wasn't even there. Her eyes looked small and colorless beneath the rim of yet another hat.

I don't know why, but I took off one of my spangled paste earrings and handed it to her. "Here's a souvenir," I said.

"How much do you want for it?" she asked.

"Take it," I said, thrusting it into her palm. "It's yours."

"I don't know what you thought you were about," he said. We lay naked in each other's arms while somewhere, I knew, Mama was searching for me, as it was nearly time to go.

"I wanted to give her a little something," I said. "To brighten up her little life."

A laugh burst from his mouth. "Does her life need brightening, then?"

"I reckon it does." I leaned across his chest and put my tongue into his mouth. Mechanically, as if he couldn't help it, he put his hands on my breasts. I pulled my face away. "I reckon I've got the best of you."

He laughed again. It was a sharp laugh, as if something hurt him. "You might at that." He began to move against me. "But you mustn't think—"

"What?"

"You mustn't think you have all of me."

"Whatever are you on about?" I looked at him and laughed, but he wasn't laughing back.

"You know exactly what I'm on about."

I stared at him, as realization began to dawn on me. "You mean you— with her? You do—this?"

"Of course we do." He looked at me in honest surprise. "Whatever did you think?"

I drew away from him and stared. He lay there, staring back at me, and suddenly he looked incredibly old. As I began to pound my fists against his ruddy, hairless chest, until he grabbed my wrists and stopped me, it was as if she had suddenly appeared there between us. He was a bit fat round the stomach, and the punches raining down on him had just seemed to disappear into his flesh. I wrested my wrists from his grasp, stood up, and backed away from him, grabbing my shirt and throwing it on, pulling on my knickers (inside out, I later found), stepping into my skirt, which was from last year and much too short. As I backed away and stood in the door of the toolshed, he lay there watching me, not saying anything. "This is filthy," I said. "This is disgusting. You are a disgusting old man."

"You wanted it," he said in a tired voice. As I ran out the door, he did nothing to stop me.


We were down in Hampshire when I began to feel sick. At first I managed to conceal it from everyone—after all, no one paid much attention to me normally. Mary was busy with her baby; my brothers were driving the lorries and chasing women in the towns we passed through. Mama was busy managing everyone, yelling at the clowns and cursing in Danish, words she didn't know we all knew. Papa often sat alone in the trailer, or stared dreamily out at the countryside while everything went on around him.

But one morning Candace, an acrobat who was one of my cousins on Papa's side, caught me being sick behind a hedgerow where I'd thought no one would see me. I wiped my mouth when I saw her and stood up as if nothing had happened. It was probably this feeble attempt at deception that made her narrow her eyes and stare at me, examining my face as if a confession might be written there. "What's all this?" she said in a voice that managed to be both mocking and kind. I had never got on too well with Candace, who was not quite old enough to be my mother but bossed me around all the time anyway. Before I was born, Candace had done my pony act. Now she still walked the high wire, but she'd grown a bit plump after the birth of her first child, and one of the clowns, who was Scottish, once told her she looked like a haggis in tights. "Are we feeling a few degrees under?" she asked, staring at me with a little smile.

"I think it's something I ate," I said, wiping a stray bit of sick off my cheek.

Candace only laughed, a coarse, nasty laugh that I somehow understood.

When everyone found out, they all wanted to go back and find who had done this to me. My brothers wanted to kill him. As I lay in bed in the trailer, figures hovered over me and fired questions at me that I refused to answer. There was a steady parade of women in and out of my tent, and I grew sicker and weaker owing to methods they used "to try to bring it off," as they put it—at first I had no idea what this meant. They all interrogated me, but somehow, I managed to never tell anyone who he was or where he lived, though I told a few people bits and bobs about him. "He was a smiler," I told Daniel the clown, who seemed to be the only person who did not utterly condemn me for my foolishness (which seemed much more culpable to everyone somehow than my lack of morals).

None of the remedies to bring it off worked, and in February, my daughter Miranda was born. By that time, the War was on, and we could no longer travel. All of our equipment was requisitioned by the military, and for the entire duration of the War—the next six years—we stayed in our winter quarters in Kent, where I no longer had to go to school but simply hung about taking care of Miranda. My brothers were all in the Army. Papa tried to enlist but was rejected, much to his regret. I think he rather fancied a suicide mission. The men who weren't in the military supported us by traveling up to London and doing little shows in department stores. The women stayed behind, and some found work on the estates nearby. It was as if time had suddenly gone wrong somehow, and the clock had run down and stayed on the same hour, the same minute, for six years.

For a while when the War ended, no one was sure how to proceed. Papa, who had spent the War years driving one of our lorries for the Army, seemed to fall back into his dreamy state, and could reach no decisions at all. Mama had aged visibly during those years, perhaps from the strain of continually managing every aspect of everyone's life, and she was unsure whether she wanted to go back on the road. The men had set up a nice business in London— their little shows had turned into a regular feature, attended by a lot of the gentry. They had moved into a small theatre in the West End and were making what we thought then was fabulous sums of money, though later when success really struck, we had to laugh about that.

But somehow, in spring of 1946, we pulled out of our winter quarters with a brand-new tent and the few lions and bears we had managed to keep alive during the War years. (We had had to shoot most of the animals because we couldn't feed them.) We made our way along the south coast, stopping at all the old towns that had loved us years ago.

Everywhere we went, people poured out to see us. We would pull into those country towns and once again, we were like royalty, and the townspeople greeted us with incredible joy and relief, as if their old lives had finally been returned to them. Miranda, who was six by then, would ride up on the top of the front wagon, wearing the little tutu Mama had made her and waving to everyone we passed as if she were Princess Elizabeth herself.

By this time, I had a sort of relationship with Daniel the clown—nothing physical went on, but it was generally understood that we were keeping company. He was always after me to marry him, and he would have made a good father to Miranda, but something always stopped me even considering it. It wasn't that he was unattractive—he was a handsome bloke, and still is—but the part of me that should have warmed to him seemed to have frozen somehow. I was still only twenty-three, and I had kept my figure, which Mama seemed quite pleased about. But something in me had turned cold and hard, as if I was not gold anymore but some ordinary metal. So I kept him at bay.

It was strange being on the road again, and especially strange to have so little to do with the show. I did a lot behind the scenes now—trained animals, mended costumes, prepared food. We had a fleet of ducks we'd bought from a farmer in Rye, and I'd trained them to do a little dance. Miranda had helped me a bit, but in the back of my mind, I tried to keep her from getting too interested—I wanted her to have as little to do with the circus as possible.

My little niece Emily had learned my pony routine (my pony, Magic, had died during the War), and Mama had even spruced up my old costume for her. Though I had no regrets at all about relinquishing my place in the ring to Emily, I must say that I managed never to have to watch her. During the show, I stayed in the trailer with Miranda.

When we got to Colchester, I was surprised at how unfamiliar it looked. Of course, I'd never seen much of it in the first place, just the marketplace and the Roman wall and the inside of a toolshed. But as we drove past the town and on to our usual encampment on its outskirts, it looked just the same as any other market town. What surprised me even more was how little I felt there. I had expected to be moved somehow, to sadness or to anger, but even though I knew that somewhere within a few miles of us was the father of my own Miranda, I felt nothing.

She looked like me, Miranda did, and I was always grateful for that. Not only because I wouldn't want anyone to recognize her face in his if they should happen to see him, but also because I was spared any reminders in her of what people had taken to calling my "mistake," as if it had only happened once. (I had never told anyone that it had gone on for three years—not even Daniel— and I never did tell.) The one bit of resemblance between Miranda and her father was her eyes—they were small and blue, like his, and seemed out of place in a face that otherwise looked just like mine and, I was coming to realize, like Mama's. I was glad she didn't look much like Jack, as I had to bring her with me into town that first day to pick up some items for tea. I drove one of the lorries into town—I had learned to drive during the War—and the whole time we were in town, I kept glancing over my shoulder, praying that I wouldn't run into Jack, or worse, his wife. When I'd loaded up the lorry with bread, meat, cheese, and milk, I herded Miranda into the passenger side and sped away, ignoring her pleas to stop a bit in town. She liked to wear her tutu into the towns so people would give her candy. As we drove away, Miranda pressed her face against the window and cried—she was a bit spoilt, as everyone constantly reminded me. When we got back to our trailer, I found I was breathing heavily, like someone who has had a narrow escape.

That night, I could hear the sounds of the show as I lay in my trailer and tried to sleep. I closed my eyes, and on the backs of my eyelids (for I was half awake) I could see myself going round and round the ring on Magic while the crowds cheered from the side seats, a blur. I pictured myself there, so many years ago, and in all those years, this was probably the only time that I cried.

"More meat," Mama said to me the next morning. "You must go into town and visit the butcher. Tell him we insist on paying." She was proud of our newfound ability to pay, and had never felt comfortable taking something for nothing.

"I'd really rather not," I said. "I have some things to do."

"Things? What things?"

"Just things. Can't someone else go?"

"What someone else? There is no someone else. Everyone else has an important job. I think it's time you began making more of a contribution." Mama had been saying variations of this to me for my entire life, as if I had never before done a bit of work but had just lain about being fanned by palm leaves. She opened up her mouth now as if a string of Danish curses lay on its threshold and could be loosed at any moment.

I went into town, leaving Miranda with Daniel, who was teaching her a handkerchief trick.

As I walked through the marketplace, past the huge stone church, past all the little market stalls, I found myself watching the faces of the people who passed. No one seemed to take any notice of me, as I was a stranger—I had grown used to not being recognized from the show. As I watched them as they passed, I found I was looking into their eyes for a sign of recognition, a sign that they knew who I had been. And then I found I was looking for Jack.

I bought some cheese at the cheese stand. The man behind the counter may have been the same boy that had been there so many years ago—I could no longer remember his face. I thanked him, and as I turned away I half expected to see Jack standing in the spot where he had been. But of course there was no one there.

That night during the show, I put Miranda to bed with her usual bedtime story. She liked to hear stories about my old pony, Magic. In the stories, Magic could talk, and she and the little girl in the stories, Rosie, had wonderful adventures in which they could fly, and they flew over Germany and dropped a giant elephant poo on Hitler and killed him, thereby saving the brave Danish people who had fought against him, not to mention the Germans, for whom they didn't care. Then Rosie and Magic had flown back to England and slid down a magic rainbow into the heart of London, where the King had asked them into Buckingham Palace for tea and had a big parade for them. And then, if Miranda hadn't fallen asleep by then, which she almost always had, Rosie and Magic would get up on a giant stage in the middle of Kensington Gardens and fly around in circles, while all the people of London cheered round them. "And they would fly and fly and fly and fly and fly," I'd say until she finally fell asleep.

That night, Miranda was asleep right after the giant elephant poo. I crept back over to my own bed and lay down, but I didn't feel the least bit sleepy. I could hear the crowd cheering in the tent, and music playing, and drums beating, and voices laughing at the clowns. I pictured the people sitting at the edge of the ring—and then I opened my eyes and sat up. "Jack," I said out loud.

Before I knew it I was up and dressed and standing in the doorway to the tent. I crouched in a shadow, partly so Mama wouldn't see me—she would never let me leave Miranda alone in the trailer for fear that she'd be stolen by gypsies—and partly because if Jack was there, I didn't want him to see me until I was ready to be seen.

But he wasn't there. I looked all round the ring, carefully studying each face. I searched the spot where he'd always sat, but no one there looked remotely like him. Of course, I knew he might have changed during the six years since I'd seen him, but I knew that in spite of anything that time or the War could have done to him, I would recognize him instantly. As my eyes pored over the light, happy faces on the ring's edge, I began to feel a weird combination of things: fear, that something had happened to him, that he'd been killed in the War. And desire—a terrible desire to see him.

The next day, I volunteered to go into town. Mama was a bit surprised, but she didn't pay much attention, just handed me the keys to the lorry and a shopping list. She didn't seem to notice that I'd gotten myself up a bit for the trip, done my hair and put on a spot of lipstick.

When I got into town, I wandered in and out of the shops. There was no market in town today, and the marketplace looked bare, as if the stalls full of vegetables and fish and cheese had all been some sort of mirage. I reckoned that was how people must have felt whenever the circus left. After I tired of strolling, I sat down on a bench in front of the church and watched people go by—old people leaning on sticks, women with prams, a few men with hats and canes going in and out of the bank, a few blokes who looked like farm laborers. When I heard the clock on the church strike eleven, I realized I'd been sitting there for nearly an hour, and that Mama would be wondering where I was, and more importantly, where the food for dinner was. I was feeling a bit peckish myself by this time, so I thought I'd go to the bakery first—I quite fancied a custard tart. I had seen a bakery across the square quite near to where I had parked.

The bakery had a small display window in its front, and a pile of granary loaves sat in a patch of sun. I stood in the window looking past the loaves at the counter inside, trying to decide if I wanted a custard pie or a flapjack. Then I noticed the woman behind the counter: it was Jack's wife.

As I stood in front of her, pointing at the things I wanted—six granary loaves, four white, three dozen scones (I had quite lost my appetite for elevenses)—my hands were shaking, but she seemed not to notice. She looked considerably older than when I had last seen her, as if time had not been kind to her, and I felt a clutch of fear in my stomach that something might have happened to Jack. "You must be with the circus," she said to me through lips so thin they looked as if her words might get cut on them.

"You've seen us, then?" I asked.

"Oh, no, we haven't been. This one's afraid of clowns." She pointed behind her. There in the corner sat a tiny girl, perhaps two or three years old. The girl was wearing a little blue frock with flowers embroidered on the pockets. "Perhaps we'll go tonight. Won't we, chickie?" she called to the little girl, who looked up at me with her mother's hard face and Jack's eyes.

As I drove home, I reasoned it out. The girl was young enough that Jack must still have been alive at least halfway through the War. The woman had said "we"—but she might have just meant herself and her daughter.

That night I watched for them in the stands, but they never came.

The next day, I once again volunteered to make the run into town, and this time Mama stopped and stared at me, opening her mouth as if about to ask me a question and then closing it again. I left Miranda with Daniel and drove off in the lorry, and as I pulled into town, the clock was once again striking eleven.

Through the front window, I could see Jack's wife and the little girl moving about. When I got into the shop, I could see that the little girl had on a red frock today.

"Did you get round to see us last night?" I asked as Jack's wife was piling loaves of bread into a box.

"No. My husband wasn't feeling well. Perhaps tonight."

"It's our last night here," I said, hearing the word "husband" and feeling as if the floor beneath me had tilted and that I was falling backwards. I grabbed onto the counter to steady myself. "Was your husband injured in the War, then?"

"Oh, no," she said, not seeming to notice that this was none of my business. "He fell out of a tractor a few months ago and did his back in. He can't sit for long periods of time anymore." She said this as if in the past, he had sat for long periods of time doing some important thing.

"Is he an older bloke, then?" I asked, smiling like she and I were quickly growing to be bosom chums.

"Oh, no. He's only thirty-nine," she said.

"Ah," I said. "So he wasn't in the War?"

"Here's your order," she said, handing me the box. "No, he managed to stay out of the War. Bad knees."

"Oh, I see. Bad knees. A knee is a tricky thing. I rode in the circus for years, and I—"

"That will be two pounds eight shillings, please."

I handed her the money. "You have a lovely little girl," I said, smiling at the little girl, who stuck her tongue out at me. "What's her name?"

"Rosie," she said, and for a moment I started, thinking that she was speaking to me.

"What a lovely name," I said to the little girl. "Hello, Rosie."

"Thanks very much," Jack's wife said, concluding our transaction.

"You must come tonight," I said. "Your little girl will love it. And it's so close if you live in town."

"We just live behind the shop," she said.

"Ah," I said again. "Well, thanks very much. Cheerio."

I took the box of bread out to the lorry, then went back to all the various other shops I needed to go to. When I'd finished, I drove the lorry round to the street just behind the bakery. Past the house in front of me, I could see what must be the back wall of the bakehouse's garden. Above the wall were windows of the house's second story. I saw no signs of life there.

On a hunch, I drove to the outskirts of town. It took me a while to find it—driving was so different from walking—but finally there it was, the Roman wall. I parked the lorry and got out. It was nearly the longest day of summer, and everything looked bright and green and golden. I started along the path on the edge of the estate, and soon I saw the toolshed beyond a patch of trees. I was just about to approach it when I saw its door open. I hid behind a tree and watched as Jack came out. He looked older—his hair had gone rather gray, and he'd gained at least a stone (of course, so had I)—but he had the same look on his face that I remembered, that gay smile as if everything was going exactly the way he'd planned it. I opened my mouth to call out to him but then, of course, I saw the girl behind him. She looked about fourteen, and she was tugging at the waistband of her skirt, which was crooked. I waited behind the tree until they'd gone. Then I drove back to our encampment and told Daniel I'd marry him.

Everyone seemed quite pleased, if a bit bewildered. After all, everyone knew he'd been after me for some time to say yes, and no one could understand why I had taken so long to do it. As Daniel kissed me that night before the show— and it was only the second time we'd kissed—I thought about Jack and the girl in the toolshed, and I returned Daniel's kiss with a passion I'm sure surprised him, and which I'm not altogether sure, looking back on it, that he liked.

When the show started, I stood on the edge of the ring—I let Miranda stay up and watch, as we were celebrating. She seemed delighted about the engagement, as she adored Daniel, and asked if she could begin calling him Papa right away. I said no, that she had to wait until we were properly married. She sat at the side of the ring and cheered so loudly for him that I thought she would make herself sick (as she sometimes did when she got too worked up). When he and a few of the other clowns made a human pyramid, I could see that behind his sad-clown makeup, he was beaming. From the top of the pyramid, he winked at me just before the other clowns all rolled aside and he fell face down in the sawdust.

The show had already started when Jack's wife came in with their little girl. She smiled and waved when she saw me, and her face looked almost pretty, kinder somehow, as if she were thoroughly excited to be there. The little girl looked quite pale with fright, and when she saw the clowns, she started screaming. The laughter and cheers of the crowd drowned her out, but I could see her little mouth open and her eyes shut as she wailed. "Life is tough, Rosie," I said to her from across the room, which of course she couldn't hear.

Halfway through the show, I took Miranda out—she was already drooping, as she was used to such an early bedtime—and put her to bed with a quick story. Then, with the noise of the crowd to drown out the sound of my motor, I took off in one of the lorries and headed into town.

\*    \*    \*

From behind his house, I could see a light just beyond his garden wall. The house I had parked in front of was completely dark—everyone had probably gone to the circus. The moon was nearly full overhead as I crept through the shadows of a yew tree and round to the back of the front house. In an instant, I was over the stone garden wall, and I felt like doing some backflips as I landed, but instead just stood there, staring at the rear of the bakehouse. It was a stone house, like all the houses in Colchester, and by moonlight the stone seemed almost to shimmer. In the small back window, I could see the yellow glow of an electric light. I moved through the moonlight gently, making no sound, and when I got near the window, I stopped. As far as I recall, I did not stop to ask myself what I was doing; instead, it seemed as if for the first moment in as long as I could remember, my life, my wild life, made some flicker of sense.

The window was a bit too high to see through. I tried to scale the wall, but I could get no purchase on the stone. I looked around for something to stand on and found a large empty flower pot by the side of the wall. As I upended it and rolled it over to the window, it made a loud scraping noise against the flagstones that had been laid in the ground. I braced myself, expecting to hear barking or to see more lights come on, but there was nothing. Standing on the upended flower pot, I peered in the window.

A large console wireless stood in the center of the room. Next to the wireless was a small gas fire. Next to the gas fire was a settee, and on the settee lay Jack, in a dressing gown and slippers, asleep. I couldn't see his face, just his hair, gray and tousled. His hand dangled over the edge of the settee, and his body moved with his breathing.

For a long time, I stood and watched him. Much later, when television was invented, it reminded me of this moment—of glimpsing through a small lighted square into another world, a dream world in which the lives of others went on like a pantomime. It was like looking through an opening into another universe, and I could hardly tear myself away from it. It seemed a miracle that it should be there at all, and that I should be able to watch it as it went on without me.

But finally I heard the clock in the church strike ten. The sound startled me, and for a moment I felt panic. I knew that the show ended round about ten, and that Jack's wife and daughter would be home within the half hour—and I would be lucky if no one checked my trailer and found that I'd gone. Without even thinking about what I was doing—and I'm not sure I had ever even considered what I was going to do once I'd reached Jack's house—I dashed round to the front of the house, found a door to the side of the shop, and rang the doorbell.

For a moment, nothing happened, and I rang again, thinking that perhaps I'd be unable to rouse him. A flicker of relief began to well up in me as I thought about how I would go home to Miranda, to Daniel, and in the morning we would roll away and perhaps never return. But a second later, the door opened, and there he was.

He stared at me. His hair was disheveled and his eyes were vague, as if his sleep had been quite a sound one. He seemed to be trying to focus on my face, as if it were familiar but he couldn't quite place it.

"Hello, Jack," I said. "It's me. Rosie. Do you remember?"

"Rosie," he said, still staring at me with a blank expression. "Do I know you?"

"Let's just say that you knew me," I said, beginning to breathe a bit heavily. "Let's just say that you knew me quite well."

"Rosie," he said again, as if trying to place me. As he spoke, I noticed that his lips had a slackness, and I realized that he was not wearing his false teeth.

"The toolshed," I said. "Before the War. You were the first man ever that I was—" I paused. "With." I did not say, "And the only man."

"Oh, yes," he said, still trying to focus on my face. "Of course. Rosie." I could tell from his voice that he did not remember me.

"I've grown," I said. "I've grown up. Surely you remember me—I was the circus girl."

"The circus girl," he repeated, and then I saw him remember. His small eyes widened. "Of course, Rosie. The circus girl. Before the War." He eyed me up and down. "Goodness me, how you've changed."

"It's been a long time," I said. "A lot has happened."

"Of course," he said, nodding as if he was quite pleased to have recalled me at last. "The War and all." There was a silence, as if he considered asking me in and then quickly rejected the idea.

For a moment I looked at him without saying anything. His eyes—my daughter's eyes—were still heavy with sleep. "You have a daughter," I said finally.

"Yes," he said. "My little Rosie. I always liked the name," he said as if in explanation, as if to assure me he hadn't named her after me.

"No," I said. "Miranda. You have a daughter named Miranda. She's six years old."

I was expecting him to react in some way to this information, but he just stared at me. "He's rather stupid," I found myself thinking.

Finally he spoke. "I remember you," he said, as if it had finally come back to him. "You went round the ring on that pony. You were the tastiest little piece, you were, and you knew it. Yes, I remember you now. And you're telling me that you have—that we have—"

"Miranda," I said. "She's mine," I added, "not yours," as if this was finally clear to me, that as far as I was concerned he no longer had anything to do with my life. "I mean, you're her father, but that's as far as it goes. I just came to tell you. I just wanted you to know. That's all."

"My golly, this is a lot to take in," he said, running a hand through his hair, which I noticed had thinned considerably on top. "I was just having forty winks over there on the settee, and I'm a bit—"

"Yes," I said. "I saw you. I was looking through your window."

"Were you?" He looked startled, and for some reason I remembered how I had felt when he had come into the tent that day, when I'd been rehearsing with Daniel. I had felt violated somehow. Then he put his hand up to his mouth, as if he suddenly realized that he had no teeth. He smiled at me, a ghastly, toothless smile, and for an instant he looked like his old self again. "You've gotten old," he said to me, still smiling. "You're too old for me now." I recognized the seductive lilt in his voice, and in spite of myself, something responded inside me. "Put on a bit of weight, too." As he smiled into my face, he reached his hand out, palm outward, then moved forward so that his palm lay flat against my breast. "Still fancy me, then?"

And at that moment, God help me, I did still fancy him, in spite of the fact that he looked old and horrible and frightening, and I found myself just about to move forward into his arms like some kind of robot, and as I got close to him I could smell him, the same smell I didn't know I remembered, when I heard a voice behind me, and when I turned, I found his wife and daughter coming up the walk.

When word went round the circus that I'd been found in the arms of a married man by the man's own wife and daughter, it was as if a bomb had gone off, like one of those land mines left from the War that lie under a farmer's field for years and years and then explode one day for no good reason. Somehow, it didn't take anyone long to figure out that Jack was Miranda's father, and if we hadn't had to move onto the next town first thing the next morning, I don't know what might have happened. My brothers made noises about breaking his kneecaps and worse, but when it came down to it, they were too busy, and perhaps too old and tired, to bother. Also, everyone tried to keep the whole thing hushed up so that Miranda would not get wind of it, as no one seemed to think it appropriate that she meet her real father, least of all me.

So as it was, after Jack's wife had left Mama's trailer, where they'd been closeted for half the morning, we packed everything up as usual, pulled up stakes, and rolled out of town the way we always had, with Miranda at the head of the caravan in her little pink tutu like a good fairy guiding us on our way. By the time we'd reached the next town, everyone seemed to have entered into an unspoken agreement never to mention the incident again, and except for a few sarcastic remarks periodically from my cousin Candace, that's the way that it stayed. Daniel and I got married as planned, and he has never even asked me what I was doing with Jack that night. I have never tried to explain, although I have spent all these years trying to prepare an answer, just in case he ever did ask me how, on the very night that I had agreed to marry him, I could steal away like a thief in the night to be with another man (of course, everyone assumed that Jack's wife had caught us parting after an evening of passion and would never have believed otherwise).

But he never has asked, and if he had, there was never an answer I could have given him that would have made any sense. All I have ever been able to think of saying is that it seemed as if all those years ago, Jack had taken something that belonged to me and that after all that time, he still had it, and that I had simply wanted it back. And that I had never recovered it, and that as far as I know, he has it to this day.

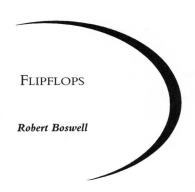

FLIPFLOPS

*Robert Boswell*

**ROBERT BOSWELL** is the author of two short-story collections (*Dancing in the Dark* and *Living to Be a Hundred*) and three novels (*Crooked Hearts, The Geography of Desire,* and *Mystery Ride*). His work has appeared in many magazines, including *The New Yorker, Esquire,* and *The Iowa Review,* as well as the O. Henry Awards and Best American Short Stories series.

"I KNOW A joke," I say.

Alice is next to me, lying on a canvas recliner in a stylish striped bathing suit, legs crossed, beads of sweat sliding across her oiled skin. Her sunglasses, perfect brown eggs, rest on the bridge of her nose at the proper angle, her lips part to the precise degree of desire. Even her feet, busy against one another, point to the sand like the feet of a dancer suspended in flight. The beach is crowded, people like us, down from the States for the long Thanksgiving weekend, escaping the cold, maybe in love. Alice and I have never been together before, never made love. We broke off relationships to come here, believing we needed distance to satisfy longing.

She lowers her sunglasses, smiles behind the perfect eggs. Her face is handsome, solid, visibly relieved that I have something to say. The boldness of our trip has made us shy, smiling at our silences in the plane, playing with our poor Spanish in the taxi, changing clothes separately in our room. The closest connection we've made so far was agreeing on identical purple flipflops in the garish hotel shop.

"There was a man with three arms," I say.

She turns on her side to face me. Arms and legs cross. "Is this a penis joke?"

"No, that's three legs." A man in long pants and shoes walks through the sand carrying a box of jewelry, opals, and obsidian, but I wave him off. Children in jagged brown cutoffs play tag with the advancing and receding water. Middle-aged women sit in the shallows, cupping water to their shoulders, talking and staring back at the beach with the flat expressions of concealed boredom. Beyond them, two men challenge one another to swim farther, waving and laughing. "The man with three arms is lonely, so he goes to a fortune-teller."

"Here?"

"Not Mexico." I shake my head, think. "Virginia, small town, has a name like a woman's name, like Rhonda. Rhonda, Virginia. The fortune-teller's name is May."

Alice laughs. "Her last name is Bee, right? May Bee, the fortune-teller."

"No, let me tell this or it'll take all day."

"I need the details."

The sun is high. An old couple, white as fence posts, hold hands and wade into the water up to their knees, thighs, hips. One young woman, her belly hanging over her sulfur yellow bikini bottom, picks her way carefully through a patch of sharp rocks on the beach. The two men dare each other out farther.

"Her last name is Josephine. May Josephine, fortune-teller. So the man with three arms . . ."

"What's his . . ."

"Ted. Ted Tommy. So Ted goes to May."

"Everyone has two first names." She lifts a knee, runs her foot along her reclining calf, toes pointed, still the feet of a dancer. The bell-shaped woman draws near, flabby-chested, hair pooched up on one side and streaked with sand.

"He asks if he will ever find a woman who'll love him despite his third arm. She looks at her cards and says yes, there's that possibility. He gets very excited and asks, 'When? How do I meet her?' And so on. The fortune-teller tells him to come back in three weeks."

Alice shakes her head. "This isn't going to be one of those long jokes that's only funny because it takes so long to get so little?"

"No, that's life. This is a joke." The sulfur bikini walks past again, returning to the water, the stem of a beachball in her mouth. The ball droops over her chin, the same partially inflated oblong of her breasts. Beyond her, one wave erases the next like a succession of thoughts. "So Ted goes around for three weeks very excited."

"What's he do?"

The sulfur bikini runs a finger around her waistband, dredging an inch of sand. The two swimmers are all arms and backs. "He's a . . . let me think." Alice and I met at work, the university. She's a graduate student in biology and I work in the office.

"A typist," she says.

"No, a milkist. A milker. He milks cows."

"They use machines for that."

"Not when there's a man with three arms."

She shakes her head and laughs, a concession, the same gesture she made when I told her I wanted to see her, have lunch, dinner, a movie, leave our lovers. I had been seeing a computer programmer who wrote poetry, wore used clothes, and shredded the three shirts I left in her closet. Alice had been dating an optometrist with perfect vision and a gap between his front teeth.

"By day he milks, by night he frets." I touch her arm, hot—we're burning up out here. Alice looks at my hand on her arm with a curious stare, as if a bird had lighted there. "Three weeks finally pass and he goes back. She lays out the cards and says he'll meet her in precisely three more weeks if all goes well."

"Sounds like a scam."

"He asks what he needs to do. She says to brush his hair, teeth, and shoes three times a day, using a different hand for each chore but the same brush."

"This is getting really silly." She laces her fingers across her chest. Alice doesn't like nonsense.

A beach waiter arrives with two sweating beers I ordered an hour ago. Alice hands me my wallet from her purse. I give the waiter a wad of pesos. He's chunky, in a long green wedding shirt that makes him look like a huge papaya. He hands most of the wad back to me, leaves before I can calculate a tip. "So Ted's shaken." I hand the wallet back to Alice. I drink. She drinks. "But he does it, brushes his hair with his right hand, his teeth with his left hand, and his shoes with his middle hand."

"Middle hand? Where does this third arm grow from?"

"His chest, right over his heart." When I say this, her face flattens slightly. We drink again. I feel there's something I want to ask her, something to do with us, but I don't know what it is, and there's the joke to finish. "So he brushes each three times a day, using his toothbrush since that's the only one that would fit in his mouth." I wait for a smile, but she doesn't so I hurry it up. "Three weeks pass. On the final day he's milking as usual and the daughter of the dairy farmer comes to him and says, 'I've been noticing you. Why do you use the same brush on your hair, teeth, and shoes?' He smiles at her. She's very pretty."

"All women in jokes are. Or very ugly. Mark used to tell jokes about ugly women. It bothered me." She shades her eyes with her hand, a black shadow slashes her face. Mark is the optometrist. He used to wait for her in the biology office, hands in his pockets, slouched against a wall, gap-toothed smile. I panic for an instant, thinking he may have told me this joke, but I decide not. It's a joke I grew up with. I just haven't told it in a while.

"He explains about the fortune-teller and that this is the day the woman who could love him should come and, sure enough, the farmer's daughter falls in love with him."

Suddenly the sulfur bikini drops her beach ball and stands bolt upright, her back to us. The women in the shallows stand and face the ocean. One of the boys in jagged brown cutoffs points. I look out over the water.

"So?" Alice asks.

"So." I shade my eyes but see nothing. "So, it just goes to show." The man with the jewelry is beside us again but ignoring us, staring out at the Pacific. "A brush in the hand," I say. "No, a brush in each hand. A third brush. Wait a minute." The man with the jewelry begins running, kicking sand against my chest. "A brush in the hand is worth a third in the chest."

"That's not it," Alice says. She sits up straight, stares at the people lining the water's edge.

"Wait," I say, looking at the people but trying to remember the punch line. "Two in the brush is worth a third in the hand. Something like that." I want to say it's the telling that matters, but she's already standing.

"Something's going on out there," she says.

I stand, look out beyond the crowd. The swimmers have gone too far. One is struggling in, the other just a waving arm, a dark head. "He's drowning," I say and begin running toward the water, across the cutting rocks, pushing between the old couple, white as fence posts. One, two, three high steps into the water, then dive beneath a surging wave, pull and kick to the surface, then it's automatic. I'm a swimmer. Fifty laps every morning at the university pool. But this water's thick, the waves insistent. Swing, pull, kick, and twist.

Well into the ocean, I do a pop-up to locate them. One brown man is within twenty yards to my right. Duck, swing, pull, kick, twist. The water is cold. I needed to stretch before I began swimming, warm up. The swimmer is there, T-shirt transparent with water. He's treading hard, slaps the water, shakes his head, says something unintelligible, points farther out. I can see his buddy spitting water, thrashing, another thirty yards, maybe more.

Swing, pull. The cold settles in my muscles. They become brittle. Kick, twist, swing. A wave slaps against my face and head. Another pop-up. Nothing. The ocean rising and falling. A hand. Twenty yards farther still. Swing, pull. I have to think it through, tell my legs to kick, kick, kick. My arms pull in next to my chest. I argue with my arms. Swing, kick, pull. I've messed up the order, working against myself. I stop, tread, my knees jerk up to my chest. The man is gone. I shiver in the water, try one dive, but I can see nothing in the murky Pacific, feel nothing but the cold, the stinging red of my eyes, the painful arguments of my muscles. I turn back.

I backstroke. The sun finds slightly more of me. Backstroking, returning to shore, my body in agreement, I take a deep breath. The man has drowned or is drowning. I backstroke. The sky is mimeo blue.

The first step in shallow water, my knees buckle, but I right myself, wait for a wave to push my thighs forward. Alice is at the water's edge, arms crossed, hands on her shoulders, striped suit, brown eggs. "I couldn't reach him," I say, but too softly, an asthmatic cough.

She runs to me, ties her arms around me. Waves rush our calves. "You're cold," she says.

As she says it, I begin to shiver. Her hands flatten against my back, move up and down in arcs. The first swimmer made it back to shore. He lies on his back in the sand. A crowd, ridiculous in beach clothes that barely cover their bodies, has gathered around him. "Bodies should be covered," I say.

"He's alive," Alice says.

"No, the others." I point at the garish crowd. We walk back toward our beach chairs. Alice is wearing her flipflops, but the rocks tear at my feet. I stop. "Would you grab my flipflops?" I ask her.

She nods, hurries across the patch of rocks and stretch of sand to our chairs. Her body twists and curves perfectly, but her stylish striped suit seems ridiculous too. She reaches the chairs, begins circling, head down. I left the flipflops by my chair, but Alice doesn't see them. I take another step. These are not rocks, I think, these are teeth.

"I can't seem to find them," she says when I finally reach the chairs. I search with her, but they're gone.

"Check your purse," I say, but nothing else is missing.

The crowd is helping the surviving swimmer walk to the hotel. His arms, flabby from fatigue, are around the shoulders of two large men. His wet T-shirt droops from his shoulders like age. Alice and I watch the group as they pass. The swimmer looks directly at me but either doesn't recognize me or chooses not to acknowledge me. The others seem to follow his example, saying nothing.

I look over their feet. Most are barefoot, some in leather thongs, a few flipflops. I scrutinize the flipflops—oranges, grays, reds, greens, one purple pair—a woman, skinny, short dark hair, a black bathing suit stretched over her body like a frown. She trudges through the sand in the rear of the crowd. Her flipflops are much too large for her feet. They're mine.

I grab Alice's shoulder, point. "My flipflops." I hurry over to the crowd, pulling Alice along. "Pardon me," I say loudly.

The crowd looks me over, even the men helping the swimmer. "Pardon me." I approach the skinny woman. "Those are my flipflops," I say.

She looks straight ahead as if she can't hear.

I grab her arm. "My flipflops," I say and point. *"Mis zapatos."*

She jerks her head in my direction. "I speak English," she says, looks away, begins walking again with the group.

"I want my flipflops."

"These are not yours." She still doesn't look at me.

Two dark men in matching bathing suits and life jackets carrying a rowboat above their heads run past us to the water. Alice puts her hands on my waist, pulls me toward her. "Forget it," she whispers.

"I want my flipflops," I say and grab the woman's arm again, jerk her around to face me.

The skinny woman glares at me, then kicks off the flipflops. One bounces off my shin; the other slaps Alice in the pelvis.

For Thanksgiving dinner, we order steaks, rare. The restaurant in the hotel overlooks the ocean, which, at dusk, is as gray as the sky. Muzak cowboy songs are playing—"Back in the Saddle Again," "Tumbling Tumbleweeds," others I don't recognize. At least one person at each of the tables near us has a decapitated pineapple with a straw growing out of it, so when Alice orders Scotch and water, I'm relieved. In a new blue blouse and white skirt, she looks as fresh as new sheets. Changing out of beach clothes has made us familiar again. All afternoon we avoided talking about the drowning by avoiding talking. I slept while she read, then stared at the ocean, the rowboat bobbing in the distance, while she took a nap. Still we're hardly talking, but the silence is more comfortable.

When I first met Alice, she had a cold, sniffling into a tissue while she explained her interest in desert biology, how life in the desert persevered against the odds. Her nose was red, eyes watery. Later I told her she was more beautiful with a cold, that hers was the kind of face that needed flaws. It's her sunburned nose that reminds me, and I begin to wonder if I'll like her best in the mornings before coffee and makeup, and that makes me wonder if there will be mornings. The steaks arrive, overcooked, with refried beans, rice, and green peas.

"I don't think I've ever had steak for Thanksgiving," Alice offers. She slices away a triangle of meat.

"One Thanksgiving, when I was an undergrad," I say, "I ate moldy cottage cheese and day-old bagels." It's a lie, but it fills the space between us.

"I remember one Christmas." She touches the cloth napkin to her lips. "The turkey hadn't thawed. My mother was sick and Father was trying to do everything. He was an awful cook but he had beautiful eyes, like yours, like . . . I want to say like spearmint, but that's a flavor." She gently prods my hand with her finger. "We ate pimento cheese sandwiches and Sara Lee pound cake."

We laugh, hold hands for a moment, then eat. The steak is more tender than it looks but, for some reason, hard to swallow. I fill up on beans and rice. Several tables away, the old couple from the beach stand and walk toward the exit. They see me watching and come to our table. The woman hangs back, smiling sadly and nodding, holding a small white purse tight against her abdomen. The man, overdressed in a white shirt and bow tie, puts a hand on my shoulder. He shakes his head, frowns, shrugs. "The ocean," he says, as if in explanation.

I nod and they leave.

"You look good in water," Alice says, her face intent, as if she's trying to remember something. "The way you just started running . . ." She's looking past me so intensely I almost turn, but she drops her gaze to her plate. "He was a long way out."

I watch her slice her steak. "I was on the swim team in high school," I tell her. "Once I swam two hundred laps for some charity. Multiple Sclerosis, I think."

"I mowed lawns for March of Dimes." She whirls her fork in a tight circle next to her face. "Baked brownies for Muscular Dystrophy. Washed cars for Battered Wives."

"Get Along Little Dogies" begins playing in the background. I smile at her, stir my beans, rice, and peas together. "The credit union donated a dollar for every lap I swam. My shoulders ached for a month."

She reaches across the table, stops me from stirring. "I was scared while you were out there." She looks out the window at the ocean. "I was afraid you might drown, then—this is awful—I tried to think how I'd explain being here with you."

"Did you come up with something?"

She nods. "Research." She giggles, and I remember that her laughter is one of the things that attracted me. "Oh, I would have told the truth, but it sounds so tragic. I hate people feeling sorry for me."

"So what is the truth?" I lean closer to her. "Why *are* you here?"

She smiles, looks at her lap, then the ocean. "Look," she says, "your friends."

The old couple, holding hands, stand near the water's edge. They're both pointing. Three men appear and, behind them, others I can't make out. The men roll up their pants, begin wading in, then spread apart, circling.

"What are they doing?" I ask.

Alice shakes her head, shrugs.

The tallest man gestures to the others. They bend over, lift a body out of the shallow water. The tall one has the hands, the others a foot each. I feel my body pull back.

"This is awful," Alice says. I don't know whether she means the scene outside or us. I turn to face her. She could be the swimmer's widow, so dark is her face. I turn back. The real widow has run barefoot across the sharp rocks to the body. Her hands go from the tangle of her short hair to her husband's bloated body. She wraps her arms around his trunk, but just as quickly she jumps back, away from the body. She drops to her knees, wipes at her arms where they touched him. The three men carry the body away.

Alice touches my arm. I jump. "What?"

"That's her, isn't it?" she says.

"Who?"

"The one who took your flipflops."

I stand, fork and napkin fall. I press my face against the window.

"That's her, isn't it?" Alice says.

I hood my eyes with my hands to stop the glare of the restaurant lights. "It can't be," I say.

"That's her," Alice says. "That's her."

The woman takes a handful of sand, rubs her arms with it.

"No," I say. "That's not her."

Alice tugs at my shirt. I sit back at the table, and we eat our Thanksgiving steaks.

Finally in bed together, I can do nothing, my penis soft and small as a child's. We hold each other. I run my hands down the soft curve of her back again and again. The walls in this room, I realize, are yellow, most yellow near the night lamp, muted by the dark in the corners. There is a painting of a brown boy in a ridiculously large sombrero standing next to a smiling mule. On the dresser, our clothes make happy shapes, like party favors.

"You know any more jokes?" Alice whispers.

Our clothes on the dresser, I think, this room. But I don't say that. I shake my head.

"What about the other? Do you remember the punch line?"

I try to remember. When I can't, I try to reconstruct it.

"A bird in the hand is worth two in the bush. Third would be bird," I say.

"Brush would be bush," she says.

"It doesn't go together. I got thrown off course."

Alice raises up on one elbow. "Maybe the daughter doesn't fall in love with him."

"Maybe." I nod and we become so quiet that I can hear the ocean rushing toward us and human sounds in the room next door.

"Maybe he falls in love with the fortune-teller," Alice says. "Or with his fortune."

"Or with the telling," I say and pull her close, but to get her really close would require something else, something like a third arm. I try to think what it might be.

Alice touches my cheek with her fingertips, then turns off the lamp and the room goes dark. "Do you think we did right coming here?" she asks.

"I don't know," I say, but it comes out a whisper and I lose track of my thoughts.

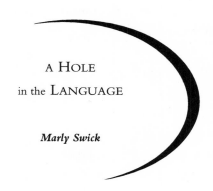

A HOLE
in the LANGUAGE

*Marly Swick*

**MARLY SWICK** is the author of two collections of short stories, *A Hole in the Language* (reprinted as *Monogamy*) and *The Summer Before the Summer of Love,* as well as a novel, *Paper Wings.* Her work has appeared in many magazines and anthologies, including *The Atlantic, Redbook, Gettysburg Review, Prize Stories 1991: The O. Henry Awards,* and *New Stories of the South.* She lives and teaches in Nebraska.

I USED TO believe there is nothing new under the sun. Now what I believe is that there are no new words under the sun—except those having to do with computers—and that is the problem. People are suspicious of anyone or anything that can't be named. It's a sin against language, a sin against community. If you can't be labeled, you're like a car without a license plate—elusive and unaccountable, yet capable of doing great damage. That is the way they see you, and in fact, you do feel a bit out of control—at the same time tentative and reckless—as if all the street signs are in a foreign alphabet, and all you have to rely on are your own split-second instincts. Which is why Elka and I are so cautious now. We live our lives like drivers with our eyes glued to the flashing red light in the rearview mirror. We are braced for the siren's wail. We keep waiting to be punished.

Andrew, my ex-husband, has been as decent under the circumstances as anyone could be, but he is confused, almost dazed. "Do the two of you consider yourselves *married?*" he asks me, his voice, as always lately, straddling the fence between curiosity and animosity.

"We don't think about it," I say. "We're just . . . together."

Till death do us part, I think to myself. As it did us join. A fearful symmetry.

"Together," he repeats blankly, as if he has never heard the word before.

It is difficult to talk to him. His emotions are constantly turning inside out like a matador's cape. He wants to do "the right thing" but is not sure what that is, although everyone else seems to be. Well-meaning friends and relatives, including my own parents, keep urging him to sue me for custody of Grace, our eight-year-old daughter, whose anxiety manifests itself in odd ways. She has nightmares, and not long after Andrew moved out, I overheard her telling the postman that her father had been run over by a UPS truck, something that happened to our dachshund when she was five. She sees a child psychologist once a week—a precautionary measure.

Sometimes, lying in bed with Elka, I just do not know how all this came about, and I wish that Andrew and Grace and I had never moved to Denver, and that I had never met Elka. Not that I am not happy with Elka. Life with another woman seems so harmonious, so easy. I feel like someone who has lived abroad for many years and then suddenly rediscovers the simple, lazy joy of speaking in her native tongue. My hands and mouth have never been so articulate; my skin has never listened so attentively. Yet I fear that maybe I am just a small-town Midwestern girl at heart and I would be happier being unhappy than deviant.

Before Andrew, Grace, and I moved to Denver, we lived in Berkeley, where Andrew lives now. When he returned from London, alone, he rented an apartment on Panoramic Way with a view of Alcatraz. Grace visited him recently and reported that the place is so small he has no bed. There are wall-to-wall tatami mats, and when it was time for bed, the two of them unrolled their sleeping bags. They also ate exclusively with chopsticks. I imagine that Andrew enjoys this footloose opportunity to go Zen, and that defuses my guilt.

Our house was in the flatlands near the Oakland border—ramshackle and overfurnished. Andrew and Peter, his partner, built harpsichords in our garage, and I taught history at a private girls school in San Francisco. All the girls wore gray flannel blazers and knee socks and had pink-dyed streaks in their hair or asymmetrically shaved skulls that put me in mind of malignant brain tumors. They were so rich they seemed immune to life and cared nothing for history. I hated the job. In the mornings, Grace went to Montessori school, and in the afternoons, Andrew was around to keep an eye on her. It was through Grace's chatter that I finally, dim-wittedly, deduced that Andrew was having an affair with one of his customers—a prize-winning children's writer who lived in a restored Victorian in San Francisco and had commissioned an Italian virginal. When I asked him point-blank, Andrew admitted it was true and promised not to see her again. When the instrument was finished, his partner delivered it to the city. I hid the books she had given Grace, and Grace stopped mentioning her name. But occasionally the phone would ring and when I answered, the caller would hang up, and I always suspected it was she. During that split second of silence before the line went dead, I imagined I could hear our two hearts thumping in sync, our hands on the receivers connected by an elaborate circuit of electricity. I never ceased to hear her silence until we loaded up two U-Hauls and moved to Denver the following summer.

In Denver I was completely happy for a month. We rented a pleasant house on the outskirts of the city. It had large sunny rooms and a small swimming pool, like a turquoise postage stamp from some Caribbean island. I had finally landed a job in my field: assistant professor of anthropology at Denver University. Andrew seemed busy and content, converting the garage into a workshop and making the rounds of the local music stores, establishing contacts. Grace made new friends quickly, inviting the neighbor kids over to swim, while her father or I played lifeguard in the ninety-plus-degree heat. Our next-door neighbors, Elka and Nigel Bentley, invited us to a Fourth of July barbecue to meet the neighbors. She was a weaver of some renown and he was a chemist for Bell Labs. Later that night, in bed, Andrew and I discussed the party, analyzed the other couples in that smugly superior way that couples have, and joked about investing in a riding lawn mower. I wrote witty notes to old friends in Berkeley about my fieldwork in the suburbs.

Andrew and I were getting along fine. We always did. The woman in San Francisco was all but forgotten. If anything, I was more curious than jealous. She represented a threat that had passed, a minor crisis swiftly dealt with. Andrew and I had grown up in the same small town, been together since our sophomore year at the University of Nebraska, could barely remember a time when we had not known one another. It was as if our past, our history, were some vital organ that we shared. It would take more than infidelity to blast us apart.

We kept meaning to invite Elka and Nigel to dinner, to return their invitation, but there never seemed to be enough time. I was busy preparing my classes for the fall, and Andrew was already working on a Flemish Double for a music professor at the university. Sometimes, in the afternoon, Elka and Max would come over. Max was only four, and Grace, who had just turned seven that spring, her maternal instincts in full bloom, hovered over him in the water. I liked to watch the tender way she strapped on his water wings and held his hand, usually against his will, as she escorted him into the house to go to the bathroom or get a cookie. However, like any mother, her patience would occasionally snap. More than once I had to yank her from the pool and send her to her room for clobbering Max with a kick-board. Elka just laughed good-naturedly and said, "He has to learn to fight his own battles."

Although he was small for his age, Max was fearless. Unfortunately, he seemed to have more courage than coordination and usually looked like a walking Band-Aid advertisement. Every few minutes, as Elka and I sat in lawn chairs or in the shallow end of the pool chatting away, I would see her start to call out to Max—"Slow down!" or "Watch out!"—and then force herself to let him be. She was thirty-nine when he was born, and she as much as admitted that she had only married Nigel because she wanted to have a baby. I assumed this was her subtle way of letting me know that she shared Andrew's and my assessment of Nigel as, at best, an odd duck and, at worst, a cold fish. He was a cartoonish cliché—the rational scientist with true British reserve—like Cary Grant in *Bringing Up Baby,* only less humorous and handsome. But once she let me know the situation, Elka never complained about him, and, at least in our presence, she always treated him affectionately.

The last week in August, Andrew and I decided to take a week off before the semester started and visit my parents in Coral Gables. Elka volunteered to water the houseplants and take in our mail, and I told her that they should feel free to use our pool. The Sunday we left, I looked out our bedroom window as I was packing and saw Nigel floating in the deep end. He was sitting perfectly upright in a Styrofoam chaise lounge, wearing a Walkman (New Wave, Country Western?) and reading a book that even from a distance looked formidably technical. His nose was plastered with zinc oxide and he was wearing his rubber sandals. Andrew and I shook our heads and smiled.

We had a pleasant visit with my parents. Thinking back to previous visits, how we used to end up arguing and sulking over everything from U.S. immigration policy to red meat, it almost scared me to see how well we now seemed to get along without even trying. I asked Andrew if he thought it meant we were even straighter than we thought, that the suburbs were working their mysterious magic on us. He said it was just the shadow of death putting us on our best behavior. (My father had recently had a double bypass, and as soon as he recovered, my mother had a double mastectomy.) It is amazing how agreeable you can be when you fear that every word you say could be the last word someone hears.

On the plane home to Denver, I felt relieved and relaxed. We watched a silly movie, and I drank a miniature carafe of wine. By the time we left the Denver airport it was late, long past Grace's bedtime. She slept with her head in my lap, her open mouth imprinting a wet rose on the fabric of my skirt during the long ride home. Andrew and I sang along to Linda Ronstadt on the tape deck. It was a hot, dry night, and as we turned the corner to our street, Andrew said, "Let's go for a swim after we put Grace to bed." I nodded and smiled, thinking that after a week of sleeping in the same room with Grace at my parents' cottage, he had more in mind than just a swim.

When we pulled into the driveway, I noticed that the mail had overflowed its box and was piled haphazardly on the doorstep. Inside the house, while Andrew carried Grace upstairs to bed, I walked from room to room, opening the windows and taking an unconscious inventory. I noticed the Boston fern looked peaked, and when I stuck my finger in the soil, it was as dry as the Kalahari. I was spritzing the plants when Andrew reappeared stark naked carrying two towels.

"I thought Elka would be more reliable," I said, heading for the kitchen to refill the atomizer. "I'm surprised."

"Come on," he said. "You can do that later."

Outside, I slipped off my sweaty clothes. Andrew was already swimming minilaps. I waded into the cool water. It was perfectly quiet and dark, except for the soft splashing and the white-goose lamp glowing in Grace's upstairs window. Andrew surfaced beside me.

"Looks like they had a little party," he said, gesturing to a couple of overturned lawn chairs.

"Maybe it was the wind." I still wanted to believe that our neighbors were trustworthy.

"A real blow-out affair."

I groaned and he tried to duck me. We made practiced love in the shallow end of the pool and then went to bed and slept peacefully. In retrospect I would like to say we tossed and turned, that we were both visited by morbid nightmares, but, in truth, we slept peacefully. The next morning, while we were eating breakfast, the telephone rang. "You get it," I told Andrew. I was busy buttering toast and arguing with Grace about how much sugar belonged on her cereal. Suddenly Andrew hung up, clamped my arm, and propelled me into the hallway.

"What the hell . . . ?" I started to shake loose, then noticed his expression. An internal siren started wailing in the back of my brain, speeding forward.

"That was Nigel," he said. "He called to tell us Max drowned last Sunday. The day we left." He let go of my arm.

"No." I pressed my hands against my ears and shut my eyes as if it were some scary part of a movie that would be over with in a second, only it was worse with my eyes closed, projecting my own images. I opened them again.

He nodded, not saying anything, keeping his eyes locked on mine, not blinking, until the precise instant he saw it hit me, the rest of it.

"Oh Jesus," I said. "Not here." I looked out through the sunny kitchen, through the sliding glass doors, at the bright shimmer of turquoise. "How?"

"I don't know. Nigel didn't say and I didn't want to ask."

"Last night," I shuddered. "How could we not have *felt* something, something in the water, how could we . . ." I started to howl—a low, throaty growl that taxied slowly from my belly to my throat, then took off. He tried to wrap his arms around me, but I slapped them away. My fingernail scraped the inside of his wrist.

Grace bolted out of her chair and raced into the hallway clutching a piece of greasy toast. "What's wrong with Mommy?" Her eyes widened. She seemed to freeze in place.

"She hurt herself," Andrew said, staring aggrieved at the razor-thin thread of blood on his wrist. "She bumped her head." He bent over and picked Grace up. "You've got a jam mustache, Amazing Grace. Let's go shave it off."

"How'd she bump her head?" Grace asked suspiciously, looking back at me over his shoulder as he carted her off.

I opened the sliding glass doors and walked outside. The sun glinting off the water hurt my eyes. It looked exactly the same. A few leaves floating on the surface, a kick-board bobbing in the deep end. I don't know what I expected to see: blood, skid marks, broken glass? I looked over at Elka's house.

This is how it happened. (I heard the story first from another neighbor and later, in more detail, from Elka herself.) It was Sunday afternoon. We had just taken off. Elka and Max were in the kitchen, and Nigel was floating in his chaise lounge in our pool. Elka, who hated to cook, was making some elaborate dessert for a dinner party that evening—the kind that requires four hands to whip the egg whites, melt the chocolate, sift the sugar, and de-stem the strawberries simultaneously. Max was kneeling on a chair at the table, stabbing some Saltines with peanut butter. I can picture his sticky fist pushing his white-blond hair out of his eyes, his peanut-butter-coated bangs spiked out like a punk rocker's. The phone rang and Elka answered it, cradling the receiver between her shoulder and neck as she continued to whip and melt and sift. It was long distance, Nigel's widowed mother in London. As she looked at the chocolate bubbling in the double boiler and assured Mother Bentley that they were all fine, she told Max, *sotto voce,* to run next door and tell Daddy to hurry to the phone. After five or so minutes, when neither Nigel nor Max had appeared, she apologized to her mother-in-law and said Nigel would have to call her back. Irritated, she hung up, turned the burners off, and cut across the backyard to our house. The gate was open, and she could see Nigel in his floating lounge chair. She hollered, but he didn't answer. More irritated, she stormed over to the pool. As she neared the water's edge, she could see that Nigel was wearing his Walkman, sound asleep, his book open in his lap, snoring. Max was nowhere in sight. Her heart started pounding in her ears like a movie sound track, and she hollered Max's name as she stooped to pick up the long-handled butterfly net we used to skim leaves and bugs from the water's surface and extended the pole to prod Nigel in the ribs. At that instant, out of the corner of her eye, she spotted Max's red-and-blue-striped T-shirt floating near the bottom of the pool, not far from Nigel's chaise lounge, in the deep end. She dropped the pole and dove for him. The pole clattering onto the cement jolted Nigel awake.

\*    \*    \*

I began spending time with Elka. I didn't know what to say. Under normal circumstances, I am not a demonstrative person, and had Elka been dry-eyed and glacial in her grief, as I imagine I might have been in her place, most likely I would have mumbled my inadequate formal apologies and then avoided her out of guilt and embarrassment. But Elka's grief was a force of nature—a flood, a quake, an avalanche of emotion—that swept us both up. There was nothing personal or private about it. That first terrible evening when I knocked tentatively on her door, trembling with irrational guilt, expecting her to call me abusive names and slap us with a lawsuit, she flung open the door and embraced me. I could see that she had been sitting there in the dark, surrounded by little piles of Max's clean clothes. A plastic laundry basket was in the middle of the living room floor next to a box of Kleenex. We drank a whole bottle of Amaretto together—the only liquor in the house—tears streaming, not bothering to light a lamp as the dusk deepened into darkness inside the house. Nigel was not at home and somehow I did not think to ask where he was. I found it impossible to talk. I had never been particularly fluent in the language of the emotions. To me, words expressed thoughts, not feelings. Embarrassed by my silence, I got up and roamed into the kitchen. A pan of crusted chocolate was sitting on the stove, a bowl of spoiled egg-whites on the counter, wilted strawberries in the sink. The fact that Elka, normally such a compulsively neat hausfrau, had let her kitchen deteriorate to this state shook something loose inside me. I began washing the dishes, and as I stood at Elka's sink and plunged my hands into the hot soapy water, I experienced a terrifying disorientation, as if I *were* Elka, trapped in my grief, and not just the neighbor come to offer my condolences. I let Elka talk. She sat at the kitchen table, pouring us snifters of Amaretto, and rambled from one topic to the next, a frantic chatter not at all like her usual slow and soothing speech. She was passed out on the couch when I left around midnight, and I threw up in the bushes outside our back door before staggering inside.

After that, hardly an evening went by that I did not stray over there. Sitting at my desk reading about male-female roles in New Guinea or puberty rites among the Zuñi Indians, my thoughts would wander to Elka sitting there alone, and I would stare out my window at the pool, floodlit with an eerie greenish light. If I stared long enough, I would see a small shadow take shape under the surface of the water, like the outline of a murder victim drawn in chalk. I tried moving my desk to face the wall, but I just found myself putting away my books and joining Elka earlier every evening. I told myself this was my fieldwork in the land of grief, more foreign to me even than Pago Pago. I refused to let Grace come with me. Whenever Elka saw us together, I felt embarrassed, as if a starving person had caught me eating a steak. Since Andrew worried and complained about my spending so much time with Elka, I began to lie—to say I was going to the store or to the library or for a walk. There was only so much he could say without sounding hard-hearted. What soft-hearted person can begrudge a grieving mother? It occurred to me that there was a hole in the language. Why was there no word like *widow* to designate the mother of a dead child?

Elka would open a bottle of wine. Nigel was always out somewhere, probably at his lab, even after midnight. They were no comfort to each other. Sometimes she would take my hand and hold it, just hold it, and I would pat her hand, stiffly at first, then less so, as the wine unstarched me. There was nothing sexual about it. We were mourners. We could have been orphaned children or ninety-year-old widows. There was something ancient and collective at work. At the end of the month, Nigel rented a furnished apartment clear across the city, packed a suitcase, a few cartons of books and tools, and was gone. Statistics show that few marriages, even healthy ones, survive the death of a child. Elka didn't seem to miss him, rarely mentioned him. In the evolution of her life, he was like some secondary characteristic—a fin or gill—that, having ceased to serve a function, disappeared.

Andrew and I argued over the swimming pool. What I wanted to do, what I dreamed one night, was that we shoveled dirt into it like an open grave, until it was filled, and then we planted grass. However, we were renting the house and I knew the landlord would object. So I figured I would do the next best thing. While Andrew was on a wood-buying trip, I called the pool maintenance company and had them drain and cover the pool. This was mid-August, still hot enough to swim for several more weeks. Andrew arrived home in the late afternoon, tired and sweaty. He kissed me hello and then went upstairs to unpack. I didn't say anything even when he came down a few minutes later in his bathing trunks. Grace was across the street at a friend's birthday party. She had been pouting ever since the pool man came. My nerves were bad, and I had actually slapped her across the face that morning, then cried until she patted my hair to comfort me. Andrew slid the glass doors open and stepped outside. My stomach muscles clenched.

"Okay," he said, "okay," when he walked back inside a split second later. "Okay." His voice was calm, soothing, as if he were gentling a spooked horse.

"You don't mind?" In the back of my brain, I heard my breathing kick on again.

"Did you think I would?"

"I don't know. I thought you might," I said. "You want a cold beer?"

"I want a cold swim!" He pounded the oak table with his fist so hard that the bowl of fruit bounced and two tangerines rolled onto the floor. "That's what I *want,* as if you cared."

"If you had any feelings, you wouldn't set foot in that pool," I shouted back. "The sight of it would make you sick."

"You're sick." He jabbed a finger at my chest. "You're obsessed." He dropped his hands to his sides suddenly, and the anger seemed to drain out through his fingertips. "Maybe you ought to see someone, a psychologist," he said more calmly. "This guilt—it's ridiculous. We had nothing to do with it. Nothing."

"I'm perfectly sane. I just don't like looking at that pool." I knelt down and retrieved the bruised tangerines. "We survived without a pool for ten years. Most of the free world lives without swimming pools in their backyard."

"That's not the point."

I shrugged.

"I think we should move," he said. "Find another house."

"No!" I rummaged in the refrigerator for two beers and attempted a more calm and pragmatic tone. "We're settled. Grace has friends here."

"Yeah, and what about your friend?" His thumb stabbed the air in the direction of Elka's house. "Whatever's going on between the two of you isn't healthy."

"There's nothing 'going on.' Do I have to remind you that you're the one who had something 'going on'?"

"That's old news. Don't try to shift the blame." He twisted the cap off his beer and took a swallow. "I can see what's happening even if you can't."

The argument never really ended. It twisted and turned and splintered and mutated, destructive and indestructible. Almost every evening, Andrew would pack his gym bag and drive to the university, where he would swim laps for an hour. He had always been a half-hearted jogger, an on-again-off-again tennis player—never a swimmer. I knew he did it as a silent reproach. I didn't care. When Elka asked me whether Andrew minded my spending so much time with her, I said, "Of course not." And she believed me because he was always so friendly and helpful—mowing her lawn, fixing the leaky faucet. Even as late as November, when we were barely speaking, he got out the ladder and put up all her storm windows.

One evening, an unusually stifling August night, Andrew mixed up a pitcher of margaritas and we sat on the side patio, drinking and sweating. We avoided the backyard. The sight of the boarded-up pool only reminded us of our differences. Grace was already in bed. We were talking lightly about this and that, nothing much, and he reached over and pulled the string on my bathing suit top. It slid down to my waist, and he fished an ice cube out of his drink and began sliding it over my breasts. The side porch was screened off by a tall hedge, and when we first moved in, we had made love there once or twice—Andrew liked the sensation of freedom—but I had checked one day recently and discovered it was possible for Elka to see us from her bedroom window. He slid his hand under the waistband of my shorts and his icy fingertips sent a shiver through me. I could see the light on in Elka's bedroom and hear her radio playing softly.

"Not here," I said. "Inside."

"It's too hot in there." He knelt down on the flagstone and put his face between my legs. I moaned, then thought of Elka over there all alone, listening to us, and pushed him away.

"What's the matter?" he said.

"Elka. I don't want her to see us."

"Why? You think she'd be jealous?" He flung my bathing suit top at me.

"No. I think she'd feel sad."

"Christ, I'm tired of this." He stood up and slid open the glass door into our bedroom. "Max may have drowned, but you're in way over your head." He slammed the door behind him, stormed into the bathroom, and turned on the shower. It sounded like heavy rain. I looked at the sky expecting to hear thunder and see lightning.

In September, I began teaching, Grace started second grade, and Andrew's father, Art the Fart, suffered a mild stroke. A retired Air Force colonel, he had rarely spoken a civil word to Andrew, his only son, since he filed for C.O. status in 1968, but Andrew promptly flew out to Monterey when his mother called with the news. I suspected that he welcomed the excuse to get away for a while, since for no rational reason things were deteriorating so rapidly between us. It was almost as if *we* were the ones who had lost our child, and occasionally when I passed by Grace's room, I would experience this chill of desolation, as if she were long dead. It was as if because the tragedy had taken place in our backyard, it was somehow meant for us; we were part owners.

It was not a good time for Andrew to be gone. I sometimes wonder if everything might simply, gradually have returned to normal if Andrew had not jumped at the first chance to escape. This may sound naive, but I believe in the domino theory—the chain reaction. At any point along the way, the chain can be broken, resistance can halt momentum. But Andrew had never been a fighter. Look how effortlessly he had relinquished his lover, the woman in San Francisco. At the time I interpreted it as a sign of his caring (for me), but later I realized it was a sign of his not caring (for her)—at least not enough to resist—and Elka was in no shape to resist anything. So that left me. Grief and love feel a lot alike, different stages of the same emotion. It's difficult to tell them apart in the dark.

With Andrew in California, someone needed to be there for Grace on the afternoons I taught my Intro class and the two evenings a week I conducted the honors seminar. Elka volunteered. After school, Grace went next door and played with Elka's collection of old German dolls—real glass eyes and human hair—while Elka worked at her floor loom. When I returned home, Elka would have a savory stew simmering on the stove, a crisp salad in the refrigerator.

"I thought you hated to cook," I said the first evening. "You don't have to do all this."

"I need to keep busy," she said. "It's good for me."

The evenings I had my seminar Elka would stay after dinner. She would watch television or play Chinese checkers with Grace until her bedtime. I had feared that Grace's presence would be a constant, wounding reminder of Max's absence, but Elka seemed to seek her out, and sometimes I would hear them laughing together about something silly. One afternoon I came home and found Elka sitting on the couch with Grace sound asleep in her lap. Elka was stroking Grace's hair, the same white-blond as Max's, weeping silently. Grace woke up as soon as I entered the room and burst into frightened tears when she saw Elka crying. Andrew and I had sat Grace down and explained to her about Max's being dead. She had listened somberly and then said, "Like Weenie?" Weenie was our dachshund, the one who had been run over, so we figured that she understood.

None of us seemed capable of sleeping alone in our solitary beds, of getting through the night. Elka postponed returning to her empty house later and later each night, until it seemed only logical that she stay. The third bedroom was my study and the couch was too short for Elka's long legs, so she slept in my bed. We balanced precariously like bookends on either edge of the bed, chaste as schoolgirls, more chaste, waiting for Grace. Grace's nightmares started while Andrew was in California. Almost every night she would wake up choking and crying, not screaming, and stumble into my bedroom. "I want Daddy," she'd whimper, then still half-asleep, she would curl up between Elka and me in bed, her body like a tight little fist, and the three of us would huddle like aborigines around a fire in the darkness, only we *were* the fire.

I had not spoken to Andrew since he called to say he had arrived safely in Monterey, his father seemed strong and alert, and his parents were driving him crazy. A cautious, civil conversation. After that, a postcard arrived every other day or so. He had been gone ten days. The last postcard said he was visiting friends of ours in Berkeley. It was postmarked San Francisco, which could have signified anything—dinner in Chinatown, an old movie at the Surf Theater, linguine and clams at Little Joe's in North Beach. We had been married ten years and lived together for two before that. You would think that after twelve years you would just *know* one way or the other, but I had no idea if he were seeing her again or not—the woman with the Italian virginal. Her name was Maggie.

As it turned out, or at least as he told me and I believe him, he had not even called her, although he had been to the city for dinner two or three times and had thought about it each time. He had told the whole story about Max and Elka and me to Peter, his former partner, over Irish coffees at the Buena Vista one evening. Peter had listened and then said, "So what's the problem? I don't get it. She feels sorry for this Elka, she spends a lot of time with her. It's a temporary situation. Let it ride."

"There's more to it," Andrew said, immediately defensive.

"What?" Peter asked. "I'm listening."

"I don't know. I don't know," Andrew laughed. "There must be something."

"And suddenly I just felt ridiculous," Andrew said when he called me from the pay phone at the Buena Vista. "I can't even remember why I've been so angry. I was trying to explain it to Peter and suddenly it just seemed like no big deal. I guess I just overreacted. I'm sorry."

"It's just been a bad time," I said. "For all of us."

"How's Elka?"

"Better," I said.

"Good. Are you still spending as much time with her?" His voice had a slight edge, although he was trying to keep it light.

"Not so much. I'm busy with classes," I mumbled.

"What?" he shouted.

I could hear loud music and talking and laughter and the clatter of dishes in the background. Elka was asleep on the couch in front of the television, where I'd found her when I came home from my seminar, and Grace was upstairs in bed. I didn't want to shout.

I cupped my hand around the mouthpiece and whispered into it. "I said not so much. We hardly see each other. Where are you?"

"The Buena Vista. I guess Peter was right. He said, in effect, I was being a jerk."

"You're not a jerk," I said. "And even if you are, I miss you."

"I miss you, too. In fact, I'm thinking . . ."

There was a loud crash, as if someone had dropped a tray full of silverware at Andrew's feet. "I can't hear you," I said.

"Never mind," he shouted. "This is ridiculous. Call you later." He hung up.

The phone call cheered me. Everything seemed lighter suddenly, as if a simple solution for some weighty problem had just occurred to me, and I hummed an old Linda Ronstadt song as I climbed the stairs and ran the water for my bath. I carried the radio into the bathroom and submerged myself in the steamy water, thinking over responses I wished I had given to student questions earlier in the evening. Whenever the bath water cooled off, I'd rotate the *Hot* faucet with my toes and let it blast until I was pleasantly scalded again. I thought about all the times Andrew had marveled and complained about my capacity to withstand heat. And I remembered a documentary about nuclear radiation in which this activist nun said that if you heated it up gradually, frogs would remain in a pot of water until they boiled themselves to death. This was supposed to be a metaphor for humanity and the arms race. When I finished draining the bath and drying myself off, I tiptoed into my bedroom for a clean nightgown. Elka and Grace were already sound asleep in bed, nestled together in the pitch dark like two small, furry animals trying to burrow into the same hole.

Hours later, Elka was shaking me. It was still dark. I was dreaming that we were swimming in the ocean in Florida, near my parents' house. Max and my father were floating in a large black inner tube garlanded with flowers.

"I heard something," Elka whispered. "Someone's downstairs."

I sat up quickly, my heart hammering, and covered Grace completely with the blanket, as if to make her invisible to danger. I heard the footsteps on the stairs. Elka and I sat there frozen. I couldn't decide if it would be better or worse to turn on the light. Where's Andrew? I thought, panicked and paralyzed, and then there he was, standing in the doorway, whispering my name: "Jane, Jane? It's Andrew. Are you awake?"

"Thank God!" I burst out and snapped on the bedside lamp. "You scared us half to death." I pressed the palm of my hand against my heart. "Be still." I was laughing with relief. He was standing there staring, glaring really, as Elka nervously buttoned the top button of her pajamas and Grace suddenly woke up and shouted, "Daddy!" She leapt out of bed and ran after him as he stormed down the stairs. I could hear their voices but not their words down below in the kitchen. Elka and I looked at each other, not quite meeting each other's eyes. For the first time I felt awkward with her. I was aware of the weight of my breasts through the thin nightgown material, and I could smell her spicy perfume on the sheets. She reached over and covered my hand with hers, a gesture of comfort, and for the first time I felt the charge between us, as if my blood were slowly heating up, and it surprised me and alarmed me. I felt Elka's trembling pass through me, and I wondered where this came from. It was as if our passion were a figment of Andrew's jealousy.

Andrew flew back to California the next day. He stayed away. He would call to talk to Grace but refuse to speak to me. He gave Grace a phone number where she could reach him and told her it was a secret. While she was at school, I searched her room until I found it taped inside the lid of her jewelry box. I left the lid open, and, sitting on my bed, I could hear the tinkly silver music through the wall as I dialed the number. A woman answered. "Hello," I said. "Andrew Lefler gave me your name as a reference. I'm thinking of buying a harpsichord."

"Oh yes," she said. "What would you like to know?"

I hung up.

He called me that evening from a pay phone. It must have been on the street. I could hear traffic noises. "What do you want?" he kept saying. "Do you really want me to come back?"

"Yes," I said. "Yes, yes, yes. How many times do I have to say it."

"All right. Two conditions. One, you find yourself a therapist. Two, you find us another house."

"Okay. How soon can you be here?" I said. "I want you to come right away."

"What's the rush? You sound scared."

"I *am* scared," I shouted, then lowered my voice. "Tomorrow? Can you come tomorrow?"

"I told you. Two conditions. I'm not coming back until—"

"You're not serious," I interrupted.

"I *am* serious. I want to know *you're* serious. Are you?"

I didn't answer right away. I stood up and paced the room. Out the window I could see the swimming pool cover sagging under a blanket of brown leaves.

"I'll call the landlord tomorrow," I said.

But I didn't. I couldn't imagine Elka living next door to strangers or the house standing empty. Nigel called her periodically. He even stopped by the house with plane tickets one evening and begged her to go away on vacation with him to Hawaii, but she refused and asked him not to come back. She spent most of her time at our house. I don't know what the neighbors thought. I don't know what we thought. We tried not to think about it, to label it. Once in the heat of a long-distance argument, Andrew called me a "dyke," and I was literally winded by the insult.

"It's not like that," I shouted and hung up, furious, then ran to the bathroom and threw up. I was too sick to come to the phone when he called back five minutes later. Elka answered it and said he'd said to tell me he was sorry. I was stretched out on the tile floor. She knelt down and sponged my face and neck with a cool washcloth. Her long hair tickled my arm. I reached up and tucked a strand back behind her ear. In the winter her hair was the color of sand and the exposed ear as delicately pink as a shell. I imagined lying next to her, pressing my ear to hers, lulled by the distant hush of ocean. She locked the door and lay down next to me on the cold tiles.

At Thanksgiving Andrew came back for five days to visit with Grace and collect his things. Elka flew to St. Paul to have Thanksgiving with her parents and brother's family. While she was away, Andrew put up her storm windows and sawed some dead limbs off the massive tree in her front yard. He no longer seemed angry, just sad—bewildered but resigned. I had papers to grade and was not in a festive mood, so the three of us had Thanksgiving dinner in a restaurant and then escorted Grace to a matinee of *Snow White* where she sat between us. Andrew and I slept in our bed and even made love twice, the first night and the last, hello and good-bye. He was going to London with Maggie— she had some grant and he was going to study harpsichord making at the London College of Furniture, something he had always wanted to do. He agreed to let Grace stay with me, temporarily at least. I promised to send her to a child psychologist once a week and to have the psychologist send him monthly reports. Part of me bristled at being put on probation like this, but another part of me was relieved to have some professional monitoring the situation, which, as far as I was concerned, was already way beyond my control. I thought of it as a kind of emotional avalanche, something apart from me, with a momentum all its own. A fluke. Something that could not happen again in a million years. Something that is neither happy nor sad. Something that defies definition.

The week after Andrew left, Elka moved in. We carried the dining room set down to the basement and moved her loom into the empty space. In my study, directly above the dining room, I can hear the shuttle slamming back and forth, back and forth. Elka works at a furious pace, as if she is trying to make up for lost time. Lately, she has begun reading through my anthropology books, which are filled with descriptions of women weaving—mats, baskets, textiles. Inspired by Elka, I am gathering notes for a scholarly paper on the role of weaving in tribal cultures. And inspired by me, she is working on a series of "mosquito bags" modeled after the elaborate, highly prized sleeping bags the Tchambuli women in New Guinea used to weave. Two of these woven bags equaled the price of one canoe.

And even Grace has developed a sudden, passionate interest in weaving. Elka has given her a small hand loom. Often, when I gravitate downstairs for a snack or study break, I find Grace sitting cross-legged on the floor next to

Elka, working away on some narrow, brightly colored belt or scarf. Their hands seem to dance in the slanting afternoon light as they work side by side in companionable silence. It is a peaceful scene—primitive, archetypal, female— and for one perfect instant I imagine the men are off in their canoes, catching fish with their bare hands. And any moment now they will appear, Andrew and Nigel holding aloft the canoe, and Max bringing up the rear, clutching the fish to his chest, the day's bountiful catch shining silver in the bright sun.

IKE and NINA

*T. Coraghessan Boyle*

**T. CORAGHESSAN BOYLE**'s short stories have appeared in *The New Yorker, The Atlantic, Playboy, The Paris Review, GQ,* and *The Antioch Review.* His recent books include *The Tortilla Curtain, Without a Hero, The Road to Wellville,* and *East Is East.* He studied music at SUNY-Potsdam before earning an M.F.A. and Ph.D. at the Iowa Writers' Workshop. He lives near Santa Barbara, California.

THE YEARS HAVE put a lid on it, the principals passed into oblivion. I think I can now, in good conscience, reveal the facts surrounding one of the most secretive and spectacular love affairs of our time: the *affaire de coeur* that linked the thirty-fourth president of the United States and the then first lady of the Soviet Union. Yes: the eagle and the bear, defrosting the Cold War with the heat of their passion, Dwight D. Eisenhower—Ike—virile, dashing, athletic, in the arms of Madame Nina Khrushcheva, the svelte and seductive school-mistress from the Ukraine. Behind closed doors, in embassy restrooms and hotel corridors, they gave themselves over to the urgency of their illicit love, while the peace and stability of the civilized world hung in the balance.

Because of the sensitive—indeed sensational—nature of what follows, I have endeavored to tell my story as dispassionately as possible, and must say in my own defense that my sole interest in coming forward at this late date is to provide succeeding generations with a keener insight into the events of those tumultuous times. Some of you will be shocked by what I report here, others moved. Still others—the inevitable naysayers and skeptics—may find it diffi-cult to believe. But before you turn a deaf ear, let me remind you how unthink-able it once seemed to credit reports of Errol Flynn's flirtation with Nazis and homosexuals, FDR's thirty-year obsession with Lucy Mercer, or Ted Kennedy's overmastering desire for an ingenuous campaign worker eleven years his junior. The truth is often hard to swallow. But no historian worth his salt, no self-respecting journalist, no faithful eyewitness to the earth-shaking and epoch-making events of human history has ever blanched at it.

Here then, is the story of Ike and Nina.

In September of 1959, I was assistant to one of Ike's junior staffers, thirty-one years old, schooled in international law, and a consultant to the Slaviclanguages program at one of our major universities.* I'd had very little contact with the president, had in fact laid eyes on him but twice in the eighteen months I'd worked for the White House (the first time, I was looking for a drinking fountain when I caught a glimpse of him—a single flash of his radiant brow—huddled in a back room with Foster Dulles and Andy Goodpaster; a week later, as I was hurrying down a corridor with a stack of reports for shredding, I spotted him slipping out a service entrance with his golf clubs). Like dozens of bright, ambitious young men apprenticed to the mighty, I was at this stage of my career a mere functionary, a paper shuffler, so deeply buried in the power structure I must actually have ranked below the pastry chef's croissant twister. I was good—I had no doubt of it—but I was as yet untried, and for all I knew unnoticed. You can imagine my surprise when early one morning I was summoned to the Oval Office.

It was muggy, and though the corridors hummed with the gentle ministrations of the air conditioners, my shirt was soaked through by the time I reached the door of the president's inner sanctum. A crewcut ramrod in uniform swung open the door, barked out my name, and ushered me into the room. I was puzzled, apprehensive, awed; the door closed behind me with a soft click and I found myself in the Oval Office, alone with the president of the United States. Ike was standing at the window, gazing out at the trees, whistling "The Flirtation Waltz," and turning a book of crossword puzzles over in his hands. "Well," he said, turning to me and extending his hand, "Mr. Paderewski, is that right?"

"Yes sir," I said. He pronounced it "Paderooski."†

"Well," he repeated, taking me in with those steely blue eyes of his as he sauntered across the room and tossed the book on his desk like a slugger casually dropping his bat after knocking the ball out of the park. He looked like a golf pro, a gymnast, a competitor, a man who could come at you with both hands and a nine iron to boot. Don't be taken in by all those accounts of his declining

---

*I choose not to name it, just as I decline to reveal my actual identity here, for obvious reasons.

†This is a pseudonym I've adopted as a concession to dramatic necessity in regard to the present narrative.

health—I saw him there that September morning in the Oval Office, broad-shouldered and trim-waisted, lithe and commanding. Successive heart attacks and a bout with ileitis hadn't slowed the old warrior a bit. A couple of weeks short of his sixty-ninth birthday, and he was jaunty as a high-schooler on prom night. Which brings me back to the reason for my summons.

"You're a good egg, aren't you, Paderewski?" Ike asked.

I replied in the affirmative.

"And you speak Russian, is that right?"

"Yes, sir, Mr. President—and Polish, Sorbian, Serbo-Croatian, and Slovene as well."

He grunted, and eased his haunch down on the corner of the desk. The light from the window played off his head till it glowed like a second sun. "You're aware of the upcoming visit of the Soviet premier and his, uh, wife?"

I nodded.

"Good, that's very good, Paderewski, because as of this moment I'm appointing you my special aide for the duration of that visit." He looked at me as if I were some odd and insignificant form of life that might bear further study under the microscope, looked at me like the man who had driven armies across Europe and laid Hitler in his grave. "Everything that happens, every order I give you, is to be held strictly confidential—top secret—is that understood?"

I was filled with a sense of mission, importance, dignity. Here I was, elevated from the ranks to lend my modest talents to the service of the first citizen of the nation, the commander-in-chief himself. "Understood, Mr. President," I said, fighting the impulse to salute.

This seemed to relax him, and he leaned back on the desk and told me a long, involved story about an article he'd come across in the *National Geographic*, something about Egyptian pyramids and how the members of a pharaoh's funeral procession were either blinded on the spot or entombed with their leaders—something along those lines. I didn't know what to make of it. So I put on my meditative look, and when he finished I flashed him a smile that would have melted ice.

Ike smiled back.

\*    \*    \*

By now, of course, I'm sure you've guessed just what my special duties were to consist of—I was to be the president's liaison with Mrs. Khrushchev, a go-between, a pillow smoother and excuse maker: I was to be Ike's panderer. Looking back on it, I can say in all honesty that I did not then, nor do I now, feel any qualms whatever regarding my role in the affair. No, I feel privileged to have witnessed one of the grand passions of our time, a love both tender and profane, a love that smoldered beneath the watchful eyes of two embattled nations and erupted in an explosion of passionate embraces and hungry kisses.

Ike, as I was later to learn, had first fallen under the spell of Madame K. in 1945, during his triumphal visit to Moscow after the fall of the Third Reich. It was the final day of his visit, a momentous day, the day Japan had thrown in the towel and the great war was at long last ended. Ambassador Harriman arranged a reception and buffet supper at the U.S. embassy by way of celebration, and to honor Ike and his comrade-in-arms, Marshal Zhukov. In addition to Ike's small party, a number of high-ranking Russian military men and politicos turned out for what evolved into an uproarious evening of singing, dancing, and congratulatory backslapping. Corks popped, vodka flowed, the exuberant clamor of voices filled the room. And then Nina Khrushcheva stepped through the door.

Ike was stunned. Suddenly nothing existed for him—not Zhukov, not Moscow, not Harriman, the armistice, or "The Song of the Volga Boatmen," which an instant before had been ringing in his ears—there was only this vision in the doorway, simple, unadorned, elegant, this true princess of the earth. He didn't know what to say, didn't know who she was; the only words of Russian he could command—*zdrav'st* and *spasibo*\*—flew to his lips like an unanswered prayer. He begged Harriman for an introduction, and then spent the rest of the evening at her side, the affable Ike, gazing into the quiet depths of her rich mud-brown eyes, entranced. He didn't need an interpreter.

It would be ten long years before their next meeting, years that would see the death of Stalin, the ascendancy of Khrushchev, and Ike's own meteoric rise to political prominence as the thirty-fourth president of the United States.

\*"Hello" and "thank you."

Through all that time, through all the growing enmity between their countries, Ike and Nina cherished that briefest memory of one another. For his part, Ike felt he had seen a vision, sipped from the cup of perfection, and that no other woman could hope to match it—not Mamie, not Ann Whitman, not even his old flame, the lovely and adept Kay Summersby. He plowed through CIA dossiers on this captivating spirit, Nina Petrovna, wife of the Soviet premier, maintained a scrapbook crammed with photos of her and news clippings detailing her husband's movements; twice, at the risk of everything, he was able to communicate with her through the offices of a discreet and devoted agent of the CIA. In July of 1955, he flew to Geneva, hungering for peaceful coexistence.

At the Geneva Conference, the two came together once again, and what had begun ten years earlier as a riveting infatuation blossomed into the mature and passionate love that would haunt them the rest of their days. Ike was sixty-five, in his prime, the erect warrior, the canny leader, a man who could shake off a stroke as if it were a head cold; Nina, ten years his junior, was in the flush of womanly maturity, lovely, solid, a soft inscrutable smile playing on her elfin lips. With a subterfuge that would have tied the intelligence networks of their respective countries in knots, the two managed to steal ten minutes here, half an hour there—they managed, despite the talks, the dinners, the receptions, and the interminable, stultifying rounds of speechmaking, to appease their desire and sanctify their love forever. "Without personal contact," Ike said at a dinner for the Russian delegation, his boyish blue eyes fixed on Mrs. Khrushchev, "you might imagine someone was fourteen feet high, with horns and a tail." Russians and Americans alike burst into spontaneous laughter and applause. Nina Petrovna, first lady of the Soviet Union, stared down at her chicken Kiev and blushed.

And so, when the gargantuan Soviet TU 114 shrieked into Andrews Air Force Base in September of 1959, I stood by my president with a lump in my throat: I alone knew just how much the Soviet visit meant to him, I alone knew by how tenuous a thread hung the balance of world peace. What could the president have been thinking as the great sleek jet touched down? I can only conjecture. Perhaps he was thinking that she'd forgotten him, or that the scrutiny of the press would make it impossible for them to steal their precious few moments together, or that her husband—that torpedo-headed bully boy—would discover them and tear the world to pieces with his rage. Consider Ike at that moment, consider the all-but-insurmountable barriers thrown in his way, and you can appreciate my calling him one of the truly impassioned lovers of all time. Romeo had nothing on him, nor Douglas Fairbanks either—even the starry-eyed Edward Windsor pales by comparison. At any rate, he leaped at his opportunity like a desert nomad delivered to the oasis: there would be an assignation that very night, and I was to be instrumental in arranging it.

After the greeting ceremonies at Andrews, during which Ike could do no more than exchange smiles and handshakes with the premier and premiersha, there was a formal state dinner at the White House. Ambassador Menshikov was there, Khrushchev and his party, Ike and Mamie, Christian Herter, Dick Nixon, and others; afterward, the ladies retired to the Red Room for coffee. I sat at Ike's side throughout dinner, and lingered in the hallway outside the Red Room directly thereafter. At dinner, Ike had kissed Madame K.'s hand and chatted animatedly with her for a few minutes, but they covered their emotions so well that no one would have guessed they were anything other than amenable strangers wearing their social faces. Only I knew better.

I caught the premiersha as she and Mamie emerged from the Red Room in a burst of photographers' flashbulbs. As instructed, I took her arm and escorted her to the East Room, for the program of American songs that would highlight the evening. I spoke to her in Russian, though to my surprise she seemed to have a rudimentary grasp of conversational English (did she recall it from her schoolteaching days, or had she boned up for Ike?). Like a Cyrano, I told her that the president yearned for her tragically, that he'd thought of nothing else in the four years since Geneva, and then I recited a love poem he'd written her in English—I can't recall the sense of it now, but it boiled with Elizabethan conceits and the imagery of war, with torn hearts, manned bastions, and references to heavy ordnance, pillboxes, and scaling the heights of love. Finally, just before we entered the East Room, I pressed a slip of paper into her hand. It read, simply: *3:00 A.M., back door, Blair House.*

At five of three, in a rented, unmarked limousine, the president and I pulled up at the curb just down the street from Blair House, where the Khrushchev party had been installed for the night. I was driving. The rear panel slid back and the president's voice leaped at me out of the darkness: "Okay, Paderewski, do your stuff—and good luck."

I eased out of the car and started up the walk. The night was warm and damp, the darkness a cloak, streetlights dulled as if they'd been shaded for the occasion. Every shadow was of course teeming with Secret Service agents— there were enough of them ringing the house to fill Memorial Stadium twice over—but they gave way for me. (Ike had arranged it thus: one person was to be allowed to enter the rear of Blair House at the stroke of three; two would be leaving an instant thereafter.)

She was waiting for me at the back door, dressed in pants and a man's overcoat and hat. "Madame Khrushcheva?" I whispered. *"Da,"* came the reply, soft as a kiss. We hurried across the yard and I handed her into the car, admiring Ike's cleverness: if anyone—including the legion of Secret Service, CIA, and FBI men—had seen us, they would have mistaken the madame for her husband and concluded that Ike had set up a private, ultrasecret conference. I slid into the driver's seat and Ike's voice, shaken with emotion, came at me again: "Drive, Paderewski," he said. "Drive us to the stars." And then the panel shot to with a passionate click.

For two hours I circled the capitol, and then, as prearranged, I returned to Blair House and parked just down the street. I could hear them—Ike and Nina, whispering, embracing, rustling clothing—as I cut the engine. She giggled. Ike was whistling. She giggled again, a lovely windchime of a sound, musical and coltish—if I hadn't known better I would have thought Ike was back there with a coed. I was thinking with some satisfaction that we'd just about pulled it off when the panel slid back and Ike said: "Okay, Paderewski—let's hit it." There was the sound of a protracted kiss, a sound we all recognize not so much through experience—who's listening, after all?—but thanks to the attention Hollywood sound men have given it. Then Ike's final words to her, delivered in a passionate susurrus, words etched in my memory as if in stone: "Till we meet again," he whispered.

Something odd happened just then, just as I swung back the door for Mrs. Khrushchev: a car was moving along the street in the opposite direction, a foreign car, and it slowed as she stepped from the limousine. Just that—it slowed—and nothing more. I hardly remarked it at the time, but that instant was to reverberate in history. The engine ticked up the street, crickets chirruped. With all dispatch, I got Mrs. Khrushchev round back of Blair House, saw her in the door, and returned to the limousine.

"Well done, Paderewski, well done," Ike said as I put the car in drive and headed up the street, and then he did something he hadn't done in years—lit a cigarette. I watched the glow of the match in the rearview mirror, and then he was exhaling with rich satisfaction, as if he'd just come back from swimming the Potomac or taming a mustang in one of those televised cigarette ads. "The White House," he said. "Chop-chop."

Six hours later, Madame K. appeared with her husband on the front steps of Blair House and fielded questions from reporters. She wore a modest gray silk chemise and a splash of lipstick. One of the reporters asked her what she was most interested in seeing while touring the U.S., and she glanced over at her husband before replying (he was grinning to show off his pointed teeth, as impervious to English as he might have been to Venusian). "Whatever is of biggest interest to Mr. Khrushchev," she said. The reporters lapped it up: flashbulbs popped, a flurry of stories went out over the wire. Who would have guessed?

From there, the Khrushchevs took a special VIP train to New York, where Madame K. attended a luncheon at the Waldorf and her husband harangued a group of business magnates in Averell Harriman's living room. "The Moscow Cha-Cha" and Jimmy Driftwood's "The Bear Flew over the Ocean" blared from every radio in town, and a special squad of NYPD's finest—six-footers, expert in jujitsu and marksmanship—formed a human wall around the premier and his wife as they took in the sights of the Big Apple. New York rolled out the red carpet, and the Khrushchevs trod it with a stately satisfaction that rapidly gave way to finger-snapping, heel-kicking glee. As the premier boarded the plane for Los Angeles, Nina at his side, he mugged for cameras, kissed babies, and shook hands so assiduously he might have been running for office.

And then the bottom fell out.

In Los Angeles, ostensibly because he was nettled at Mayor Paulson's hard-line speech and because he discovered that Disneyland would not be on his itinerary, the raging, tabletop-pounding, Magyar-cowing Khrushchev came to the fore: he threw a tantrum. The people of the United States were inhospitable boors—they'd invited him to fly halfway round the world simply to abuse him. He'd had enough. He was curtailing the trip and heading back to Moscow.

I was with Ike when the first reports of the premier's explosion flashed across the TV screen. Big-bellied and truculent, Khrushchev was lecturing the nation on points of etiquette, jowls atremble, fists beating the air, while Nina, her head bowed, stood meekly at his side. Ike's voice was so pinched it could have come from a ventriloquist's dummy: "My God," he whispered, "he knows." (I suddenly remembered the car slowing, the flash of a pale face behind the darkened glass, and thought of Alger Hiss, the Rosenbergs, the vast net-work of Soviet spies operating unchecked in the land of the free: they'd seen her after all.) Shaking his head, Ike got up, crossed the room, and lit another verboten cigarette. He looked weary, immeasurably old, Rip Van Winkle wak-ing beside his rusted gun. "Well, Paderewski," he sighed, a blue haze playing round the wisps of silver hair at his temples, "I guess now the shit's really going to hit the fan."

He was right, but only partially. To his credit, Khrushchev covered himself like a trouper—after all, how could he reveal so shocking and outrageous a business as this without losing face himself, without transforming himself in that instant from the virile, bellicose, iron-fisted ruler of the Soviet masses to a pudgy, pathetic cuckold? He allowed himself to be mollified by apologies from Paulson and Cabot Lodge over the supposed insult, posed for a photograph with Shirley MacLaine at Twentieth Century–Fox, and then flew on to San Francisco for a tense visit. He made a dilatory stop in Iowa on his way back to Washington and the inevitable confrontation with the man who had suddenly emerged as his rival in love as well as ideology. (I'm sure you recall the cele-brated photographs in *Life, Look,* and *Newsweek*—Khrushchev leering at a phal-lic ear of corn, patting the belly of a crewcut interloper at the Garst farm in Iowa, hefting a piglet by the scruff of its neck. Study them today—especially in contrast to the pre–Los Angeles photos—and you'll be struck by the mixture of jealous rage and incomprehension playing across the premier's features, and the soft, tragic, downcast look in his wife's eyes.)

I sat beside the president on the way out to Camp David for the talks that would culminate the Khrushchev visit. He was subdued, desolated, the animation gone out of his voice. He'd planned for these talks as he'd planned for the European Campaign, devising stratagems and feints, studying floorplans, mapping the territory, confident he could spirit away his inamorata for an idyllic hour or two beneath the pines. Now there was no chance of it. No chance, in fact, that he'd ever see her again. He was slumped in his seat, his head thrown back against the bulletproof glass as if he no longer had the will to hold it up. And then—I've never seen anything so moving, so emotionally ravaging in my life—he began to cry. I offered him my handkerchief but he motioned me away, great wet heaving sobs tearing at his lungs, the riveting blue eyes that had gazed with equanimity on the most heinous scenes of devastation known to civilized man reddened with a sorrow beyond despair. "Nina," he choked, and buried his face in his hands.

You know the rest. The "tough" talks at Camp David (ostensibly over the question of the Berlin Wall), the Soviet premier's postponement of Ike's reciprocal visit till the spring, "when things are in bloom," the eventual rescinding of the invitation altogether, and the virulent anti-Eisenhower speech Khrushchev delivered in the wake of the U-2 incident. Then there was Ike's final year in office, his loss of animation, his heart troubles (*heart troubles*—could anything be more ironic?), the way in which he so rapidly and visibly aged, as if each moment of each day weighed on him like an eternity. And finally, our last picture of him: the affable, slightly foggy old duffer chasing a white ball across the links as if it were some part of himself he'd misplaced.

As for myself, I was rapidly demoted after the Khrushchev visit—it almost seemed as if I were an embarrassment to Ike, and in a way I guess I was, having seen him with his defenses down and his soul laid bare. I left the government a few months later and have pursued a rewarding academic career ever since, and am in fact looking forward to qualifying for tenure in the upcoming year. It has been a rich and satisfying life, one that has had its ups and downs, its years of quotidian existence and its few breathless moments at the summit of human history. Through it all, through all the myriad events I've witnessed, the loves I've known, the emotions stirred in my breast by the tragic events of our times, I can say with a sense of reverent gratitude and the deepest sincerity that nothing has so moved and tenderly astonished me as the joy, the sorrow, the epic sweep of the star-crossed love of Ike and Nina. I think of the Cold War, of nuclear proliferation, of Hungary, Korea, and the U-2 incident, and it all finally pales beside this: he loved her, and she loved him.

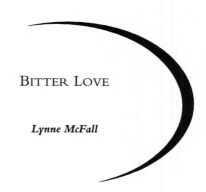

BITTER LOVE

*Lynne McFall*

**LYNNE MCFALL** is the author of two novels, *The One True Story of the World* and *Dancer with Bruised Knees,* and a philosophical study, *Happiness.* She is at work on a new novel, *The Way Out.*

I LOST MY right eye in a pool-playing accident in the Sea Horse Saloon on January 27, the day of my thirty-ninth birthday. I'd tell you the story but everyone I've told it to so far—man or woman—starts making retching noises and backing away. But you can use your imagination: a pool cue, a jealous woman, one blue eye.

I would like to tell you about the man, however. His name was Jake and he was a steam-pipe fitter. He drove a rusted-out, puke-green Maverick that he bought with some money he won playing liars' dice. There was a hole the size of a bowling ball in the floorboard. No rugs except for some little frayed pieces of green still stuck to the metal. The tape player ate every tape you put into it. I remember how I cried the day it ate my Bonnie Raitt. When you turned the heater on it smelled like dirty socks burning, and it didn't put out any heat. His driving was worse than his car. Every time we went anywhere together, I'd end up with a knot as big as a fist in my stomach and violent inner trembling from the many times I'd nearly died. An eighteen-wheeler would screech to a halt inches from my door, and he'd smile like a manic child. He looked behind him *after* he changed lanes, used his rearview mirror mostly for picking his teeth, which he'd do with a silver dental instrument while driving eighty miles an hour. When the light, any light, turned green, he'd floor it, apparently untouched by the months of gas rationing most of us remember. He took every corner like he was at Indy, cut people off without even a gesture toward his blinkers, turned on his lights at night only as an afterthought. He was dangerous.

Two weeks after he left me he wrote me a letter. He said he felt like he'd been driving for a long time through the dark toward some glorious city. That he'd taken the back roads because he couldn't find the main highway. It was a longer route, he knew, but he thought he'd get there eventually. Sometimes he thought he could see lights, but like a mirage of water they would vanish as he got closer. But he kept on driving, too stubborn and stupid to stop and ask someone. What they would have told him, he said, is that that road didn't go there.

I guess I was supposed to be the glorious city. Or maybe it was "true love" he was driving at. I'm not sure. I wanted to write back and say that maybe, it's just a thought, per*haps* he should consider this: the reason he didn't make it to the glorious city is that his car is shit and he's a lousy driver. I wanted to say that there are some good places you can't find on a map. I didn't, of course. I wouldn't want him to think I was bitter.

But he cured me of country music, I'll give him that. I used to drink rum and Coke and play Patsy Cline or Hank Williams and cry myself sick. He taught me the true meaning of self-pity. I no longer need the cheap fix.

I remember Patsy was singing the night we met. I had gone to the Sea Horse Saloon in a mood of drink-yourself-blind. I was upset, not about anything in particular but just about the general strain of living—that a person has to *work* for a living, for example. I am a photographer by chosen profession, but I was working for Ted's Typing Service at the time, on Geary Boulevard. Drunks off the street would bring you in some legal form to type up—they were suing their landlord, they were writing up their last will and testament—and they would breathe whiskey in your face and threaten you with nonpayment for fixing their spelling errors. Working at some low-level job for peon wages at great aggravation instead of pursuing one's *art,* what kind of life is that?

He came in and sat down with two barstools between us. Friendly but not pushy. I looked up out of polite curiosity but just quickly, no smile. Dark hair, a beard, heavyset. Pretty brown eyes, so kind, they reminded me of my grand-mother's. Some guys, you look into their eyes and know it's only a matter of time until they pick you up and throw you against a wall. This guy wouldn't do it. Or if he did, he'd regret it instantly and forever.

When he smiled I wanted him. It was the kind of smile that would not only take you home and tuck you in afterwards, but would fix you breakfast.

"I want! I want!" This is something I would yell at odd moments during our days together. Then Jake would come to me, take off my clothes, first the blouse, unbuttoned slowly from the bottom, each article of clothing—taking his time with me, making me wait, teasing me with his hands, his tongue.

"What do you want?" he would say and smile at me like I was really something. Something precious. Something you would always want in your line of sight.

I guess not.

I should have seen it coming. But in his life no one had ever been loyal, had ever stood up for him, stuck with him when things got tough. I wanted to be the one. Noble me.

Maybe he didn't like having someone around who was always pointing out the half-eaten worm in the rotten apple. I have a gift for the negative, I admit. But even those who are difficult need to be loved, and in that I am no exception.

He had a complicated system of merits and demerits as to love. How harsh you were last night to my friend Alex. That's seven demerits. Janice and Rick *liked* you, that's three for you. Why must you keep badmouthing Big John? Don't you know that'll cost you an arm and a leg? Big John was his boss, but I think Jake thought of Big John as his father. His real father walked out on him and his mother when he was little. Maybe that's where he got the talent.

He was always walking out. This is the picture that sticks in my mind: him slamming his things together and stuffing them into the trunk of his Maverick. It would take several trips, and he would keep his face in a rage the whole time. He walked this ridiculous indignant cartoon strut when he was mad. I'd be crying, wondering what went wrong this time, saying I was sorry, or saying I wished I'd never put myself in his hands, whichever was appropriate.

He hated what he called "scenes." That's me screaming and him stuffing his things into the trunk of his Maverick. But he wouldn't talk to you in an ordinary human voice about anything of significance. I would try to get him drunk, hoping he would tell me where I stood, once and for all. But he could never tell me the truth, as if it took some superhuman courage he just couldn't summon. So I was always trying to read the signs, begging for bad news. "It looks like you don't love me enough," I would say softly. "But maybe you don't have the guts to tell me." We'd be at the Surf, listening to "You're Not the Man" on the jukebox, that saxophone like someone moaning. "No," he'd say, too carefully. "I love you." But the look of his eyes in the light of the Coors sign was not convincing. Finally it was me who'd get drunk and start screaming. Patience is not its own reward.

He was very punishing but in a passive way. He wouldn't call, he would be silent long hours of a Sunday, he would pinch his lips together and harden his eyes to a fine glint. He withheld the word "love" from his cards and letters for the entire last six months, then he signs his goodbye letter "Love, Jake." It was, to put it simply, more than I could take. It's the small things that destroy us.

If I knew his side of the story, I would tell it. But here I am as usual having to make it up, trying to stuff all these painful memories and ragged feelings into some kind of trunk. I hate people—I'm trying for a light tone here—who have no sense of an ending, no need of a proper burial.

I've been going through some letters he wrote me. Reading them over for clues. He said in one that what he felt for me was not love because love was not fierce enough. But reading that didn't make me feel better. If someone has decided to rewrite the past, old letters prove nothing.

When I got a temporary job down in L.A. (photographing zoo animals) and he moved into the latest new place that was chosen without me in mind, he got rid of my favorite chair. Looking back, that was a sign.

He took up with this woman, Sally. Dumb as shit and bright pink lipstick. That was the second sign. I guess she was a glorious city he could find on his frayed atlas. She liked to torment me with it. For example, she'd say, when I saw her at the bar, that she and Jake had spent last weekend fucking their brains out. I said I bet it didn't take all weekend. Her idea of independence was to always have more than one lover. I used to ridicule this.

Some people, when they are gone, leave you less than you were. He wasn't one of these. There were good things. But remembering them pierces me.

I bought him this white silk teddy for his birthday. Me in it was the present. But I was too shy to put it on. He kept asking and I finally did. He had me turn this way and that in the soft light in the dark room. He looked at me then like he loved me enough. I can remember every instant of that night, the urgency, my pounding heart, the way I moved above him. Those are the things that make the loss of an eye seem a kindness.

It was hard that last year to keep taking off my clothes, to keep making myself vulnerable to him, when he was doing the final tally. Sometimes I would look at him and see him moving his lips and know that he was adding things up, trying to be fair. It would be interesting to know which point was the clincher.

I have a talent for sleeping. Nine or ten hours a night is usual. When he left I woke up crying every night at three A.M. and couldn't get back to sleep. Images of us together, in different postures, filled my head. Every night, like a video, I would see us.

Pale thighs against a dark-haired chest. I am sitting on his lap, in the large red leather chair, my knees up under his armpits. I am rocking back and forth, back and forth. He is making a sound I have never heard before, his eyes half closed, his mouth open. I kiss him hard, bite his bottom lip until I taste blood.

After a month I went to see Dr. Glass. I said, "I can't sleep." There were blue shadows under my eyes. I said, "If you're not careful you can see through my skin." I held up my translucent wrists, helpless. "I see him. I see him everywhere." She said it was only grief.

Then she recommended something called counterimagining. "For example." She held up her two forefingers like goal posts. "Imagine putting all his letters in a box in the backyard. Burn it. Or," she said, "put *him* in a closet. Firmly close the door."

I liked this idea. But it didn't work. I cried at the pyre of letters, let him out after five minutes.

But she'd given me a thought. That's when I started trying to imagine a better ending, thinking this might allow me to put this man behind me, give me some peace.

This is the way it really happened. He called me to say it was over. Just like that. (I didn't think you could walk out over the telephone; that's one on me.) I had been supposed to come and stay with him that weekend, to celebrate my birthday. I thought we had been working things out. I had been trying to change in some of the ways he needed (for example, quit screaming), trying to fathom what it was like to be him, trying to understand what made him the tender man he was. Now I know: too much sympathy can kill you.

Anyway, he calls up and after five minutes of clearing his throat like he was choking on a goddamn chicken bone—and slow me saying, "What? What is it? Can't you *breathe?*"—he just says this: "I don't want us to be together anymore. I don't want you to come out here this weekend." I asked him why. He said he didn't think he could make it clear. He said that living with me was like riding on a roller coaster and he wanted to get off. He said he loved me but not enough. He said there was someone else. "That's pretty clear," I said. "Jesus Christ," I said, "any one of those reasons would have been sufficient." But he said he was trying to be honest for once. Nice change for him, I thought, but I was trying to keep from being beaten to death by my own heart. And I'd bought a nonrefundable ticket. There I was, all fucked up and no place to go.

Telling me over the phone like that—I didn't think it showed respect for what we had been to each other. We'd had a life together (four years, on and off) and I deserved better than a phone call. I was only thirty-nine but I'd already learned that it's not so much what is done to you as the manner in which it is done.

So I used the ticket. Air West. Free drinks. During takeoff I closed my eyes and the images started to come. Now it wasn't just at night, when I couldn't sleep. Thoughts of him were taking over my life. I closed my eyes tighter but the images still came.

This time we're standing on the balcony overlooking the ocean. It is night. I have my long black nightgown on. I stand in front, the top railing just above my waist, an edge against my ribs. He is behind, the only warmth in the cold night, his thighs against the backs of my thighs. He slips the spaghetti straps off my shoulders, cups his warm hands under my breasts, uses his thumb and forefinger to make me arch my back. I feel him lift the slippery material up to my waist, feel him push himself inside me, easy at first, then harder. I stand on tiptoe, feel my feet rise off the wooden planks as I watch the white of the slow-breaking waves.

Liar! I started tying him up, first his arms, behind his back, handcuffed to emphasize a point, then his legs. When I was through he couldn't move. I made the rope so tight it burned his ankles. Betrayer! I put masking tape over his mouth. He made a "Mm-mmm" sound, but this time I didn't give in. A person has limits.

I got into town around eight that evening and took a cab to the Sea Horse, knowing he would be there with his latest glorious city. I thought I deserved a more fitting ending and I intended to have it.

The cab driver was tight-lipped and sullen but I gave him a ten-dollar tip, for flair and courage, then walked through the heavy black curtains. Made an entrance, you might say.

This woman, call her Poughkeepsie, was bigger than I expected. Hair the color of mouse. Thin. Pale. Not too glamorous. No Paris.

I remember the song on the jukebox. Lenny Welch. "Since I Fell for You." Jesus.

I walked up to the bar where they were sitting with their backs to me. I said, "Hi. My name's Sarah," and stuck out my hand. I can be civilized when I have to be.

But she didn't seem to understand my desire to have things out with the man whose thigh she had her hand on. So I tried to give her a little history, let her know where I stood in the order of things.

"Fuck off," she explained.

I grabbed the dice cup and shook the bartender, Judy, for the music. I lost. But she gave me four quarters anyway. I put on Hank Williams singing "Your Cheatin' Heart" with "I'm So Lonesome I Could Cry" as a chaser. Six times.

I had a few more Bacardi and Cokes and then tried to convince her again. "Four years," I said. "You are only a few nights. Maybe *good* nights, but still . . ."

She was not impressed with this line of reasoning and pushed me backwards off the barstool where I had been trying to make my case.

All this time Jake is looking at me like I'm in the wrong movie. I thought, *Jake*. It's *me*. Sarah. Don't you recognize me? At my final undoing, I had believed, at my attempted massacre, he would be on my side. At a minimum. No. Maybe she was a few more nights than I imagined.

I was down and I didn't have the will to get up. I just lay there, near defeat, close to a whimper. The boots around my head seemed way too big for human feet.

When I picked myself up off the floor Poughkeepsie was right in my face.

That's when I picked up the pool cue. Never pick up a pool cue if you don't intend to use it. Never brandish a pool cue at someone larger and meaner than yourself. I play these useless admonitions over and over in my head, the way a person might repeat a prayer for improved health over the deceased.

I had believed the human eye to be a tenacious thing. I think that woman must have been an oyster shucker before she took up with Jake. She popped that thing out of there as easy as opening a longneck, like removing a cork with a crowbar, like playing tiddlywinks. I thought my face was on fire. I tried to put it out with my fingernails.

I was in the hospital for six weeks. You can have too much time to think. I stared at the white walls so long I went snow-blind. Once in a while I would put my right hand over the bandages on the right side of my face, the way you do when you're trying to see something more clearly. I thought about Jake, the old movies, the old reruns. No counterimagining could touch the way his skin felt next to my skin, like you're in warm water and sinking.

This time we are in bed, on Christmas Eve. He has given me a toy and we are trying it out, children laughing in the dark. "Like this?" he says, moving the head of the machine. "Like this?" I wiggle until it's where I want it, then I begin to writhe, making sounds of mock ecstasy. He takes me almost roughly, his thrusting hard and steady, his hands on my shoulders, holding them down, as if he were trying to teach me a lesson, his thrusting now hard and irregular, probing, as if he were trying to locate the wound. I don't know him. My eyes are wide open and the only sound in the room is the muffled whirring of the small motor trapped in the blue comforter.

My last week in the hospital the candy striper lady brought in some books on a cart, but she didn't smile. She looked at me as if hers were a serious mission, full of mortality and risk. I picked out *Crooked Hearts. Endless Love.* I looked up at her. She shook her head, back and forth, eyes that saw everything. I put the books back on the cart.

Instead I started rereading Nietzsche—something I hadn't looked at since my days at Modesto J.C., something I thought I'd never use, perfectly useless, like trigonometry. The part I concentrated on is the part about *amor fati,* loving one's fate even when it's harsh, especially when it's harsh. What he's talking about is pain, great pain, that long, slow pain in which we are burned with green wood, pain that takes its time with us, like a good lover.

The morning they took the bandages off and I saw the place where my eye had been, I cried. Tears seeping through the red twisted skin. An obscene wink. It was the most sickening sight I had ever seen, and it was a permanent part of my face. But I refused the black patch. I have made a lot of mistakes in my life but I am not a coward.

Nietzsche says that only this kind of pain forces us to go down into our depths, to put away all trust, all good-naturedness, all that would veil, all mildness, all that is medium—things in which we have formerly found our humanness.

For weeks I howled like a coyote. I could not look in a mirror. I wanted, more than to be whole again, someone to hold me. I said, "Nothing is as good when you have it as it is bad when it's gone." It didn't ring true. I said, "Rejection is the great aphrodisiac." So what? I said, "I have been wounded in an accident of my own choosing, and there is no way I can undo it."

Out of such long and dangerous exercises in self-mastery, Nietzsche says, one emerges as a different person, with a few *more* question marks—above all, with the will to question more persistently, more deeply, severely, harshly, evilly, and quietly than has ever been questioned on this earth before. The trust in life is gone; life itself has become a problem.

I'm not a religious person, but when I read that part I said it out loud: "Amen."

Yet one should not jump to the conclusion, Nietzsche says, that with all this a man (or a one-eyed woman, I would add) has necessarily become a barn owl. Even the love of life is still possible—only one loves differently. It is the love for a woman who raises doubts in us.

Maybe I've got him wrong but I think what he's talking about is bitter love. The kind of love that sees the withered eye in the mirror and doesn't cringe. It's a love that comes out of strength rather than weakness, but it has no illusions. It does not expect something for nothing. (It does not expect something for something.) It knows that for every inarticulate joy there is some bright grief.

People are always saying, "You're so bitter." As if this were something one should endeavor to avoid. I say, "Look at this eye." I say, "If you're not bitter you haven't been paying attention." But would there be so much bitterness if there wasn't still love? That's the hard question I have to ask myself.

I haven't got the answer yet but last night, for the first time, I could sleep. I slept through almost to morning, without dreaming. When I woke up I didn't raise the blinds. In that shallow half-light, with my one good eye, I could see his real face. The soft brown eyes so like my dead grandmother's, the heavy nostrils flaring, full lips, those straight white teeth, the ugly mole just beneath his jawline.

I don't know why but I decided to let him go. It was at first merely an internal gesture, like intending one person rather than another when you use a common name. But then it gathered momentum. I untied his arms and legs, unlocked the handcuffs with the small key I keep on the chain around my neck, loosened the straitjacket in back, so it no longer looked like he was hugging himself, ripped the masking tape from his mouth—fast, so it wouldn't hurt.

In spite of the rope burns and the welts, I think he smiled, nodded a thank-you. Is this what love is? Out of gratitude he took a step toward me, looked at me for the first time as if I were human. But before he could open his arms, I gave him his heart back.

He didn't know how to take what was his. I understand that now. That's why he always laughed so hard at the part in *Midnight Cowboy* where Ratso Rizzo is stuffing the salami into his pockets. That's why he needed me: gifted and greedy.

In my imagination I could see him opening outward. I set him free to become whatever he is. Thief. Ordinary man. Truth-teller. I watched him bloom, even in the dark, like a nightflower.

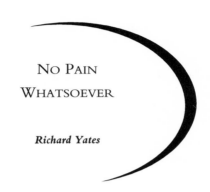

NO PAIN
WHATSOEVER

*Richard Yates*

RICHARD YATES was the author of two short-story collections (*Eleven Kinds of Loneliness* and *Liars in Love*) and seven novels (*Revolutionary Road, A Special Providence, Disturbing the Peace, The Easter Parade, A Good School, Young Hearts Crying,* and *Cold Spring Harbor*). He died in 1992.

MYRA STRAIGHTENED HERSELF in the back seat and smoothed her skirt, pushing Jack's hand away.

"All right, baby," he whispered, smiling, "take it easy."

"You take it easy, Jack," she told him. "I mean it, now."

His hand yielded, limp, but his arm stayed indolently around her shoulders. Myra ignored him and stared out the window. It was early Sunday evening, late in December, and the Long Island streets looked stale; dirty crusts of snow lay shriveled on the sidewalk, and cardboard images of Santa Claus leered out of closed liquor stores.

"I still don't feel right about you driving me all the way out here," Myra called to Marty, who was driving, to be polite.

" 'S all right," Marty grumbled. Then he sounded his horn and added, to the back of a slow truck, "Get that son of a bitch outa the way."

Myra was annoyed—why did Marty always have to be such a grouch?— but Irene, Marty's wife, squirmed around in the front seat with her friendly grin. "Marty don't mind," she said. "It's good for 'm, getting out on a Sunday insteada laying around the house."

"Well," Myra said, "I certainly do appreciate it." The truth was that she would much rather have taken the bus, alone, as usual. In the four years she had been coming out here to visit her husband every Sunday she had grown used to the long ride, and she liked stopping at a little cafeteria in Hempstead, where you had to change buses, for coffee and cake on the way home. But today she and Jack had gone over to Irene and Marty's for dinner, and the dinner was so late that Marty had to offer to drive her out to the hospital, and she had to accept. And then of course Irene had to come along, and Jack too, and they all acted as if they were doing her a favor. But you had to be polite. "It certainly is nice," Myra called, "to be riding out here in a car, instead of a—*don't,* Jack!"

Jack said, "*Sh-h-h,* take it easy, baby," but she threw off his hand and twisted away. Watching them, Irene put her tongue between her teeth and giggled, and Myra felt herself blushing. It wasn't that there was anything to be ashamed of—Irene and Marty knew all about Jack and everything; most of her friends did, and nobody blamed her (after all, wasn't it almost like being a widow?)—it was just that Jack ought to know better. Couldn't he at least have the decency to keep his hands to himself now, of all times?

"There," Marty said. "Now we'll make some time." The truck had turned off and they were picking up speed, leaving the streetcar tracks and stores behind as the street became a road and then a highway.

"Care to hear the radio, kids?" Irene called. She clicked one of the dial tabs and a voice urged everyone to enjoy television in their own homes, now, tonight. She clicked another and a voice said, "Yes, your money buys more in a Crawford store!"

"Turn that son of a bitch off," Marty said, and sounding the horn again, he pulled out into the fast lane.

When the car entered the hospital grounds, Irene turned around in the front seat and said, "Say, this is a beautiful place. I mean it, isn't this a beautiful place? Oh, look, they got a Christmas tree up, with lights and all."

"Well," Marty said, "where to?"

"Straight ahead," Myra told him, "down to that big circle, where the Christmas tree is. Then you turn right, out around the Administration Building, and on out to the end of that street." He made the turn correctly, and as they approached the long, low TB building, she said, "Here it is, Marty, this one right here." He drew up to the curb and stopped, and she gathered together the magazines she had brought for her husband and stepped out on the thin gray snow.

Irene hunched her shoulders and turned around, hugging herself. "Oo-oo, it's *cold* out there, isn't it? Listen, honey, what time is it you'll be through, now? Eight o'clock, is it?"

"That's right," Myra said, "but listen, why don't you people go on home? I can just as soon take the bus back, like I always do."

"Whaddya think I am, crazy?" Irene said. "You think I want to drive all the way home with Jack moping there in the back seat?" She giggled and winked. "Be hard enough just trying to keep him happy while you're inside, let alone driving all the way home. No, listen, we'll cruise around a little, honey, maybe have a little drink or something, and then we'll come back here for you at eight o'clock sharp."

"Well okay, but I'd really just as soon—"

"Right here," Irene said. "We'll see you right here in front of the building at eight o'clock sharp. Now hurry up and shut the door before we all freeze to death."

Myra smiled as she slammed the door, but Jack, sulking, did not look up to smile back, or wave. Then the car rolled away and she walked up the path and the steps to the TB building.

The small waiting room smelled of steam heat and wet overshoes, and she hurried through it, past the door marked NURSES' OFFICE—CLEAN AREA and into the big, noisy center ward. There were thirty-six beds in the center ward, divided in half by a wide aisle and subdivided by shoulder-high partitions into open cubicles of six beds each. All the sheets and the hospital pajamas were dyed yellow, to distinguish them from uncontaminated linen in the hospital laundry, and this combined with the pale green of the walls made a sickly color scheme that Myra could never get used to. The noise was terrible too; each patient had a radio, and they all seemed to be playing different stations at once. There were clumps of visitors at some of the beds—one of the newer men lay with his arms around his wife in a kiss—but at other beds the men looked lonely, reading or listening to their radios.

Myra's husband didn't see her until she was right beside his bed. He was sitting up, cross-legged, frowning over something in his lap. "Hello, Harry," she said.

He looked up. "Oh, hi there, honey, didn't see you coming."

She leaned over and kissed him quickly on the cheek. Sometimes they kissed on the lips, but you weren't supposed to.

Harry glanced at his watch. "You're late. Was the bus late?"

"I didn't come on the bus," she said, taking off her coat. "I got a ride out. Irene, the girl that works in my office? She and her husband drove me out in their car."

"Oh, that's nice. Whyn't you bring 'em on in?"

"Oh, they couldn't stay—they had someplace else to go. But they both said to give you their regards. Here, I brought you these."

"Oh, thanks, that's swell." He took the magazines and spread them out on the bed: *Life, Collier's* and *Popular Science*. "That's swell, honey. Sit down and stay awhile."

Myra laid her coat over the back of the bedside chair and sat down. "Hello there, Mr. Chance," she said to a very long Negro in the next bed who was nodding and grinning at her.

"How're you, Mrs. Wilson?"

"Fine, thanks, and you?"

"Oh, no use complaining," Mr. Chance said.

She peered across Harry's bed at Red O'Meara, who lay listening to his radio on the other side. "Hi there, Red."

"Oh, hi, Mrs. Wilson. Didn't see you come in."

"Your wife coming in tonight, Red?"

"She comes Saturdays now. She was here last night."

"Oh," Myra said, "well, tell her I said hello."

"I sure will, Mrs. Wilson."

Then she smiled at the elderly man across the cubicle whose name she could never remember, who never had any visitors, and he smiled back, looking rather shy. She settled herself on the little steel chair, opening her handbag for cigarettes. "What's that thing on your lap, Harry?" It was a ring of blond wood a foot wide, with a great deal of blue knitting wool attached to little pegs around its edge.

"Oh, this?" Harry said, holding it up. "It's what they call rake-knitting. Something I got from occupational therapy."

"*What*-knitting?"

"Rake-knitting. See, what you do, you take this little hook and kind of pry the wool up and over each peg, like that, and you keep on doing that around and around the ring until you got yourself a muffler or a stocking cap—something like that."

"Oh, *I see,*" Myra said. "It's like what we used to do when I was a kid, only we did it with a regular little spool, with nails stuck in it? You wind string around the nails and pull it through the spool and it makes sort of a knitted rope, like."

"Oh, yeah?" Harry said. "With a spool, huh? Yeah, I think my sister used to do that too, now that I think of it. With a spool. You're right, this is the same principle, only bigger."

"What're you going to make?"

"Oh, I don't know, I'm just fooling around with it. Thought I might make a stocking cap or something. I don't know." He inspected his work, turning the knitting-rake around in his hands, then leaned over and put it away in his bed stand. "It's just something to do."

She offered him the pack and he took a cigarette. When he bent forward to take the match the yellow pajamas gaped open and she saw his chest, unbelievably thin, partly caved-in on one side where the ribs were gone. She could just see the end of the ugly, newly healed scar from the last operation.

"Thanks, honey," he said, the cigarette wagging in his lips, and he leaned back against the pillows, stretching out his socked feet on the spread.

"How're you feeling, Harry?" she said.

"Feeling fine."

"You're looking better," she lied. "If you can gain a little weight now, you'll look fine."

"Pay up," said a voice over the din of the radios, and Myra looked around to see a little man coming down the center aisle in a wheelchair, walking the chair slowly with his feet, as all TB patients did to avoid the chest strain of turning the wheels with their hands. He was headed for Harry's bed, grinning with yellow teeth. "Pay up," he said again as the wheelchair came to a stop beside the bed. A piece of rubber tubing protruded from some kind of bandage on his chest. It coiled across his pajama top, held in place by a safety pin, and ended in a small rubber-capped bottle which rode heavily in his breast pocket. "Come on, come on," he said. "Pay up."

"Oh, yeah!" Harry said, laughing. "I forgot all about it, Walter." From the drawer of his bed stand he got out a dollar bill and handed it to the man, who folded it with thin fingers and put it in his pocket, along with the bottle.

"Okay, Harry," he said. "All squared away now, right?"

"Right, Walter."

He backed the wheelchair up and turned it around, and Myra saw that his chest, back and shoulders were crumpled and misshapen. "Sorry to butt in," he said, turning the sickly grin on Myra.

She smiled. "That's all right." When he had gone up the aisle again, she said, "What was that all about?"

"Oh, we had a bet on the fight Friday night. I'd forgotten all about it."

"Oh. Have I met him before?"

"Who, Walter? Sure, I think so, honey. You must've met him when I was over in surgery. Old Walter was in surgery more'n two years; they just brought him back here last week. Kid's had a rough time of it. He's got plenty of guts."

"What's that thing on his pajamas? That bottle?"

"He's draining," Harry said, settling back against the yellow pillows. "Old Walter's a good guy; I'm glad he's back." Then he lowered his voice, confidentially. "Matter of fact, he's one of the few really good guys left in this ward, with so many of the old crowd gone now, or over in surgery."

"Don't you like the new boys?" Myra asked, keeping her own voice low so that Red O'Meara, who was relatively new, wouldn't hear. "They seem perfectly nice to me."

"Oh, they're all right, I guess," Harry said. "I just mean, well, I get along better with guys like Walter, that's all. We been through a lot together, or something. I don't know. These new guys get on your nerves sometimes, the way they talk. For instance, there's not one of them knows anything about TB, and they all of them think they know it all; you can't tell them anything. I mean, a thing like that can get on your nerves."

Myra said she guessed she saw what he meant, and then it seemed that the best thing to do was change the subject. "Irene thought the hospital looked real pretty, with the Christmas tree and all."

"Oh, yeah?" Very carefully, Harry reached over and flicked his cigarette into the spotless ashtray on his bed stand. All his habits were precise and neat from living so long in bed. "How're things going at the office, honey?"

"Oh, all right, I guess. Remember I told you about that girl Janet that got fired for staying out too long at lunch, and we were all scared they'd start cracking down on that half-hour lunch period?"

"Oh, yeah," Harry said, but she could tell he didn't remember and wasn't really listening.

"Well, it seems to be all blown over now, because last week Irene and three other girls stayed out almost two hours and nobody said a word. And one of them, a girl named Rose, has been kind of expecting to get fired for a couple of months now, and they didn't even say anything to her."

"Oh, yeah?" Harry said. "Well, that's good."

There was a pause. "Harry?" she said.

"What, honey?"

"Have they told you anything new?"

"Anything new?"

"I mean, about whether or not you're going to need the operation on the other side."

"Oh, *no,* honey. I told you, we can't expect to hear anything on that for quite some time yet—I thought I explained all that." His mouth was smiling and his eyes frowning to show it had been a foolish question. It was the same look he always used to give her at first, long ago, when she would say, "But when do you *think* they'll let you come home?" Now he said, "Thing is, I've still got to get over this *last* one. You got to do one thing at a time in this business; you need a long postoperative period before you're really in the clear, especially with a record of breakdowns like I've had in the last—what is it, now—four years? No, what they'll do is wait awhile, I don't know, maybe six months, maybe longer, and see how this side's coming along. Then they'll decide about the other side. Might give me more surgery and they might not. You can't count on anything in this business, honey, you know that."

"No, of course, Harry, I'm sorry. I don't mean to ask stupid questions. I just meant, well, how're you feeling and everything. You still have any pain?"

"None at all, anymore," Harry said. "I mean, as long as I don't go raising my arm too high or anything. When I do that it hurts, and sometimes I start to roll over on that side in my sleep, and that hurts too, but as long as I stay—you know—more or less in a normal position, why, there's no pain whatsoever."

"That's good," she said. "I'm awfully glad to hear that, anyway."

Neither of them spoke for what seemed a long time, and in the noise of radios and the noise of laughing and coughing from other beds, their silence seemed strange. Harry began to riffle *Popular Science* absently with his thumb. Myra's eyes strayed to the framed picture on his bed stand, an enlarged snapshot of the two of them just before their marriage, taken in her mother's back yard in Michigan. She looked very young in the picture, leggy in her 1945 skirt, not knowing how to dress or even how to stand, knowing nothing and ready for anything with a child's smile. And Harry—but the surprising thing was that Harry looked older in the picture, somehow, than he did now. Probably it was the thicker face and build, and of course the clothes helped—the dark, decorated Eisenhower jacket and the gleaming boots. Oh, he'd been good-looking, all right, with his set jaw and hard gray eyes—much better looking, for instance, than a too stocky, too solid man like Jack. But now with the loss of weight there had been a softening about the lips and eyes that gave him the look of a thin little boy. His face had changed to suit the pajamas.

"Sure am glad you brought me this," Harry said of his *Popular Science*. "They got an article in here I want to read."

"Good," she said, and she wanted to say: Can't it wait until I've gone?

Harry flipped the magazine on its face, fighting the urge to read, and said, "How's everything else, honey? Outside of the office, I mean."

"All right," she said. "I had a letter from Mother the other day, kind of a Christmas letter. She sent you her best regards."

"Good," Harry said, but the magazine was winning. He flipped it over again, opened it to his article and read a few lines very casually—as if only to make sure it was the right article—and then he lost himself in it.

Myra lighted a fresh cigarette from the butt of her last one, picked up the *Life* and began to turn the pages. From time to time she looked up to watch him; he lay biting a knuckle as he read, scratching the sole of one socked foot with the curled toe of the other.

They spent the rest of the visiting hour that way. Shortly before eight o'clock a group of people came down the aisle, smiling and trundling a studio piano on rubber-tired casters—the Sunday night Red Cross entertainers. Mrs.

Balacheck led the procession; a kindly, heavyset woman in uniform, who played. Then came the piano, pushed by a pale young tenor whose lips were always wet, and then the female singers: a swollen soprano in a taffeta dress that looked tight under the arms and a stern-faced, lean contralto with a briefcase. They wheeled the piano close to Harry's bed, in the approximate middle of the ward, and began to unpack their sheet music.

Harry looked up from his reading. "Evening, Mrs. Balacheck."

Her glasses gleamed at him. "How're you tonight, Harry? Like to hear a few Christmas carols tonight?"

"Yes, ma'am."

One by one the radios were turned off and the chattering died. But just before Mrs. Balacheck hit the keys a stocky nurse intervened, thumping rubber-heeled down the aisle with a hand outstretched to ward off the music until she could make an announcement. Mrs. Balacheck sat back, and the nurse, craning her neck, called, "Visiting hour's over!" to one end of the ward and, "Visiting hour's over!" to the other. Then she nodded to Mrs. Balacheck, smiling behind her sterilized linen mask, and thumped away again. After a moment's whispered counsel, Mrs. Balacheck began to play an introductory "Jingle Bells," her cheeks wobbling, to cover the disturbance of departing visitors, while the singers retired to cough quietly among themselves; they would wait until their audience settled down.

"Gee," Harry said, "I didn't realize it was that late. Here, I'll walk you out to the door." He sat up slowly and swung his feet to the floor.

"No, don't bother, Harry," Myra said. "You lie still."

"No, that's all right," he said, wriggling into his slippers. "Will you hand me the robe, honey?" He stood up, and she helped him on with a corduroy VA bathrobe that was too short for him.

"Good night, Mr. Chance," Myra said, and Mr. Chance grinned and nodded. Then she said good night to Red O'Meara and the elderly man, and as they passed his wheelchair in the aisle, she said goodnight to Walter. She took Harry's arm, startled at its thinness, and matched his slow steps very carefully. They stood facing each other in the small awkward crowd of visitors that lingered in the waiting room.

"Well," Harry said, "take care of yourself now, honey. See you next week."

"Oo-oo," somebody's mother said, plodding hump-shouldered out the door, "it *is* cold tonight." She turned back to wave to her son, then grasped her husband's arm and went down the steps to the snow-blown path. Someone else caught the door and held it open for other visitors to pass through, filling the room with a cold draft, and then it closed again, and Myra and Harry were alone.

"All right, Harry," Myra said, "you go back to bed and listen to the music, now." He looked very frail standing there with his robe hanging open. She reached up and closed it neatly over his chest, took the dangling belt and knotted it firmly, while he smiled down at her. "Now you go on back in there before you catch cold."

"Okay. Good night, honey."

"Good night," she said, and standing on tiptoe, she kissed his cheek. "Good night, Harry."

At the door she turned to watch him walk back to the ward in the tight, high-waisted robe. Then she went outside and down the steps, turning up her coat collar in the sudden cold. Marty's car was not there; the road was bare except for the dwindling backs of the other visitors, passing under a street lamp now as they made their way down to the bus stop near the Administration Building. She drew the coat more closely around her and stood close to the building for shelter from the wind.

"Jingle Bells" ended inside, to muffled applause, and after a moment the program began in earnest. A few solemn chords sounded on the piano, and then the voices came through:

Hark, the herald angels sing,
Glory to the new-born King . . .

All at once Myra's throat closed up and the streetlights swam in her eyes. Then half her fist was in her mouth and she was sobbing wretchedly, making little puffs of mist that floated away in the dark. It took her a long time to stop, and each sniffling intake of breath made a high sharp noise that sounded as if it could be heard for miles. Finally it was over, or nearly over; she managed to control her shoulders, to blow her nose and put her handkerchief away, closing her bag with a reassuring, businesslike snap.

Then the lights of the car came probing up the road. She ran down the path and stood waiting in the wind.

Inside the car a warm smell of whiskey hung among the cherry-red points of cigarettes, and Irene's voice squealed, "Oo-oo! Hurry up and shut the *door!*"

Jack's arms gathered her close as the door slammed, and in a thick whisper he said, "Hello, baby."

They were all a little drunk; even Marty was in high spirits. "Hold tight, everybody!" he called, as they swung around the Administration Building, past the Christmas tree, and leveled off for the straightaway to the gate, gaining speed. "Everybody hold tight!"

Irene's face floated chattering over the back of the front seat. "Myra, honey, listen, we found the most adorable little place down the road, kind of a roadhouse, like, only real inexpensive and everything? So listen, we wanna take you back there for a little drink, okay?"

"Sure," Myra said, "fine."

" 'Cause I mean, we're way ahead of you now anyway, and anyway I want you to see this place . . . Marty, will you take it *easy!*" She laughed. "Honestly, anybody else driving this car with what he's had to drink in him, I'd be scared to death, you know it? But you never got to worry about old Marty. He's the best old driver in the world, drunk, sober, I don't care *what* he is."

But they weren't listening. Deep in a kiss, Jack slipped his hand inside her coat, expertly around and inside all the other layers until it held the flesh of her breast. "All over being mad at me, baby?" he mumbled against her lips. "Wanna go have a little drink?"

Her hands gripped the bulk of his back and clung there. Then she let herself be turned so that his other hand could creep secretly up her thigh. "All right," she whispered, "but let's only have one and then afterwards—"

"Okay, baby, okay."

"—and then afterwards, darling, let's go right home."

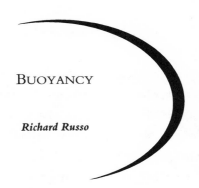

BUOYANCY

*Richard Russo*

RICHARD RUSSO is the author of three novels:
*Mohawk, The Risk Pool,* and *Nobody's Fool*. His novel *Straight*
*Man* is forthcoming.

FOR SOME TIME they'd been sliding from summer into autumn, from lush green to sepia. Everywhere there were downed trees, slender birches and lindens supported by power lines, tree trunks chainsawed into revealing cross-sections and left by the side of the road, broken limbs, themselves the size of small trees, stacked alongside gray-shingled houses. The trees that survived the hurricane were all damaged too, their trunks stripped, naked and pink, under the early September sky. Brittle leaves along the shoulder of the road danced and twirled, like distant memories, in the wake of automobiles.

"Oh dear," said the professor's wife, her voice a rich mixture of sadness and disappointment. She'd been worrying the white, scarlike crease of skin on the third finger of her left hand.

At the wheel, her husband, Paul Snow, professor emeritus, eyed her gravely but didn't say anything, waiting instead for her to elaborate, though he was not surprised when she didn't. June had always been a woman given to small exclamations that she would then decline to explain. Her "Oh dear's" were usually the tip of some emotional iceberg. To keep from colliding with them head on, Professor Snow acknowledged their existence, sensing he was supposed to do this, then navigated around them with care, lest his wife reveal the full nine tenths below the surface. She'd done that only once, years before, but her life-litany of long-held grievances, of womanly disappointments, had all come out in an amazing torrent, beginning in rage against himself, but ending in almost unbearable regret and sadness from which, it now seemed to Professor Snow, that June had never fully recovered, never become her old self. Their family physician had assured him that his wife's emotional equilibrium had stabilized, that she was right to wean herself of her medication, that he needn't watch her so carefully anymore. Professor Snow had been relieved to hear this, but it seemed to him that June's moods still turned on a dime, without warning and without, it appeared to him, apparent cause. Or without immediate cause. It was, of course, the immediate cause he was always trying to locate, having no wish to revisit the remote or the universal.

"What?" said Professor Snow.

By way of response, his wife failed to entirely suppress a shiver.

"Perhaps if we opened the windows," he suggested, rolling his own down and turning off the air conditioner. When the warmer air outside began to swirl through the car, he realized that he himself had been cold for some time. "Is that better, June?"

"Yes," his wife said unconvincingly. "Much."

But with the warmer outside air came the rich odor of decaying leaves, and again Snow felt the confused and disorienting sense of approaching winter. This time it was he himself who shivered. At first he thought his wife had not noticed because she was looking straight ahead, not at him, and because it took her such a long time to say, abstractedly, "We've come too late, haven't we."

On the ferry though, under the bright, late summer sky, the breeze on the upper deck billowing their clothes, they both cheered up. Out on the open water there was, of course, no evidence of the recent hurricane, no hint of autumn, much less of winter. Here, the early September sun warming their skin, the Snows compared notes on what they remembered, what they'd forgotten, what had changed in the nearly thirty years since their last visit to the island. "The main thing that's changed," the professor remarked, "is that we now have enough money to stay at an inn." They'd been very poor that previous trip, as poor as a young assistant professor and his new, even younger graduate student wife could be. They'd rented the cheapest cottage they could find in Oak Bluffs and still had to leave the island three days early when they ran out of money.

In truth, Snow had forgotten nearly all the details of their previous visit, or thought he had forgotten, until many came rushing back to him—the way the cars were loaded, bumper to bumper in the dark belly of the island ferry, the way the gulls followed effortlessly along the upper deck, patiently awaiting a handout. The coin-operated View Finders were still mounted on both the port and starboard railings, promising to bring into focus the far-off details of where you were going, where you'd been.

Halfway to the island, June Snow, who was wearing a pale yellow cotton sweater, pulled it over her head so she could feel the sun on her arms, and her husband, who felt his heart go into his throat, imagined for a moment that she'd forgotten herself and intended to sun in her brassiere on the upper deck of the ferry. Instinctively he reached out his hand to prevent her.

How foolish, he thought, in the long moment his hand was extended. He knew she was wearing a blouse underneath, remembered her pulling the sweater on over it as they left the house that morning. And of course he had also momentarily forgotten who she was, this woman, his wife. All of which left him, hand extended, trying to prevent what didn't need preventing.

But fate was kind and offered him an opportunity to save face. "I seem to be snagged," June said, her voice muffled inside the sweater, its fabric having caught on a button, and so there, even as she spoke, was his ready, helpful hand, as if to suggest that he was capable of anticipating her every need.

When they arrived at the Captain Clement House, the front entrance was locked, a note affixed to the inside of the glass, printed, in script: *Please Enter Through Garden.* They went around back and through a trellised archway into a manicured green world left miraculously untouched by the hurricane. Outside on the terrace the giant oak had been stripped bare, but the garden, surrounded and protected on three sides, was unscathed. Several dozen varieties of perennials were in defiant bloom, and perhaps because of these there were yellow bees everywhere. The Snows did not linger.

"I'm so glad you're here," said Mrs. Childress, the owner, a small, trim woman of difficult-to-read middle age, with a not-quite British accent and dark circles under her eyes. "For the moment you have the inn to yourselves. I'm rather concerned about the Robbins party. They're sailing up from Newport and I was given to expect them several hours ago. But I'm sure they'll be docking momentarily." With this she gave an elegant, sweeping gesture in the direction of the garden, as if to suggest that the schooner in question might this very second be tying up just beyond the French doors. "We islanders are all a prey to foreboding these days," the Childress woman confided to Mrs. Snow as the professor signed the guest register. "A remnant of the storm, no doubt. I'm sure they'll arrive safely."

Professor Snow agreed, remarking that nothing untoward ever happened to people from Newport who owned sailing craft.

"Well, I don't know these particular people," Mrs. Childress said, as if to suggest that therefore she had no idea whether they might be susceptible to sudden squalls at sea, "but they were quite delighted to learn we'd have a distinguished professor of American history in our midst. I warn you in advance that we're all bracing for a weekend of scintillating conversation."

"Ah," said Professor Snow, who was not a professor of history, but rather of literature, "I'm retired, I'm afraid."

Mrs. Childress blinked, as if at some misunderstanding.

"I no longer scintillate," he explained, "though of course I used to."

Mrs. Childress clapped her hands appreciatively and turned to June. "Isn't he the droll one?"

The Snows were shown to a room on the third floor, from which they had an excellent view of the town and, in the distance, the harbor. When the Childress woman left them alone, Professor Snow followed his wife out to the balcony, where they lingered for only a moment because of the bees. He was relieved to see that June was smiling.

Back home in Ithaca, they had made gentle fun of the language of the Captain Clement House brochure, in which the word "resplendent" had occurred three times. But Professor Snow had insisted that it was just the place for them. He suspected that despite their easy mockery, June secretly had her heart set on just such a place as the Captain Clement with its "meticulously preserved, graceful formalities" ("We're snots!" they'd glossed at home, reading the brochure out loud), its "artful blending of American and English, 18th- and 19th-century antiques" ("Try and guess!"), its "finishing touches of crystal and porcelain appointments" ("Crystal commodes! Porcelain chandeliers!"), its "romantic ambience and elegant grandeur" ("Pre-payment requested").

It was, after all, thanks to Professor Snow that their return to the island, so long planned, kept getting put off. For how long? A decade? Twice their reservations had actually been made and then canceled to accommodate some necessary academic conference. The most recent last-minute cancellation had occurred just last Christmas when Snow had let himself be talked into his least favorite conference so that he could be one of the committee to interview short-list candidates for his own position. He should have known better, of course, though he never would have guessed that his colleagues would hire, over his strenuous objections, a young fool whose academic specialty wasn't even literature at all, but rather, as he proudly proclaimed, "culture." In the interview the young fellow had spoken in the latest critical jargon and assured Snow's puzzled colleagues that of course his research was strictly "cutting edge." A month later, when the boy (he seemed no more than twenty, though his vita suggested thirty) visited the campus, he'd shown no deference to the department's senior scholars and exhibited smirking contempt for Snow's own books. That so many of the professor's colleagues seemed taken with the boy suggested to Snow that perhaps they shared the young fellow's opinion of his work and himself, a realization so bitter that Snow had behaved badly, suggesting at the question-and-answer session following the young man's presentation (which had been entitled "Gender Otherness and Othering") that students taking his courses might satisfy in this fashion their foreign language requirement.

But the boy was hired and Snow retired, willingly enough when all was said and done. The young fool would get his. In no time he'd be a tenured and promoted and fully vested *old* fool, by which time Snow himself would be contentedly, happily, cold and dead. Until that time, he had to face June, a woman who seemed to understand that with his retirement he'd just run out of excuses. "The Captain Clement is for us," he'd insisted. "We'll traverse floorboards worn to a glowing patina by two centuries of perpetual footsteps."

The morning after their arrival at the Captain Clement the Snows slept in and went down to late breakfast in the small dining room. The only other diners were the two couples they'd met the afternoon before at tea, the people from Newport that Mrs. Childress had been awaiting so anxiously. The three couples had mingled rather uncomfortably, for an hour or so, the gathering supervised by the Childress woman, who seemed intent on holding it together by the sheer force of her will and a tray of sticky pastries. Later that night at a nearby restaurant, when the Snows had casually mentioned where they were staying, they'd learned from a loose-talking bartender some of the reasons for the Childress woman's anxiety. The Childresses (there had been a Mr. Childress at one point) had bought the Captain Clement only three years before and, according to the bartender, paid too much for it, reportedly in the neighborhood of two and a half million dollars ("You got any idea how many hotel rooms you gotta rent to make back three mill?" the bartender had asked, one eyebrow arched significantly). The Childresses had no sooner purchased the inn than the bottom fell out of island real estate (as well as their marriage), and now the woman was good and stuck. The bartender explained confidently and without visible empathy that the hurricane, which had ruined the last month of the summer season, would be the final nail in her coffin. ("You got the place to yourself, I bet.")

Very nearly. The Captain Clement was host only to the Snows and the Newport foursome. Robbins, the man who owned the yacht, was retired military, and Professor Snow was unable to decide whether the man was just naturally loud or whether he was going deaf. Having been informed that Snow's area of study was American history, Major Robbins quickly cornered the professor and announced that he himself was something of a Civil War buff and then proceeded to regale Snow on the subject of a single obscure battle, the tactical details of which he had apparently committed to memory. Snow, loath to offend, first feigned interest, then abstraction, and finally (when the major said, "Now here's where it gets complicated") intellectual exhaustion. Robbins was not the only one who appeared disappointed when the Snows made excuses and escaped through the garden. The major's traveling companions watched the Snows depart with the weary expression of people who'd been promised a lengthy reprieve and cheated of it.

This morning, in the Captain Clement's dining room, Robbins's companions looked haggard, as though none of them had slept well, or as though a single night's sleep had not been sufficient for them to face this new day, though the major himself looked fresh and ready for anything. All four were dressed in beach attire and Professor Snow noted with relief that they were nearly finished with their breakfasts and unlikely to invite the Snows to join them. June, who professed to having enjoyed her conversation with the major's companions, seemed to be on the verge of veering sociably toward their table until Snow touched her elbow and successfully guided her to the other side of the dining room. "Try the Mexican eggs," Major Robbins bellowed.

"I will," Snow promised, holding June's chair for her, a gesture that seemed appropriate here at the Captain Clement.

Mrs. Childress, who had been in the kitchen, came out to greet them and to inquire how they'd slept. Snow had slept badly, but insisted otherwise. "What a shame we can't offer you breakfast in the garden," the Childress woman said, as if the word "shame" were not nearly potent enough to convey her own personal disappointment. "But the bees have claimed it, I fear."

From where they sat, the Snows could see that the garden was indeed set up for dining, pristine white tables scattered among the flowers and hedges. They could also see bees swarming beyond the French doors.

"Are bees the price of such lovely flowers?" June wondered.

"Alas no," the Childress woman said, her faintly British accent kicking in again. "It's the storm. The bees are disoriented, or so we're told. They think it's spring."

Major Robbins was noisily pushing back his chair now. "The beach!" he cried, as if announcing a dangerous amphibious assault, one he planned to lead personally. His troops looked potentially mutinous. The major's wife, first through the French doors, let out a whoop when the bees closed in and she bolted for the white trellised arch, arms flying about her head, her companions close behind, also waving in the air.

The Snows' waitress was a pretty girl named Jennifer who had a dark, remarkably even tan, the professor noted when she bent over to pick up a fork she managed to knock on the floor. Snow wondered whether it was the girl's clumsiness or her willingness to bend over in her scoop-necked uniform that caused the Childress woman to roll her eyes at June before disappearing into the kitchen.

"South Shore has the best beaches," the girl explained in response to Snow's question about where they might spend the afternoon. "Really primo body surfing."

As the girl said this, Professor Snow thought he saw a trace of doubt flicker across her heretofore untroubled features. As if it might have registered, somewhere, that body surfing might not be what these people she was waiting on had in mind.

"Oak Bluffs is nice too," she added hastily. "That's got a lagoon."

Another flicker of doubt. Had she insulted them? The girl smiled weakly, as if to concede she wasn't the person to ask. She didn't know what older people like the Snows did or where they did it. Or why.

Her plight was so touching that Snow decided to help her off the hook. "Which is the beach with the cliffs?" he asked, recalling it from their previous trip.

"Gay Head, you mean?" the girl said in surprise. "That's clothing optional."

"Oh," June said, with a wry smile, "well *that's* out then."

"Right," the girl said sympathetically, though the source of that sympathy was unclear to Professor Snow. Was she unwilling to shed her clothes in public now, or was she looking ahead thirty years? Actually, she went on to explain, the whole beach wasn't nudist. If they stayed right around the area where the trail joined the beach, they'd be fine. It was only farther down the beach beneath the bluff, where the nudists gathered. They liked to cover their bodies with moist clay from the cliffs, then dry in the sun. The clay was a primo skin conditioner, she explained. "And don't worry about the name. Some people think it's a gay beach, but it's not," she concluded, as if she felt it her duty to allay their fears on this score at least. "They probably ought to change the name."

"They could call it Primo Beach," June mocked when the girl was gone.

While June was in the bathroom changing into the new bathing suit she'd bought on impulse the day before while they were waiting for the ferry, Professor Snow called his old colleague, Professor Loudener, whom they would visit in Manhattan on their way back to Ithaca. David Loudener was one of very few people who knew any of the details of what had happened when June suffered her breakdown. In fact he had been with Professor Snow when the police had called to say that June had been found at a nearby shopping mall, where she had attracted notice by staring into the empty display window of a vacant store. Together, they had gathered June up and taken her home, grateful that no harm had come to her. The only consequence of her brief disappearance seemed to be that she had given her wedding ring to a stranger. This was years ago, but "How is June?" was David Loudener's first question, and Professor Snow imagined he heard in his old friend's voice a doubt, even a fear perhaps. It reminded Snow that he had worried at the time that Loudener had blamed him, at least in part, for what had befallen June. "You're going to have to be careful of her," he'd warned Snow after June was released from the hospital, and there was something in the tone of his friend's voice that suggested to Professor Snow that David Loudener doubted that caring for June was a task he was cut out for.

"We're both fine," the professor said, aware that June was probably able to hear the conversation through the bathroom door. "Anxious to see you and Elaine." And once again he took down the complicated directions he'd need to follow into Manhattan.

"This is way too young, isn't it," June said when she emerged from the bathroom, modeling the new white swimsuit.

Snow couldn't tell whether it was too young or whether there was something in his wife's posture that suggested, defiantly almost, a woman determined to act her age. June was still trim, athletic-looking even, but she was also in one of those moods where she wasn't about to cut herself any slack. She'd been in a sunny mood when she entered the bathroom to change, but now she appeared discouraged, uncertain. "You look wonderful," he assured her. "Come here."

She ignored this invitation. "It's cut too high in the leg," she said, tracing the line of the suit with her index fingers.

"It's the way they're wearing them," Snow said, though now that she'd drawn his attention to it, he saw what she meant.

"It's the way twenty-year-olds are wearing them," she said. "Twenty-year-olds with primo bodies."

"You look lovely, June," he said.

"You'd let me go out in public looking like a fool, wouldn't you?" she said. "Dear God."

"At least I had enough sense to buy this," she said, slipping a yellow cotton cover-up over the suit.

As they drove up-island, the devastation of the hurricane became even more pronounced. Apparently, island cleanup had been prioritized and the less populated side was still awaiting attention. Here, along the winding road, trees still bowed, power lines and downed limbs and other wind-blown objects littered the narrow shoulder of the roadway, awaiting disposal. The air was thick with yellow bees, which pinged angrily off their windshield.

But farther on the topography changed, the land opening up as the road bent toward the shore, rewarding them every quarter mile or so with a glimpse of blue ocean, until finally the road climbed and narrowed and there was blue sky and ocean on both sides. June's mood seemed to lift as the car climbed the final stretch toward the lighthouse perched on the cliff. Halfway down the boardwalk path to the beach, they stopped so June could pull off the cotton cover-up, and when she did this she surrendered a grudging smile. "There," she said. "Are you happy now?"

"I *was* happy," he protested. "I *am* happy."

"Feel that breeze," she said.

By the time they got to the beach, Professor Snow realized he was out of shape, and he allowed June to carry the beach chairs the rest of the way in exchange for the shoulder bag that contained their towels and suntan lotion, his wallet, her purse. Her mood was so generous that she did not remind him that she had warned against these particular chairs, framed of heavy metal, backed and seated with thick canvas. June had been in favor of the lighter aluminum jobs with the plastic straps, but these had looked flimsy to Professor Snow, who'd refused to economize. They would sleep in a good sturdy inn and recline in good sturdy beach chairs.

Where the boardwalk path joined the beach it was relatively crowded with bathers, but the Snows observed that by trekking a ways they could have a stretch of sand more or less to themselves. "By all means," June agreed. "In this suit I want to be as far away from people as I can get."

It looked to be about three hundred yards from where the path met the beach to the rocky point, the red-gray clay cliffs rising gently along the way. When they'd gone not quite a hundred yards, June dropped their chairs in the sand and said, "This is as far as I go, buddy boy. Look up and you'll see why."

Professor Snow, who was more tired than he cared to admit, had been slogging forward through the sand with his head down. "What?" he said.

Farther up the beach, directly beneath the tallest cliffs, was another smaller cluster of bathers, which caused him to wonder if there'd been another path they'd missed, a more direct one down to the beach.

"Those people are naked," his wife said.

Professor Snow squinted, salty perspiration stinging his eyes. "Are you certain?" The figures down the beach were recognizably human but too far away to be gender specific.

"You need glasses," she told him, setting up her chair.

He dropped their bag in the sand. "I need binoculars."

Overheated by their trek, they went for a swim. The September water was still wonderfully warm, and Professor Snow, who had loved to swim as a young man, dove into the surf and swam out beyond where the waves were breaking and there did a leisurely crawl before letting the surf bear him back in. June was not the sort of woman who plunged right into anything, much less the Atlantic Ocean, and he was not surprised to see that she was still feeling her way. He watched her do this with genuine amusement and pleasure. She had always been a graceful woman, and now, in her middle fifties, still was. She had a way of meeting the swells that seemed to Snow the very essence of woman. The waves never broke over her, never knocked her back. Rather, at the last moment, she rose with the water, right up to the crest and then went gently down again. How long, he tried to recall, since they had made love?

Perhaps his wife was thinking the same thing, because as he swam toward her, she surrendered to him a smile that contained not a single reservation, though its cause may have been merely the joy of water, the thrill of buoyancy. "Oh, this is grand," she admitted, water beading in her hair and lashes. When they embraced, she whispered urgently into his ear, "I'm sorry I've been such a pill."

Such a pill. As Professor Snow embraced his wife, it occurred to him that the last time she'd used this phrase, she'd been a young woman, and their love for each other had been so effortless that whatever had momentarily come between them could be effectively banished with such a benign phrase. What that same phrase conveyed to him now was not just a sudden and powerful resurgence of affection and trust, but also its implied promise—that the difficulties of their marriage during the last decade might even now be banished by a mutual act of will. They would simply decide and it would be done. They would be their old, younger selves again. They would be in love.

Later as they stood in the warm sand, toweling themselves dry, June looked down at herself and said, "Thank heavens it's just us." The bathing suit which had caused her so much anxiety dry now proved to be less than opaque wet, and her nipples showed clearly through the wet fabric, as did the dark triangle of her pubic hair. To Professor Snow's surprise, she seemed less upset to discover this than she had been when she emerged from their bathroom at the Captain Clement, insisting the suit was too young, that she looked foolish.

"Let's move our chairs up under the bank," she suggested, something mischievous in her eye, something Snow hadn't witnessed in a long time.

"Why?"

But she was already carting her own chair, plus the beach bag, toward the bank. Folding up the remaining chair, he followed, tired, happy, suspicious. High tides had eroded irregularly, of course, and the spot where June set up her chair, he realized, was semiprivate. Still he was astonished when his wife peeled off her bathing suit and stood naked before him, this woman who for years had changed into her nightgown in the bathroom. "Well?" she said.

"Well what?"

"Let me know if we have company," June said settling into her beach chair and putting on sunglasses. "Unless you're embarrassed . . ."

"Why should I be embarrassed?" he said, staring down at her.

"Good." She smiled, taking a book out of the beach bag.

Professor Snow set up his beach chair next to his wife's. Apparently a challenge had been issued, and there was nothing to do but answer it. When he dropped his bathing trunks, she looked at him critically over the rim of her sunglasses. "I *beg* your pardon," she said.

Last night, after they'd returned from dinner and Professor Snow realized he'd neglected to pack reading material, he'd slipped into a pair of Bermuda shorts and a T-shirt and padded downstairs in his bare feet to check out the book-lined room where tea had been served that afternoon. What he found there was discouraging, if not surprising. Many of the volumes were *Reader's*

*Digest* condensed books, and as he scanned the shelves for something worth reading, he realized that there could be only one possible explanation for such a bizarre library. These books must have been purchased in bulk, for no other reason than to provide what the Captain Clement advertised as "gracious ambience." Some of the books were water damaged, their brown, brittle pages stuck together. Others were upside down.

Perhaps because it was one of the upside-down ones, Professor Snow did not immediately recognize his own book on Emily Dickinson. He had to remove it from the shelf to be sure, but there he was, twenty years younger, staring back at himself seriously from the dust jacket. How strange, he considered, to discover himself in a place like the Captain Clement. How had he come to be here, inverted, next to (far more predictably) Thomas Costain? He examined the book curiously, including the inside flap, which bore an endorsement: "Snow," the blurb read, "goes a long way toward laying bare the secrets of one of our literature's most private lives."

This was precisely the sort of notion, of course, that the young fellow hired to replace him had scoffed at. A twentieth-century male scholar "penetrating" the secrets of a nineteenth-century woman poet? What effrontery! According to the new thinking, all such a study could possibly succeed in doing would be to reveal the prejudices and assumptions of the author's own culture and gender. Insight? Hardly. How the young fellow would have snickered, Professor Snow thought with regret, to know that the best of Professor Snow's work had found a resting place at the Captain Clement "amidst the gentler elegance of a bygone day." Instead of returning the book to its former place on the shelf, Snow laid it flat on top of the row where the Childress woman might notice it in a week or so, and perhaps recognize her guest from the dust jacket photo.

Returning with a magazine to their room, Professor Snow paused at the foot of the stairs, rooted there by the muffled, distant sound of a woman weeping. Although he had left June engrossed in a book, his first thought was that this grief, although sudden and unannounced, must be hers, and so he remained where he was, paralyzed in the dark, until he realized that the sound was not coming down to him from above, but rather from behind the door that marked the entrance to the Childress woman's quarters. To Professor Snow's relief, he found June safely asleep in their room, facing the window, its sheer curtains stirring in the warm autumn breeze. Still, though the grief he'd heard below was not his to share, it haunted Professor Snow's slumbers, and he was awakened several times during the night by the sound of distant weeping carried upward along the Captain Clement's ancient ducts and floor registers, and he lay in the dark for what seemed like hours, alert to the measured sound of June's breathing, on guard against the possibility that some deep sympathy with another woman's grief would reawaken her own. But she continued to sleep peacefully. Once she changed positions and murmured a word softly, and he noticed that she massaged her ring finger before rolling over again, but she did not wake and her sleep seemed untroubled. Since giving away her wedding ring, she'd refused to let him replace it, though he made up his mind to broach the subject again before they left the island.

Perhaps because he had remained awake during so much of the night, he now fell deeply asleep on the beach, drawn downward by the rhythm of the waves, his anxious watchfulness relaxed. When he awoke, it was to the realization that he'd been asleep for some time. He remembered vaguely that just before he'd drifted off June had touched his arm gently and suggested he put on sun screen, but there had been a cool breeze off the water, and he was enjoying the feeling of his skin tightening as it dried in the sun. His skin felt warm now, but he still felt no urgency about waking completely. How pleasant it was just to lie there with his eyes closed, thinking of June's warm embrace in the waves, her acceptance of him, listening to the surf and the pleasant sounds of beach activity around them.

He opened one eye. When he'd gone to sleep, there hadn't *been* any activity. He and June had been alone. No longer. A few yards away a young woman was just releasing a Frisbee, and he followed its flight toward the water. A small dog leaped into the air, caught the Frisbee in its mouth and trotted back to the girl. She was wearing a T-shirt and when she turned to fling the Frisbee again he noticed that she was wearing the smallest black bikini bottom he'd ever seen. No. Check that. She was wearing no bikini bottom at all. At which point he remembered he'd fallen asleep naked himself. Sitting up straight, he saw that he still was.

Also that June's beach chair was empty.

*        *        *

Of course, he assured himself, she had gone for a walk or a swim. Except that he didn't see her in the water, and when he looked for the beach bag containing their things he saw it was no longer sitting alongside her chair. Surely she wouldn't have taken the bag if she'd just gone for a walk. And anyway, she would not have gone for a walk. Not up a stretch of beach populated, as this one was, however sporadically, by nudists. The sand was still not crowded—the nudists, mostly young and in couples, had bivouacked discreet distances from each other. The only person who wasn't young was a gray-haired man standing at the water's edge, looking out to sea. Even from where he sat, Snow could tell the man had an enormous belly. Apparently he occupied a nearby blanket, and Snow was able to deduce from this what must have happened. In his mind's eye he saw the man, clothed, coming up the beach toward them, June looking up from her book when he arrived (she would have put her own suit back on, Snow was certain, when the first bather arrived along their stretch of beach). She'd probably flashed the man a noncommittal smile, an acknowledgment of their similarities, of age and, presumably, attitude toward public nudity. The man probably smiled back as he disrobed. Lord, Snow thought.

Then an even worse scenario occurred to him. Perhaps June too had fallen asleep under the seductive sun and awakened suddenly, as he himself had done, naked and surrounded by beautiful young nudists, feeling humiliated and old. He imagined her on the verge of tears, struggling awkwardly into the bathing suit she'd considered immodest that morning, losing her balance in the sand, convinced that everyone was staring at her. She wouldn't have been satisfied once she got into the suit either. She'd have put on the cotton cover-up. But why hadn't she awakened him? Because she never did, not when things were worst for her. She'd given him no sign the morning of her breakdown. She simply hadn't been there when he returned home. And their family physician, an old friend of the professor's, had warned Snow that, while unlikely, it was possible that once off her medication, June might suffer a relapse into her former depression. Be vigilant, he had warned them both. To battle depression you must first recognize its onset, its early-warning signals.

Professor Snow stood, shading his eyes with his hands, and gazed up the beach in the direction they'd come, half expecting to see his wife's fleeing form. The beach stretched on forever.

Hastily drawing his bathing trunks back on, Professor Snow considered what to do. The most important thing, he told himself, was to reach June as quickly as possible. She was probably weeping quietly in their car at the summit. It *had* been June he'd heard weeping last night in the Captain Clement, he was suddenly, irrationally, certain.

The top of the lighthouse was just visible from where he stood, an impossibly long way off, it seemed to him, since he'd have to retrace his steps up the beach, locate the winding boardwalk path that snaked its leisurely way up the cliffs. He noticed again that at the rocky base of the cliffs, maybe a hundred yards down the beach, there was that other concentration of bathers, and he reasoned again that there had to be another trail up the cliffs. A shortcut. Steep perhaps, but more direct. Depending on how much of a head start June had, he might actually intercept her.

Regardless of which way he went, he would have to leave the chairs. He couldn't carry them so far if he returned the way they'd come, and he certainly couldn't pack them up the side of the cliff when he found the path those other bathers must have used. Leave the chairs, he decided. He didn't want the chairs. He wanted June. He thought about how, just a short time ago, they had embraced in the waves, about his sudden optimism that all would be made right between them. Had he been foolish to think it possible? To imagine their marriage as buoyant as water, their mistakes weightless and inconsequential in the sudden swell of affection?

Professor Snow started down the beach toward the cliffs, hot sand giving beneath his feet with every step.

The rocky promontory was farther than it looked. Much. The cliffs continued to rise as Professor Snow made his way down the beach, and by the time he'd gone fifty yards the top of the lighthouse had disappeared. The cliffs themselves loomed up, high and jagged and steep. In some stretches the clay was bright red, in others gray. From a distance these alternating striations appeared to be narrow ribbons, but they actually extended on for thirty-yard intervals. He kept an eye out for a path but every place that looked promising was posted with a sign forbidding bathers to climb.

What had appeared to be a concentration of bathers at the foot of a single cliff face, turned out to be isolated, spread-out, privacy-seeking nudists. Despite this, Snow continued down the narrowing beach, the bright blue ocean on his left, the cliffs climbing ever higher on his right, the hot sun at his back. He'd forgotten what it was like to try to hurry in the sand, and when his calf muscles began to throb and his lower back to ache, he slowed, fearing that he would not have the strength to climb the cliff when he finally found the path.

It was only when he'd gone—what?—maybe three hundred yards, his lower back pulsating, his breathing labored now, that he was certain of the error of his reasoning. Here at the promontory the beach turned north and before him lay another stretch of sand as long as that which he had just traversed, this one entirely devoid of bathers. Staring up at the cliffs, he now realized, there *was* no other path, no shortcut. The top of the lighthouse had come into view again, but it was behind him now, and at the sight of it, his heart plunged. How far he had come! He'd be lucky to make it back to the beach chairs, much less to the boardwalk path that led the long way up the cliffs toward what remained of his marriage.

And what did remain of it? In his exhaustion Professor Snow now recalled the litany of anguish and accusation that June had laid before him years ago in the hospital. By marrying her, he had stolen her own bright career, made her a dinner party hostess to people who should have been her colleagues. Did he have any idea how badly she had wanted children? And did he realize that she knew, had known for years, about the long affair he'd had with one of his graduate students? When he told her how ashamed he was, that he bitterly regretted his infidelity, June had said, with genuine rancor, that she was sorry to hear it, because she'd had an affair of her own that she did not regret in the least. Professor Snow had not believed this confession, concluding that June simply wanted to wound him, and later when she asked him to forget everything she'd said, to write it off as menopause, he found to his surprise that he was able to, eager to, in fact.

It was almost too far to return now, he thought, staring up the beach and into the immediate future. There would be the drive back to the ridiculous Captain Clement, and then, in another day, the complicated journey to Manhattan, to the city that seemed more confusing each time they visited, where he sometimes got lost and no longer possessed the knack of knowing where he and June would be safe. Then the return to Ithaca, a place too familiar and small to get lost in, at least for a while.

As he started back, his knees jellied, his back throbbing, Professor Snow discovered that even now, he felt lost. All he had to do, of course, was return the way he had come. He knew that. With the cliffs on one side, the sea on the other, it wasn't like there was any possibility of taking a wrong turn, but the sun was in his eyes now, doubly it seemed, because of the glare off the water, and the beach stretched on, unbroken. If he wasn't careful he'd walk right past the beach chairs in their secluded alcove. And how would he know when he'd arrived at the place where the beach joined that path? The huge beach was impossible to miss from the path, but not the tiny path from the beach. He imagined himself marching stupidly, doggedly up this beach forever.

Still, there was nothing to do but keep moving. Because of the glare off the water and the stinging perspiration in his eyes, Professor Snow sometimes did not see sunbathers until he was almost on top of them, and one young woman, startled by his sudden nearness, quickly rolled onto her stomach and glared over her shoulder at him angrily. When she nudged the sleeping boy next to her, Snow mumbled an apology and hurried on, staggering in the sand. How could he have been so foolish as to come this way? Why had he persisted so long in his folly by assuming the existence of a second path? He plunged forward, blindly now, on the verge of panic. His sunburn—he was suddenly aware of it—was making him lightheaded. He was inhabiting a nightmare where everything was inverted. Instead of discovering himself naked in a crowd of friendly, well-dressed strangers—wasn't this the way such dreams usually worked?—here he was, an old man in baggy swimming trunks, adrift in a sea of angry, naked strangers. And what phantasm, dear God, was this, not chasing him, but coming languidly toward him down the beach?

Professor Snow, transfixed, slowed at the sight, certain he had lost his mind. Was it a young woman approaching or a hag? Incredibly, she was both. Her skin, from head to toe, was a dry, cracking, lifeless gray. The figure resembled, frighteningly, a photographic negative. Its naked breasts were large and full, the dry seaweed between her legs the color of pale ash. Only her eyes were white until she smiled at him, lewdly he thought, revealing rows of sharp, perfect white teeth.

"Dear God," he said, dropping heavily to his knees, far too exhausted to flee another step. "Dear God, be merciful."

Perhaps because the dry hand on his shoulder was both warm and gentle, he found the courage to look up at the gray skull, which was fearful still, though no longer grinning. Its expression seemed almost apprehensive, the last thing he would have expected, now that he'd recognized the figure, its allegorical significance.

"Not now," he pleaded. He could feel his heart thudding dangerously in his chest. "Please. Not now."

June drove. The trip back down-island took almost an hour. An eternity. The world had finally righted itself, but at Professor Snow's expense, it seemed to him. He felt like a man with very little time left. June, at the wheel, looked less old than shattered. Her part in what had transpired she'd been able to explain in a few terrible, clipped sentences. When he'd awakened, she'd been swimming. The current had borne her a ways down the beach. She'd seen him stand and look for her, and she'd waved, unsure whether he'd seen her or not. Then he'd pulled on his bathing trunks and started up the beach, for a walk, she'd assumed, to look at all the pretty naked girls. She'd felt self-conscious about her own nakedness at first, but the sensation had quickly vanished, replaced by an odd, pleasant sense of liberation. Before going into the water, she'd stuffed the bag that contained their things under the beach chair he was sleeping in. He'd have seen it there if he'd looked.

Their arrival back at the Captain Clement had been the final humiliation. June had had to lead Snow like a blind man under the trellised arch, and halfway to the French doors the garden path had begun to swim before him and he'd slumped heavily onto one of the wicker benches. It was several minutes before he was able to stand again. June had remained there with him, though she refused to sit or speak, the two of them, silent, in the center of a dense cloud of bees, in full view of the dining room where the Robbins foursome and the Childress woman had gathered for tea.

Shortly after, June went out in search of first aid cream, leaving him in their room at the top of the Captain Clement. They would be cutting short their stay on the island a second time, and Snow was certain June would call David Loudener and cancel their visit to the city. What excuse she would offer, he had no idea. Nor did he care. June had been gone only a few minutes when there was a knock at the door, and Professor Snow, who couldn't think of a single person in the world that he wanted at that moment to see, was rewarded for his misanthropy by the sight of that person who in all the wide world he wanted to see least.

"We're gonna be checkin' out early," Major Robbins explained. "I don't think we could take another night in this place," he said, glancing around the Captain Clement contemptuously. When it became clear that Professor Snow did not follow this, he continued, "You didn't hear that caterwauling last night?"

Professor Snow remained confused. How could the half-deaf major have heard June's grief?

"You're lucky you're up here on the third floor," Robbins said, rolling his eyes. "I don't know what's wrong with our hostess, but she bawled half the night. The wife and I are right over her bedroom."

"The poor woman," Professor Snow said.

"Well . . . yeah . . . sure," the major conceded, "but Christ Almighty."

"Would you like to come in?" Snow offered, standing aside. "My wife just—"

"Yeah, I saw her go," Robbins admitted. "I just wanted to make sure you were okay. That's some sunburn you got."

"I'm feeling better now," Snow lied, though in truth he was still feverish. Each time he touched the tender skin along his forearm, his fingerprint remained like a scar.

"I'm glad," Major Robbins said, though he looked skeptical. "Personally, I think it was those Mexican eggs. Between you and me, I been crapping little green razor blades all afternoon."

"I didn't have them," Snow admitted.

"Oh." The major looked hurt to learn this, and Snow recalled he'd promised to order them. "Anyhow I came up to tell you I saw that book you wrote. Down there in the library? It looked real interesting."

"I'm told it's passé," Snow admitted.

The major dismissed this view with a wave. "I always thought it would be real satisfying to write a book. Leave something behind for people to remember you by. Like history, almost."

The two men shook hands then, and when Professor Snow closed the door, he listened to the major lumber heavily down the two flights of stairs, a kinder man than he had imagined. The whole Robbins party must have gone out through the bee-filled garden, because Snow heard the women whooping. Instead of lying back down on the bed and risking a feverish sleep, he went over to the window and looked down in time to see the Robbins foursome come out through the trellised arch and head toward the harbor. They were dressed in shorts and white cotton sweaters and canvas deck shoes, spry, all of them, for their age.

It was still difficult for Professor Snow to credit the events of the afternoon. He couldn't decide whether what had transpired was sudden or if it had all been approaching for years in increments so slow as to be undetectable as motion to the human eye. How long the world had remained tilted! How slowly his rationality had returned, and how little comfort trailed in its wake. The figure on the beach had intuited blind confusion before he himself had understood. "You wait right here," it had instructed him, unnecessarily, since he lacked both the strength and equilibrium to get to his feet. He'd watched the figure dart into the ocean, into a breaking, thigh-high wave, and when the water receded, taking with it much of the dried clay, leaving its legs flesh-colored, he'd stared at the miracle without comprehending. Even after the next larger wave completed the transformation and the young woman emerged glistening, reborn, from the sea, he still couldn't make it work.

She'd had a name (already forgotten) and a boyfriend, and once they'd clothed themselves, they took him by the elbow and guided him, an invalid, back up the beach. They'd pointed to each woman they passed who could conceivably have been Professor Snow's wife, asking him, are you sure, because he remained confused and disoriented, answering, "I don't think so," after examining one woman with heavy, sagging breasts, another with round, fleshy hips, a third with the wrong color hair. In truth, he was terrified of not recognizing June at a distance, of telling them no, this was not the woman he'd been married to for thirty years, and then being wrong. The sun made him feel faint and distant from his own body, and after each new woman proved not to be June, he'd lost interest in the search, certain that she was long gone.

In the end it was June who saw them coming, saw the professor limping up the beach toward her, looking as if he would surely collapse were it not for the support of the young couple. She'd risen tentatively, fearfully at first, then come hurrying toward them. He had seen her without truly recognizing her, occupied as his wandering mind was with the problem of how to explain his delusion, how to make anyone understand that he had met Death in the figure of this young woman and been granted what he now felt to be a temporary reprieve. He still had not thought of a way to make a more heartfelt apology to his wife than he had managed to do on that terrible day when he and Paul Loudener had found her, lost and forlorn, staring into the vacant storefront display window.

And now June had come swimming into his ken too soon, making him aware of the two young people who were supporting him, especially of the handsome young fellow at his left elbow, and so, with a world of difficult, maybe impossible things to say, he'd felt himself rise up and say the cruel thing that was so easy, that seemed to give him strength. "Cover yourself, June," he'd heard himself instruct her. "For God's sake."

And so now, Paul Snow, professor emeritus, author of four books, three of them biographies, stood at the third-floor window of the Captain Clement as dusk gathered in the street below, waiting for his wife to return. It *was* foolish and arrogant, he had to concede, to think you could imagine the truth of another human life, to unlock its secrets, probe its mysteries, as he had been credited with doing in his book on Emily Dickinson. What, in the end, could he know of what was in her heart? Maybe the young fellow they'd hired to replace him was right to scoff. But there *were* things you could know, even when you didn't want to. Pain, humiliation, fear of inadequacy—these were knowable things. He had known them, felt them, shared them that moment when he'd told his wife to cover herself. He wasn't a different species, despite his flaws. Maybe he'd forgotten who June was. Maybe he'd never known. But how exquisitely he, who had caused her pain, had felt and shared it in that moment, was sharing it still.

Down in the street in the gathering dark Professor Snow saw a woman who looked like June, though he couldn't be sure, not anymore. She had stopped at a crosswalk, though there was no traffic in the empty street, and no signal. The woman seemed uncertain whether to head up the street toward him, or away. She appeared to be listening, as if for the distant sound of the ocean, perhaps imagining how it had felt to be borne gently aloft on a wave.

CLEANING HOUSE

*Alyce Miller*

**ALYCE MILLER**'s collection *The Nature of Longing* won the Flannery O'Connor Award and was republished in paperback. She has completed a forthcoming novel and two more collections of short fiction. Her work has appeared in numerous magazines, including *Story, Kenyon Review,* and *Glimmer Train.* She and her husband live in Bloomington, Indiana, where she teaches in the M.F.A. program at Indiana University.

HER LOVER'S NAME is William and his fingers work faster than a shuttle on a loom. He's volunteered to scour the bathroom while she tidies the bedroom. There is a feverish quality to their efforts, almost a celebratory spirit. The bathroom and the bedroom are the two rooms where she and William spend most of their time in leisurely showers and leisurely naps, oblivious to the hour on the clock. These are the rooms where, with shades drawn, they have whiled away their hermetic days. Ordered out for pizza, canceled appointments, unplugged the phone, gone in late to work or not at all, and gorged themselves on the luxury of two weeks, which have coiled around them to the point of near suffocation. Sometimes she doesn't leave the bed even for a drink of water, but lies parched, removed, staring at the ceiling from the tight, pungent circle of William's arms.

Sometimes they pretend they are two people stranded on a desert island, hopeless about ever being found, resigned to their fate: a slow undoing of life. Death hovers on the horizon, not in the form of sun or frost, but in the subtle draining of passion. They lie lifeless for what seems like hours. At those moments there's nothing left to say; each has been milked to unconsciousness. It is only when one moves that the other is aware of separateness.

"I'm using bleach in the bathtub," William announces, kneeling on the bathroom floor. A steamy vapor rises up from the porcelain.

"Paul will think I've hired someone to clean."

"In a way you have." William winks.

She's vacuumed the bedroom for so long she's sure the rugs have gone threadbare. She's like Lady Macbeth with her damned spot.

Tomorrow, Paul will return. This is as much as she has told William about Paul. You'd think little things would seep out through the pores of intimacy, when she and William lie in bed together. But they don't. She has drawn an uncrossable line in her mind. When she is with William, she refuses all references to Paul. She forgets, happily, about everything. Most importantly, with William, she stops holding her breath.

"Why did you ever marry Paul?" William asks on this, their last night together. He normally doesn't ask personal questions.

"I've forgotten," she says, and puts a stop to it.

Paul is as familiar as the weather and the seasons. She half expects him to someday fade like the paint on the walls.

Perhaps if they'd had children. But children weren't possible, and this is something else she has never told William, who asked once, but only perfunctorily, if she had any. William has two children of his own who live in another state. He carries pictures as proof. She prefers to let him believe whatever he wants about her. Ironic, she used to think, that her own husband skillfully delivered into the world more than four thousand babies belonging to other women. It occurred to her she might have viewed those deliveries as a form of betrayal, but that would be too obvious. Besides, what does it matter now, she is past the point of wanting children. That desire belonged to a different time.

She won't talk about these matters concerning herself or Paul, with William or with anyone for that matter. She will not have them exposed, criticized, analyzed, or laughed at by the man she sleeps with. She keeps Paul's study door locked when William is there. Far more intimate to poke through a man's books and papers than to sleep with his wife, she figures. And, during William's stay, she does not, under any circumstances, allow either of them to borrow Paul's books, his pens, his telephone, or his writing tablets.

It is after midnight and she and William have exhausted themselves with cleaning and now lie side by side like two corpses. But they grow restless. The chill of late autumn hovers over the ledge of the open window. It is not a hot night. Yet they pull apart as if it were, as if the very touch of the other is too much.

Lying there, she feels her heart pulse more rapidly, growing wilder in her chest, until she is convinced she hears the thump of Paul's step on the porch, the key in the front lock, and the scrape of shoe on the mat inside the door.

William pretends to be asleep. She can tell by his breathing that he isn't. She gets up for the third time and prowls gently through the house, without turning on lights. She knows exactly how many steps there are from the second to the first floor, how many steps it takes her to move through the dining room into the kitchen. There are shadows of tree leaves and lights from the street; there is the hiss of water in the pipes as she opens the faucet and pours a glass of water. She drinks slowly in the darkened kitchen, watching the shadowplay on the walls, finding her own quivering silhouette among the others.

In her mind she plans for Paul's dinner tomorrow night when he returns. She reminds herself to check under the bed once again to be certain that William hasn't left behind a stray sock or Kleenex.

And first thing, in the morning, when William and she have parted, and she has rechecked the closets and the drawers, and made sure one of his razor blades hasn't fallen under the tub, she will take their bed sheets, softened and soured by frenzied tussles, and drive them to the city dump, five miles away.

They can never be washed clean enough, she doesn't dare risk putting them in the trash cans out back, and she can't take the chance of being seen depositing them in a public trash can, like a crook.

There is anonymity at the city dump, as well as finality. Here it is that castoff objects have collected in an anonymous pit tended by men in orange shirts and caps who shovel it all together. No danger of these objects ever reappearing. They lie beyond recognition in their open grave.

The man in the weighing booth, a heavyset, humorless fellow in a Harley cap, jots down the weight of the car as it enters, and then again as it exits. He never seems fazed that her car going out will weigh exactly what it weighed coming in.

"Ten dollars," he murmurs every time, quoting the minimum, without looking out at her from his glass cage.

Someday, she thinks, as the bill passes from her hand through the slot in the window, he may raise his eyes and actually look at her. He will separate her from all the other drivers of all the other cars moving through, and ask her, "What is it you dump here every couple of months, lady, air?"

She has anticipated that moment, when the man who guards the hellish pits of discarded junk stubs out his cigar and considers her odd journey past the toxic waste site and the recycled glass to where the white painted arrows lead, to dump something that weighs almost the same as nothing, something so light she might as well be passing through in an empty car. She has practiced numerous and humorous responses, none of which she will ever have the nerve to use. And, she realizes, he will never ask.

She sets down the empty water glass and stares around at the kitchen walls.

Instead of going directly upstairs, she leans over on the countertop and lowers her head gently onto her curved arms. Her forehead finds comfort in the cool hardness of the tile. She can go no farther. Inside the dark circle of her arms, she inhales and exhales softly, twice. She pictures Paul's carefully locked study, tomorrow's bed made up with fresh sheets and quilt, all the care she has taken with him in his absence. In this way, she assures herself, she has been most faithful.

The MIDDLEMAN

*Bharati Mukherjee*

BHARATI MUKHERJEE was born in Calcutta, India, in 1940. She won the National Book Critics Circle Award for her collection *The Middleman and Other Stories.* Her novels include *The Holder of the World, Jasmine,* and *The Tiger's Daughter.* She and her husband, Clark Blaise, have lived in Canada, India, and the United States. She teaches at the University of California, Berkeley.

THERE ARE ONLY two seasons in this country, the dusty and the wet. I already know the dusty and I'll get to know the wet. I've seen worse. I've seen Baghdad, Bombay, Queens—and now this moldering spread deep in Mayan country. Aztecs, Toltecs, mestizos, even some bashful whites with German accents. All that and a lot of Texans. I'll learn the ropes.

Forget the extradition order, I'm not a sinful man. I've listened to bad advice. I've placed my faith in dubious associates. My first American wife said, in the dog-eat-dog, Alfred, you're a beagle. My name is Alfie Judah, of the once-illustrious Smyrna, Aleppo, Baghdad—and now Flushing, Queens—Judahs.

I intend to make it back.

This place is owned by one Clovis T. Ransome. He reached here from Waco with fifteen million in petty cash hours ahead of a posse from the SEC. That doesn't buy much down here, a few thousand acres, residency papers and the right to swim with the sharks a few feet off the bottom. Me? I make a living from things that fall. The big fat belly of Clovis T. Ransome bobs above me like whale shit at high tide.

The president's name is Gutiérrez. Like everyone else he has enemies, right and left. He's on retainer from men like Ransome, from the *contras,* maybe from the Sandinistas as well.

The woman's name is Maria. She came with the ranch, or with the protection, no one knows.

President Gutiérrez's country has definite possibilities. All day I sit by the lime green swimming pool, sun-screened so I won't turn black, going through my routine of isometrics while Ransome's *indios* hack away the virgin forests. Their hate is intoxicating. They hate gringos—from which my darkness exempts me—even more than Gutiérrez. They hate in order to keep up their intensity. I hear a litany of presidents' names, Hollywood names, Detroit names—Carter, *chop,* Reagan, *slash,* Buick, *thump*—bounce off the vines as machetes clear the jungle greenness. We spoke a form of Spanish in my old Baghdad home. I always understand more than I let on.

In this season the air's so dry it could scratch your lungs. Bright-feathered birds screech, snakeskins glitter, as the jungle peels away. Iguanas the size of wallabies leap from behind macheted bushes. The pool is greener than the ocean waves, cloudy with chemicals that Ransome has trucked over the mountains. When toads fall in, the water blisters their skin. I've heard their cries.

Possibilities, oh, yes.

I must confess my weakness. It's women.

In the old Baghdad when I was young, we had the hots for blondes. We'd stroll up to the diplomatic enclaves just to look at women. Solly Nathan, cross-eyed Itzie, Naim, and me. Pinkish flesh could turn our blood to boiling lust. British matrons with freckled calves, painted toenails through thin-strapped sandals, the onset of varicose, the brassiness of prewar bleach jobs—all of that could thrill us like cleavage. We were twelve and already visiting whores during those hot Levantine lunch hours when our French masters intoned the rules of food, rest, and good digestion. We'd roll up our fried flat bread smeared with spicy potatoes, pool our change, and bargain with the daughters of washer-women while our lips and fingers still glistened with succulent grease. But the only girls cheap enough for boys our age with unspecified urgencies were swamp Arabs from Basra and black girls from Baluchistan, the broken toys discarded by our older brothers.

Thank God those European women couldn't see us. It's comforting at times just to be a native, invisible to our masters. *They* were worthy of our lust. Local girls were for amusement only, a dark place to spend some time, like a video arcade.


"You chose a real bad time to come, Al," he says. He may have been born on the wrong side of Waco, but he's spent his adult life in tropical paradises playing God. "The rains'll be here soon, a day or two at most." He makes a whooping noise and drinks Jack Daniel's from a flask.

"My options were limited." A modest provident fund I'd been maintaining for New Jersey judges was discovered. My fresh new citizenship is always in jeopardy. My dealings can't stand too much investigation.

"Bud and I can keep you from getting bored."

Bud Wilkins should be over in his pickup anytime now. Meanwhile, Ransome rubs Cutter over his face and neck. They're supposed to go deep-sea fishing today, though it looks to me as if he's dressed for the jungle. A wetted-down hand towel is tucked firmly under the back of his baseball cap. He's a Braves man. Bud ships him cassettes of all the Braves games. There are aspects of American life I came too late for and will never understand. It isn't love of the game, he told me last week. It's love of Ted Turner, the man.

His teams. His stations. His America's Cup, his yachts, his network.

If he could clone himself after anyone in the world, he'd choose Ted Turner. Then he leaned close and told me his wife, Maria—once the mistress of Gutiérrez himself, as if I could miss her charms, or underestimate their price in a seller's market—told him she'd put out all night if he looked like Ted Turner. "Christ, Al, here I've got this setup and I gotta beg her for it!" There *are* things I can relate to, and a man in such agony is one of them. That was last week, and he was drunk and I was new on the scene. Now he snorts more JD and lets out a whoop.

"Wanna come fishing? Won't cost you extra, Al."

"Thanks, no," I say. "Too hot."

The only thing I like about Clovis Ransome is that he doesn't snicker when I, an Arab to some, an Indian to others, complain of the heat. Even dry heat I despise.

"Suit yourself," he says.

Why do I suspect he wants me along as a witness? I don't want any part of their schemes. Bud Wilkins got here first. He's entrenched, doing little things for many people, building up a fleet of trucks, of planes, of buses. Like Ari Onassis, he started small. That's the legitimate side. The rest of it is no secret. A man with cash and private planes can clear a fortune in Latin America. The story is Bud was exposed as a CIA agent, forced into public life and made to go semipublic with his arms deals and transfer fees.

"I don't mind you staying back, you know. She wants Bud."

Maria.

I didn't notice Maria for the first days of my visit. She was *here,* but in the background. And she was dark, native, and I have my prejudices. But what can I say—is there deeper pleasure, a darker thrill than prejudice squarely faced, suppressed, fought against, and then slowly, secretively surrendered to?

Now I think a single word: adultery.

On cue, Maria floats toward us out of the green shadows. She's been swimming in the ocean, her hair is wet, her big-boned, dark-skinned body is streaked with sand. The talk is Maria was an aristocrat, a near-Miss World whom Ransome partially bought and partially seduced away from Gutiérrez, so he's never sure if the president owes him one, or wants to kill him. With her thick dark hair and smooth dark skin, she has to be mostly Indian. In her pink Lycra bikini she arouses new passion. Who wants pale, thin, pink flesh, who wants limp, curly blond hair, when you can have lustrous browns, purple-blacks?

Adultery and dark-eyed young women are forever entwined in my memory. It is a memory, even now, that fills me with chills and terror and terrible, terrible desire. When I was a child, one of our servants took me to his village. He wanted me to see something special from the old Iraqi culture. Otherwise, he feared, my lenient Jewish upbringing would later betray me. A young woman, possibly adulterous but certainly bold and brave and beautiful enough to excite rumors of promiscuity, was stoned to death that day. What I remember now is the breathlessness of waiting as the husband encircled her, as she struggled against the rope, as the stake barely swayed to her writhing. I remember the dull thwock and the servant's strong fingers shaking my shoulders as the first stone struck.

I realize I am one of the very few Americans who knows the sound of rocks cutting through flesh and striking bone. One of the few to count the costs of adultery.

Maria drops her beach towel on the patio floor, close to my deck chair, and straightens the towel's edge with her toes. She has to have been a dancer before becoming Ransome's bride and before Gutiérrez plucked her out of convent school to become his mistress. Only ballerinas have such blunted, misshapen toes. But she knows, to the right eyes, even her toes are desirable.

"I want to hear about New York, Alfred." She lets herself fall like a dancer on the bright red towel. Her husband is helping Eduardo, the houseboy, load the jeep with the day's gear, and it's him she seems to be talking to. "My husband won't let me visit the States. He absolutely won't."

"She's putting you on, Al," Ransome shouts. He's just carried a case of beer out to the jeep. "She prefers St. Moritz."

"You ski?"

I can feel the heat rising from her, or from the towel. I can imagine as the water beads on her shoulders how cool her flesh will be for just a few more minutes.

"Do I look as though I ski?"

I don't want to get involved in domestic squabbles. The *indios* watch us. A solemn teenager hefts his machete. We are to have an uncomplicated view of the ocean from the citadel of this patio.

"My husband is referring to the fact that I met John Travolta in St. Moritz," she says, defiantly.

"Sweets," says Ransome. The way he says it, it's a threat.

"He has a body of one long muscle, like an eel," she says.

Ransome is closer now. "Make sure Eduardo doesn't forget the crates," he says.

"Okay, okay," she shouts back, "excuse me," and I watch her corkscrew to her feet. I'm so close I can hear her ligaments pop.

Soon after, Bud Wilkins roars into the cleared patch that serves as the main parking lot. He backs his pickup so hard against a shade tree that a bird wheels up from its perch. Bud lines it up with an imaginary pistol and curls his finger twice in its direction. I'm not saying he has no feeling for wildlife. He's in boots and camouflage pants, but his hair, what there is of it, is blow-dried.

He stalks my chair. "We could use you, buddy." He uncaps a beer bottle with, what else, his teeth. "You've seen some hot spots."

"He doesn't want to fish." Ransome is drinking beer, too. "We wouldn't want to leave Maria unprotected." He waits for a retort, but Bud's too much the gentleman. Ransome stares at me and winks, but he's angry. It could get ugly, wherever they're going.

They drink more beer. Finally Eduardo comes out with a crate. He carries it bowlegged, in mincing little half-running steps. The fishing tackle, of course. The crate is dumped into Bud's pickup. He comes out with a second and third, equally heavy, and drops them all in Bud's truck. I can guess what I'm watching. Low-grade arms transfer, rifles, ammo and maybe medicine.

"*Ciao, amigo,*" says Bud in his heavy-duty Texas accent.

He and Ransome roar into the jungle in Ransome's jeep.

"I hope you're not too hungry, Alfie." It's Maria calling from the kitchen. Alfred to Alfie before the jeep can have made it off the property.

"I'm not a big eater." What I mean to say is, I'm adaptable. What I'm hoping is, let us not waste time with food.

"Eduardo!" The houseboy, probably herniated by now, comes to her for instructions. "We just want a salad and fruit. But make it fast, I have to run into San Vincente today." That's the nearest market town. I've been there, it's not much.

She stands at the front door about to join me on the patio when Eduardo rushes us, broom in hand. "*Vaya!*" he screams.

But she is calm. "It must be behind the stove, stupid," she tells the servant. "It can't have made it out this far without us seeing it."

Eduardo wields his broom like a night stick and retreats into the kitchen. We follow. I can't see it. I can only hear desperate clawing and scraping on the tiles behind the stove.

Maria stomps the floor to scare it out. The houseboy shoves the broom handle in the dark space. I think first, being a child of the overheated deserts, giant scorpions. But there are two fugitives, not one, a pair of ocean crabs. The crabs, their shiny purple backs dotted with yellow, try to get by us to the beach where they can hear the waves.

How do mating ocean crabs scuttle their way into Clovis T. Ransome's kitchen? I feel for them.

The broom comes down, thwack, thwack, and bashes the shells in loud, succulent cracks. *Ransome, Gringo,* I hear.

He sticks his dagger into the burlap sacks of green chemicals. He rips, he cuts.

"Eduardo, it's all right. Everything's fine." She sounds stern, authoritative, the years in the presidential palace have served her well. She moves toward him, stops just short of taking his arm.

He spits out, "He kills everything." At least, that's the drift. The language of Cervantes does not stretch around the world without a few skips in transmission. Eduardo's litany includes crabs, the chemicals, the sulfurous pool, the dead birds and snakes and lizards.

"You have my promise," Maria says. "It's going to work out. Now I want you to go to your room, I want you to rest."

We hustle him into his room but he doesn't seem to notice his surroundings. His body has gone slack. I hear the word Santa Simona, a new saint for me. I maneuver him to the cot and keep him pinned down while Maria checks out a rusty medicine cabinet.

He looks up at me. "You drive *Doña* Maria where she goes?"

"If she wants me to, sure."

"Eduardo, go to sleep. I'm giving you something to help." She has water and a blue pill ready.

While she hovers over him, I check out his room. It's automatic with me. There are crates under the bed. There's a table covered with oilcloth. The oilcloth is cracked and grimy. A chair by the table is a catchall for clothes, shorts, even a bowl of fruit. Guavas. Eduardo could have snuck in caviar, imported cheeses, Godiva candies, but it's guavas he's chosen to stash for siesta hour hunger pains. The walls are hung with icons of saints. Posters of stars I'd never have heard of if I hadn't been forced to drop out. Baby-faced men and women. The women are sensual in an old-fashioned, Latin way, with red curvy lips, big breasts and tiny waists. Like Maria. Quite a few are unconvincing blondes, in that brassy Latin way. The men have greater range. Some are young versions of Fernando Lamas, some are in fatigues and boots, striking Robin Hood poses. The handsomest is dressed as a guerrilla with all the right accessories: beret, black boots, bandolier. Maybe he'd played Che Guevara in some B-budget Argentine melodrama.

"What's in the crates?" I ask Maria.

"I respect people's privacy," she says. "Even a servant's." She pushes me roughly toward the door. "So should you."

\*     \*     \*

The daylight seems too bright on the patio. The bashed shells are on the tiles. Ants have already discovered the flattened meat of ocean crabs, the blistered bodies of clumsy toads.

Maria tells me to set the table. Every day we use a lace cloth, heavy silverware, roses in a vase. Every day we drink champagne. Some mornings the Ransomes start on the champagne with breakfast. Bud owns an air-taxi service and flies in cases of Épernay, caviar, any damned thing his friends desire.

She comes out with a tray. Two plates, two fluted glasses, chèvre cheese on a bit of glossy banana leaf, water biscuits. "I'm afraid this will have to do. Anyway, you said you weren't hungry."

I spread a biscuit and hand it to her.

"If you feel all right, I was hoping you'd drive me to San Vincente." She gestures at Bud Wilkins's pickup truck. "I don't like to drive that thing."

"What if I didn't want to?"

"You won't. Say no to me, I mean. I'm a terrific judge of character." She shrugs, and her breasts are slower than her shoulders in coming down.

"The keys are on the kitchen counter. Do you mind if I use your w.c. instead of going back upstairs? Don't worry, I don't have horrible communicable diseases." She laughs.

This may be intimacy. "How could I mind? It's your house."

"Alfie, don't pretend innocence. It's Ransome's house. This isn't *my* house."

I get the key to Bud's pickup and wait for her by the bruised tree. I don't want to know the contents of the crates, though the stencilling says "fruits" and doubtless the top layer preserves the fiction. How easily I've been recruited, when a bystander is all I wanted to be. The Indians put down their machetes and make signs to me: *Hi, mom, we're Number One.* They must have been watching Ransome's tapes. They're all wearing Braves caps.

The road to San Vincente is rough. Deep ruts have been cut into the surface by army trucks. Whole convoys must have passed this way during the last rainy season. I don't want to know whose trucks, I don't want to know why.

Forty minutes into the trip Maria says, "When you get to the T, take a left. I have to stop off near here to run an errand." It's a strange word for the middle of a jungle.

"Don't let it take you too long," I say. "We want to be back before hubby gets home." I'm feeling jaunty. She touches me when she talks.

"So Clovis scares you." Her hand finds its way to my shoulder.

"Shouldn't he?"

I make the left. I make it sharper than I intended. Bud Wilkins's pickup sputters up a dusty rise. A pond appears and around it shacks with vegetable gardens.

"Where are we?"

"In Santa Simona," Maria says. "I was born here, can you imagine?"

This isn't a village, it's a camp for guerrillas. I see some women here, and kids, roosters, dogs. What Santa Simona is is a rest stop for families on the run. I deny simple parallels. Ransome's ranch is just a ranch.

"You could park by the pond."

I step on the brake and glide to the rutted edge of the pond. Whole convoys must have parked here during the rainy season. The ruts hint at secrets. Now in the dry season what might be a lake has shrunk into a muddy pit. Ducks float on green scum.

Young men in khaki begin to close in on Bud's truck.

Maria motions me to get out. "I bet you could use a drink." We make our way up to the shacks. The way her bottom bounces inside those cutoffs could drive a man crazy. I don't turn back but I can hear the unloading of the truck.

So: Bud Wilkins's little shipment has been hijacked, and I'm the culprit. Some job for a middleman.

"*This* is my house, Alfie."

I should be upset. Maria's turned me into a chauffeur. You bet I could use a drink.

We pass by the first shack. There's a garage in the back where there would be the usual large, cement laundry tub. Three men come at me, twirling tire irons the way night sticks are fondled by Manhattan cops. "I'm with her."

Maria laughs at me. "It's not you they want."

And I wonder, *who* was she supposed to deliver? Bud, perhaps, if Clovis hadn't taken him out? Or Clovis himself?

We pass the second shack, and a third. Then a tall guerrilla in full battle dress floats out of nowhere and blocks our path. Maria shrieks and throws herself on him and he holds her face in his hands, and in no time they're swaying and moaning like connubial visitors at a prison farm. She has her back to me. His big hands cup and squeeze her halter top. I've seen him somewhere. Eduardo's poster.

"Hey," I try. When that doesn't work, I start to cough.

"Sorry." Maria swings around still in his arms. "This is Al Judah. He's staying at the ranch."

The soldier is called Andreas something. He looks me over. "Yudah?" he asks Maria, frowning.

She shrugs. "You want to make something of it?"

He says something rapidly, locally, that I can't make out. She translates, "He says you need a drink," which I don't believe.

We go inside the command shack. It's a one-room affair, very clean, but dark and cluttered. I'm not sure I should sit on the narrow cot; it seems to be a catchall for the domestic details of revolution—sleeping bags, maps and charts, an empty canteen, two pairs of secondhand army boots. I need a comfortable place to deal with my traumas. There is a sofa of sorts, actually a car seat pushed tight against a wall and stabilized with bits of lumber. There are bullet holes through the fabric, and rusty stains that can only be blood. I reject the sofa. There are no tables, no chairs, no posters, no wall decorations of any kind, unless you count a crucifix. Above the cot, a sad, dark, plaster crucified Jesus recalls His time in the desert.

"Beer?" Maria doesn't wait for an answer. She walks behind a curtain and pulls a six-pack of Heinekens from a noisy refrigerator. I believe I am being offered one of Bud Wilkins's unwitting contributions to the guerrilla effort. I should know it's best not to ask how Dutch beer and refrigerators and '57 two-tone Plymouths with fins and chrome make their way to nowhere jungle clearings. Because of guys like me, in better times, that's how. There's just demand and supply running the universe.

"Take your time, Alfie." Maria is beaming so hard at me it's unreal. "We'll be back soon. You'll be cool and rested in here."

Andreas manages a contemptuous wave, then holding hands, he and Maria vault over the railing of the back porch and disappear.

She's given me beer, plenty of beer, but no church key. I look around the room. Ransome or Bud would have used his teeth. From His perch, Jesus stares at me out of huge, sad, Levantine eyes. In this alien jungle, we're fellow Arabs. You should see what's happened to the old stomping grounds, compadre.

I test my teeth against a moist, corrugated bottle cap. It's no good. I whack the bottle cap with the heel of my hand against the metal edge of the cot. It foams and hisses. The second time it opens. New World skill. Somewhere in the back of the shack, a parakeet begins to squawk. It's a sad, ugly sound. I go out to the back porch to give myself something to do, maybe snoop. By the communal laundry tub there's a cage and inside the cage a mean, molting bird. A kid of ten or twelve teases the bird with bits of lettuce. Its beak snaps open for the greens and scrapes the rusty sides of the bar. The kid looks defective, dull-eyed, thin but flabby.

"Gringo," he calls out to me. "Gringo, gum."

I check my pockets. No Dentyne, no Tums, just the plastic cover for spent traveler's checks. My life has changed. I don't have to worry about bad breath or gas pains turning off clients.

"Gringo, Chiclets."

The voice is husky.

I turn my palms outward. "Sorry, you're out of luck."

The kid leaps on me with moronic fury. I want to throw him down, toss him in the scummy vat of soaking clothes, but he's probably some sort of sacred mascot. "How about this pen?" It's a forty-nine-cent disposable, the perfect thing for poking a bird. I go back inside.

I am sitting in the HQ of the Guerrilla Insurgency, drinking Heineken, nursing my indignation. A one-armed man opens the door. "Maria?" he calls. *"Prego."* Which translates, indirectly, as "The truck is unloaded and the guns are ready and should I kill this guy?" I direct him to find Andreas.

She wakes me, maybe an hour later. I sleep as I rarely have, arm across my eyes like a bedouin, on top of the mounds of boots and gear. She has worked her fingers around my buttons and pulls my hair, my nipples. I can't tell the degree of mockery, what spillover of passion she might still be feeling. Andreas and the idiot boy stand framed in the bleaching light of the door, the boy's huge head pushing the bandolier askew. Father and son, it suddenly dawns. Andreas holds the birdcage.

"They've finished," she explains. "Let's go."

Andreas let us pass, smirking, I think, and follows us down the rutted trail to Bud's truck. He puts the birdcage in the driver's seat, and in case I miss it, points at the bird, then at me, and laughs. Very funny, I think. His boy finds it hilarious. I will *not* be mocked like this. The bird is so ill-fed, so cramped and tortured and clumsy it flutters wildly, losing more feathers merely to keep its perch.

"*Viva la revolución, eh?* A leetle gift for helping the people."

No, I think, a leetle sign to Clovis Ransome and all the pretenders to Maria's bed that we're just a bunch of scrawny blackbirds and he doesn't care who knows it. I have no feeling for revolution, only for outfitting the participants.

"Why?" I beg on the way back. The road is dark. "You hate your husband, so get a divorce. Why blow up the country?"

Maria smiles. "Clovis has nothing to do with this." She shifts her sandals on the birdcage. The bird is dizzy, flat on its back. Some of them die, just like that.

"Run off with Andreas, then."

"We were going to be married," she says. "Then Gutiérrez came to my school one day and took me away. I was fourteen and he was minister of education. Then Clovis took me away from him. Maybe you should take me away from Clovis. I like you, and you'd like it, too, wouldn't you?"

"Don't be crazy. Try Bud Wilkins."

"Bud Wilkins is, you say, dog meat." She smiles.

"Oh, sure," I say.

I concentrate on the road. I'm no hero, I calculate margins. I could not calculate the cost of a night with Maria, a month with Maria, though for the first time in my life it was a cost I might have borne.

Her voice is matter-of-fact. "Clovis wanted a cut of Bud's action. But Bud refused and that got Clovis mad. Clovis even offered money, but Bud said no way. Clovis pushed me on him, so he took but he still didn't budge. So—"

"You're serious, aren't you? Oh, God."

"Of course I am serious. Now Clovis can fly in his own champagne and baseball games."

She has unbuttoned more of the halter and I feel pressure on my chest, in my mouth, against my slacks, that I have never felt.

All the lights are on in the villa when I lurch Bud's pickup into the parking lot. We can see Clovis T. Ransome, very drunk, slack-postured, trying out wicker chairs on the porch. Maria is carrying the birdcage.

He's settled on the love seat. No preliminaries, no questions. He squints at the cage. "Buying presents for Maria already, Al?" He tries to laugh.

"What's that supposed to mean?" She swings the cage in giant arcs, like a bucket of water.

"Where's Bud?" I ask.

"They jumped him, old buddy. Gang of guerrillas not more'n half a mile down the road. Pumped twenty bullets in him. These are fierce little people, Al. I don't know how I got away." He's watching us for effect.

I suspect it helps when they're in your pay, I think, and you give them Ted Turner caps.

"Al, grab yourself a glass if you want some Scotch. Me, I'm stinking drunk already."

He's noticed Bud's truck now. The emptiness of Bud's truck.

"That's a crazy thing to do," Maria says. "I warned you." She sets the cage down on the patio table. "Bud's no good to anyone, dead or alive. You said it yourself, he's dog meat." She slips onto the love seat beside her husband. I watch her. I can't take my eyes off her. She snakes her strong, long torso until her lips touch the cage's rusted metal. "Kiss me," she coos. "Kiss me, kiss, kiss, sweetheart."

Ransome's eyes are on her, too. "Sweets, who gave you that filthy crow?"

Maria says, "Kiss me, loverboy."

"Sweetie, I asked you who gave you that filthy crow."

I back off to the kitchen. I could use a shot of Scotch. I can feel the damp, Bombay grittiness of the air. The rains will be here, maybe tonight.

When I get back, Ransome is snoring on the love seat. Maria is standing over him, and the birdcage is on his lap. Its door is open and Clovis's fat hand is half inside. The bird pecks, it's raised blood, but Clovis is out for the night.

"Why is it," she asks, "that I don't feel pride when men kill for me?"

But she does, deep down. She wants to believe that Clovis, mad jealous Clovis, has killed for her. I just hate to think of Maria's pretty face when Clovis wakes up and remembers the munitions are gone. It's all a family plot in countries like this; revolutions fought for a schoolgirl in white with blunted toes. I, too, would kill for her.

"Kill it, Alfie, please," she says. "I can't stand it. See, Clovis tried but his hand was too fat."

"I'll free it," I say.

"Don't be a fool—that boy broke its wings. Let it out, and the crabs will kill it."

Around eleven that night I have to carry Ransome up the stairs to the spare bedroom. He's a heavy man. I don't bother with the niceties of getting him out of his blue jeans and into his pajamas. The secrets of Clovis T. Ransome, whatever they are, are safe with me. I abandon him on top of the bedspread in his dusty cowboy boots. Maria won't want him tonight. She's already told me so.

But she isn't waiting for me on the patio. Maybe that's just as well. Tonight love will be hard to handle. The dirty glasses, the booze and soda bottles, the Styrofoam-lidded bowl we used for ice cubes are still on the wicker-and-glass coffee table. Eduardo doesn't seem to be around. I bring the glasses into the kitchen. He must have disappeared hours ago. I've never seen the kitchen in this bad a mess. He's not in the villa. His door has swung open, but I can't hear the noises of sleeping servants in the tropics. So, Eduardo has vanished. I accept this as data. I dare not shout for Maria. If it's ever to be, it must be tonight. Tomorrow, I can tell, this cozy little hacienda will come to grief.

Someone should go from room to room and turn out the lights. But not me. I make it fast back to my room.

"You must shut doors quickly behind you in the tropics. Otherwise bugs get in."

Casually, she is unbuttoning her top, untying the bottom tabs. The cutoffs have to be tugged off, around her hips. There is a rush of passion I have never known, and my fingers tremble as I tug at my belt. She is in my giant bed, propped up, and her breasts keep the sheet from falling.

"Alfie, close the door."

Her long thighs press and squeeze. She tries to hold me, to contain me, and it is a moment I would die to prolong. In a frenzy, I conjugate crabs with toads and the squawking bird, and I hear the low moans of turtles on the beach. It is a moment I fear too much, a woman I fear too much, and I yield. I begin again, immediately, this time concentrating on blankness, on burned-out objects whirling in space, and she pushes against me murmuring, "No," and pulls away.

Later, she says, "You don't understand hate, Alfie. You don't understand what hate can do." She tells stories; I moan to mount her again. "No," she says, and the stories pour out. Not just the beatings; the humiliations. Loaning her out, dangling her on a leash like a cheetah, then the beatings for what he suspects. It's the power game, I try to tell her. That's how power is played.

Sometime around three, I wake to a scooter's thin roar. She has not been asleep. The rainy season must have started an hour or two before. It's like steam out there. I kneel on the pillows to look out the small bedroom windows. The parking lot is a mudslide. Uprooted shrubs, snakes, crabs, turtles are washed down to the shore.

Maria, object of my wildest ecstasy, lies inches from me. She doesn't ask what I see. The scooter's lights weave in the rain.

"Andreas," she says. "It's working out."

But it isn't Andreas who forces the door to my room. It is a tall, thin Indian with a calamitous face. The scooter's engine has been shut off, and rain slaps the patio in waves.

"*Americano.*" The Indian spits out the word. "Gringo."

Maria calmly ties her halter tabs, slowly buttons up. She says something rapidly and the Indian steps outside while she finds her cutoffs.

"Quickly," she says, and I reach for my pants. It's already cold.

When the Indian returns, I hear her say "Jew" and "Israel." He seems to lose interest. *"Americano?"* he asks again. "Gringo?"

Two more Indians invade my room. Maria runs out to the hall and I follow to the stairs. I point upwards and try out my Spanish. "Gringo is sleeping, drunk."

The revolution has convened outside Clovis's bedroom. Eduardo is there, Andreas, more Indians in Ted Turner caps, the one-armed man from Santa Simona. Andreas opens the door.

"Gringo," he calls softly. "Wake up."

I am surprised, truly astonished, at the recuperative powers of Clovis T. Ransome. Not only does he wake, but he sits, boots on the floor, ignoring the intrusion. His Spanish, the first time I've heard him use it, is excellent, even respectful.

"I believe, sir, you have me at a disadvantage," he says. He scans the intruders, his eyes settling on me. "Button your fly, man," he says to me. He stares at Maria, up and down, his jaw working. He says, "Well, sweets? What now?"

Andreas holds a pistol against his thigh.

"Take her," Ransome says. "You want her? You got her. You want money, you got that too. Dollars, marks, Swiss francs. Just take her—and him—" he says, pointing to me, "out of here."

"I will take your dollars, of course."

"Eduardo—" Ransome jerks his head in the direction, perhaps, of a safe. The servant seems to know where it is.

"And I will take her, of course."

"Good riddance."

"But not him. He can rot."

Eduardo and three Indians lug out a metal trunk. They throw away the pillows and start stuffing pillow cases with bundles of dollars, more pure currency than I've ever seen. They stuff the rest inside their shirts. What must it feel like? I wonder.

"Well, *Señor* Andreas, you've got the money and the woman. Now what's it to be—a little torture? A little fun with me before the sun comes up? Or what about him—I bet you'd have more fun with him. I don't scream, *Señor* Andreas, I warn you now. You can kill me but you can't break me."

I hear the safety clicking off. So does Clovis.

I know I would scream. I know I am no hero. I know none of this is worth suffering for, let alone dying for.

Andreas looks at Maria as though to say, "You decide." She holds out her hand, and Andreas slips the pistol in it. This seems to amuse Clovis Ransome. He stands, presenting an enormous target. "Sweetie—" he starts, and she blasts away and when I open my eyes he is across the bed, sprawled in the far corner of the room.

She stands at the foot of their bed, limp and amused, like a woman disappointed in love. Smoke rises from the gun barrel, her breath condenses in little clouds, and there is a halo of condensation around her hair, her neck, her arms.

When she turns, I feel it could be any of us next. Andreas holds out his hand but she doesn't return the gun. She lines me up, low, genital-level, like Bud Wilkins with a bird, then sweeps around to Andreas, and smiles.

She has made love to me three times tonight. With Andreas today, doubtless more. Never has a truth been burned so deeply in me, what I owe my life to, how simple the rules of survival are. She passes the gun to Andreas who holsters it, and they leave.

In the next few days when I run out of food, I will walk down the muddy road to San Vincente, to the German bar with the pay phone: I'll wear Clovis's Braves cap and I'll salute the Indians. "Turtle eggs," I'll say. "Number One," they'll answer back. Bud's truck has been commandeered. Along with Clovis's finer cars. Someone in the capital will be happy to know about Santa Simona, about Bud, Clovis. There must be something worth trading in the troubles I have seen.

# HAIRBALL

*Margaret Atwood*

MARGARET ATWOOD's first poem was published when she was nineteen. She has since published more than twenty books, including the novels *The Handmaid's Tale,* *Cat's Eye,* and *The Robber Bride,* the short-story collection *Wilderness Tips* (from which "Hairball" is taken), and a volume of poetry, *Morning in the Burned House.* She lives in Toronto with novelist Graeme Gibson and their daughter Jess.

ON THE THIRTEENTH of November, day of unluck, month of the dead, Kat went into the Toronto General Hospital for an operation. It was for an ovarian cyst, a large one.

Many women had them, the doctor told her. Nobody knew why. There wasn't any way of finding out whether the thing was malignant, whether it contained, already, the spores of death. Not before they went in. He spoke of "going in" the way she'd heard old veterans in TV documentaries speak of assaults on enemy territory. There was the same tensing of the jaw, the same fierce gritting of the teeth, the same grim enjoyment. Except that what he would be going into was her body. Counting down, waiting for the anesthetic, Kat too gritted her teeth fiercely. She was terrified, but also she was curious. Curiosity has got her through a lot.

She'd made the doctor promise to save the thing for her, whatever it was, so she could have a look. She was intensely interested in her own body, in anything it might choose to do or produce; although when flaky Dania, who did layout at the magazine, told her this growth was a message to her from her body and she ought to sleep with an amethyst under her pillow to calm her vibrations, Kat told her to stuff it.

The cyst turned out to be a benign tumor. Kat liked that use of *benign,* as if the thing had a soul and wished her well. It was big as a grapefruit, the doctor said. "Big as a coconut," said Kat. Other people had grapefruits. "Coconut" was better. It conveyed the hardness of it, and the hairiness, too.

The hair in it was red—long strands of it wound round and round inside, like a ball of wet wool gone berserk or like the guck you pulled out of a clogged bathroom-sink drain. There were little bones in it too, or fragments of bone; bird bones, the bones of a sparrow crushed by a car. There was a scattering of nails, toe or finger. There were five perfectly formed teeth.

"Is this abnormal?" Kat asked the doctor, who smiled. Now that he had gone in and come out again, unscathed, he was less clenched.

"Abnormal? No," he said carefully, as if breaking the news to a mother about a freakish accident to her newborn. "Let's just say it's fairly common." Kat was a little disappointed. She would have preferred uniqueness.

She asked for a bottle of formaldehyde, and put the cut-open tumor into it. It was hers, it was benign, it did not deserve to be thrown away. She took it back to her apartment and stuck it on the mantelpiece. She named it Hairball. It isn't that different from having a stuffed bear's head or a preserved ex-pet or anything else with fur and teeth looming over your fireplace; or she pretends it isn't. Anyway, it certainly makes an impression.

Ger doesn't like it. Despite his supposed yen for the new and outré, he is a squeamish man. The first time he comes around (sneaks around, creeps around) after the operation, he tells Kat to throw Hairball out. He calls it "disgusting." Kat refuses point-blank, and says she'd rather have Hairball in a bottle on her mantelpiece than the soppy dead flowers he's brought her, which will anyway rot a lot sooner than Hairball will. As a mantelpiece ornament, Hairball is far superior. Ger says Kat has a tendency to push things to extremes, to go over the edge, merely from a juvenile desire to shock, which is hardly a substitute for wit. One of these days, he says, she will go way too far. Too far for him, is what he means.

"That's why you hired me, isn't it?" she says. "Because I go way too far." But he's in one of his analyzing moods. He can see these tendencies of hers reflected in her work on the magazine, he says. All that leather and those grotesque and tortured-looking poses are heading down a track he and others are not at all sure they should continue to follow. Does she see what he means, does she take his point? It's a point that's been made before. She shakes her head slightly, says nothing. She knows how that translates: there have been complaints from the advertisers. *Too bizarre, too kinky*. Tough.

"Want to see my scar?" she says. "Don't make me laugh, though, you'll crack it open." Stuff like that makes him dizzy: anything with a hint of blood, anything gynecological. He almost threw up in the delivery room when his wife had a baby two years ago. He'd told her that with pride. Kat thinks about sticking a cigarette into the side of her mouth, as in a black-and-white movie of the forties. She thinks about blowing the smoke into his face.

Her insolence used to excite him, during their arguments. Then there would be a grab of her upper arms, a smoldering, violent kiss. He kisses her as if he thinks someone else is watching him, judging the image they make together. Kissing the latest thing, hard and shiny, purple-mouthed, crop-headed; kissing a girl, a woman, a girl, in a little crotch-hugger skirt and skintight leggings. He likes mirrors.

But he isn't excited now. And she can't decoy him into bed; she isn't ready for that yet, she isn't healed. He has a drink, which he doesn't finish, holds her hand as an afterthought, gives her a couple of avuncular pats on the off-white outsized alpaca shoulder, leaves too quickly.

"Goodbye, Gerald," she says. She pronounces the name with mockery. It's a negation of him, an abolishment of him, like ripping a medal off his chest. It's a warning.

He'd been Gerald when they first met. It was she who transformed him, first to Gerry, then to Ger. (Rhymed with *flair*, rhymed with *dare*.) She made him get rid of those sucky pursed-mouth ties, told him what shoes to wear, got him to buy a loose-cut Italian suit, redid his hair. A lot of his current tastes—in food, in drink, in recreational drugs, in women's entertainment underwear—were once hers. In his new phase, with his new, hard, stripped-down name ending on the sharpened note of *r*, he is her creation.

As she is her own. During her childhood she was a romanticized Katherine, dressed by her misty-eyed, fussy mother in dresses that looked like ruffled pillowcases. By high school she'd shed the frills and emerged as a bouncy, round-faced Kathy, with gleaming freshly washed hair and enviable teeth, eager to please and no more interesting than a health-food ad. At university she was Kath, blunt and no-bullshit in her Take-Back-the-Night jeans and checked shirt and her bricklayer-style striped-denim peaked hat. When she ran away to England, she sliced herself down to Kat. It was economical, street-feline, and pointed as a nail. It was also unusual. In England you had to do something to get their attention, especially if you weren't English. Safe in this incarnation, she Ramboed through the eighties.

It was the name, she still thinks, that got her the interview and then the job. The job with an avant-garde magazine, the kind that was printed on matte stock in black and white, with overexposed close-ups of women with hair blowing over their eyes, one nostril prominent: *the razor's edge,* it was called. Haircuts as art, some real art, film reviews, a little stardust, wardrobes of ideas that were clothes and of clothes that were ideas—the metaphysical shoulder pad. She learned her trade well, hands-on. She learned what worked.

She made her way up the ladder, from layout to design, then to the supervision of whole spreads, and then whole issues. It wasn't easy, but it was worth it. She had become a creator; she created total looks. After a while she could walk down the street in Soho or stand in the lobby at openings and witness her handiwork incarnate, strolling around in outfits she'd put together, spouting her warmed-over pronouncements. It was like being God, only God had never got around to off-the-rack lines.

By that time her face had lost its roundness, though the teeth of course remained: there was something to be said for North American dentistry. She'd shaved off most of her hair, worked on the drop-dead stare, perfected a certain turn of the neck that conveyed an aloof inner authority. What you had to make them believe was that you knew something they didn't know yet. What you also had to make them believe was that they too could know this thing, this thing that would give them eminence and power and sexual allure, that would attract envy to them—but for a price. The price of the magazine. What they could never get through their heads was that it was done entirely with cameras. Frozen light, frozen time. Given the angle, she could make any woman look ugly. Any man as well. She could make anyone look beautiful, or at least interesting. It was all photography, it was all iconography. It was all in the choosing eye. This was the thing that could never be bought, no matter how much of your pitiful monthly wage you blew on snakeskin.

Despite the status, *the razor's edge* was fairly low-paying. Kat herself could not afford many of the things she contextualized so well. The grottiness and expense of London began to get to her; she got tired of gorging on the canapés at literary launches in order to scrimp on groceries, tired of the fuggy smell of cigarettes ground into the red-and-maroon carpeting of pubs, tired of the pipes bursting every time it froze in winter, and of the Clarissas and Melissas and Penelopes at the magazine rabbiting on about how they had been literally, absolutely, totally freezing all night, and how it literally, absolutely, totally, usually never got that cold. It always got that cold. The pipes always burst. Nobody thought of putting in real pipes, ones that would not burst next time. Burst pipes were an English tradition, like so many others.

Like, for instance, English men. Charm the knickers off you with their mellow vowels and frivolous verbiage, and then, once they'd got them off, panic and run. Or else stay and whinge. The English called it *whinging* instead of whining. It was better, really. Like a creaking hinge. It was a traditional compliment to be whinged at by an Englishman. It was his way of saying he trusted you, he was conferring upon you the privilege of getting to know the real him. The inner, whinging him. That was how they thought of women, secretly: whinge receptacles. Kat could play it, but that didn't mean she liked it.

She had an advantage over the English women, though: she was of no class. She had no class. She was in a class of her own. She could roll around among the English men, all different kinds of them, secure in the knowledge that she was not being measured against the class yardsticks and accent-detectors they carried around in their back pockets, was not subject to the petty snobberies and resentments that lent such richness to their inner lives. The flip side of this freedom was that she was beyond the pale. She was a colonial—how fresh, how vital, how anonymous, how finally of no consequence. Like a hole in the wall, she could be told all secrets and then be abandoned with no guilt.

She was too smart, of course. The English men were very competitive; they liked to win. Several times it hurt. Twice she had abortions, because the men in question were not up for the alternative. She learned to say that she didn't want children anyway, that if she longed for a rug-rat she would buy a gerbil. Her life began to seem long. Her adrenaline was running out. Soon she would be thirty, and all she could see ahead was more of the same.

This was how things were when Gerald turned up. "You're terrific," he said, and she was ready to hear it, even from him, even though *terrific* was a word that had probably gone out with fifties crew cuts. She was ready for his voice by that time too: the flat, metallic nasal tone of the Great Lakes, with its clear hard *r*'s and its absence of theatricality. Dull normal. The speech of her people. It came to her suddenly that she was an exile.

Gerald was scouting, Gerald was recruiting. He'd heard about her, looked at her work, sought her out. One of the big companies back in Toronto was launching a new fashion-oriented magazine, he said: upmarket, international in its coverage, of course, but with some Canadian fashion in it too, and with lists of stores where the items portrayed could actually be bought. In that respect they felt they'd have it all over the competition, those American magazines that assumed you could only get Gucci in New York or Los Angeles. Heck, times had changed, you could get it in Edmonton! You could get it in Winnipeg!

Kat had been away too long. There was Canadian fashion now? The English quip would be to say that "Canadian fashion" was an oxymoron. She refrained from making it, lit a cigarette with her cyanide-green Covent Garden–boutique leather-covered lighter (as featured in the May issue of *the razor's edge*), looked Gerald in the eye. "London is a lot to give up," she said levelly. She glanced around the see-me-here Mayfair restaurant where they were finishing lunch, a restaurant she'd chosen because she'd known he was paying. She'd never spend that kind of money on food otherwise. "Where would I eat?"

Gerald assured her that Toronto was now the restaurant capital of Canada. He himself would be happy to be her guide. There was a great Chinatown, there was world-class Italian. Then he paused, took a breath. "I've been meaning to ask you," he said. "About the name. Is that Kat as in Krazy?" He thought this was suggestive. She'd heard it before.

"No," she said. "It's Kat as in KitKat. That's a chocolate bar. Melts in your mouth." She gave him her stare, quirked her mouth, just a twitch.

Gerald became flustered, but he pushed on. They wanted her, they needed her, they loved her, he said in essence. Someone with her fresh, innovative approach and her experience would be worth a lot of money to them, relatively speaking. But there were rewards other than the money. She would be in on the initial concept, she would have a formative influence, she would have a free hand. He named a sum that made her gasp, inaudibly of course. By now she knew better than to betray desire.

So she made the journey back, did her three months of culture shock, tried the world-class Italian and the great Chinese, and seduced Gerald at the first opportunity, right in his junior vice-presidential office. It was the first time Gerald had been seduced in such a location, or perhaps ever. Even though it was after hours, the danger frenzied him. It was the idea of it. The daring. The image of Kat kneeling on the broadloom, in a legendary bra that until now he'd seen only in the lingerie ads of the Sunday *New York Times,* unzipping him in full view of the silver-framed engagement portrait of his wife that complemented the impossible ball-point pen set on his desk. At that time he was so straight he felt compelled to take off his wedding ring and place it carefully in the ashtray first. The next day he brought her a box of David Wood Food Shop chocolate truffles. They were the best, he told her, anxious that she should recognize their quality. She found the gesture banal, but also sweet. The banality, the sweetness, the hunger to impress: that was Gerald.

Gerald was the kind of man she wouldn't have bothered with in London. He was not funny, he was not knowledgeable, he had little verbal charm. But he was eager, he was tractable, he was blank paper. Although he was eight years older than she was, he seemed much younger. She took pleasure from his furtive, boyish delight in his own wickedness. And he was so grateful. "I can hardly believe this is happening," he said, more frequently than was necessary and usually in bed.

His wife, whom Kat encountered (and still encounters) at many tedious company events, helped to explain his gratitude. The wife was a priss. Her name was Cheryl. Her hair looked as if she still used big rollers and embalm-your-hairdo spray; her mind was room-by-room Laura Ashley wallpaper: tiny, unopened pastel buds arranged in straight rows. She probably put on rubber gloves to make love, and checked it off on a list afterwards. One more messy household chore. She looked at Kat as if she'd like to spritz her with air de-odorizer. Kat revenged herself by picturing Cheryl's bathrooms: hand towels embroidered with lilies, fuzzy covers on the toilet seats.

The magazine itself got off to a rocky start. Although Kat had lots of lovely money to play with, and although it was a challenge to be working in color, she did not have the free hand Gerald had promised her. She had to contend with the company board of directors, who were all men, who were all accountants or indistinguishable from them, who were cautious and slow as moles.

"It's simple," Kat told them. "You bombard them with images of what they ought to be, and you make them feel grotty for being the way they are. You're working with the gap between reality and perception. That's why you have to hit them with something new, something they've never seen before, something they aren't. Nothing sells like anxiety."

The board, on the other hand, felt that the readership should simply be offered more of what they already had. More fur, more sumptuous leather, more cashmere. More established names. The board had no sense of improvisation, no wish to take risks; no sporting instincts, no desire to put one over on the readers just for the hell of it. "Fashion is like hunting," Kat told them, hoping to appeal to their male hormones, if any. "It's playful, it's intense, it's predatory. It's blood and guts. It's erotic." But to them it was about good taste. They wanted Dress-for-Success. Kat wanted scattergun ambush.

Everything became a compromise. Kat had wanted to call the magazine *All the Rage,* but the board was put off by the vibrations of anger in the word "rage." They thought it was too feminist, of all things. "It's a *forties* sound," Kat said. "Forties is *back.* Don't you get it?" But they didn't. They wanted to call it *Or.* French for *gold,* and blatant enough in its values, but without any base note, as Kat told them. They sawed off at *Felice,* which had qualities each side wanted. It was vaguely French-sounding, it meant "happy" (so much less threatening than rage), and, although you couldn't expect the others to notice, for Kat it had a feline bouquet which counteracted the laciness. She had it done in hot-pink lipstick-scrawl, which helped some. She could live with it, but it had not been her first love.

This battle has been fought and refought over every innovation in design, every new angle Kat has tried to bring in, every innocuous bit of semi-kink. There was a big row over a spread that did lingerie, half pulled off and with broken glass perfume bottles strewn on the floor. There was an uproar over the two nouveau-stockinged legs, one tied to a chair with a third, different-colored stocking. They had not understood the man's three-hundred-dollar leather gloves positioned ambiguously around a neck.

And so it has gone on, for five years.

*     *     *

After Gerald has left, Kat paces her living room. Pace, pace. Her stitches pull. She's not looking forward to her solitary dinner of microwaved leftovers. She's not sure now why she came back here, to this flat burg beside the polluted inland sea. Was it Ger? Ludicrous thought but no longer out of the question. Is he the reason she stays, despite her growing impatience with him?

He's no longer fully rewarding. They've learned each other too well, they take shortcuts now; their time together has shrunk from whole stolen rolling and sensuous afternoons to a few hours snatched between work and dinnertime. She no longer knows what she wants from him. She tells herself she's worth more, she should branch out; but she doesn't see other men, she can't, somehow. She's tried once or twice but it didn't work. Sometimes she goes out to dinner or a flick with one of the gay designers. She likes the gossip.

Maybe she misses London. She feels caged, in this country, in this city, in this room. She could start with the room, she could open a window. It's too stuffy in here. There's an undertone of formaldehyde, from Hairball's bottle. The flowers she got for the operation are mostly wilted, all except Gerald's from today. Come to think of it, why didn't he send her any at the hospital? Did he forget, or was it a message?

"Hairball," she says, "I wish you could talk. I could have a more intelligent conversation with you than with most of the losers in this turkey farm." Hairball's baby teeth glint in the light; it looks as if it's about to speak.

Kat feels her own forehead. She wonders if she's running a temperature. Something ominous is going on, behind her back. There haven't been enough phone calls from the magazine; they've been able to muddle on without her, which is bad news. Reigning queens should never go on vacation, or have operations either. Uneasy lies the head. She has a sixth sense about these things, she's been involved in enough palace coups to know the signs, she has sensitive antennae for the footfalls of impending treachery.

The next morning she pulls herself together, downs an espresso from her mini-machine, picks out an aggressive touch-me-if-you-dare suede outfit in armor gray, and drags herself to the office, although she isn't due in till next week. Surprise, surprise. Whispering knots break up in the corridors, greet her with false welcome as she limps past. She settles herself at her minimalist desk, checks her mail. Her head is pounding, her stitches hurt. Ger gets wind of her arrival; he wants to see her a.s.a.p., and not for lunch.

He awaits her in his newly done wheat-on-white office, with the eighteenth-century desk they chose together, the Victorian inkstand, the framed blow-ups from the magazine, the hands in maroon leather, wrists manacled with pearls, the Hermès scarf twisted into a blindfold, the model's mouth blossoming lusciously beneath it. Some of her best stuff. He's beautifully done up, in a lick-my-neck silk shirt open at the throat, an eat-your-heart-out Italian silk-and-wool loose-knit sweater. Oh, cool insouciance. Oh, eyebrow language. He's a money man who lusted after art, and now he's got some, now he is some. Body art. Her art. She's done her job well; he's finally sexy.

He's smooth as lacquer. "I didn't want to break this to you until next week," he says. He breaks it to her. It's the board of directors. They think she's too bizarre, they think she goes way too far. Nothing he could do about it, although naturally he tried.

Naturally. Betrayal. The monster has turned on its own mad scientist. "I gave you life!" she wants to scream at him.

She isn't in good shape. She can hardly stand. She stands, despite his offer of a chair. She sees now what she's wanted, what she's been missing. Gerald is what she's been missing—the stable, unfashionable, previous, tight-assed Gerald. Not Ger, not the one she's made in her own image. The other one, before he got ruined. The Gerald with a house and a small child and a picture of his wife in a silver frame on his desk. She wants to be in that silver frame. She wants the child. She's been robbed.

"And who is my lucky replacement?" she says. She needs a cigarette, but does not want to reveal her shaking hands.

"Actually, it's me," he says, trying for modesty.

This is too absurd. Gerald couldn't edit a phone book. "You?" she says faintly. She has the good sense not to laugh.

"I've always wanted to get out of the money end of things here," he says, "into the creative area. I knew you'd understand, since it can't be you at any rate. I knew you'd prefer someone who could, well, sort of build on your foundations." Pompous asshole. She looks at his neck. She longs for him, hates herself for it, and is powerless.

The room wavers. He slides towards her across the wheat-colored broadloom, takes her by the gray suede upper arms. "I'll write you a good reference," he says. "Don't worry about that. Of course, we can still see one another. I'd miss our afternoons."

"Of course," she says. He kisses her, a voluptuous kiss, or it would look like one to a third party, and she lets him. *In a pig's ear.*

She makes it home in a taxi. The driver is rude to her and gets away with it; she doesn't have the energy. In her mailbox is an engraved invitation: Ger and Cheryl are having a drinks party, tomorrow evening. Postmarked five days ago. Cheryl is behind the times.

Kat undresses, runs a shallow bath. There's not much to drink around here, there's nothing to sniff or smoke. What an oversight; she's stuck with herself. There are other jobs. There are other men, or that's the theory. Still, something's been ripped out of her. How could this have happened to her? When knives were slated for backs, she'd always done the stabbing. Any headed her way she'd seen coming in time, and thwarted. Maybe she's losing her edge.

She stares into the bathroom mirror, assesses her face in the misted glass. A face of the eighties, a mask face, a bottom-line face; push the weak to the wall and grab what you can. But now it's the nineties. Is she out of style, so soon? She's only thirty-five, and she's already losing track of what people ten years younger are thinking. That could be fatal. As time goes by she'll have to race faster and faster to keep up, and for what? Part of the life she should have had is just a gap, it isn't there, it's nothing. What can be salvaged from it, what can be redone, what can be done at all?

When she climbs out of the tub after her sponge bath, she almost falls. She has a fever, no doubt about it. Inside her something is leaking, or else festering; she can hear it, like a dripping tap. A running sore, a sore from running so hard. She should go to the Emergency ward at some hospital, get herself shot up with antibiotics. Instead she lurches into the living room, takes Hairball down from the mantelpiece in its bottle, places it on the coffee table. She sits cross-legged, listens. Filaments wave. She can hear a kind of buzz, like bees at work.

She'd asked the doctor if it could have started as a child, a fertilized egg that escaped somehow and got into the wrong place. No, said the doctor. Some people thought this kind of tumor was present in seedling form from birth, or before it. It might be the woman's undeveloped twin. What they really were was unknown. They had many kinds of tissue, though. Even brain tissue. Though of course all of these tissues lack structure.

Still, sitting here on the rug looking in at it, she pictures it as a child. It has come out of her, after all. It is flesh of her flesh. Her child with Gerald, her thwarted child, not allowed to grow normally. Her warped child, taking its revenge.

"Hairball," she says. "You're so ugly. Only a mother could love you." She feels sorry for it. She feels loss. Tears run down her face. Crying is not something she does, not normally, not lately.

Hairball speaks to her, without words. It is irreducible, it has the texture of reality, it is not an image. What it tells her is everything she's never wanted to hear about herself. This is new knowledge, dark and precious and necessary. It cuts.

She shakes her head. What are you doing, sitting on the floor and talking to a hairball? You are sick, she tells herself. Take a Tylenol and go to bed.

The next day she feels a little better. Dania from layout calls her and makes dovelike, sympathetic coos at her, and wants to drop by during lunch hour to take a look at her aura. Kat tells her to come off it. Dania gets huffy, and says that Kat's losing her job is a price for immoral behavior in a previous life. Kat tells her to stuff it; anyway, she's done enough immoral behavior in this life to account for the whole thing. "Why are you so full of hate?" asks Dania. She doesn't say it like a point she's making, she sounds truly baffled.

"I don't know," says Kat. It's a straight answer.

After she hangs up she paces the floor. She's crackling inside, like hot fat under the broiler. What she's thinking about is Cheryl, bustling about her cozy house, preparing for the party. Cheryl fiddles with her freeze-framed hair, positions an overloaded vase of flowers, fusses about the caterers. Gerald comes in, kisses her lightly on the cheek. A connubial scene. His conscience is nicely washed. The witch is dead, his foot is on the body, the trophy; he's had his dirty fling, he's ready now for the rest of his life.

Kat takes a taxi to the David Wood Food Shop and buys two dozen chocolate truffles. She has them put into an oversized box, then into an oversized bag with the store logo on it. Then she goes home and takes Hairball out of its bottle. She drains it in the kitchen strainer and pats it damp-dry, tenderly, with paper towels. She sprinkles it with powdered cocoa, which forms a brown pasty crust. It still smells like formaldehyde, so she wraps it in Saran Wrap and then in tinfoil, and then in pink tissue paper, which she ties with a mauve bow. She places it in the David Wood box in a bed of shredded tissue, with the truffles nestled around. She closes the box, tapes it, puts it into the bag, stuffs several sheets of pink paper on top. It's her gift, valuable and dangerous. It's her messenger, but the message it will deliver is its own. It will tell the truth, to whoever asks. It's right that Gerald should have it; after all, it's his child too.

She prints on the card, "Gerald, Sorry I couldn't be with you. This is all the rage. Love, K."

When evening has fallen and the party must be in full swing, she calls a delivery taxi. Cheryl will not distrust anything that arrives in such an expensive bag. She will open it in public, in front of everyone. There will be distress, there will be questions. Secrets will be unearthed. There will be pain. After that, everything will go way too far.

She is not well; her heart is pounding, space is wavering once more. But outside the window it's snowing, the soft, damp, windless flakes of her childhood. She puts on her coat and goes out, foolishly. She intends to walk just to the corner, but when she reaches the corner she goes on. The snow melts against her face like small fingers touching. She has done an outrageous thing, but she doesn't feel guilty. She feels light and peaceful and filled with charity, and temporarily without a name.

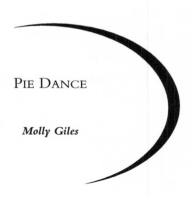

# Pie Dance

*Molly Giles*

**MOLLY GILES** was born in California in 1940. She was educated at the University of California, Berkeley, and at San Francisco State University, where she now teaches in the creative writing department. Her stories have appeared in *Shenandoah, Redbook, North American Review, McCall's,* and *Ascent.* Her short-story collection *Rough Translations* won the 1985 Flannery O'Connor Award for Short Fiction. Her forthcoming book is *Creek Walk.*

I DON'T KNOW what to do about my husband's new wife. She won't come in. She sits on the front porch and smokes. She won't knock or ring the bell, and the only way I know she's there at all is because the dog points in the living room. The minute I see Stray standing with one paw up and his tail straight out I say, "Shhh. It's Pauline." I stroke his coarse fur and lean on the broom and we wait. We hear the creak of a board, the click of a purse, a cigarette being lit, a sad, tiny cough. At last I give up and open the door. "Pauline?" The afternoon light hurts my eyes. "Would you like to come in?"

"No," says Pauline.

Sometimes she sits on the stoop, picking at the paint, and sometimes she sits on the edge of an empty planter box. Today she's perched on the railing. She frowns when she sees me and lifts her small chin. She wears the same black velvet jacket she always wears, the same formal silk blouse, the same huge dark glasses. "Just passing by," she explains.

I nod. Pauline lives thirty miles to the east, in the city, with Konrad. "Passing by" would take her one toll bridge, one freeway, and two backcountry roads from their flat. But lies are the least of our problems, Pauline's and mine, so I nod again, bunch my bathrobe a little tighter around my waist, try to cover one bare foot with the other, and repeat my invitation. She shakes her head so vigorously the railing lurches. "Konrad," she says in her high young voice, "expects me. You know how he is."

I do, or I did—I'm not sure I know now—but I nod, and she flushes, staring so hard at something right behind me that I turn too and tell Stray, who is still posing in the doorway, to cancel the act and come say hello. Stray drops his front paw and pads forward, nose to the ground. Pauline blows cigarette smoke into the wisteria vine and draws her feet close to the railing. "What kind is it?" she asks, looking down.

I tell her we don't know, we think he's part Irish setter and part golden retriever; what happened was someone drove him out here to the country and abandoned him and he howled outside our house until one of the children let him come in. Pauline nods as if this were very interesting and says, "Oh really?" but I stop abruptly; I know I am boring. I am growing dull as Mrs. Dixon, Konrad's mother, who goes on and on about her poodle and who, for a time, actually sent us birthday cards and Christmas presents signed with a poodle paw print. I clasp the broom with both hands and gaze fondly at Stray. I am too young to love a dog; at the same time I am beginning to realize there isn't that much to love in this world. So when Pauline says, "Can it do tricks?" I try to keep the rush of passion from my eyes; I try to keep my voice down.

"He can dance," I admit.

"How great," she says, swaying on the railing. "Truly great."

"Yes," I agree. I do not elaborate. I do not tell Pauline that at night, when the children are asleep, I often dance with him. Nor do I confess that the two of us, Stray and I, have outgrown the waltz and are deep into reggae. Stray is a gay and affable partner, willing to learn, delighted to lead. I could boast about him forever, but Pauline, I see, already looks tired. "And you?" I ask. "How have you been?"

For answer she coughs, flexing her small hand so the big gold wedding ring flashes a lot in the sun; she smiles for the first time and makes a great show of pounding her heart as she coughs. She doesn't look well. She's lost weight since the marriage and seems far too pale. "Water?" I ask. "Or how about tea? We have peppermint, jasmine, mocha, and lemon."

"Oh no!" she cries, choking.

"We've honey. We've cream."

"Oh no! But thank you! So much!"

After a bit she stops coughing and resumes smoking and I realize we both are staring at Stray again. "People," Pauline says with a sigh, "are so cruel. Don't you think?"

I do; I think yes. I tell her Stray was half-starved and mangy when we found him; he had been beaten and kicked, but we gave him raw eggs and corn oil for his coat and had his ear sewn up and took him to the vet's for all the right shots and look at him now. We continue to look at him now. Stray, glad to be noticed, and flattered, immediately trots to the driveway and pees on the wheel of Pauline's new Mustang. "Of course," I complain, "he's worse than a child."

Pauline bows her head and picks one of Stray's hairs off her black velvet jacket. "I guess," she says. She smiles. She really has a very nice smile. It was the first thing I noticed when Konrad introduced us; it's a wide smile, glamorous and trembly, like a movie star's. I once dreamt I had to kiss her and it wasn't bad, I didn't mind. In the dream Konrad held us by the hair with our faces shoved together. It was claustrophobic but not at all disgusting. I remember thinking, when I awoke: Poor Konrad, he doesn't even know how to punish people, and it's a shame, because he wants to so much. Later I noticed that Pauline's lips, when she's not smiling, are exactly like Konrad's, full and loose and purplish, sad. I wonder if when they kiss they feel they're making a mirror; I would. Whether the rest of Pauline mirrors Konrad is anyone's guess. I have never seen her eyes, of course, because of the dark glasses. Her hair is blond and so fine that the tips of her ears poke through. She is scarcely taller than one of the children, and it is difficult to think of her as Konrad's "executive assistant"; she seems a child, dressed up. She favors what the magazines call the "layered look"—I suspect because she is ashamed of her bottom. She has thin shoulders but a heavy bottom. Well, I want to tell her, who is not ashamed of their bottom. If not their bottom their thighs or their breasts or their wobbly female bellies; who among us is perfect, Pauline.

Instead of saying a word of this, of course, I sigh and say, "Some days it seems all I do is sweep up after that dog." Stray, good boy, rolls in dry leaves and vomits some grass. As if more were needed, as if Stray and I together are conducting an illustrated lecture, I swish the broom several times on the painted porch floor. The straw scrapes my toes. What Pauline doesn't know—because I haven't told her and because she won't come inside—is that I keep the broom by the front door for show. I keep it to show the Moonies, Mormons, and Jehovah's Witnesses who stop by the house that I've no time to be saved, can't be converted. I use it to lean on when I'm listening, lean on when I'm not; I use it to convince prowlers of my prowess and neighbors of my virtue; I use it for everything, in fact, but cleaning the house. I feel no need to clean house, and certainly not with a broom. The rooms at my back are stacked to the rafters with dead flowers and song sheets, stuffed bears and bird nests, junk mail and seashells, but to Pauline, perhaps, my house is vast, scoured, and full of light—to Pauline, perhaps, my house is in order. But who knows, with Pauline. She gives me her beautiful smile, then drops her eyes to my bathrobe hem and gives me her faint, formal frown. She pinches the dog hair between her fingers and tries to wipe it behind a leaf on the yellowing vine.

"I don't know how you manage" is what she says. She shakes her head. "Between the dog," she says, grinding her cigarette out on the railing, "and the children . . ." She sits huddled in the wan freckled sunlight with the dead cigarette curled in the palm of her hand, and after a minute, during which neither of us can think of one more thing to say, she lights up another. "It was the children," she says at last, "I really wanted to see."

"They'll be sorry they missed you," I tell her politely.

"Yes," Pauline says. "I'd hoped . . ."

"Had you but phoned," I add, just as politely, dropping my eyes and sweeping my toes. The children are not far away. They said they were going to the end of the lane to pick blackberries for pie, but what they are actually doing is showing their bare bottoms to passing cars and screaming "Hooey hooey." I know this because little Dixie Steadman, who used to baby-sit before she got her Master's Degree in Female Processes, saw them and called me. "Why are you letting your daughters celebrate their femininity in this burlesque?" Dixie asked. Her voice was calm and reasonable and I wanted to answer, but before I could there was a brisk papery rustle and she began to read rape statistics to me, and I had to hold the phone at arm's length and finally I put it to Stray's ear and even he yawned, showing all his large yellow teeth, and then I put the receiver down, very gently, and we tiptoed away. What I'm wondering now is what "hooey" means. I'd ask Pauline, who would be only too glad to look it up for me (her curiosity and industry made her, Konrad said, an invaluable assistant, right from the start), but I'm afraid she'd mention it to Konrad and then he would start threatening to take the children away; he does that; he can't help it; it's like a nervous tic. He loves to go to court. Of course he's a lawyer, he has to. Even so, I think he overdoes it. I never understood the rush to divorce me and marry Pauline; we were fine as we were, but he says my problem is that I have no morals and perhaps he's right, perhaps

I don't. Both my divorce and Pauline's wedding were executed in court, and I think both by Judge Benson. The marriage couldn't have been statelier than the dissolution, and if I were Pauline, only twenty-four and getting married for the very first time, I would have been bitter. I would have insisted on white lace or beige anyway and candles and lots of fresh flowers, but Pauline is not one to complain. Perhaps she feels lucky to be married at all; perhaps she feels lucky to be married to Konrad. Her shoulders always droop a little when she's with him, I've noticed, and she listens to him with her chin tucked in and her wrists poised, as if she were waiting to take dictation. Maybe she adores him. But if she does she must learn not to take him too seriously or treat him as if he matters; he hates that; he can't deal with that at all. I should tell her this, but there are some things she'll have to find out for herself. All I tell her is that the girls are gone, up the lane, picking berries.

"How wonderful," she says, exhaling. "Berries."

"Blackberries," I tell her. "They grow wild here. They grow all over."

"In the city," she says, making an effort, "a dinky little carton costs eighty-nine cents." She smiles. "Say you needed three cartons to make one pie," she asks me, "how much would that cost?"

I blink, one hand on my bathrobe collar.

"Two-sixty-seven." Her smile deepens, dimples. "Two-sixty-seven plus tax when you can buy a whole frozen pie for one-fifty-six, giving you a savings of one-eleven at least. They don't call them convenience foods," Pauline says, "for nothing."

"Are you sure," I ask, after a minute, "you don't want some tea?"

"Oh no!"

"Some coffee?"

"Oh no!"

"A fast glass of wine?"

She chuckles, cheerful, but will not answer. I scan the sky. It's close, but cloudless. If there were to be a thunderstorm—and we often have thunderstorms this time of year—Pauline would have to come in. Or would she? I see her, erect and dripping, defiant.

"Mrs. Dixon," I offer, "had a wonderful recipe for blackber . . ."

"Mrs. Dixon?"

For a second I almost see Pauline's eyes. They are small and tired and very angry. Then she tips her head to the sun and the glasses cloud over again.

"Konrad's mother."

"Yes," she says. She lights another cigarette, shakes the match out slowly. "I know."

"A wonderful recipe for blackberry cake. She used to say that Konrad never liked pie."

"I know."

"Just cake."

"I know."

"What I found out, Pauline, is that he likes both."

"We never eat dessert," Pauline says, her lips small and sad again. "It isn't good for us and we just don't have it."

Stray begins to bark and wheel around the garden and a second later the children appear, Letty first, her blond hair tangled and brambly like mine, then Alicia, brown-eyed like Konrad, and then Sophie, who looks like no one un-less—yes—with her small proud head, a bit like Pauline. The children are giggling and they deliberately smash into each other as they zigzag down the driveway. "Oops," they cry, with elaborate formality, "do forgive me. My mis-take." As they come closer we see that all three are scratched and bloody with berry juice. One holds a Mason jar half full and one has a leaky colander and one boasts a ruined pocket. Pauline closes her eyes tight behind her dark glasses and holds out her arms. The girls, giggling, jostle toward her. They're wild for Pauline. She tells them stories about kidnappers and lets them use her calcu-lator. With each kiss the wooden railing rocks and lurches; if these visits keep up I will have to rebuild the porch, renew the insurance. I carry the berries into the kitchen, rinse them off, and set them to drain. When I come back outside Pauline stands alone on the porch. Stains bloom on her blouse and along her out-thrust chin.

"Come in," I urge, "and wash yourself off."

She shakes her head very fast and smiles at the floor. "No," she says. "You see, I have to go."

The children are turning handsprings on the lawn, calling "Watch me!

me! me!" as Stray dashes between them, licking their faces. I walk down the driveway to see Pauline off. As I lift my hand to wave she turns and stares past me, toward the house; I turn too, see nothing, no one, only an old wooden homestead, covered with yellowing vines, a curtain aflutter in an upstairs window, a red door ajar on a dark brown room.

"Thank you," she cries. Then she throws her last cigarette onto the gravel and grinds it out and gets into her car and backs out the driveway and down to the street and away.

Once she turns the corner I drop my hand and bite the knuckles, hard. Then I look back at the house. Konrad steps out, a towel gripped to his waist. He is scowling; angry, I know, because he's spent the last half hour hiding in the shower with the cat litter box and the tortoise. He shouts for his shoes. I find them toed out in flight, one in the bedroom, one down the hall. As he hurries to tie them I tell him a strange thing has happened: it seems I've grown morals.

"What?" Konrad snaps. He combs his hair with his fingers when he can't find my brush.

"Us," I say. "You. Me. Pauline. It's a lot of hooey," I tell Konrad. "It is."

Konrad turns his face this way, that way, scrubs a space clear in the mirror. "Do you know what you're saying?" he says to the mirror.

I think. I think, Yes. I know what I'm saying. I'm saying good-bye. I'm saying, Go home.

And when he has gone and the girls are asleep and the house is night-still, I remember the pie. I roll out the rich dough, flute it, and fill it with berries and sugar, lemons and spice. We'll have it for breakfast, the children and I; we'll share with Stray. "Would you like that?" I ask him. Stray thumps his tail, but he's not looking at me; his head is cocked, he's listening to something else. I listen too. A faint beat comes from the radio on the kitchen counter. Even before I turn it up I can tell it's a reggae beat, strong and sassy. I'm not sure I can catch it. Not sure I should try. Still, when Stray bows, I curtsy. And when the song starts, we dance.

The FIRST SNOW

*Daniel Lyons*

**DANIEL LYONS**'s collection of short stories *The Last Good Man* won the AWP Short Fiction Award. Lyons's stories have appeared in *Playboy, GQ, Redbook,* and *Story,* among others. He has received a National Endowment for the Arts literary grant and was a semifinalist in *Granta*'s "Best of the Young American Novelists" competition. His first novel, *Coco,* is forthcoming. Lyons lives in Ann Arbor, Michigan, and works as a journalist.

THE NEWSPAPER PRINTS their names, and I admit that makes it worse. There are sixteen of them, and my father, whose name begins with A, is at the top of the list: Henry Abbott.

There was a rest area in Derry, apparently, and a path into the woods, and a giant hollow sycamore in the meeting place where they were arrested. The story in the *Gazette* says New Hampshire state troopers have been watching for weeks, camouflaged. They have videotapes.

The phone calls begin: more words for *fag* than I knew existed. Mom takes a call, listens, and slams down the phone. Her hair is matted to her head, her blouse is wrinkled, her eyes are bloodshot from not sleeping: she looks the way she did the time Jenny's appendix burst and we sat up all night in the hospital waiting room. She unplugs the phone.

"Visiting his mother," she says, disgusted. That was the excuse Dad used when he went out yesterday. I'm trying to remember how long he's been visiting Nana on Sundays.

She lights a cigarette and then stubs it out, so hard that it snaps. "Bob, I'm sorry," she tells me, "but I won't live with this."

Dad spent the night in jail. Mom said she couldn't handle the police station, all the smirks and snickers. He was arraigned this morning, and now, six hours later, he's still at his lawyer's office. I imagine this is a first for Mr. Pangione. He's a contract man: wills, taxes, divorce—the last, I think, may be of use when the criminal case is finished. I picture the two of them in their big leather chairs: Mr. Pangione embarrassed and looking down at his desk, my father fidgeting, afraid to go home.

Dad does more than jump into strange cars in rest areas. The big surprise is that he has a steady. All I can gather from the conversation taking place behind the bedroom door upstairs is that the steady is married, and that he too is shocked about Dad's adventures in the woods.

"What, and do you love him? Do you love him? I can't believe I'm asking this! My husband! I'm going to be sick."

Dad starts to cry. I can hear his wet words, but I can't make them out. Oddly, the news of the steady doesn't seem so bad.

Jenny and Nelson are in the family room playing Chutes and Ladders, oblivious. Jenny is seven and Nelson is five—both, I hope, too young to remember this. I, however, am seventeen.

I spread the *Gazette* out on the kitchen table and read the list of names again, wondering which one was the one with my father. What an image: all those men, moving silently in the woods, my father among them.

I fold the paper and put it up on top of the refrigerator, where Jenny and Nelson won't find it. I think about stupid things: Should I still do my homework? Will we have Thanksgiving? What are we doing for dinner tonight?

Mom solves the last one: Kentucky Fried Chicken. We sit, the five of us, at what I suppose will be our own Last Supper. Jenny and Nelson make castles with their mashed potatoes and Mom doesn't scold them; Dad grips the drumstick Mom gave him—at least she's got her sense of humor—and makes fake small talk about school, where he did not teach today; Mom gives him polite fake responses between gulps from her tumbler of gin; I watch for a while, then stare straight into my plate, not wanting to meet any of their eyes.

Later, Mom packs suitcases and duffel bags and moves with Jenny and Nelson to the Driscolls' house. I tell her I'm going to stay at home.

Mom puts the kids in the car, then comes in to ask me once more to come with her. For a moment I am literally standing between them: Mom at the open door, angry; Dad by the fireplace, drumming his fingers on the mantel, looking away. He is a schoolteacher, a man accustomed to dignity, which he is now working hard to maintain.

"Well?" she says.

The fact is, I feel bad for my father. I'm not going to leave him here alone.

"You go on without me," I say.

Just like any other night, Dad sits slack-gutted in his recliner in the family room, watching television. I go in and sit on the couch. The show is NFL highlights.

"Look at that hit," he says. "Jesus Christ."

There is a slow-motion replay: the arms stretching for the pass, the safety spearing in from behind, the tiny moment when there is no motion, then the legs lifting up, the head snapping back like a car crash dummy's, the ball tumbling free.

"Jesus Christ," he says again. He grabs a handful of peanuts from the can, shakes them in his hand like dice, and looks at me. "You going to stay for the game?" he says.

The air in the room feels overpressurized, like in a submarine that has surfaced too quickly.

"I don't know," I say.

"Well," he says, smiling, "I'm glad you decided to stay."

Suddenly I want to reach over and smack him for being so happy; I'd like to wipe that smile off his face.

"I'm glad you're in such a good mood," I say.

He sits up and says, "Bob, look—"

But I turn my back. I mumble something about homework and run upstairs to my room.

I'm on the phone with Drew—yes, everyone knows; some jerk has already started a joke—when another call comes in. It's Mr. Ryan, Dad's principal. I click back to Drew, tell him I've got to go, then call down to Dad.

"Well, I don't need to go to school tomorrow," he says when he arrives upstairs a few minutes later.

He tries to smile, then stands slope-shouldered in my doorway, looking old and paunchy in his cardigan sweater—more like an old fart at the Elks Club than some fairy running around in the woods. "I'm suspended," he says.

In homeroom there are eyes on me. I keep my head down. I write my name, over and over, in a spiral notebook. When Miss Moynihan calls my name there are snickers from the back of the room, but she stares them down. So she knows too, I think. We watch a video about nuclear weapons.

In the hall people make faces and whisper to each other, but they stay away, which is the best I can expect. It's not like I've got an army of friends who would rush to defend me. Drew comes up and fake punches me in the stomach—I guess to let me know that we're still manly men and to let everyone else know that he, at least, is on my side. He is five-foot-three and plays snare drum in the marching band. "So, Meester Elwood," he says. "You learn the Jetsons Theme?"

"The what?"

He pushes his glasses up the bridge of his nose. "Fuck you. The cartoon medley."

I make a face.

"For today? Rehearsal? The Turkey Day game?" He waves his hand back and forth in front of my face. "Hello? Hello?"

I explain that I am dropping band. Playing clarinet is just one of several things I will not do in public for a long, long time. Others: wear pink shirts, sharpen pencils, eat bananas. Beer in long-neck bottles. Anything to do with flowers.

On the door of my locker, in indelible black Magic Marker, is a drawing of a man, naked, kneeling down, with another man kneeling behind him, a giant third leg standing up from his abdomen. "Gee, Dad," the cartoon voice balloon says, "why can't we just go camping, like other families?"

The *Gazette* runs a front-page story about the arraignment. There is a priest, a banker, a man who runs a Sunoco station. Then there's my father, the menace of the J. G. Whittier Middle School.

A group of parents is calling for an investigation. "We want to know, has he ever chaperoned dances? Has he supervised gym?" a man named Ralph Leighton says.

A New Hampshire state trooper describes "the activities observed at the location." He uses words like "sodomy" and "fondling." During the arrest, he says, officers wore thick rubber gloves to keep from getting AIDS. Suddenly I think of our plates, our glasses, our toilet seat: but no, I think, that's ridiculous.

A Derry selectman says he doesn't care what these guys do as long as they do it in someone else's town. "I don't hate queers," he says.

After dinner, no kidding—Dad is cleaning his shotgun. He laughs when he sees the look on my face.

"For Christ's sake, Bob." He's wearing his most Dad outfit: corduroys from L. L. Bean, a polo shirt, and a golf sweater. "I thought we'd go down to Plum Island on Saturday. Ducks are open."

We really do hunt, he and I. Deer, ducks. But Jesus, I'm thinking—what's next? A pickup truck? Drinking contests? Washing whites with colors?

Dad is sunk so deep into his recliner that he and the chair look like all one piece, as if it grew out of his back. The remarkable thing is how much like a Dad he is. He is a little too fat in the belly and ass, and his brown hair is thin on top and shot with gray on the sides. He even wears brown tortoiseshell half-glasses when he reads the newspaper.

I snap on the television and pretend to watch, but when he's not looking I study his face, looking for clues. For three days I've wondered how he managed to fool us all for so long. Wasn't there anything different about him? Yes, I realize now, there is a certain softness in his cheeks, a slackness at the edges of his mouth, which I hadn't noticed before.

"What?" he says, looking up from oiling the barrel.

"Nothing. Is that the Remington?"

He scowls. I turn back to the television and pretend to watch the commercial.

The phone rings. I jump up. "I'll unplug it."

"No," he says. He groans getting out of his chair. "Hello?" he says. Then, in a voice I've never heard: "Hi! Yes, I was hoping! I called this afternoon. Right. Oh, wait a minute." He hands me the phone. "Hang this up when I get upstairs?" Before I hang up I hear him say, "So, Mark."

In the night the phone rings. I reach, wondering how long it's been ringing. A voice says, "You know how fags—"

I hang up. My breath rises in short, quick bursts. I think about school tomorrow. The phone rings again, and I unplug the cord, forgetting the other phones: the ringing continues in the kitchen, in the family room, in my father's room. My father says hello.

Then, groggy, he says, "Pardon me?"

I turn my face into my pillow. In the morning he pours me coffee and apologizes for the calls. "We'll get an answering machine," he says.

*    *    *

Mom says the Driscolls have room for me. I tell her I'm fine. "We're going hunting," I tell her. She rolls her eyes.

It's Wednesday. We're having dinner at Beshara's, a Lebanese place on South Union Street.

"Anyway, you can't all stay with the Driscolls," I say. "I mean, forever."

She says she is fully aware of what she can and can't do. She reminds me that she is my mother. I tell her I'm fully aware of that. I tell her that Dad is still Dad; that in most ways, nothing has changed. She uses words like "denial" and "trauma." She talks about lawyers and restraining orders. She pushes a cube of lamb back and forth on her plate.

"Are you going to eat that?" I say.

"Here." She slides her plate toward me.

I tell her my theory, which is that Dad has a brain tumor. Yesterday Drew told me about an uncle of his who one day at breakfast told his wife he was leaving her and the children to become a painter. And then did.

"That was Gauguin," she says.

"What?"

"Never mind."

"Anyway, something like a year later the guy had a seizure, and when they took him to the hospital they found out he had a tumor on his brain, the size of a grapefruit."

She lights a cigarette. "Why is it that tumors are always the size of a grapefruit? They're never the size of an orange. Or a cantaloupe."

This has been harder on her than I'd realized. I push on, though, explaining to her how Drew's uncle woke after surgery and didn't even know he'd left his family—the whole thing had been a mistake.

"And they all lived happily ever after," she says.

"Not really."

She raises an eyebrow. I shake my head.

"It doesn't matter. What *does* matter is that we get Dad in for a brain scan—fast."

Finally, I make her laugh.

\*    \*    \*

Our house leaks cold air through every joint, and the frame shudders and groans in the November wind. This house has been in the Abbott family since Ralph Waldo Emerson lived in our town. Emerson, in fact, ate dinner here, with my great-great-great-uncle, Walter Henry Abbott.

I can't sleep. I lie still as a stone beneath two blankets and wonder whether my father fantasizes about me.

He must think about men. Young men: he must like the way we look. Does he think about me? Does he look at me? Has he ever? I cast back, but I can't remember any incidents. He sees me in the morning, though, scampering cold in a towel from the bathroom to my bedroom. I think about him eyeing me, wanting to take me in his mouth.

For a moment I wish him dead: I wonder what it would be like if he were gone. It is as if I have discovered that the man in the other room is not who he says he is; that he has been in a witness protection program and his real name is not Henry Abbott, but something else altogether, something sinister and Italian; that he is not my father at all.

I wonder if I will inherit this. I had a dream, once. But just once. And there was Art Brancato, a senior when I was a freshman: hairy-chested in the locker room, lounging naked, unafraid, a full-grown man at seventeen; I studied the way he squinted when he laughed, and for a while I tried to walk the way he did, rolling my shoulders. But no. That's not the same.

In the morning there is frost on the lawn and someone has spray-painted "Honk If You Love Men" on both sides of the Cutlass. The front of the house is spattered with eggs—it looks as if something big has sneezed on us.

Thanksgiving is a week away. Drew says I can come to his family's house, but I have to turn him down. Dad says he's going to cook dinner. He's counting on me. Secretly I'm hoping that someone will invite us—Aunt Marian, maybe—but I realize that's unlikely. We are pariahs, the unclean. So we will end up, the two of us, leaning over our little turkey and thanking God—for what? For not being run over by a train? For not being hit by lightning? "Well," I imagine Dad saying in his phony classroom voice, "we've still got two good arms and two good legs. That's more than some can say."

He calls the Driscolls to see if Mom and the kids will come home for the holiday. He has not spoken to her since she left. His hand shakes so much that he misses the number and has to hang up and dial again.

"Bill? Henry. Thanks," he says when Mr. Driscoll answers. "That means a lot right now. Right. I know. It's tough on all of us. I'm calling for Kate, actually. Oh. Well, I mean, you could tell her, all I want to do is talk. I mean, what harm—OK. All right. Maybe later, then."

But later she won't take his call, either.

He goes upstairs. I hear him on the phone with Mark. I imagine he's inviting him for Thanksgiving. Before our Norman Rockwell holiday scene can take form in my mind, I hear a sound like coughing from behind his door.

"For Christ's sake," he says. "For Christ's sake. All right then. I won't. I said I won't. Bye."


I dread gym but I don't ask to be excused. Afterward, in the locker room, I can't help it: I glance at their bodies. Not between their legs, but at the legs themselves. The long muscles of the thighs. The arms, the shoulders, the chests. The curved, wing-shaped backs.

I want to know if this excites me. I have always insisted that it doesn't, but I've never actually checked.

I look at their shapes, pink in the steam of the shower room. There is something, maybe. My looks are too furtive to tell. If I stared I might feel more. Or I might feel less.

It's Thursday afternoon. Walking home I hear the band practicing in the field behind the auditorium, and I hate my father for bringing me to this.


At home, Aunt Marian, Dad's sister, is sitting on the couch. She has brought a coffee cake; she makes them for funerals. She fidgets with the cellophane wrapping. Dad's family is pure Yankee, as tight with their feelings as they are with their money. They're not equipped for this.

"Well," she says.

He plants himself into his recliner. "So, yes," he says. "Nice of you."

Kindness lasts as long as a cup of tea. She avoids all references to Thanksgiving and instead chatters on about family gossip: which cousin got which piece of furniture from Grandmother Wilkinson's house in Gloucester, why Cousin Richard needed electroshock therapy. Then, her support shown, her duty endured, she rises to leave.

At the door she says, "Has Mom called?"

"Maybe I should call her."

"Poor dear Henry." She kisses his cheek. She turns to me and I get the same kiss. "Take care, Robert."

Twice that afternoon he starts to call, then hangs up. He putters. He fixes the leak in the roof in the back porch. He cleans leaves from the rain gutters.

Mom is taking Jenny and Nelson to spend Thanksgiving in Ohio with her sister. They might not come back, she says.

She and Dad are in the kitchen, Friday afternoon. I'm in the family room, wondering what we'll call this room now. Den, maybe.

Dad says she's using her children as bargaining chips.

"There's no bargaining going on here," she says. She tells him he should get a lawyer.

He sits at the kitchen table. He looks like a guy in a Vietnam movie, mumbling about all his dead friends, too shell-shocked to think straight.

She takes out a piece of paper and begins running down a list of what they own and what their debts are. Suddenly he interrupts her, slams his hand on the table, and says, "Look, you can't goddamn *do* this. You can't."

More and more he is angry. I take this as a good sign. At least he's acting like a man. In the scenario I dread, he slides the other way: he gets a fancy haircut, shrieks at jokes, flips his hands as he speaks.

Mom doesn't flinch. She folds the paper, puts it in her purse, and snaps it shut. "Good-bye, then," she says.

I walk her to the car. We sit in the driveway. She lights a new cigarette from the old one. Her hands tremble. She says, "I really don't think you should be staying here."

"Look," I say, "I'm not going to sleep on some couch in some basement."

"Does the other guy—" She drags, then exhales. "Does he come over?"

"I think they broke up."

"Broke up." She shakes her head. "Jesus Christ." She laughs. She seems fragile, as if she's grown old too fast, like the plants in those sped-up film clips. I can't look at her. "Bob," she says, "I want you to come with us to Ohio."

Don't do this, I'm thinking. Don't make me choose. In seven months I will finish school and then I will leave them all; but for now I want things to stay the same.

"I can get a court order," she says. "You're a minor."

Across the street, Mr. Gauthier is on his lawn, raking leaves and watching us. I wave at him. He looks away.

"Bob, please," she says.

"Reveille," Dad says. It's Saturday morning, still dark out. "Rise and shine."

We stop at Big Bear for coffee and cinnamon rolls. On the way to Plum Island I fall back to sleep, and when I wake up we are backing down the boat ramp. We have rented a Nissan Sentra while the Cutlass is being painted.

I winch out the boat, a twelve-foot Sears aluminum rowboat with a three-horse Evinrude motor, then drag it ashore with the bowline while Dad parks.

We sputter down the channel into the thick of the salt marsh, then sit and wait. The dawn sky is sick gray. I worry that it might rain. Dad loads five shells into the chamber of his gas-action Remington and hands me two for my over-and-under, the gun he used as a boy. We sit facing each other, barrels across our laps. We wait. We wait some more.

"Open those sardines," he says.

This is our hunting breakfast, a habit he got from his father. It's a tradition I don't plan to carry on.

The tin cover sticks at first. I take off my gloves to get a better grip, and when I pull harder the lid suddenly tears off in my hand and runs a long, curved slice across the meat of my thumb. "Fuck," I say, because we swear when we hunt. "Motherfucker," I say, as a line of blood fills the cut.

Dad reaches across and takes my hand. "Let's have a look," he says, but his touch is like a spark, and I pull away.

He stops. His eyes are wide open. He starts to say something, then doesn't.

I look out over the marsh. There is nothing but water and sky, all gray. I imagine us from above, in black and white, so small on the water. I place the tin of sardines on the bench seat between us. I squeeze my thumb in the palm of my other hand. A drop of blood hits the bottom of the boat with a splat. Another falls; then another.

He reaches back to the first-aid box and takes out a Band-Aid. "Here," he says. I hold out my thumb, and he wraps the cut.

We sit. He doesn't say anything. He stares at me. I put my gloves back on. The wake from a boat crossing the marsh rocks us clumsily. He's still staring.

"I'm sorry," I say finally. "I just can't understand."

He fidgets with his wool cap. "I know."

"Maybe someday. I don't know."

"But you still love your old man, don't you?"

I kick my boots together. "Don't ask me things like that."

I look up. His eyes are reaching. I'm thinking that whatever happens, I don't want to see him cry.

"I need to know that," he says. "It's important."

He tries to take my hand again, but again I pull away.

"Stop it," I say. I sit back away from him. "Just don't."

He droops. I consider starting the engine and heading out of the marsh. But as awful as this moment is, I am unable to let it go. I feel on the edge of a discovery, as if some truth is about to reveal itself.

It doesn't. We sit and wait without talking. The water is calm, and now that the sun has come up, it's almost warm. We eat the sardines on crackers.

Suddenly shots are booming out over the water all around us—I realize now we're not alone here—and looking up I see the first line of ducks arcing down into the marsh. I point over his shoulder and he wheels and drops to one knee but already we're too late, they're past us and banking off, but he fires and fires anyway, long after the others have stopped. With each shot the recoil kicks his right shoulder back, as if it might spin him around. The spent shells leap from his chamber and hit the bottom of the boat still smoking, and he fires, fires, and fires into the empty sky.

He collapses into the curve of the bow. He turns his face away. I crawl over and kneel by him. "Dad," I say, "they're gone." He takes my hand, and this time I let him keep it.

Our new Code-A-Phone is chirping, and the message light blinks in time with it. Dad drops his hunting gear in the corner and, still in his plaid wool coat and right in front of me, he rushes to the machine like a schoolgirl. There is a man's voice, and I'm thinking, I really don't want to hear this.

But it's a man named Duncan Gardner, a lawyer. He represents Mom. "From now on, if you want to talk, I'd like you to talk to me," he says.

There are no other messages. Dad stands there, realizing, I guess, how foolish he looks. He takes a bottle to bed.

Later, past midnight, I lie awake in bed. Outside, the first snow of the season is falling against the night sky, tumbling through the tree branches and ticking against my window, and it's as if all the trouble in the world is coming down on us. Our old house creaks. I watch the snow toss and mingle in the air.

Dad is stirring in his room. Then his door opens and he pads down the stairs, through the hall and across the kitchen. I hold myself still, expecting— and I admit, half-hoping—to hear the crack of a muffled report from the garage. At least then we all could get over this. Instead there is the hum of the refrigerator, the clink of a bottle, a kitchen chair scraping on the linoleum floor. I cannot imagine why, but my poor father has decided to trudge on, and I know there are worse times ahead.

I think of him down there alone in the dark. I think of my mother, sleeping on a couch in someone's house. I think of Drew's uncle with the brain tumor, whose wife was so glad to have him back from the hospital that she decorated the house with balloons and streamers and threw a party for him. What they couldn't know, as they passed around the pieces of cake and danced to Ray Charles records, was that in three months his liver and lungs would be rotten with cancer, and that a month after that he'd be dead, leaving his friends to feel small and stupid—scared of the future, and stunned by the secrets life buries in us.

SILENT PARTNERS

*Robley Wilson*

ROBLEY WILSON, editor of *The North American Review,* has been a Guggenheim Fellow in Fiction and a Nicholl Fellow in Screenwriting. He is a former Drue Heinz winner (for *Dancing for Men* in 1982), and received the 1986 Starrett Prize (for *Kingdoms of the Ordinary*) and the 1990 Society of Midland Authors Prize for Poetry (for *A Pleasure Tree*). His most recent story collection is *Terrible Kisses.* He lives in Iowa and Florida, and is married to fiction writer Susan Hubbard.

LATELY, ALEX SEES his rival, whose name is Jennifer, almost every afternoon in the dim corridor, fourth floor, of the new language building. A small young woman, moon-faced and owl-eyed in her round glasses, Jennifer is hanging out, waiting to meet Pauline after class.

Pauline is his ex-wife. Jennifer is her lover. The two women have lived together for nearly a year.

At first Alex blamed himself. Sitting with Pauline in the student cafeteria, overlooking a river dotted with brown ducks, he had tried to understand.

"We rented a place across the river, near the hospital," Pauline told him. "I know you're disgusted. I just thought you ought to know, even if you aren't my husband anymore."

"No, no," he said. "I'm not disgusted. Just surprised."

"Surprise is good. You mustn't ever take things for granted."

"Do I know her?"

"Jennifer," Pauline said. "You met her once; she stayed behind to help me clean up, the night we gave the election party."

"And you're happy."

She studied him. "I truly am. Probably for the first time since before you and I were married."

"Truly?" He repeated the word as if it were from another language.

"My God," Pauline said, "do you want an affidavit from Jennifer?"

Now, thinking back to his courtship of Pauline, to their meetings when classes were done for the day, he remembers her swagger, overconfident and mannish, as if she carried a chip on her shoulder. He remembers that she smoked cigarettes like a poker player, a factory hand. When he also remembers their times in bed—her passion, her sensitivity to his own desires—he blames her for subterfuge, for sexual deception. Sometimes he admits to himself that he is going out of his way to disown his past with her.

Not to mention his past with other men in her life, before she met him.

That fiancé of hers, Timothy. When Pauline and Alex first began making love in her tiny apartment just down the hill from the university, Timothy's photograph hung in plain view on the wall at the foot of the bed.

"Close your eyes," Pauline said when he suggested that she ought to take down the picture. "Don't look at a man when you're loving me."

One day they were driving in the city where the fiancé lived. It is still an uncomfortable memory of Alex's.

"Tim's apartment isn't far from here," Pauline had said.

"Terrific."

"I'm not trying to make you jealous," she said. "But it's a nice place. You'd like it."

"Maybe I would," Alex said.

"I happen to know he's out of town."

"Even more terrific."

"And I still have a key."

He marvels now—he marveled then—at her apparent contempt for Tim, a man she was promised to. Yet it was exciting: going there, whispering in the hallway while Pauline unlocked the door, drinking Timothy's whiskey, thrashing in Timothy's bed. Pauline insisted they leave the bed rumpled and unmade, so Tim would know.

Alex wonders if Jennifer guesses how cruel Pauline can be—if she will someday learn, for instance, that not long ago, after they had met by chance at the shopping center downtown, he and Pauline went to the apartment near the hospital and made love. When will Pauline tell her?

Jennifer knows who he is. Pauline has introduced them: "My friend, Jennifer. My once-upon-a-time, Alex." He told Jennifer he was pleased to meet her. Jennifer seemed frightened and shy.

When he was in bed with Pauline, he had said, "What's it like, to make love to a woman?" As soon as he asked, he wished he hadn't.

Pauline avoided the question. "Loving is loving," she said.

"I'm sorry," he said. "It was a dumb thing to ask." He was ashamed to have brought it up.

"It isn't dumb," Pauline said. "It just can't be answered."

Later, when he was putting on his clothes in the bedroom she shared with Jennifer, Alex caught Pauline watching him out of the dresser mirror. "This is my first time with a man in more than a year," she said, not turning to face him. "It wasn't *so* bad."

This Monday afternoon he comes down the west stairwell of the language building on his way to the parking lot, having just taken a German Poetry quiz he knows he has failed. On the third-floor landing a small group of students has come out of a sign-language class, and they are continuing to make silent conversation. Alex has watched them before; he is fascinated by their gestures, by the animation of their faces despite the absence of spoken words, by the apparent ease of their communication. He thinks of how many ways there are for men and women to relate to one another and, in the same thought, What about me?

At the moment he isn't relating to anyone. He is an otherwise normal twenty-nine-year-old man alone in a world of pairs, divorced by a wife he lived with for five years, having no genuine hope of replacing her. His dreams— finishing graduate school, finding a decent job, raising a family—are like so much smoke, swept aside on the winds of sexual freedom. Pauline may continue to be his friend, but not the mother of his children.

While he is feeling sorry for himself, Pauline emerges from the classroom, mingles with the other students, then notices Alex.

"What a surprise," she says.

He hasn't seen her in nearly three weeks; she seems paler, thinner, but the brightness of her eyes does not suggest sadness. "Are you studying that stuff?" he says.

"Yes. For Jennifer. I'm getting pretty good at it."

"For Jennifer?"

Pauline raises an eyebrow. "You didn't know she was deaf?"

"No."

"Since she was eight," Pauline says. "Some weird complication from measles." She considers Alex's look of disbelief. "Can't you imagine two people being happy and quiet at the same time?"

"But she isn't—" He stumbles on the word. Pauline has fallen into step alongside him, descending the cement steps that echo harshly under her heels.

"She isn't mute," Pauline says. "She's just not good at talk—like someone with a slight speech impediment. Anyway, I prefer silence when I'm alone with her. That's why I've been learning to sign."

"And you're really good at it?"

"Good enough to carry on an argument." As they go out the back door into the parking lot, she gives him a sly, sidelong glance. "Want to try me?"

"No," he says. He wonders if this isn't a good time to tell her how lonely he is. "Can I give you a lift?"

"Jennifer's picking me up." Pauline shields her eyes from the afternoon sun and surveys the parking lot. "There she is."

Alex looks where she is pointing. Jennifer is standing by an opened car door. She waves. Pauline waves back, and runs to the car, still waving.

Now when Alex sees Jennifer he feels differently toward her. Now he is more hopeful of reconciling with Pauline, redrawing his dreams of family and of ordinary success, for perhaps it is not love she feels for Jennifer after all. Perhaps it is sympathy, or pity, of the sort sensitive people feel for the handicapped. Poor Jennifer. She has—what do they call it now?—a "communicative disorder." He looks forward to meeting her in the university halls or on the campus walks. He says "hello" to her, out loud, pretending still to be unaware of her deafness. Jennifer doesn't know that Alex is patronizing her, just as she seems not to know that Pauline has been unfaithful to her, not so very long ago.

One evening Pauline telephones, weeping, and asks him to come to the apartment. By the time he arrives, he is a man who has come courting; he lacks only the bouquet of flowers, the box of chocolates.

When Pauline opens the door, Alex is shocked. Tonight her eyes reflect the sleeplessness he has looked for earlier, and she seems as unhappy as—in his perverse desire for reunion with her—he has sometimes wished.

"I had to talk to someone," she says. "Jennifer's moved out."

Alex can't think how to respond.

"I'm going crazy," Pauline says. She motions him to a chair, and sits on one end of the sofa, across the room from him.

"What happened?"

She shakes her head. "There was no note or anything. Just empty bureau drawers, all her clothes gone from the closet. I've called everyone I can think of who knows her."

Alex sits helplessly. Pauline has never worn much makeup, but what little she does wear is streaked with tears that have not quite dried. Her hair is uncombed. She has on a blue peignoir that shows her thighs. He watches her reach for a cigarette and light it.

"You asked me once what it was like to love a woman," she says.

"It was an improper question. I felt guilty about it for a week."

"And those were the days when you didn't know about Jennifer—that she was deaf."

"I just thought she was terribly shy. I imagined she was afraid of me, or resented me."

"I told you then," Pauline says, "that loving was loving, and that the object of it didn't really make a difference—but that wasn't true. It isn't true."

She looks at him through the blue curl of cigarette smoke. "The delicacy of loving a woman," she says. "The intimate way we understand ourselves. It's like a welcome peace." She lays the cigarette in the ashtray and folds her hands in her lap. "When I made the signs for 'I love you,' I'd make them very slowly, and I'd feel my heart flutter against the word 'love.' Then sometimes I'd take her fingers and press them against my throat, and say it out loud: 'I love you.' Letting her feel the resonance of the words."

Alex looks away. His ex-wife is embarrassing him, he thinks.

"Or I'd put my mouth against her skin—anywhere—and say those words over and over and over. I swear, after a while I could feel her whole body singing with love-words."

"Jesus, Pauline," he says.

Pauline smiles. "I told you: the question wasn't improper. Just difficult." She rubs the heels of her palms against her damp cheeks. "Thank you," she says. "I feel better, talking about it."

"And what now?"

"I don't know. Tell me how to go about winning someone back."

He wants to say something clumsy about how easily he could be won back, but he can tell—by her sadness, her tears, the passion of all she has told him—that the time is not right. "Well," he says instead, "I guess you just have to hang in there."

When Alex comes down the west stairwell after class the next day, two women are standing against the light at the third-floor landing. When he has passed and looks back, he sees that one of them is Jennifer. The other is a dark-haired older woman he doesn't recognize. They are deep in the artful conversation of the deaf, and he stops for a moment, two or three steps below the landing, to watch them. It is wonderful: the eloquence of Jennifer's signs, the expressiveness of her gestures. Her lips move slightly, as if she is saying to herself the words she passes to her partner—giving them a silent rehearsal before turning them over to the easy instrument of her hands. He can almost see why Pauline is attracted to Jennifer. Alex wishes he were able to read these words, to understand the connections women enjoy that shut him out so entirely.

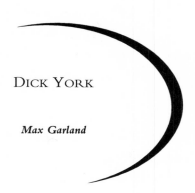

## Dick York

*Max Garland*

**MAX GARLAND** is a former rural mail carrier who now teaches at the University of Wisconsin–Eau Claire. His fiction has appeared in *Gettysburg Review, New England Review,* and *Best American Short Stories, 1995. The Postal Confessions,* his first book of poems, was awarded the 1994 Juniper Prize. Other awards include a National Endowment for the Arts Poetry Fellowship and a James Michener Fiction Fellowship.

THE EX-FARMERS WERE a beer-and-a-half into the morning, watching *Be-witched* again, one of the vintage black-and-white episodes. Since it was his fourth morning stopping into the bar for coffee, Jack sidled one stool closer to the three men. From the ex-farmers he had learned that most of the figures strutting and fretting across the screen were already dead. Agnes Moorehead, who portrayed the vengeful witch, Endora, was gone. Aunt Clara, Uncle Arthur, a host of assorted wraiths and warlocks had departed. Dick York, who played the constantly befuddled mortal who married into the witches, was reportedly near death, penniless and housebound somewhere in the Midwest. In fact, of the principals, only the actress who played Samantha, the blond suburban witch, still flourished, appearing in dinner theater and the occasional made-for-TV movie. Even some of the voices on the laugh track had undoubtedly perished, Jack realized, their only audible remains the anonymous chuckles and canned guffaws spilling over the bar and through the cigarette smoke of the ex-farmers.

"You can't tell me they'd make a show like that now." Roy was honing a familiar point. "People would say it was satanic. Fire off a batch of letters and get the preachers behind them. Probably wind up changing Samantha into an angel or something, like they did with Little Joe."

Since it was the beginning of February, the day before Groundhog's, and the furnace had not quite kicked the chill, Jack still wore the expensive if not entirely convincing bomber jacket Sylvia had given him for Christmas. Sylvia and Jack had lived together three years. More and more, however, it seemed they were constantly waving goodbye as Jack left for his week-long Shakespeare-in-the-Schools residencies.

"We'll talk tonight," Sylvia would call from the doorway as Jack walked to his car, and he would think of her as he drove, crossing the state to deliver Shakespeare to the children of dying farm towns. It was a long, complicated process, losing someone. There were so many little mirages, islands of happiness and nostalgia, when several endings still seemed possible. Nevertheless, Jack was pretty sure of the signs. As he drove, he would try to focus on what was ahead, try to plan his school presentations. But it was the waving goodbye that hung in his mind, the persistent afterimage of Sylvia at the door. What was it about the restlessness of a woman that turned a man into a clown? he wondered. Pratfalls, painted frown, sad floppy shoes. Where did it start? And was there any way, once it started, to stop the losing of ground?

Fashionably crinkled, prematurely faded, the bomber jacket had been an innocent enough gift. Given the current state of their affections, however, Jack was finding symbolism everywhere. As he tried on the leather jacket at Christmas, it had occurred to him, momentarily, that Sylvia was actually sending him to war. He checked all the many pockets, flapped and zippered. A farewell note? A coded map? A suicide vial?

Alongside him at the bar, the ex-farmers were still several layers deep in flannel and down. Truman, who sat next to Roy, registered the shift from drowsiness to melancholy by blindly peeling the label from his beer. Olney, occupying the next stool, watched the television through thick, dark-rimmed glasses. Olney wore a lifelong bachelor's stubble and rarely spoke, although he did move his beer in small damp circles and hesitations on the bar, much in the manner of a man playing Ouija.

On screen, the white witch Samantha, played by Elizabeth Montgomery, lifted the slim gable of an eyebrow to mark the arrival of havoc. Her hair was swept back from her forehead, sprayed into a downward spill, then flipped up at the shoulders, framing her face in a lush, blond bell.

"And after they turned her into an angel, they'd give her a divorce and a family to raise. Maybe throw in an orphan or two," Roy speculated, adding the unlikely angelic divorce for the benefit of Truman, who wasn't listening, but whose wife had left some years earlier for the lights of Des Moines. A widower himself, Roy tapped an ash neatly into his palm.

Meanwhile, Samantha cooed and pouted, tenderly stroking the mane of her husband, who had been transformed into a Shetland pony. Evidence pointed sharply toward the mother-in-law, Endora, who stood in a doorway, arms crossed defiantly, hair screwed tight and high, eyes made up to resemble the eyes of a large cat. Samantha's voice was the very syrup of consolation as she promised Darrin he would somehow be returned to natural form. Her face betrayed only the slightest trace of amusement, as if she had very briefly considered keeping the beast. Samantha wore a tight black Ban-Lon sweater chosen for its effectiveness in the numerous profile shots. A pearl nestled in the lobe of each ear, and a heart-shaped locket bobbed hypnotically about her chest, drawing Olney, at least, into the grip of a low-grade spell.

"That's the third time this winter," Roy continued, "the third time he's been some kind of horse." The beers and cigarettes ascended to the lips of the other two in a pattern of almost tidal regularity. After a quiet sip, Truman replaced his bottle and exhaled wearily. He rewarded himself for this piece of work with a loose drag from his cigarette, and as he released the chestful of smoke, Olney lifted *his* beer and moved through the same deliberate stations. Even the frequent bouts of coughing came according to turn. Truman barked briefly into his fist, then readjusted himself on the stool as if the outburst had thrown him temporarily from a delicate orbit. A few beats later, Olney was visited by a slightly darker version of the same cough.

"Mister Shakespeare," Roy tossed amiably across the stools to where Jack sat huddled over his coffee. "You got them reciting *Hamlet* yet?" A 900 number was flashing across the TV screen. It seemed you could make a personal call to Barbie.

"Actually, we did a scene from *Hamlet* yesterday. They're pretty ferocious little sword-fighters." Jack had armed the fourth graders with cardboard swords covered with aluminum foil. With a good deal of spontaneous editing and bowdlerizing, he was introducing the elementary schoolers to snippets of the plays. Sporting construction-paper crowns for the roles of kings and queens, or camouflaged in fern leaves for the final assault on Macbeth, the fourth graders of Farley Elementary were proving to be willing pretenders.

"Well, it's something new for them. Wake things up a bit, right?" Roy asked, completing the slow swivel toward Jack. "You haven't found any little geniuses over there, have you?"

"Plenty of geniuses," Jack answered. As on the previous mornings, no one seemed to be running the place, and again he poured his own coffee, folding a dollar bill beneath the edge of the nearest napkin holder.

"Well, they come by it honestly, don't they, Truman?" Roy gave a faint nod to the man next to him, "Truman has about a half-dozen grandkids over there."

"Three girls," Truman corrected, rotating politely in Jack's direction and pulling a deflated cigarette pack from his vest. "But they're already up at the middle school. I don't expect they know Shakespeare from Adam. Smart kids, though."

"They've got plenty of time," Jack said. "You never know. One of them might turn out to be a writer herself and put Farley on the map," although as soon as he spoke, Jack realized he had insulted the town.

"Oh, we're on the map." Roy glanced into the muzzle of his beer, then turned to Jack. "But that's about all. They've got a little dot for us about the size of a flyspeck. The whole outfit can blow away and they still keep you on the map like there was somebody home."

*Bewitched* resumed, and the three men swung in formation back to the set. At this hour of the morning the television served as the bar's primary light source. The beer signs with their cursive Germanic logos were still unplugged. The morning sun, though hysterically bright off the snow outside, barely fazed the tinted front windows.

Apparently lacking the power to unravel Endora's spell, Samantha had resorted to conventional feminine pleading on her husband's behalf. Still a pony, Darrin nuzzled his wife along the left hip, nickering softly. Samantha ran through a broad repertoire of hand-wringing, exasperated sighs, and frowns of almost Kabuki proportion, her dilemma sweeping forth in a gray wash over the bottles and spigots of the bar. Samantha's conflict had been basically the same in each of the episodes Jack had seen during the week. On the one hand, there was Darrin, her scarecrow love, the man who continually insisted she abandon witchcraft for the more prosaic joys of simple wifery. No traveling through time, no rhymed incantations, no housekeeping by the twitch of a nose. On the other hand, there was her mother, her long magical ancestry, her own strangely riddled blood, the ancient telekinetics rustling just below her carefully lacquered fingertips.

Jack had to admit it wasn't bad. After four mornings, he was picking up the devices pretty clearly—men into animals, reversals of time, the appearance of evil twins. Whoever wrote *Bewitched* had more than a nodding acquaintance with classical mythology. But it wasn't only the mythology that struck Jack. There was something else, something that had happened in the twenty-odd years since the show had originally aired, years that included Jack's entire adolescence and adult life. What had been written as a slapstick comedy of love, now seemed a rather obvious and somewhat pathetic struggle for power. Darrin, with his ad campaigns, his piggish clients, his "Honey, I'm home." His world hanging by a frayed thread. Samantha, clearly out of his league, yet waving him off cheerfully each morning, reassuring him, like a parent playing a game with a doomed child, trying desperately to lose.

Of course, Jack had just finished his third cup of coffee, the caffeine kicking in, doubling back on itself, and possibly swamping his judgment on the matter.

Still, he felt himself drawn. He had friends at the university, Sylvia's friends really, who made decent livings, were able to purchase homes and major appliances by conjuring up relevance from programs like *Bewitched. Iconography of the Media* was the name of one such course; "The Car as Closet: A Post-Hetero Reading of *Route 66*," the title of a much discussed dissertation. You had to admire the imagination, not to mention the sheer nerve it took to carve something of such nothings, from waves and splashes of electron babble.

Not that he was on much firmer ground these days. Shakespeare for fourth graders? Tiny farm boys weeping for Ophelia? But at least the name *Shakespeare* hung above the project, a legitimating ghost, a name to adorn the grade-school memory along with the names of the Founding Fathers and the inventor of the light bulb.

Jack was sure *Bewitched* had been rediscovered. He felt certain the program had already been tossed through the bright hoops of academic jargon—Samantha as Isis, as Hera, as the enduring image of Eve, the dim scroll of attendant footnotes.

And what would they make of Darrin? Petulant, devoted, knuckleheaded Darrin, desperately trying to hold his lover to earth. Jack felt an increasing jitteriness—the coffee, the distinct chill in the room. He also felt rather ridiculous sitting there in his tough-guy pilot's jacket—bomber of cities, strafer of railways. He thought of Sylvia, possibly still sleeping at this hour, and fought off a nervous impulse to call her. And say what? *Are you awake?*

Jack looked across at the ex-farmers and was struck by the unfortunate feeling that he was one of them, that they were all part of some lost Sad-Sack platoon. He felt there was some great abandoning in progress, women leaving in seas and droves, looking back on their doltish husbands and lovers, like outgrown grade-school friends.

Into the fourth cup of coffee, however, the speculations began floating away, and Jack's entire skull seemed to be lifting slightly. He noticed that his attention had strayed considerably from the screen. The bewildered pony had vanished from the TV living room and Dick York had reappeared, wearing his slick black suit and Vitalisized hair, the only signs of his ordeal a touch of stiffness in his back and a slightly rumpled collar where the pony bridle had been.

"How many of you have ever been, or plan to be, or are at this very moment, in love?" A predictable wave of queasy laughter swept the room. Only two girls, sitting side by side and dressed in identical Paula Abdul T-shirts, raised their hands. A small boy in distressed jeans and huge unwieldy basketball sneakers attempted to raise the arm of the boy in front of him, but was easily beaten back.

"Well, love is something William Shakespeare liked to put his characters through," Jack said. "Listen to this:

"Give me my Romeo, and, when he shall die,
Take him and cut him out in little stars,
And he will make the face of heaven so fine
That all the world will be in love with night
And pay no worship to the garish sun."

Jack was actually somewhat puzzled by this quotation himself. It was either very beautiful, he thought, or extremely gruesome, all those bloody little stars. Nevertheless, glossing the word *garish* with an unkind reference to the music teacher's choice of neckties, Jack wrote the lines on the chalkboard.

"Okay, who wants to be Romeo?" A flurry of hands shot upward and wagged. "Good. Remember now, what we're going to do is carve Romeo up into a bunch of stars." The hands wilted downward, hesitated, approximately a third of them rising a second time. Jack chose a slightly hefty boy who had instantly reminded him of someone to whom he had been needlessly cruel in his own youth. In spite of a certain bravado, a pinkish taint of embarrassment rose in the boy's face as he found himself before his classmates.

For Juliet, Jack picked a girl who had already tumbled from her desk in a fit of theatrical arm waving. Like many of the others, she wore an obvious Christmas gift—a bright red sweater embroidered with leaping white figures that appeared to be sheep, or possibly exuberant ghosts.

"Romeo, I'm afraid you're already history at this point in the story. What you need to do is lie down on the floor and pretend to be dead." Romeo balked at this, as if slightly offended.

"Wait, you're right, you need something to say before you die." Jack thought a moment. "Okay, say this: 'He jests at scars that never felt a wound.' " Jack repeated the line. He had long ago abandoned the sanctity of context in his Shakespeare presentations. In fact, he had a crazy idea that if he could just arrive at the proper scrambling of lines, the exact confusion of characters— Julius Caesar confronting Macbeth, Juliet confiding in Cleopatra—something would be revealed to him. Some fourth grader, wearing a bath towel for a tunic, would stand up and in flat Midwestern tones, unwittingly solve the mystery of human love.

He did worry about this technique, however, and half-expected someone, a well-versed teacher, an undercover Shakespearean scholar, a fourth-grade prodigy, to call him to account. Perhaps at least to question whether or not the themes of romantic love and metaphor-laced death were proper meat for the tender years.

On the other hand, Jack discovered that elementary students were surprisingly capable of weeding through the Shakespearean tangles. The notions of love and death were already prowling through their lives, and for the most part they seemed intrigued by the prospects. If the old biblical angels never came down to wrestle children, Jack decided, it wasn't out of any fear for the *children's* welfare.

Jack hurried Romeo toward his death. "That's all you have to say. Got it?"

"He jets at scars that never felled a womb?" was the approximation that came forth, Romeo flopping harmlessly dead to the delight of his classmates.

"Juliet, your part is what I read earlier. It's already on the board." Jack began to repeat the lines and Juliet, a quick study, immediately shot ahead of him:

".. . and cut him out in little stars,
And he will make the face of heaven so fine
That all the world will be in love . . ."

Jack handed Juliet a large pair of scissors as the class looked on hopefully. "So Juliet, instead of actually carving up poor Romeo and making a huge mess, maybe we should pretend to cut his body into stars and use these instead." Jack tossed the double handful of silver and gold attendance stars over the boy. "Now why don't you gather up all the stars of Romeo."

Juliet began dutifully collecting the stars from Romeo's chest and the surrounding floor. The boy struggled to remain dead, his face bright as a radish.

"And where do you think we should put these stars?" Jack asked.

"On the wall?" one of the Paula Abduls suggested.

"On Miss Bennett," another student offered, referring to their regular teacher who had finally glanced up from her paperwork to cast a cold eye on Juliet's scissors.

"Yes, but think," Jack said, "and I want you to raise your hand if you remember. Where does William Shakespeare say the stars of Romeo will go?"

Several hands rose, including the hand of the dead Romeo. The quotation was, after all, still written across the board. Before Jack could call on anyone, however, Juliet answered the question herself. Only four years younger than Shakespeare's Juliet, and obviously warmed to the part, she answered without bothering to raise her hand. "They go in heaven," she said impatiently, continuing to gather the stars from the floor.

Shakespeare-in-the-Schools was life in waiting. It was one of the things that happened to playwrights when their own plays were praised with such compound redundancies as ". . . quietly contemplative, though certainly not devoid of occasional flashes of an almost poetic . . . ," which meant no plot, no action to speak of, and no one, even in the tenderhearted Midwest, would pay to sit through them. Farley Elementary was Jack's third residency of the new year.

Not that he knew all that much about Shakespeare. In fact, even in his own house, Jack was not the expert. With a joint appointment in the Drama and English departments of the state university, it was Sylvia who could separate the truly occasional plays, the ones that were little more than elaborate royal flatteries, from the plays that merely hid their potency beneath swirls of contrivance and manners. It was Sylvia who had made the pilgrimages to the Folger Library, and who, when questioned by students, could tear the various authorship claims, from Francis Bacon to the Earl of Oxford, into quick erudite tatters. Sitting in on one of her classes, Jack had listened with both pride and an inkling of fear as Sylvia traced the evolution of the ancient King Llyr from Geoffrey of Monmouth, through Holinshed and Spenser, all the way to his final Shakespearean, "Pray you undo this button."

Even before that, even from the very beginning, there had been this edge to Jack's feelings for Sylvia, this dark urge to meddle in his own happiness. They had met after a production of one of Jack's plays at the community theatre, and he had been immediately attracted, and at the same time flattered, that someone who actually knew drama had enjoyed his work. During their courtship, he tried to shake this flattered feeling, tried to rid himself of the suspicion that this beautiful and otherwise intelligent woman had made a fundamental, almost wacky mistake and was on the verge of discovering her error. Occasionally, he tried to trace this doubt back to his childhood, some scrap of maternal love withheld, something Greek and primal in the cradle. He wondered if this sense of unworthiness had seeped into his heart while listening to too many Methodist hymns as a child.

"Isn't that a little silly?" Sylvia had asked when he suggested keeping his own apartment. "This isn't the thirteenth century, Jack. You don't have to worship from afar. You can come in now."

And she had been right for a while. There had been a romantic and somewhat clandestine quality about their living together. The sweet awkwardness of her mother's first visit, the pharmaceutical erotics of the shared medicine chest. There were months, whole seasons, when Jack was almost swept into forgetting his apprehensions.

"Beta-endorphins," a biologist friend explained to him. "It's the body's opium, Jack. It's love potion. That's why passionate love lasts two, two and a half years at the most. The cells develop a tolerance." His friend went on to talk about man's nomadic ancestry, cycles of pregnancy and weaning. Jack was skeptical. "Oh, you can stay together forever," the biologist said, "but the love part, the part they write songs about, that's good for about two years. That's all we've got the drugs for."

Scientists amazed Jack. People who dug down and got to be certain about things, even preposterous things.

Jack's own approach to research was less rigorous, and involved picking out his favorite moments from the few Shakespearean plays he remotely understood, and adapting them for grade-school children. It was a strange way to make a living, traveling from district to district, sleeping in guest rooms or ousted children's beds. Jack would find himself sitting in cafeterias in tiny molded chairs, lunching on grilled cheese and brightly dyed vegetables—carrot slices that practically glowed, corn as bright as costume jewelry. He sat, often serenely, as if on another planet, trading the stale cookie for the canned peach-half that tended to slide from under the fork like some sweet, flamboyant mollusk. The children's conversations mounted into a comfortable static, broke apart, regathered. Now and then a spoon dropped and rang on the tile. There were the dutiful sounds of paper straws slurping the dregs from tiny milk cartons.

For his week in Farley, Jack was staying with the Stottlemans, Roland and Glenda. Roland was the principal at Farley Elementary, and Glenda the science teacher at the adjoining middle school. The Stottlemans were an extremely kind and very tall couple. Had Jack written them into a play, the Stottlemans would have fallen in love at an athletic event, possibly a high-school track meet.

Their house was a large two-story, typical of the latter-day plains. Painted a local shade of Protestant white, it was unadorned except for a broken fringe of icicles along the eaves. Inside, the hardwood floors were stripped to a powdery blond. Jack thought of the tall Stottlemans down in the region of knees and vapors, scrubbing the grime from between the boards. He wasn't sure exactly how floors were stripped, if in fact knees and vapors were still required, but in his dull, happy play about the Stottlemans, they worked side by side, giddy from the fumes, swabbing like a couple of merry deckhands.

Jack slept in the room of the Stottlemans' eight-year-old daughter Rosemary, who was sacrificing gamely by bunking in the den, which, she proudly pointed out, was the former bedroom of her older brother Paul, a senior at the university.

Each night Jack spoke to Sylvia over the phone, an old, increasingly thin habit. Jack lay in the little girl's bed, surrounded by an array of stuffed animals, skating trophies, and legions of dolls. The dolls stood on dressers and windowsills, peered over the edge of a bassinet, even leaned along the baseboard. Some were only inches high, some the size and shape of human babies. There were plain and faceless Mennonite dolls, and others frighteningly real, eyes bright, little hands dimpled and nimble.

During his week-long absences of the past two years, Jack and Sylvia's conversations had followed an arc-like pattern. Monday nights of froth and minutiae. Jack described the town, the children, the taste of the local tap water. There was university gossip, updated by Sylvia, kindly slanders of mutual friends. Tuesday nights were more practical: discussions of mail, late-breaking physical news—mysteries of the lower back, viral suspicions. If a new murmur occurred in the pre-war plumbing of the house, it was invariably mentioned on Tuesday.

Wednesday nights became nights of phone love. Somehow the distance had done its best work by then. The arc swept upward in a tense, unsustainable bow. They would describe in detail how much they missed each other, and precisely where. Sylvia, phoning after her bath, might wear the sashless blue kimono. Jack, in some child's bed, listened through the crackle of deregulated phone lines. Now and then, a bit of someone else's conversation spilled recklessly into theirs. Jack would lie in his tiny frozen town waiting for Sylvia to mention some small but crucial detail, the phone cord twisted tightly around her left wrist, for example.

It was, in fact, just about the time Jack realized the midweek calls had become the high points of his relationship that the love talk began to dwindle, and soon quietly ended. Sometimes there were hopes, Sylvia speaking his name in a kind of whisper, but for the most part it became hard to distinguish Wednesday's calls from the others. Occasionally, Jack would call on Wednesday night and be answered by his own recorded voice, politely articulating his own sad number.

There was no concrete evidence of Sylvia's affair. More and more, however, it was something Jack came to believe in, the way the truly religious find God in the wildflower or the lowly pebble. There were the growing pauses in their nightly conversations, the increasing tonal omissions. Sometimes it seemed the long-distance static was actually increasing when they spoke, as if unfaithfulness issued its own frantic code. When Jack returned for the weekends, their mutual furniture had a shrinking, sheepish quality about it; sunlight fell through the curtains in a single graceless bolt.

In a play about their lives, the affair would have featured a younger man, cleaner in ambition, more sterling in aspect. Maybe even one of Sylvia's students. Perhaps it had all been set in motion on the very day Jack visited Sylvia's class for the lecture on *King Lear*. The lover-to-be noticing Jack and beginning to size up his chances. What had seemed impossible edging into the realm of the merely unlikely. In the play, Sylvia would finger her own blouse as she spoke of the undoing of buttons. Maybe she, in fact, did this. Or maybe it was just before the button line, when Sylvia leaned over the lectern and breathed Lear's famous *Never, never, never, never, never,* that the student-lover felt himself drawn forward, lured from his hesitations as surely as if she had dropped five black handkerchiefs in his path.

Even for one of his plays, Jack realized it was a convenience, this reducing the fading of love to the mechanics of enticement, to a simple choice of men. He might as well blame it on the chemicals his biologist friend had mentioned, the endorphin well run dry. At any rate, after the death of Wednesday nights, the other calls, Thursday's in particular, became little more than stilted rehearsals for Jack's weekend homecomings.

The Thursday night in Farley was made even bleaker by the news of an actual death in the Stottleman family. Roland received word of his father's heart failure while still at school, and by the time Jack finished his classes, the Stottlemans had packed and driven off for the northeast corner of the state where Roland had been born. There was a note scrawled on an envelope taped to the phone, mail scattered over the kitchen table, a packet of pork chops thawing in a widening pool on the counter.

Alone in the house, Jack felt like a petty thief. He poked through the refrigerator, baked two of the wilted chops, and worked awhile on Friday's presentation. In a caffeine-induced moment of inspiration that morning in the bar, he had decided his finale would be a sort of homage to *Bewitched*. He rustled the yellowed pages of his *Complete Shakespeare* looking for usable witches. He had already instructed the fourth graders to dress accordingly.

After dinner Jack switched TV channels mindlessly, picked up the phone and dialed half the digits to Sylvia, then replaced the receiver, deciding to wait for her call later. He was counting such tiny victories now, hoping they might add up. Jack scanned the coffee-table books, even peeked into a family photograph album he discovered beneath the television. There were sunburned and snow-swept versions of the Stottlemans; babes in arms, spilling pyramids of Christmas gifts; even a shot of Paul, the older son, in graduation cap and gown.

Jack couldn't help but feel the sweep of domestic envy as he put the album away, checked the front door, and flicked off the downstairs lights. The Stottlemans' world had a fullness about it, even in the presence of death. There was a layering, a sedimentary quality that made Jack feel his own life had been erected on water. He remembered the period when he and Sylvia had spent long afternoons in bed, toying with the future, playing little baby-naming games. *"Titus,"* Sylvia had suggested, *"Fortinbras, Ferdinand."* "How about *Ruthie?"* Jack had offered, because it sounded like someone's best friend.

A cold gale wrapped itself around the house as Jack lay in his bedroom of dolls. A north window rattled in its frame. Something groaned in a heat duct. Later, when the phone rang, Jack felt the familiar acidic jolt that now accompanied Sylvia's calls, a sharp, quick, intestinal withering he both dreaded and depended upon. Though they always mouthed the old assurances over the phone, planned for the weekends, inserted the word *love* in its traditional slot, the nightly calls continued to grow more brittle. A new speed was picking up. There often seemed to be more vital conversations traveling through the braid of lines, the intrusions no longer romantic. Something truly gnawed at the wires.

"Hello," Jack tried to answer in a bright tone.

"Hello, who is this?" a voice asked, and Jack found himself speaking not to Sylvia, but to Paul Stottleman, the elder son. Apparently the family had been unable to reach him, for it was immediately clear that Paul had no inkling of his grandfather's death.

After blundering through an explanation for his presence in the house, Jack broke the news and read Paul the scribbled note his parents had left. "I'm sorry. Of course you don't know me, but I want to say I'm sorry," Jack repeated, envisioning the thin boy in the graduation gown. "It's so sad when this happens. Your grandfather . . ." Jack tried to think of something to say about a man he'd never met, but Paul seemed to have put the receiver aside. A minute later the dial tone resumed.

The second call was from Sylvia, dutiful and remote, the chorus of phantom voices chattering in the lines. Jack told her how long the drive home would take tomorrow and suggested she have dinner without him. "No, I'll wait. Nine o'clock is fine," Sylvia said. *Fine.* Jack tried to remember when that weightless word had entered their lives.

Nevertheless, after the call he tried to hold her in mind awhile, tried to visualize a happy return from Farley. Weren't there still moments, evenings, whole days when the initial sweep of infatuation came back? Wasn't that how people lived together—the sweep, the lull, the nick-of-time rescue? The affair, after all, was possibly his own invention, a mere plot device for another play he would never get around to writing.

Jack lay surrounded by the populations of dolls. Atop Rosemary's skating trophies, tiny silver figures glided in place, each poised on a single skate. The sliding door of the closet had slipped from its roller, leaving it partially open. By the child's lamplight Jack could see the small gallery of dresses, skating outfits, the jumble of tiny shoes casting their chilly heels over the moment. Instead of the kimono version of Sylvia, Jack remembered her as he had, in fact, last seen her: standing at the door waving goodbye, in jeans and turtleneck, a teacup in one hand, the other sweeping calmly above her as if brushing something inconsequential from the air.

"You ever see a set of ears like that in your life?" Roy asked, referring to Dick York, who was flailing his arms about the screen as if conducting an angry stretch of Wagner. "That man's got Prince Charles beat in the ear department."

Next to Roy, Truman breathed an elegant plume of smoke. Olney promptly tilted back a beer, the image of Samantha skating in duplicate across the lenses of his glasses. Samantha wore the typical TV housewife's attire—wasp-waisted party dress, black heels, nylons that shimmered as if woven from dew. She rushed toward Darrin, begging forgiveness. Her powers had gotten out of hand again—chairs had spun, houseguests mysteriously floated away. A portrait winked from a wall. More dramatically, the front lawn had been transformed into a misty coastline, complete with wheeling gulls, sailboats, and the clang of distant ships' bells.

Jack hadn't slept well, and this morning even coffee seemed powerless, producing little more than a low electrical hum in the brain. On this last morning, he felt particularly depressed by the bar, the antics of Samantha and Darrin, the early rising drinkers living on their pinpoint of the map. Outside, the morning was white and bitterly clear. In the bar, the television gave the rows of bottles, cash register, and stools the appearance of being trapped in ice.

Jack looked at the three men beside him. In another unwritten play, the ex-farmers became as unreal and emblematic as the characters on *Bewitched*. A trio of Midwestern Fates. No, more like opposites of the Fates—the ex-farmers would sit on their stools facing the audience and respectively spin out, measure, and snip not the future, but the past, the long cocksure past, into ribbons.

The *Bewitched* theme trickled forth, and Jack realized he had missed the resolution of the morning's episode, although by now he thought he could guess—the furniture resettled and docile, the meddlesome Endora banished. Darrin soothed by a long, tongueless living room kiss. The gulls flown away. The lawn come back, neat as a napkin.

The nine-year-old Hecate, dressed in a slightly oversized choir robe, continued:

"Upon the corner of the moon
There hangs a wondrous drop profound,
I'll catch it ere it comes to ground;

And that distilled by magic sleights
Shall raise such artificial sprites."

The sprites sprang forth from the back of the classroom in leftover Halloween costumes and assorted sleepwear. Not quite as convincing as Juliet had been, Hecate still spouted a credible

"As by the strengths of these illusions
Shall draw him on to his confusion. . . ."

Jack had thrown in whatever witches and apparitions he could find, although the scene was primarily *Macbeth* with a touch of *A Midsummer Night's Dream*. "Double, double, toil and trouble," the fourth graders chanted, more or less in unison. "Eye of newt and toe of frog," a tiny witch dressed like a ballerina spoke as she stirred the huge cafeteria pot.

Jack wondered if he had gone too far this time. What would be next, Beckett for first graders? Lorca for toddlers? What truths was he trying to put in the mouths of such babes? Did he really think they might explain to him why love burned and faded? In an effort to brighten things a bit, Jack arranged for Puck to appear at the end of the commotion and declare the whole affair a dream. The boy who played Puck had apparently misunderstood Jack's instructions the previous day and came to school in full baseball uniform, including his glove. "If we but shadows have offended," the baseball Puck read,

"Think but this, and all is mended—
That you have but slumbered here
While these visions . . ."

But Jack didn't think it was mended. Walking back from school to the Stottleman house where he had already packed for the drive home, he tried to see the clear sky as an omen. The blue of homecoming. For what other reason would there be a sky this blue unless *someone* meant well, unless there was still a little beauty to burn?

He walked past the bar and cut across an untracked lawn, bomber jacket zipped to the throat, boots falling through the snow with a muffled crunch, or faint tearing sound, as if someone were ripping heavy cloth in the distance. He thought of the ex-farmers, the disembodied voices, the fabricated lover. In spite of the evidence of the sky, he couldn't ignore the feeling that something had started unraveling too long ago, and how could he or anyone put it back now, or even find the end of it? Out of habit, he imagined a play in which he walked in a similar snow. The sky was as blue as the actual sky, although a slight wind tore through it. And in the snow play, it was only a matter of mileage, one step, then another, and at the end: open arms, heart, kimono. He knew it was naive, pathetic even. But the audience sat spellbound, hardly a cougher among them.

SPATS

*Valerie Martin*

**VALERIE MARTIN** is the author of five novels—
*The Great Divorce, Mary Reilly, A Recent Martyr, Alexandra,*
and *Set in Motion*—and two collections of short stories, *The
Consolation of Nature* and *Love.* Born in Missouri and raised in
New Orleans, she now lives in Montague, Massachusetts, and
Rome.

THE DOGS ARE scratching at the kitchen door. How long, Lydia thinks, has she been lost in the thought of her rival dead? She passes her hand over her eyes, an unconscious effort to push the hot red edge off everything she sees, and goes to the door to let them in.

When Ivan confessed that he was in love with another woman, Lydia thought she could ride it out. She told him what she had so often told him in the turbulent course of their marriage, that he was a fool, that he would be sorry. Even as she watched his friends loading his possessions into the truck, even when she stood alone in the silent half-empty house contemplating a pale patch on the wall where one of his pictures had been, even then she didn't believe he was gone. Now she has only one hope to hold on to: he has left the dogs with her and this must mean he will be coming back.

When she opens the door Gretta hangs back, as she always does, but Spats pushes his way in as soon as she has turned the knob, knocking the door back against her shins and barreling past her, his heavy tail slapping the wood repeatedly. No sooner is he inside than he turns to block the door so that Gretta can't get past him. He lowers his big head and nips at her forelegs; it's play, it's all in fun, but Gretta only edges past him, pressing close to Lydia, who pushes at the bigger dog with her foot. "Spats," she says, "leave her alone." Spats backs away, but he is only waiting until she is gone; then he will try again. Lydia is struck with the inevitability of this scene. It happens every day, several times a day, and it is always the same. The dogs gambol into the kitchen, knocking against the table legs, turning about in ever-narrowing circles, until they throw themselves down a few feet apart and settle for their naps. Gretta always sleeps curled tightly in a semicircle, her only defense against attacks from her mate, who sleeps on his side, his long legs extended, his neck stretched out, the open, deep sleep of the innocent or the oppressor.

Lydia stands at the door looking back at the dogs. Sometimes Ivan got right down on the floor with Spats, lay beside him holding his big black head against his chest and talking to him. "Did you have a good time at the park today?" he'd croon. "Did you swim? Are you really tired now? Are you happy?" This memory causes Lydia's upper lip to pull back from her teeth. How often had she wanted to kick him right in his handsome face when he did that, crooning over the dog as if it were his child or his mistress. What about me? she thought. What about my day? But she never said that; instead she turned away, biting back her anger and confusion, for she couldn't admit that she was jealous of a dog.

Spats is asleep immediately, his jaws slack and his tongue lolling out over his black lips. As Lydia looks at him she has an unexpected thought: she could kill him. It is certainly in her power. No one would do anything about it, and it would hurt Ivan as nothing else could. She could poison him, or shoot him, or she could take him to a vet and say he was vicious and have him put away.

She lights a match against the grout in the countertop and turns the stove burner on. It is too cold, and she is so numb with the loss of her husband that she watches the flame wearily, hopelessly; it can do so little for her. She could plunge her hand into it and burn it, or she could stand close to it and still be cold. Then she puts the kettle over the flame and turns away.

She had argued with Ivan about everything for years, so often and so intensely that it seemed natural to her. She held him responsible for the hot flush that rose to her cheeks, the bitter taste that flooded her mouth at the very thought of him. She believed that she was ill; sometimes she believed her life was nearly over and she hated Ivan for this too, that he was killing her with these arguments and that he didn't care.

When the water is boiling she fills a cup with coffee and takes it to the table. She sits quietly in the still house; the only sound is the clink of the cup as she sets it back in the saucer. She goes through a cycle of resolutions. The first is a simple one: she will make her husband come back. It is inconceivable that she will fail. They always had these arguments, they even separated a few times, but he always came back and so he always would. He would tire of this other woman in a few weeks and then he would be back. After all, she asked herself, what did this woman have that she didn't have? An education? And what good was that? If Ivan loved this woman for her education, it wasn't really as if he loved her for herself. He loved her for something she had acquired. And Lydia was certain that Ivan had loved *her*, had married her, and must still love her, only for herself, because she was so apparent, so undisguised; there wasn't anything else to love her for.

So this first resolution is a calm one: she will wait for her husband and he will return and she will take him back.

She sets the cup down roughly on the table, for the inevitable question is upon her: How long can she wait? This has been going on for two months, and she is sick of waiting. There must be something she can do. The thought of action stiffens her spine, and her jaw clenches involuntarily. Now comes the terrible vision of her revenge, which never fails to take her so by surprise that she sighs as she lays herself open to it; revenge is her only lover now. She will see a lawyer, sue Ivan for adultery, and get every cent she can out of him, everything, for the rest of his life. But this is unsatisfactory, promising, as it does, nothing better than a long life without him, a life in which he continues to love someone else. She would do better to buy a gun and shoot him. She could call him late at night, when the other woman is asleep, and beg him to come over. He will come; she can scare him into it. And then when he lets himself in with his key she will shoot him in the living room. He left her, she will tell the court. She bought the gun to protect herself because she was alone. How was she to know he would let himself in so late at night? He told her he was never coming back and she had assumed the footsteps in the living room came from the man every lonely woman lies in bed at night listening for, the man who has found out her secret, who knows she is alone, whose mission, which is sanctioned by the male world, is to break the spirit if not the bones of those rebellious women who have the temerity to sleep at night without a man. So she shot him. She wasn't going to ask any questions and live to see him get off in court. How could she have known it was her husband, who had abandoned her?

Yes, yes, that would work. It would be easily accomplished, but wouldn't she only end up as she was now? Better to murder the other woman, who was, after all, the cause of all this intolerable pain. She knew her name, knew where she lived, where she worked. She had called her several times just to hear her voice, her cheerful hello, in which Lydia always heard Ivan's presence, as if he were standing right next to the woman and she had turned away from kissing him to answer the insistent phone. Lydia had heard of a man who killed people for money. She could pay this man, and then the woman would be gone.

The kettle is screaming; she has forgotten to turn off the flame. So she could drink another cup of coffee, then take a bath. But that would take only an hour or so and she has to get through the whole day. The silence in the house is intense, though she knows it is no more quiet than usual. Ivan was never home much in the daytime. What did she do before? It seems to her that that life was another life, one she will never know again, the life in which each day ended with the appearance of her husband. Sometimes, she admitted, she had not been happy to see him, but her certainty that she would see him made the question of whether she was happy or sad a matter of indifference to her. Often she didn't see him until late at night, when he appeared at one of the clubs where she was singing. He took a place in the audience and when she saw him she always sang for him. Then they were both happy. He knew she was admired, and that pleased him, as if she were his reflection and what others saw when they looked at her was more of him. Sometimes he gave her that same affectionate look he gave himself in mirrors, and when he did it made her lightheaded, and she would sing, holding her hands out a little before her, one index finger stretched out as if she were pointing at something, and she would wait until the inevitable line about how it was "you" she loved, wanted, hated, couldn't get free of, couldn't live without, and at that "you" she would make her moving hands be still and with her eyes as well as her hands she would point to her husband in the crowd. Those were the happiest moments they had, though neither of them was really conscious of them, nor did they ever speak of this happiness. When, during the break, they did speak, it was usually to argue about something.

She thinks of this as she stares dully at the dogs, Ivan's dogs. Later she will drive through the cold afternoon light to Larry's cold garage, where they will rehearse. They will have dinner together; Larry and Simon will try to cheer her up, and Kenneth, the drummer, will sit looking on in his usual daze. They will take drugs if anyone has any, cocaine or marijuana, and Simon will drink a six-pack of beer.

Then they will go to the club and she will sing as best she can. She will sing and sing, into the drunken faces of the audience, over the bobbing heads of the frenzied dancers; she will sing like some blinded bird lost in a dark forest trying to find her way out by listening to the echo of her own voice. The truth is that she sings better than she ever has. Everyone tells her so. Her voice is so full of suffering that hearing it would move a stone, though it will not move her husband, because he won't be there. Yet she can't stop looking for him in the audience, as she always has. And as she sings and looks for him she will remember exactly what it was like to find herself in his eyes. That was how she had first seen him, sitting at a table on the edge of the floor, watching her closely. He was carrying on a conversation with a tired-looking woman across from him but he watched Lydia so closely that she could feel his eyes on her. She smiled. She was aware of herself as the surprising creation she really was, a woman who was beautiful to look at and beautiful to hear. She was, at that moment, so self-conscious and so contented that she didn't notice what an oddity he was, a man who was both beautiful and masculine. Her attachment to his appearance, to his gestures, the suddenness of his smile, the coldness of his eyes, came later. At that moment it was herself in his eyes that she loved; as fatal a love match as she would ever know.

The phone rings. She hesitates, then gets up and crosses to the counter. She picks up the receiver and holds it to her ear.

"Hello," Ivan says. "Lydia?"

She says nothing.

"Talk to me!" he exclaims.

"Why should I?"

"Are you all right?"

"No."

"What are you doing?"

"Why are you calling me?"

"About the dogs."

"What about them?"

"Are they OK?"

She sighs. "Yes." Then, patiently, "When are you coming to get them?"

"I can't," he says. "I can't take them. I can't keep them here."

"Why?"

"There's no fenced yard. Vivian's landlord doesn't allow dogs."

At the mention of her rival's name, Lydia feels a sudden rush of blood to her face. "You bastard," she hisses.

"Baby, please," he says, "try to understand."

She slams the receiver down into the cradle. "Bastard," she says again. Her fingers tighten on the edge of the counter until the knuckles are white. He doesn't want the dogs. He doesn't want her. He isn't coming back. "I really can't stand it," she says into the empty kitchen. "I don't think I will be able to stand it."


She is feeding the dogs. They have to eat at either end of the kitchen because Spats will eat Gretta's dinner if he can. Gretta has to be fed first; then Spats is lured away from her bowl with his own. Gretta eats quickly, swallowing one big bite after another, for she knows she has only the time it takes Spats to finish his meal before he will push her away from hers. Tonight Spats is in a bad humor. He growls at Gretta when Lydia sets her bowl down. Gretta hangs her head and backs away. "Spats!" Lydia says. "Leave her alone." She pushes him away with one hand, holding out his bowl before him with the other.

But he growls again, turning his face toward her, and she sees that his teeth are bared and his threat is serious. "Spats," she says firmly, but she backs away. His eyes glaze over with something deep and vicious, and she knows that he no longer hears her. She drops the bowl. The sound of the bowl hitting the linoleum and the sight of his food scattered before him brings Spats back to himself. He falls to eating off the floor. Gretta lifts her head to watch him, then returns to her hurried eating.

Lydia leans against the stove. Her legs are weak and her heart beats absurdly in her ears. In the midst of all this weakness a habitual ambivalence goes hard as stone. Gretta, she thinks, certainly deserves to eat in peace.

She looks down at Spats. Now he is the big, awkward, playful, good fellow again.

"You just killed yourself," Lydia says. Spats looks back at her, his expression friendly, affable. He no longer remembers his fit of bad temper.

Lydia smiles at him. "You just killed yourself and you don't even have the sense to know it," she says.


It is nearly dawn. Lydia lies in her bed alone. She used to sleep on her back when Ivan was with her. Now she sleeps on her side, her legs drawn up to her chest. Or rather, she reminds herself, she lies awake in this position and waits for the sleep that doesn't come.

As far as she is concerned she is still married. Her husband is gone, but marriage, in her view, is not a condition that can be dissolved by external circumstances. She has always believed this; she told Ivan this when she married him, and he agreed or said he agreed. They were bound together for life. He had said he wanted nothing more.

She still believes it. It is all she understands marriage to be. They must cling to each other and let the great nightmarish flood of time wash over them as it will; at the end they would be found wherever they were left, washed onto whatever alien shore, dead or alive, still together, their lives entwined as surely as their bodies, inseparably, eternally. How many times in that last year, in the midst of the interminable quarrels that constituted their life together, had she seen pass across his face an expression that filled her with rage, for she saw that he knew she was drowning and he feared she would pull him down with her. So even as she raged at him, she clung to him more tightly, and the lovemaking that followed their arguments was so intense, so filled with her need of him that, she told herself, he must know, wherever she was going, he was going with her.

Now, she confesses to herself, she is drowning. Alone, at night, in the moonless sea of her bed, where she is tossed from nightmare to nightmare so that she wakes gasping for air, throwing her arms out before her, she is drowning alone in the dark and there is nothing to hold on to.


Lydia sits on the floor in the veterinarian's office. Spats lies next to her; his head rests in her lap. He is unconscious but his heart is still beating feebly.

Lydia can feel it beneath her palm, which she has pressed against his side. His mouth has gone dry and his dry tongue lolls out to one side. His black lips are slack and there is no sign of the sharp canine teeth that he used to bare so viciously at the slightest provocation. Lydia sits watching his closed eyes and she is afflicted with the horror of what she has done.

He is four years old; she has known him all his life. When Ivan brought him home he was barely weaned and he cried all that first night, a helpless baby whimpering for his lost mother. But he was a sturdy, healthy animal, greedy for life, and he transferred his affections to Ivan and to his food bowl in a matter of days. Before he was half her size he had terrorized Gretta into the role he and Ivan had worked out for her: dog-wife, mother to his children. She would never have a moment's freedom as long as he lived, no sleep that could not be destroyed by his sudden desire for play, no meal that he did not oversee and covet. She was more intelligent than he, and his brutishness wore her down. She became a nervous, quiet animal who would rather be patted than fed, who barricaded herself under desks, behind chairs, wherever she could find a space Spats couldn't occupy at the same time.

Spats was well trained; Ivan saw to that. He always came when he was called and he followed just at his master's heel when they went out for their walks every day. But it ran against his grain; every muscle in his body was tensed for that moment when Ivan would say "Go ahead," and then he would spring forward and run as hard as he could for as long as he was allowed. He was a fine swimmer and loved to fetch sticks thrown into the water.

When he was a year old, his naturally territorial disposition began to show signs of something amiss. He attacked a neighbor who made the mistake of walking into his yard, and bit him twice, on the arm and on the hand. Lydia stood in the doorway screaming at him, and Ivan was there instantly, shouting at Spats and pulling him away from the startled neighbor, who kept muttering that it was his own fault; he shouldn't have come into the yard. Lydia had seen the attack from the start; she had, she realized, seen it coming and not known it. What disturbed her was that Spats had tried to bite the man's face or his throat, and that he had given his victim almost no notice of his intention. One moment he was wagging his tail and barking, she told Ivan; then, with a snarl, he was on the man.

Ivan made excuses for the animal, and Lydia admitted that it was freakish behavior. But in the years that followed, it happened again and again. Lydia had used this evidence against him, had convicted him on the grounds of it; in the last two years he had bitten seven people. Between these attacks he was normal, friendly, playful, and he grew into such a beautiful animal, his big head was so noble, his carriage so powerful and impressive, that people were drawn to him and often stopped to ask about him. He enjoyed everything in his life; he did everything—eating, running, swimming—with such gusto that it was a pleasure to watch him. He was so full of energy, of such inexhaustible force, it was as if he embodied life, and death must stand back a little in awe at the sight of him.

Now Lydia strokes his head, which seems to be getting heavier every moment, and she says his name softly. It's odd, she thinks, that I would like to die but I have to live, and he would like to live but he has to die.

In the last weeks she has wept for herself, for her lost love, for her husband, for her empty life, but the tears that fill her eyes now are for the dying animal she holds in her arms. She is looking straight into the natural beauty that was his life and she sees resting over it, like a relentless cloud of doom, the empty lovelessness that is her own. His big heart has stopped; he is gone.

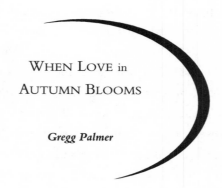

WHEN LOVE in
AUTUMN BLOOMS

*Gregg Palmer*

**GREGG PALMER**, a graduate of the Iowa Writers'
Workshop, has published fiction in *The Georgia Review, Alaska
Quarterly Review, Cream City Review, Quarterly West,* and else-
where. A special-education teacher, he lives in Frankfort,
Maine, with his wife, Leslie. He has completed his first novel,
*Census.*

"YOU SAVED MY life," Stuart told Shirley, again.

And she nodded slightly, knowing it wasn't true. Someone had—his lover, she thought. It hadn't been Shirley's doing, even though she'd decided to take the credit. "So?" she asked.

Stuart laughed. "So? So a man owes you his life," he said and kissed her dry lips and brushed the dry hair out of her eyes. "How about a *Family Circle* and a can of peaches? You love that," he told her.

"Yes," she said, flinching. He had never, in eighteen years, bought her anything or even offered. Then she took revenge, because that was easy now. "Remember the day we had the peach fight?" she lied. "We buried the pits but nothing grew." She listened to Stuart laugh too loud, pretending to remember the splatter and the smell of rotted peaches. It had never happened, of course, but he didn't remember that, either.

"I'll be back in an hour," he said, still chuckling.

Shirley wondered about the woman who read *Family Circle* and ate canned peaches, who had been Stuart's lover for at least ten years, and who apparently had saved his life. Whoever she was, she was forgotten by Stuart now—replaced in his shriveled memory by his wife, making it Shirley who had acted so calmly a month ago when his vessel exploded, and the blood was soaking through his brain.

Shirley tried to imagine the other woman's shoulders straining as she dragged Stuart across some linoleum floor and propped him against the oven or against an olive-green refrigerator whose motor chugged in the heat. Or maybe he had just crumpled in her bed, or thudded to the carpet or tile, the beer she'd poured him spilling across the floor.

Now he jigged down the sidewalk, his step too light for a sick man's. The doctor—an Oriental missing half his left thumb—had described Stuart's stroke as merely a tiny rupture. A nuisance. Two days after the operation, when she first visited Stuart, the man had scooted up. "Your husband brags about you," he said, his black hair slicked to one side. "You've had a beautiful life."

Shirley had turned away, ashamed at being confused with some other woman whose life had actually worked out. But soon she began to wonder if the misunderstanding might be a way out of her own existence. She wanted more. He *had* bragged about her to the nurses and the doctor as soon as he'd woken, and it was that second life—the one she didn't know about yet—that she wanted to steal.

Out front, the last few leaves curled on the tips of the maple's branches like withered hands. In two days it would be their nineteenth wedding anniversary. A celebration—but of what? That, like everything now, was up to her.

"What did you like most about our wedding?" Stuart had asked her as she'd sat in his hospital room.

"The wine," she said, remembering the cases of cheap beer. "Why?"

"Yes," he said, rubbing his bandages over and over. "What else?"

She laughed. "The perfect start to our perfect lives."

He stared at her. "But what else? Exactly."

He listened intently, pretending to know the things she was fabricating: "You kept nibbling my ears at the reception."

He grinned as he memorized this new detail. "I couldn't keep my hands off you."

"It was very beautiful," Shirley agreed, and he smiled and he nodded.

In truth, Stuart had postponed the wedding two weeks so that the reception could be a Halloween party, with the two of them already dressed as bride and groom. The guests poured in: hunchbacks and witches, warlocks, kings and queens, skeletons and hobgoblins. His friends drooled and screamed and roared. They bobbed for apples that had *It's A Boy!* or *It's A Girl!* cut into the skins, but Shirley, on her single dunk, came up dripping and empty, with Stuart gone. Signs of things to come. Someone played "The Monster Mash" twenty-seven times, until it stuck on the word *smash*.

She had wanted to drive to the hotel, make love and rest together, whisper across fresh sheets. But Stuart was dancing with a werewolf when Shirley asked him to take her away, trying to be sexy and conspiratorial and pleasant on her first night as his wife. He winked and whirled the werewolf into the crowd. A howl rose up with a snarl of laughter. He drank more beer and only later waltzed with Shirley under the skull lights.

"This is fun," he had said.

"I know, but I want you alone, and it's a long drive tomorrow."

"Here comes the nagging, right?"

She forced a smile. "No, but . . ."

"You live one stinking time is all. You're the bride—enjoy it," he'd said, breaking away to dance with two witches, then with the werewolf again and again. Years later, whenever he showed no concern over Shirley's sterility, a werewolf howled deep in her mind.

Now Stuart reached out from his hospital bed, but she was far away. "Every time I breathed I thought about your ears," he said. "It was a perfect night." Two nurses sprinted past the room, and then an aide pushing a gurney. "I won't ever forget it," he said and stared at her closely.

One week later, they paced the hospital corridors whose pale-green walls now depressed him. "All this reminds me of something," he had said.

"Your aunt's house," she lied.

"I was never in any danger," he said, fingering the bandages. "A thumbnail of blood. But I believed I was. And in my dreams about it sometimes you forget to call the ambulance." He paused, then raised a shaking hand. "Someone died here last night."

"It's a hospital," she said.

"I woke up at 3:30 this morning, and I was cold even though the room was hot. They rolled him out after the other patients fell asleep, but I knew." He stopped near a window that looked down on the river twisting along the city limits. A storm staggered across the sky. "You saved my life," he said. "I looked up through all that blood, and you were there. You said you loved me, told me to hold on to that. You made me live."

Lines of traffic streamed over the bridges below, car lights so close to one another they seemed connected. Separate people in their own hurries, she thought. The only thing they have in common is the cold rain their wipers push away.

*       *       *

Shirley tossed in bed alone and listened to skateboards clicking down the street. The storm must have blown through.

Their bed had always seemed too tall, she thought, high enough to be dangerous. People can get hurt easily at home, slipping in the shower, sleepwalking, or even rolling out of bed while dreaming about sharks and colors in the thick woods of love. She'd always tucked the sheets down tightly on her side.

Next to the bed stood a yellow bureau with a lamp, its shade gone—smashed. Stuart had thrown it at her one Sunday afternoon: *"Yes,"* he had whispered into the downstairs phone, the hiss creeping up to the bedroom, where dust landed on her pointed knees. "We'll go," he promised the other voice that whispered from some other house, while children and a tall husband lunged at tag in the backyard. "I swear to God I need this now," he said, and Shirley had swirled the radio full volume, to smother his voice. Holst's *Planets,* she remembered: "Jupiter, the Bringer of Jollity." Then Stuart had slammed up the stairs, torn the lamp out of the socket, and flung it at her. Her husband.

The skateboards faded off down the street. All those years, she thought. Now she could hurt *him*—there was a need for that, to even the score. Maybe she'd disappear, since she controlled the money. Or she could blackmail him about the past: send anonymous letters on scented paper, recounting his sins, threatening to tell his poor dear wife unless he paid. Bleed him dry, then vanish.

Or forgive him and forget? She looked over their cheap furniture. Lamps and bureaus and desks. The phone cord was stretched out—melted, in spots, to thin wire. Some homes are filled with love and patience, she thought, but these possessions were soaked in hate, lying, and cheating. Stains like smoke. Shouldn't he pay for this rot?

The house and the street were quiet when the phone rang once and cut off. Only a few minutes passed before the same thing happened, and then again. A code, maybe—something they'd promised to use in emergencies. Shirley wanted to answer, to help this woman and to love her, but she needed to salvage her own life. Later, she twitched and dreamed she had scrubbed the house until all the filth dissolved. But another storm wandered over the town, and lightning slashed too close. When the thunder woke her, she was still alone, and the lamp was still shadeless. Nothing ever changed.

\*     \*     \*

"You look nice," he'd said when they left the hospital. Wind corkscrewed across the sunken lot, sweeping red and yellow leaves into the sides of cars. "You know what I miss most?" he asked. "Air-conditioning," he said, as he opened her door for the first time in years. "We need a car with AC."

"It's cold," she said, wondering if he might be faking all this, searching a new angle. Or had he forgotten everything? Stealing their savings over the years. No vacations, no Christmas gifts or meals out, a second mortgage. And no air-conditioning.

"You're roasting," he said, damping the sweat off her forehead as she pulled out of the lot and drove through the noon-filled streets. "I'll tell you what I'd like to do," he went on, glancing at her. "Let's drive north. Rent a cabin and canoe, like we did that time. The city's about to explode. People hate people. You can feel it."

She could.

"Find that yellow dress I bought you," he said. "That's when I really fell in love. God, it was the best time in my life." He reached over and touched her.

"Yes," Shirley said, running a red light. Behind them tires screeched and drivers were yelling at her. Canoe? Yellow dress? He'd never taken *her* north. Her hands looked horribly thin, the knuckles like walnuts, as the car sobbed through traffic that strung backwards through forgotten miles.

That evening, after Stuart fell asleep early, she sneaked away and bought the yellow dress she would have chosen when she was young—if they'd taken a vacation together then or ever. Much later, she smoothed her husband's pale skin, goosefleshed against the blue sheets as he dreamed his scrambled dreams. And she lay next to him, slamming her eyes shut. Then her mind started replaying scenes from the cheap, wasted times that she begged not to see again but couldn't stop.

He'd hit Shirley, once—almost two years after their marriage. They were standing in the Bangor terminal, waiting for the plane to visit her parents for the first time since the wedding. Dead leaves stuck to their shoes.

He'd been complaining about the money for weeks, she remembered.

"Who spends this much to visit us?" he kept asking. Had he already taken his yellow-dressed lover to the lake by then?

"They're old," Shirley had said.

"No one is too old to be wheeled onto a plane."

"They gave us half the money, Stuart."

"Is that why we don't go running off to my mommy and daddy every goddamn day of the week?"

"Once. Once in two years," Shirley pointed out, her voice lost behind the blast of takeoffs. "And you've hated your parents since they threw you out."

"Sure. That's right. I hate them all. Lucky goddamn thing, too, so you can love everyone so fucking much."

"What do you want?" She set her bag on the green carpet and faced him. "I'll take the bus. I'll walk to Virginia—all right?"

When the blow landed over her right ear, she thought part of the ceiling had caved in. She reached out to make sure he was all right, tearing a pearl button off his shirt as she sank to one knee. People jostled past. A young policeman sat a few yards away, chewing a hot dog, swallowing. He glanced at her, barely interested, as Stuart dragged her onto the plane to fly south.

That weekend, Stuart had golfed with Shirley's father, who had melanoma and a lifetime membership in three clubs. And each night she lay in bed alone, while Stuart crept through the house till dawn. Shirley had almost believed that he wanted to touch her past, or felt too guilty to face her. She should forgive him, she had thought then—someday that would make a difference. The old house moaned as she waited for a sign, for one second of love to blow down the wide halls.

Stuart parked their grocery cart in the pantry and carried bags into the kitchen. "Hope I got everything."

"Thanks," she said, noticing how quickly he had returned.

"You've been so quiet since I left the hospital," he said, placing a can of tomatoes into the cupboard above her head. "It's me," he said. "I've done something to you. Shirl?" He set his hands on her thickening waist. She barely felt him. "Do you like me?"

Years ago—the first night he hadn't come home—she had dialed the police but hung up again and again. Their third year of marriage. She knew. She was peeling the shell off a boiled egg when he walked in at 8:00 A.M. "Hi," he said.

"I could divorce you. I should."

"For what?"

"For everything. Forgetting the milk. Fucking strangers."

"Who needs milk?" he said. "Besides, I've known her for a while." Dark rings circled the eyes above his wide grin.

"Oh," she said, fingering the egg. "And I'm supposed to just live with this. Until I kill you and everyone's surprised. Right?"

"No way." He pulled off his T-shirt.

"Tell me!" she screamed, heaving the egg that exploded behind him and slipped down the wall—she never boiled them long enough. "You left me alone." She grabbed a fork. "I was by myself, and you—"

He moved to her quickly and cradled her head. She raised the fork. "This is all over with now," he lied. He massaged her temples and made promises he'd never keep, while she ran the fork tines over his spine, tracing each notch, probing the soft spaces for pain and solutions.

Eventually, Shirley had given up, of course. Wounded, she chose to match her perfume to that lingering in his hair, threaded into the fibers of his shirts. She made that decision on a windy day, a year or so later. He was happy, so she hoarded her small peace, and that had been their life for years.

Now she wiped the sweat off the milk. "Of course I like you," she said.

"I got to the market and there was a sale on beets, and I couldn't remember eating beets. I thought I'd hurt you and you knew it. So I called the camps at the lake." He sat down, still weak from the operation. "We've got reservations for tomorrow," he announced proudly.

Shirley rubbed her dry hands. She wanted to stop this. "But you've always hated traveling on Fridays—ever since we were attacked," she lied.

"I don't remember that."

"What?" she asked. "How could you forget that gorilla in the diner who pinched my ass? I slapped him, but you were so scared. You remember, Stuart. Right? You remember."

"Our anniversary, Shirl." Stuart clamped his soft hands around hers.

"When I dialed the number, I figured you live one time is all. I saw us up there, happy again. You only live one time."

"That's right," Shirley agreed, even though she knew that was just another cliché people trusted without reason. He needed to believe that, she realized, and she told him yes again because, despite the truth, she needed it too.

That night she lay awake, listening to him breathe; shadows glanced across the bed.

She had tried to murder him one Halloween. Never in their nine years of marriage had they gone out to celebrate an anniversary—and she had been fixing a special meal when he announced he had to leave right after supper on a "business weekend."

"Where?" she had asked.

"It's business," he said, dropping a striped tie and weak suntan lotion into his suitcase. "Without business you couldn't live like this. Think about it."

While roasting the duck she had crushed the cyanide and sprinkled it into his dark beer, stirring with a Flex-Straw. Pumpkins leered from neighbors' porches, their slanted eyes flickering. Vivaldi's *Four Seasons* trickled off the radio.

"I hate that shit," he said as he came downstairs.

"I'll turn it down."

"Turn it off."

She got his beer. Steam rose from the duck as she reached across the table and handed him the bottle, but she didn't let go when he pulled. The weight hung between them: a man's life.

"Give me the goddamn beer or don't."

The doorbell rang, and feet scrambled away. A pumpkin lay crushed on their steps, its stringy innards splashed across the cement. Stuart charged into the street, swearing at skeletons that had vanished into thin air. When he came back she served wine instead. A child had cackled outside their door. Maybe it was just the wind.

How much, she wondered, had he forgotten? Would it all rush back in one second—tomorrow or the day after, while they clipped the yard? Would he drop his shears and look at her, knowing instantly that she hadn't saved him, that she'd only stolen some love when she had the chance? Then he would really laugh at her.

Streetlamps growled and telephone poles warped like insane men, and her husband breathed the thin rhythm of his life.

They had been on the road for two hours. "Almost there," he said. Pine and fir spread away from the interstate, swaying. The small beams of their headlights spit into more dark.

"It's not the same dress," he said.

"No," she said.

"Hey—here it is!" he said, suddenly swerving up an off-ramp. "I thought I'd forgotten."

"No," Shirley said. "Just smell it."

He took a breath and smiled at other memories. Beautiful times. The smaller road twisted blindly away under the silhouettes of slanting trees, their branches groping out of sight. Birches hovered thin and straight, like ghosts.

The lake shimmered, stretching into nothing. Something skimmed the surface and flapped into the sky. Stuart took her hand and led her to the log cabin, its porch facing black water. Others lined the shore, all dark but one, four buildings away, where light bled out a window. They could hear men laughing. "That's life," one voice floated out. "Deal, deal."

There was, she knew, always the other possibility: that Stuart would never remember, that maybe the doctor had missed a smaller leak and fresh blood was building even as they watched the glassy water, clotting his memories further, making him love her more and more. Killing him. He could collapse in a few weeks, maybe even in minutes.

Stuart wrapped his arms around her. "Happy anniversary, Shirl."

Soon he would find the key hooked under the eaves and unlock the door. She knew the air inside would feel damp and stale, but she found herself moving closer to him, trying to fade into this affair, trying not to care about other women who were always beaten and cheated and forgotten, not to worry about tomorrow in any way, trying just to be in love on a night exactly like this.

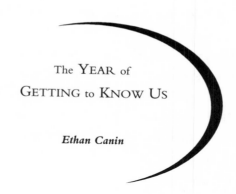

The YEAR of
GETTING to KNOW US

*Ethan Canin*

ETHAN CANIN was born in 1960 in Ann Arbor, Michigan. He studied English at Stanford University. He holds an M.F.A. from the Iowa Writers' Workshop and an M.D. from Harvard Medical School. He is the author of *Emperor of the Air, Blue River,* and *The Palace Thief.* He is married to a high-school English teacher and lives in San Francisco.

I TOLD MY father not to worry, that love is what matters, and that in the end, when he is loosed from his body, he can look back and say without blinking that he did all right by me, his son, and that I loved him.

And he said, "Don't talk about things you know nothing about."

We were in San Francisco, in a hospital room. IV tubes were plugged into my father's arms; little round Band-Aids were on his chest. Next to his bed was a table with a vase of yellow roses and a card that my wife, Anne, had brought him. On the front of the card was a photograph of a golf green. On the wall above my father's head an electric monitor traced his heartbeat. He was watching the news on a TV that stood in the corner next to his girlfriend, Lorraine. Lorraine was reading a magazine.

I was watching his heartbeat. It seemed all right to me: the blips made steady peaks and drops, moved across the screen, went out at one end, and then came back at the other. It seemed that this was all a heart could do. I'm an English teacher, though, and I don't know much about it.

"It looks strong," I'd said to my mother that afternoon over the phone. She was in Pasadena. "It's going right across, pretty steady. Big bumps. Solid."

"Is he eating all right?"

"I think so."

"Is *she* there?"

"Is Lorraine here, you mean?"

She paused. "Yes, Lorraine."

"No," I said. "She's not."

"Your poor father," she whispered.

I'm an only child, and I grew up in a big wood-frame house on Huron Avenue in Pasadena, California. The house had three empty bedrooms and in the back yard a section of grass that had been stripped and leveled, then seeded and mowed like a putting green. Twice a week a Mexican gardener came to trim it, wearing special moccasins my father had bought him. They had soft hide soles that left no imprints.

My father was in love with golf. He played seven times every week and talked about the game as if it were a science that he was about to figure out. "Cut through the outer rim for a high iron," he used to say at dinner, looking out the window into the yard while my mother passed him the carved-wood salad bowl, or "In hot weather hit a high-compression ball." When conversations paused, he made little putting motions with his hands. He was a top amateur and in another situation might have been a pro. When I was sixteen, the year I was arrested, he let me caddie for the first time. Before that all I knew about golf was his clubs—the Spalding made-to-measure woods and irons, Dynamiter sand wedge, St. Andrews putter—which he kept in an Abercrombie & Fitch bag in the trunk of his Lincoln, and the white leather shoes with long tongues and screw-in spikes, which he stored upside down in the hall closet. When he wasn't playing, he covered the club heads with socks that had little yellow dingo balls on the ends.

He never taught me to play. I was a decent athlete—could run, catch, throw a perfect spiral—but he never took me to the golf course. In the summer he played every day. Sometimes my mother asked if he would take me along with him. "Why should I?" he answered. "Neither of us would like it."

Every afternoon after work he played nine holes; he played eighteen on Saturday, and nine again on Sunday morning. On Sunday afternoon, at four o'clock, he went for a drive by himself in his white Lincoln Continental. Nobody was allowed to come with him on the drives. He was usually gone for a couple of hours. "Today I drove in the country," he would say at dinner, as he put out his cigarette, or "This afternoon I looked at the ocean," and we were to take from this that he had driven north on the coastal highway. He almost never said more, and across our blue-and-white tablecloth, when I looked at him, my silent father, I imagined in his eyes a pure gaze with which he read the waves and currents of the sea. He had made a fortune in business and owed it to being able to see the truth in any situation. For this reason, he said, he liked to drive with all the windows down. When he returned from his trips his face was red from the wind and his thinning hair lay fitfully on his head.

My mother baked on Sunday afternoons while he was gone, walnut pies or macaroons that she prepared on the kitchen counter, which looked out over his putting green.

I teach English in a high school now, and my wife, Anne, is a journalist. I've played golf a half-dozen times in ten years and don't like it any more than most beginners, though the two or three times I've hit a drive that sails, that takes flight with its own power, I've felt something that I think must be unique to the game. These were the drives my father used to hit. Explosions off the tee, bird flights. But golf isn't my game, and it never has been, and I wouldn't think about it at all if not for my father.

Anne and I were visiting in California, first my mother, in Los Angeles, and then my father and Lorraine, north in Sausalito, and Anne suggested that I ask him to play nine holes one morning. She'd been wanting me to talk to him. It's part of the project we've started, part of her theory of what's wrong— although I don't think that much is. She had told me that twenty-five years changes things, and since we had the time, why not go out to California.

She said, "It's not too late to talk to him."

My best friend in high school was named Nickie Apple. Nickie had a thick chest and a voice that had been damaged somehow, made a little hoarse, and sometimes people thought he was twenty years old. He lived in a four-story house that had a separate floor for the kids. It was the top story, and his father, who was divorced and a lawyer, had agreed never to come up there. That was where we sat around after school. Because of the agreement, no parents were there, only kids. Nine or ten of us, usually. Some of them had slept the night on the big pillows that were scattered against the walls: friends of his older brothers', in Stetson hats and flannel shirts; girls I had never seen before.

Nickie and I went to Shrier Academy, where all the students carried around blue-and-gray notebooks embossed with the school's heraldic seal. SUMUS PRIMI, the seal said. Our gray wool sweaters said it; our green exam books said it; the rear window decal my mother brought home said it. My father wouldn't put the sticker on the Lincoln, so she pressed it onto the window above her kitchen sink instead. ІМІЯЧ 2UMU2, I read whenever I washed my hands. At Shrier we learned Latin in the eighth grade and art history in the ninth, and in the tenth I started getting into some trouble. Little things: cigarettes, graffiti. Mr. Goldman, the student counselor, called my mother in for a premonition visit. "I have a premonition about Leonard," he told her in the counseling office one afternoon in the warm October when I was sixteen. The office was full of plants and had five floor-to-ceiling windows that let in sun like a greenhouse. They looked over grassy, bushless knolls. "I just have a feeling about him."

That October he started talking to me about it. He called me in and asked me why I was friends with Nickie Apple, a boy going nowhere. I was looking out the big windows, opening and closing my fists beneath the desk top. He said, "Lenny, you're a bright kid—what are you trying to tell us?" And I said, "Nothing. I'm not trying to tell you anything."

Then we started stealing, Nickie and I. He did it first, and took things I didn't expect: steaks, expensive cuts that we cooked on a grill by the window in the top story of his house; garden machinery; luggage. We didn't sell it and we didn't use it, but every afternoon we went someplace new. In November he distracted a store clerk and I took a necklace that we thought was diamonds. In December we went for a ride in someone else's car, and over Christmas vacation, when only gardeners were on the school grounds, we threw ten rocks, one by one, as if we'd paid for them at a carnival stand, through the five windows in Mr. Goldman's office.

"You look like a train station," I said to my father as he lay in the hospital bed. "All those lines coming and going everywhere."

He looked at me. I put some things down, tried to make a little bustle. I could see Anne standing in the hall just beyond the door.

"Are you comfortable, Dad?"

"What do you mean, 'comfortable'? My heart's full of holes, leaking all over the place. Am I comfortable? No, I'm dying."

"You're not dying," I said, and I sat down next to him. "You'll be swinging the five iron in two weeks."

I touched one of the tubes in his arm. Where it entered the vein, the needle disappeared under a piece of tape. I hated the sight of this. I moved the bed-sheets a little bit, tucked them in. Anne had wanted me to be alone with him. She was in the hall, waiting to head off Lorraine.

"What's the matter with her?" he asked, pointing at Anne.

"She thought we might want to talk."

"What's so urgent?"

Anne and I had discussed it the night before. "Tell him what you feel," she said. "Tell him you love him." We were eating dinner in a fish restaurant. "Or if you don't love him, tell him you don't."

"Look, Pop," I said now.

"What?"

I was forty-two years old. We were in a hospital and he had tubes in his arms. All kinds of everything: needles, air, tape. I said it again.

"Look, Pop."

Anne and I have seen a counselor, who told me that I had to learn to accept kindness from people. He saw Anne and me together, then Anne alone, then me. Children's toys were scattered on the floor of his office. "You sound as if you don't want to let people near you," he said. "Right?"

"I'm a reasonably happy man," I answered.

I hadn't wanted to see the counselor. Anne and I have been married seven years, and sometimes I think the history of marriage can be written like this: People Want Too Much. Anne and I have suffered no plague; we sleep late two mornings a week; we laugh at most of the same things; we have a decent house in a suburb of Boston, where, after the commuter traffic has eased, a quiet descends and the world is at peace. She writes for a newspaper, and I teach the children of lawyers and insurance men. At times I'm alone, and need to be alone; at times she does too. But I can always count on a moment, sometimes once in a day, sometimes more, when I see her patting down the sheets on the bed, or watering the front window violets, and I am struck by the good fortune of my life.

Still, Anne says I don't feel things.

It comes up at dinner, outside in the yard, in airports as we wait for planes.

You don't let yourself feel, she tells me; and I tell her that I think it's a crazy thing, all this talk about feeling. What do the African Bushmen say? They say, Will we eat tomorrow? Will there be rain?

When I was sixteen, sitting in the back seat of a squad car, the policeman stopped in front of our house on Huron Avenue, turned around against the headrest, and asked me if I was sure this was where I lived.

"Yes, sir," I said.

He spoke through a metal grate. "Your daddy owns this house?"

"Yes, sir."

"But for some reason you don't like windows."

He got out and opened my door, and we walked up the porch steps. The swirling lights on the squad car were making crazy patterns in the French panes of the living room bays. He knocked. "What's your daddy do?"

I heard lights snapping on, my mother moving through the house. "He's in business," I said. "But he won't be home now." The policeman wrote something on his notepad. I saw my mother's eye through the glass in the door, and then the locks were being unlatched, one by one, from the top.

When Anne and I came to California to visit, we stayed at my mother's for three days. On her refrigerator door was a calendar with men's names marked on it—dinner dates, theater—and I knew this was done for our benefit. My mother has been alone for fifteen years. She's still thin, and her eyes still water, and I noticed that books were lying open all through the house. Thick paperbacks—*Doctor Zhivago*, *The Thorn Birds*—in the bathroom and the studio and the bedroom. We never mentioned my father, but at the end of our stay, when we had packed the car for our drive north along the coast, after she'd hugged us both and we'd backed out of the driveway, she came down off the lawn into the street, her arms crossed over her chest, leaned into the window, and said, "You might say hello to your father for me."

We made the drive north on Highway 1. We passed mission towns, fields of butter lettuce, long stretches of pumpkin farms south of San Francisco. It was the first time we were going to see my father with Lorraine. She was a hairdresser. He'd met her a few years after coming north, and one of the first things they'd done together was take a trip around the world. We got postcards from the Nile delta and Bangkok. When I was young, my father had never taken us out of California.

His house in Sausalito was on a cliff above a finger of San Francisco Bay. A new Lincoln stood in the carport. In his bedroom was a teak-framed king-size waterbed, and on the walls were bits of African artwork—opium pipes, metal figurines. Lorraine looked the same age as Anne. One wall of the living room was glass, and after the first night's dinner, while we sat on the leather sofa watching tankers and yachts move under the Golden Gate Bridge, my father put down his Scotch and water, touched his jaw, and said, "Lenny, call Dr. Farmer."

It was his second one. The first had been two years earlier, on the golf course in Monterey, where he'd had to kneel, then sit, then lie down on the fairway.

At dinner the night after I was arrested, my mother introduced her idea. "We're going to try something," she said. She had brought out a chicken casserole, and it was steaming in front of her. "That's what we're going to do. Max, are you listening? This next year, starting tonight, is going to be the year of getting to know us better." She stopped speaking and dished my father some chicken.

"What do you mean?" I asked.

"I mean it will be to a small extent a theme year. Nothing that's going to change every day of our lives, but in this next year I thought we'd all make an attempt to get to know each other better. Especially you, Leonard. Dad and I are going to make a better effort to know you."

"I'm not sure what you mean," said my father.

"All kinds of things, Max. We'll go to movies together, and Lenny can throw a party here at the house. And I personally would like to take a trip, all of us together, to the American Southwest."

"Sounds all right to me," I said.

"And Max," she said, "you can take Lenny with you to play golf. For example." She looked at my father.

"Neither of us would like it," he said.

"Lenny never sees you."

I looked out the window. The trees were turning, dropping their leaves onto the putting green. I didn't care what he said, one way or the other. My mother spooned a chicken thigh onto my plate and covered it with sauce. "All right," my father said. "He can caddie."

"And as preparation for our trip," my mother said, "can you take him on your Sunday rides?"

My father took off his glasses. "The Southwest," he said, wiping the lenses with a napkin, "is exactly like any other part of the country."

Anne had an affair once with a man she met on an assignment. He was young, much younger than either of us—in his late twenties, I would say from the one time I saw him. I saw them because one day on the road home I passed Anne's car in the lot of a Denny's restaurant. I parked around the block and went in to surprise her. I took a table at the back, but from my seat in the corner I didn't realize for several minutes that the youngish-looking woman leaning forward and whispering to the man with a beard was my wife.

I didn't get up and pull the man out with me into the parking lot, or even join them at the table, as I have since thought might have been a good idea. Instead I sat and watched them. I could see that under the table they were holding hands. His back was to me, and I noticed that it was broad, as mine is not. I remember thinking that she probably liked this broadness. Other than that, though, I didn't feel very much. I ordered another cup of coffee just to hear myself talk, but my voice wasn't quavering or fearful. When the waitress left, I took out a napkin and wrote on it, "You are a forty-year-old man with no children and your wife is having an affair." Then I put some money on the table and left the restaurant.

"I think we should see somebody," Anne said to me a few weeks later. It was a Sunday morning, and we were eating breakfast on the porch.

"About what?" I asked.

On a Sunday afternoon when I was sixteen I went out to the garage with a plan my mother had given me. That morning my father had washed the

Lincoln. He had detergent-scrubbed the finish and then sun-dried it on Huron Avenue, so that in the workshop light of the garage its highlights shone. The windshield molding, the grille, the chrome side markers, had been cloth-dried to erase water spots. The keys hung from their magnetic sling near the door to the kitchen. I took them out and opened the trunk. Then I hung them up again and sat on the rear quarter panel to consider what to do. It was almost four o'clock. The trunk of my father's car was large enough for a half-dozen suitcases and had been upholstered in a gray medium-pile carpet that was cut to hug the wheel wells and the spare-tire berth. In one corner, fastened down by straps, was his toolbox, and along the back lay the golf bag. In the shadows the yellow dingos of the club socks looked like baby chicks. He was going to come out in a few minutes. I reached in, took off four of the club socks, and made a pillow for my head. Then I stepped into the trunk. The shocks bounced once and stopped. I lay down with my head propped on the quarter panel and my feet resting in the taillight berth, and then I reached up, slammed down the trunk, and was in the dark.

This didn't frighten me. When I was very young, I liked to sleep with the shades drawn and the door closed so that no light entered my room. I used to hold my hand in front of my eyes and see if I could imagine its presence. It was too dark to see anything. I was blind then, lying in my bed, listening for every sound. I used to move my hand back and forth, close to my eyes, until I had the sensation that it was there but had in some way been amputated. I had heard of soldiers who had lost limbs but still felt them attached. Now I held my open hand before my eyes. It was dense black inside the trunk, colorless, without light.

When my father started the car, all the sounds were huge, magnified as if they were inside my own skull. The metal scratched, creaked, slammed when he got in; the bolt of the starter shook all the way through to the trunk; the idle rose and leveled; then the gears changed and the car lurched. I heard the garage door glide up. Then it curled into its housing, bumped once, began descending again. The seams of the trunk lid lightened in the sun. We were in the street now, heading downhill. I lay back and felt the road, listened to the gravel pocking in the wheel wells.

I followed our route in my mind. Left off Huron onto Telscher, where the car bottomed in the rain gulley as we turned, then up the hill to Santa Ana. As we waited for the light, the idle made its change, shifting down, so that below my head I heard the individual piston blasts in the exhaust pipe. Left on Santa Ana, counting the flat stretches where I felt my father tap the brakes, numbering the intersections as we headed west toward the ocean. I heard cars pull up next to us, accelerate, slow down, make turns. Bits of gravel echoed inside the quarter panels. I pulled off more club socks and enlarged my pillow. We slowed down, stopped, and then we accelerated, the soft piston explosions becoming a hiss as we turned onto the Pasadena freeway.

"Dad's rides," my mother had said to me the night before, as I lay in bed, "would be a good way for him to get to know you." It was the first week of the year of getting to know us better. She was sitting at my desk.

"But he won't let me go," I said.

"You're right." She moved some things around on a shelf. The room wasn't quite dark, and I could see the outline of her white blouse. "I talked to Mr. Goldman," she said.

"Mr. Goldman doesn't know me."

"He says you're angry." My mother stood up, and I watched her white blouse move to the window. She pulled back the shade until a triangle of light from the streetlamp fell on my sheets. "Are you angry?"

"I don't know," I said. "I don't think so."

"I don't think so either." She replaced the shade, came over and kissed me on the forehead, and then went out into the hall. In the dark I looked for my hand.

A few minutes later the door opened again. She put her head in. "If he won't let you come," she said, "sneak along."

On the freeway the thermal seams whizzed and popped in my ears. The ride had smoothed out now, as the shocks settled into the high speed, hardly dipping on curves, muffling everything as if we were under water. As far as I could tell, we were still driving west, toward the ocean. I sat halfway up and rested my back against the golf bag. I could see shapes now inside the trunk. When we slowed down and the blinker went on, I attempted bearings, but the sun was the same in all directions and the trunk lid was without shadow. We braked hard. I felt the car leave the freeway. We made turns. We went straight. Then more turns, and as we slowed down and I was stretching out, uncurling my body along the diagonal, we made a sharp right onto gravel and pulled over and stopped.

My father opened the door. The car dipped and rocked, shuddered. The engine clicked. Then the passenger door opened. I waited.

If I heard her voice today, twenty-six years later, I would recognize it.

"Angel," she said.

I heard the weight of their bodies sliding across the back seat, first hers, then his. They weren't three feet away. I curled up, crouched into the low space between the golf bag and the back of the passenger compartment. There were two firm points in the cushion where it was displaced. As I lay there, I went over the voice again in my head: it was nobody I knew. I heard a laugh from her, and then something low from him. I felt the shift of the trunk's false rear, and then, as I lay behind them, I heard the contact: the crinkle of clothing, arms wrapping, and the half-delicate, muscular sounds. It was like hearing a television in the next room. His voice once more, and then the rising of their breath, slow; a minute of this, maybe another; then shifting again, the friction of cloth on the leather seat and the car's soft rocking. "Dad," I whispered. Then rocking again; my father's sudden panting, harder and harder, his half-words. The car shook violently. "Dad," I whispered. I shouted, "Dad!"

The door opened.

His steps kicked up gravel. I heard jingling metal, the sound of the key in the trunk lock. He was standing over me in an explosion of light.

He said, "Put back the club socks."

I did and got out of the car to stand next to him. He rubbed his hands down the front of his shirt.

"What the hell," he said.

"I was in the trunk."

"I know," he said. "What the goddamn."

The year I graduated from college, I found a job teaching junior high school in Boston. The school was a cement building with small windows well up from the street, and dark classrooms in which I spent a lot of time maintaining discipline. In the middle of an afternoon that first winter a boy knocked on my door to tell me I had a phone call. I knew who it was going to be.

"Dad's gone," my mother said.

He'd taken his things in the Lincoln, she told me, and driven away that morning before dawn. On the kitchen table he'd left a note and some cash. "A lot of cash," my mother added, lowering her voice. "Twenty thousand dollars."

I imagined the sheaf of bills on our breakfast table, held down by the ceramic butter dish, the bank notes ruffling in the breeze from the louvered windows that opened onto his green. In the note he said he had gone north and would call her when he'd settled. It was December. I told my mother that I would visit in a week, when school was out for Christmas. I told her to go to her sister's and stay there, and then I said that I was working and had to get back to my class. She didn't say anything on the other end of the line, and in the silence I imagined my father crisscrossing the state of California, driving north, stopping in Palm Springs and Carmel, the Lincoln riding low with the weight.

"Leonard," my mother said, "did you know anything like this was happening?"

During the spring of the year of getting to know us better I caddied for him a few times. On Saturdays he played early in the morning, when the course was mostly empty and the grass was still wet from the night. I learned to fetch the higher irons as the sun rose over the back nine and the ball, on drying ground, rolled farther. He hit skybound approach shots with backspin, chips that bit into the green and stopped. He played in a foursome with three other men, and in the locker room, as they changed their shoes, they told jokes and poked one another in the belly. The lockers were shiny green metal, the floor clean white tiles that clicked under the shoe spikes. Beneath the mirrors were jars of combs in green disinfectant. When I combed my hair with them it stayed in place and smelled like limes.

We were on the course at dawn. At the first fairway the other men dug in their spikes, shifted their weight from leg to leg, dummy-swung at an empty tee while my father lit a cigarette and looked out over the hole. "The big gun," he said to me, or, if it was a par three, "The lady." He stepped on his cigarette. I wiped the head with the club sock before I handed it to him. When he took the club, he felt its balance point, rested it on one finger, and then, in slow motion, he gripped the shaft. Left hand first, then right, the fingers wrapping pinkie to index. Then he leaned down over the ball. On a perfect drive the tee flew straight up in the air and landed in front of his feet.

Over the weekend his heart lost its rhythm for a few seconds. It happened Saturday night, when Anne and I were at the house in Sausalito, and we didn't hear about it until Sunday. "Ventricular fibrillation," the intern said. "Circus movements." The condition was always a danger after a heart attack. He had been given a shock and his heartbeat had returned to normal.

"But I'll be honest with you," the intern said. We were in the hall. He looked down, touched his stethoscope. "It isn't a good sign."

The heart gets bigger as it dies, he told me. Soon it spreads across the X ray. He brought me with him to a room and showed me strips of paper with the electric tracings: certain formations. The muscle was dying in patches, he said. He said things might get better, they might not.

My mother called that afternoon. "Should I come up?"

"He was a bastard to you," I said.

When Lorraine and Anne were eating dinner, I found the intern again. "I want to know," I said. "Tell me the truth." The intern was tall and thin, sick-looking himself. So were the other doctors I had seen around the place. Everything in that hospital was pale—the walls, the coats, the skin.

He said, "What truth?"

I told him that I'd been reading about heart disease. I'd read about EKGs, knew about the medicines—lidocaine, propranolol. I knew that the lungs filled up with water, that heart failure was death by drowning. I said, "The truth about my father."

The afternoon I had hidden in the trunk, we came home while my mother was cooking dinner. I walked up the path from the garage behind my father, watching the pearls of sweat on his neck. He was whistling a tune. At the door he kissed my mother's cheek. He touched the small of her back. She was cooking vegetables, and the steam had fogged up the kitchen windows and dampened her hair. My father sat down in the chair by the window and opened the newspaper. I thought of the way the trunk rear had shifted when he and the woman had moved into the back of the Lincoln. My mother was smiling.

"Well?" she said.

"What's for dinner?" I asked.

"Well?" she said again.

"It's chicken," I said. "Isn't it?"

"Max, aren't you going to tell me if anything unusual happened today?"

My father didn't look up from the newspaper. "Did anything unusual happen today?" he said. He turned the page, folded it back smartly. "Why don't you ask Lenny?"

She smiled at me.

"I surprised him," I said. Then I turned and looked out the window.


"I have something to tell you," Anne said to me one Sunday morning in the fifth year of our marriage. We were lying in bed. I knew what was coming.

"I already know," I said.

"What do you already know?"

"I know about your lover."

She didn't say anything.

"It's all right," I said.

It was winter. The sky was gray, and although the sun had risen only a few hours earlier, it seemed like late afternoon. I waited for Anne to say something more. We were silent for several minutes. Then she said, "I wanted to hurt you." She got out of bed and began straightening out the bureau. She pulled my sweaters from the drawer and refolded them. She returned all our shoes to the closet. Then she came back to the bed, sat down, and began to cry. Her back was toward me. It shook with her gasps, and I put my hand out and touched her. "It's all right," I said.

"We only saw each other a few times," she answered. "I'd take it back if I could. I'd make it never happen."

"I know you would."

"For some reason I thought I couldn't really hurt you."

She had stopped crying. I looked out the window at the tree branches hung low with snow. It didn't seem I had to say anything.

"I don't know why I thought I couldn't hurt you," she said. "Of course I can hurt you."

"I forgive you."

Her back was still toward me. Outside, a few snowflakes drifted up in the air.

"*Did* I hurt you?"

"Yes, you did. I saw you two in a restaurant."

"Where?"

"At Denny's."

"No," she said. "I mean, where did I hurt you?"


The night he died, Anne stayed awake with me in bed. "Tell me about him," she said.

"What about?"

"Stories. Tell me what it was like growing up, things you did together."

"We didn't do that much," I said. "I caddied for him. He taught me things about golf."

That night I never went to sleep. Lorraine was at a friend's apartment and we were alone in my father's empty house, but we pulled out the sheets anyway, and the two wool blankets, and we lay on the fold-out sofa in the den. I told stories about my father until I couldn't think of any more, and then I talked about my mother until Anne fell asleep.

In the middle of the night I got up and went into the living room. Through the glass I could see lights across the water, the bridges, Belvedere and San Francisco, ships. It was clear outside, and when I walked out to the cement carport the sky was lit with stars. The breeze moved inside my nightclothes. Next to the garage the Lincoln stood half-lit in the porch floodlight. I opened the door and got in. The seats were red leather and smelled of limes and cigarettes. I rolled down the window and took the key from the glove compartment. I thought of writing a note for Anne, but didn't. Instead I coasted down the driveway in neutral and didn't close the door or turn on the lights until the bottom of the hill, or start the engine until I had swung around the corner, so that the house was out of sight and the brine smell of the marina was coming through the open windows of the car. The pistons were almost silent.

I felt urgent, though I had no route in mind. I ran one stop sign, then one red light, and when I reached the ramp onto Highway 101, I squeezed the accelerator and felt the surge of the fuel-injected, computer-sparked V-8. The dash lights glowed. I drove south and crossed over the Golden Gate Bridge at seventy miles an hour, its suspension cables swaying in the wind and the span rocking slowly, ocean to bay. The lanes were narrow. Reflectors zinged when the wheels strayed. If Anne woke, she might come out to the living room and then check for me outside. A light rain began to fall. Drops wet my knees, splattered my cheek. I kept the window open and turned on the radio; the car filled up with wind and music. Brass sounds. Trumpets. Sounds that filled my heart.

The Lincoln drove like a dream. South of San Francisco the road opened up, and in the gulley of a shallow hill I took it up over a hundred. The arrow nosed rightward in the dash. Shapes flattened out. "Dad," I said. The wind sounds changed pitch. I said, "The year of getting to know us." Signposts and power poles were flying by. Only a few cars were on the road, and most moved over before I arrived. In the mirror I could see the faces as I passed. I went through San Mateo, Pacifica, Redwood City, until, underneath a concrete over-pass, the radio began pulling in static and I realized that I might die at this speed. I slowed down. At seventy drizzle wandered in the windows again. At fifty-five the scenery stopped moving. In Menlo Park I got off the freeway.

It was dark still, and off the interstate I found myself on a road without streetlights. It entered the center of town and then left again, curving up into shallow hills. The houses were large on either side. They were spaced far apart, three and four stories tall, with white shutters or ornament work that shone in the perimeter of the Lincoln's headlamps. The yards were large, dotted with eucalyptus and laurel. Here and there a light was on. Sometimes I saw faces:

someone on an upstairs balcony; a man inside the breakfast room, awake at this hour, peering through the glass to see what car could be passing. I drove slowly, and when I came to a high school with its low buildings and long athletic field I pulled over and stopped.

The drizzle had become mist. I left the headlights on and got out and stood on the grass. I thought, This is the night your father has passed. I looked up at the lightening sky. I said it, "This is the night your father has passed," but I didn't feel what I thought I would. Just the wind on my throat, the chill of the morning. A pickup drove by and flashed its lights at me on the lawn. Then I went to the trunk of the Lincoln, because this was what my father would have done, and I got out the golf bag. It was heavier than I remembered, and the leather was stiff in the cool air. On the damp sod I set up: dimpled white ball, yellow tee. My father would have swung, would have hit drives the length of the football field, high irons that disappeared into the gray sky, but as I stood there I didn't even take the clubs out of the bag. Instead I imagined his stance. I pictured the even weight, the deliberate grip, and after I had stood there for a few moments, I picked up the ball and tee, replaced them in the bag, and drove home to my wife.

The year I was sixteen we never made it to the American Southwest. My mother bought maps anyway, and planned our trip, talking to me about it at night in the dark, taking us in her mind across the Colorado River at the California border, where the water was opal green, into Arizona and along the stretch of desert highway to New Mexico. There, she said, the canyons were a mile deep. The road was lined with sagebrush and a type of cactus, jumping cholla, that launched its spines. Above the desert, where a man could die of dehydration in an afternoon and a morning, the peaks of the Rocky Mountains turned blue with sun and ice.

We didn't ever go. Every weekend my father played golf, and at last, in August, my parents agreed to a compromise. One Sunday morning, before I started the eleventh grade, we drove north in the Lincoln to a state park along the ocean. Above the shore the cliffs were planted with ice plant to resist erosion. Pelicans soared in the thermal currents. My mother had made chicken sandwiches, which we ate on the beach, and after lunch, while I looked at the crabs and swaying fronds in the tide pools, my parents walked to the base of the cliffs. I watched their progress on the shallow dunes. Once when I looked, my father was holding her in his arms and they were kissing.

She bent backward in his hands. I looked into the tide pool where, on the surface, the blue sky, the clouds, the reddish cliffs, were shining. Below them rock crabs scurried between submerged stones. The afternoon my father found me in the trunk, he introduced me to the woman in the back seat. Her name was Christine. She smelled of perfume. The gravel drive where we had parked was behind a warehouse, and after we shook hands through the open window of the car, she got out and went inside. It was low and long, and the metal door slammed behind her. On the drive home, wind blowing all around us in the car, my father and I didn't say much. I watched his hands on the steering wheel. They were big and red-knuckled, the hands of a butcher or a carpenter, and I tried to imagine them on the bend of Christine's back.

Later that afternoon on the beach, while my mother walked along the shore, my father and I climbed a steep trail up the cliffs. From above, where we stood in the carpet of ice plant, we could see the hue of the Pacific change to a more translucent blue—the drop-off and the outline of the shoal where the breakers rose. I tried to see what my father was seeing as he gazed out over the water. He picked up a rock and tossed it over the cliff. "You know," he said without looking at me, "you could be all right on the course." We approached the edge of the palisade, where the ice plant thinned into eroded cuts of sand. "Listen," he said. "We're here on this trip so we can get to know each other a little bit." A hundred yards below us waves broke on the rocks. He lowered his voice. "But I'm not sure about that. Anyway, you don't *have* to get to know me. You know why?"

"Why?" I asked.

"You don't have to get to know me," he said, "because one day you're going to grow up and then you're going to *be* me." He looked at me and then out over the water. "So what I'm going to do is teach you how to hit." He picked up a long stick and put it in my hand. Then he showed me the back-swing. "You've got to know one thing to drive a golf ball," he told me, "and that's that the club is part of you." He stood behind me and showed me how to keep the left arm still. "The club is your hand," he said. "It's your bone. It's your whole arm and your skeleton and your heart." Below us on the beach I could see my mother walking the waterline. We took cut after cut, and he taught me to visualize the impact, to sense it. He told me to whittle down the point of energy so that the ball would fly. When I swung he held my head in position. "Don't just watch," he said. *"See."* I looked. The ice plant was watery-looking and fat, and at the edge of my vision I could see the tips of my father's shoes. I was sixteen years old and waiting for the next thing he would tell me.

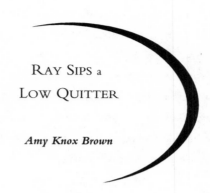

# Ray Sips a
# Low Quitter

*Amy Knox Brown*

**AMY KNOX BROWN**, a past winner of the Henfield/*Transatlantic Review* Award, holds a B.F.A. and an M.A. in English and a J.D., and is presently finishing a Ph.D. Her fiction has appeared in many magazines, including *The Missouri Review, Witness, Gallery, descant,* and *Voices West*. She lives in Iowa City, Iowa, with her two dogs, Chloe and Yogi, and is at work on a novel.

IT'S BAR DAY minus 4, early afternoon. Elise stands in the bathroom, vomiting. Afterward she washes her face, brushes her teeth, and walks, resting one hand against the wall, back into the den where she's studying with Daren. Under her feet, the carpet feels rougher than usual.

"Are you okay?" he asks.

"Yeah," she says. "Maybe I just drank too much coffee." The room is dim and messy—drawn shades, piles of books and outlines on the floor, Hi-Liters scattered like discarded shotgun shells. A pale film of cigarette smoke hovers near the ceiling.

"All right," Elise says, settling into a nest of pillows arranged in one corner. "Now a bilateral contract consists of mutual promises, while a unilateral k consists of a promise on one side and performance on the other, correct?"

"Correct," Daren says. He's still looking at her with concern. "Do you want to take a break? We could go for a walk or something."

"I'm fine," Elise says. She picks up a cup of cold coffee sitting by the pillows and takes a sip. The liquid sloshes dangerously in her stomach for a second, then settles.

"What's *res ipsa loquitur*?" Daren says.

"Latin for *the thing speaks for itself.*"

"Describe the function of *res ipsa* in tort law." Daren's staring at her, though the words he's spoken sound like something read.

"Don't you sound like a lawyer," Elise says.

"Don't I," Daren says.

"*Res ipsa,*" Elise says, "has to do with a presumption of negligence, whether an accident was someone's fault."

"Right," Daren says and looks away. Then he looks back. "You know Toby and I came up with kind of a joke about *res ipsa*—the whole thing sounds like Ray Sips a Low Quitter. Like a drink some guy named Ray might have."

"A Low Quitter," Elise says. "That's funny." She knows why he's changed the subject: he's married, and Elise and Daren are sleeping together. Fault is not something he wants to think about.

Outside, shouts of the neighborhood children rise in the air and the drone of insects, tires on asphalt, fill the hot afternoon. Elise and Daren move together on her bed; she's on top, looking over her shoulder at the mirror he set against the back of the closed door, watching him slide in and out between her spread legs as she raises and lowers herself above him.

She looks down at him, into his huge pupils. "We're very bad," she says.

"Yeah," he says. His hands press against her hips, holding her down as his back arches, his eyes close. "Very bad," he whispers.

Sometimes, staring in the bathroom mirror when she wakes or before she goes to bed at night, she recites a scrap from the litany of law she and Daren have been trying to cram into their brains. "The duty of care a landowner owes to trespassers is—" "The elements of adverse possession require that the claimant's possession be hostile, exclusive, for the length of time required statutorily—" Other times she carries on a conversation with her reflection. This reminds Elise of her mother, ironing; Elise would watch her mother waving the bottle of starch and muttering aloud, "So I said, 'What difference does it make? I mean, really, who cares?' " "What are you doing?" Elise asked once. "Thinking out loud," her mother said.

After she'd thrown up, Elise looked at herself in the mirror. *I should be studying harder and not sitting around drinking and screwing a married man.* She watched her lips form the words *screwing* and *married man.* These two facts are ones she tries not to think about, afraid that in the finite space of her brain there's only room for the duties, elements, and statutes she has to memorize for the bar.

Yesterday, Daren's wife called, looking for him. He'd gone to the liquor store on Twenty-seventh Street to get a bottle of wine.

"Sally," Elise said, "he's out at the library, running off some old exams, then I think he was going over to Toby's." She tried to combine the facts she knew of Sally—blond, short, impatient—into a cohesive whole. Sally was probably in the kitchen, holding the phone against her shoulder, wiping down the counter. "Do you want me to have him call you if he comes back?"

"No, I'll just see him when he gets home," Sally said, cheerful, oblivious. Elise didn't think Sally could tell she was drunk.

Later in the afternoon, Daren's friend Toby—a fellow Phi Delt who'd graduated from law school at the University of Kansas and was back in Lincoln to take the bar—comes over with the property outline he's been working on. This visit is part of the routine that's evolved in the month before the bar; Elise and Daren study together for most of the day, then Toby stops by and they sit around, complaining, and have a beer.

"Jesus Christ," Toby says. "It's not like the exam tests you over anything that has to do with real life—it's not like you have to give a client an answer the minute he tells you the problem. You say, 'Maybe we've got a case. I'll get my law clerks to look into it.' "

"So that should be the only answer we have to know," Elise says, finishing her beer and standing. "We just need to know how to say, 'I'll get my law clerks to look into it.' " She points at Daren's and Toby's bottles. "More beer?"

"Not for me," Toby says. "I've got to go over that Civ Pro shit again tonight."

"I'll have another one," Daren says.

Toby has the front door open when Elise returns from the kitchen with two Bud Lights. "Don't get drunk, you guys," he says.

"Of course not," Daren says. "We'll go over the Civ Pro section, then we can talk about it tomorrow or Tuesday."

"Okay," Toby says.

Elise and Daren don't study; instead they get drunk. With each beer, the nightmare of the bar exam—which is, after all, only four days away—fades into something smaller and more manageable: a bad dream . . . a dream . . . *it's a while away, we'll do fine,* they tell each other after the fifth beer. . . . *Who cares if we flunk, we can always take it again in December.*

\*      \*      \*

Elise and Daren became friends a few weeks before graduation. She'd known his name, but she'd never had a conversation with him until Waco Day, a traditional event: the law school seniors rented a bus to take them to a bar called The Sweet Hereafter in Waco, Nebraska, where they did their best to drink the place dry. On the ride home, Elise found herself sitting next to Daren. They were both drunk, like everyone else on the bus, and he started telling her about his wife: she seemed nuts, he said, withdrawn, angry, refusing to talk. He didn't know why. They'd been married six months and things seemed to go wrong from the start.

"She just gets so mad when I don't get the dishes done right after dinner—I tell her I have to study, you know, I'll do them before I go to bed but she still gets mad."

"Hm," Elise said. She was conscious, on the one hand, that everything he was saying was a cliché—*my wife doesn't understand me* was a line she'd heard in dozens of movies—but on the other hand, she'd never known someone her own age, twenty-six, who was married and having problems: up to this point, all her friends were single or if they were married, they acted like everything was perfect.

Law school seemed to be made up of sudden, violently intimate friendships—you'd sit by someone in contracts and then you'd be on the phone every night for two hours, talking about Professor Walter's chicken hypothetical or Professor Walter's alleged affairs with students—and inside jokes: impressions of the professors' voices, other students. Sometimes a word: *Tortfeased,* for instance. Or *Palsgraf,* a famous case. So Elise wasn't entirely surprised when, after Waco Day, Daren called her to ask about the tax review session on Saturday, or when they ended up going to Madsen's to shoot pool after the review. They talked about torts, which had been the class they'd both liked best freshman year. "I love *Palsgraf*," Daren said, shooting at and missing the eight ball. "I'm going to get a dog and name him Palsgraf."

Leaning on her cue, Elise tried to remember the case—it had something to do with a train, a porter, and a traveler carrying a sack of fireworks. Boarding the train, the traveler dropped the fireworks (or did he hand the sack to the porter, who dropped it?). The fireworks exploded, causing a chain reaction of damages: a scale at the far end of the train station fell over and landed on someone's ankle. Ultimately what remained in her mind about *Palsgraf* was chaos—sparks, fire, flames, and the question of blame: whose fault was this mess?

"Do you want to study for the bar together?" Daren asked.

Elise swallowed; she'd heard horror stories about the bar exam—*Buddy Mitchell was on* Law Review *and he took the bar twice and failed it, he just choked. I heard some girl from the class of '84 had a job with Barston Edward lined up but they dumped her after she failed the bar and now she's selling real estate*—and in her own life, the exam loomed as such an obstacle that it precluded any idea of what would happen afterward: she had to get a job, of course, act like an adult in high heels and suits, but the exam seemed like a wall she couldn't see beyond until she walked right up to it. She imagined this was how prisoners who've planned an escape from jail must feel. There's the escape—then what? "Sure," Elise said. She leaned over the table, aimed at the eight ball, and watched it roll into the corner pocket.

"I owe you a beer for that," Daren said.

They split a pitcher and watched the sky darken outside the windows. Daren walked Elise to her car and she was only a little surprised when he said, "You're so nice," and kissed her.

They began studying together in June. Daren arrived at Elise's apartment with his BarBri books and a six-pack. The air conditioner wasn't working and they slumped against the wall in the living room, deciding who'd outline what, drawing up a schedule, holding the bottles of beer against their faces and necks.

"I hate tax," Elise said. "I mean, Cezzarini finding the money in the piano was interesting, but the rest of it's just too much math."

"I know," Daren said. "Maybe we can get Toby to outline it."

"Good idea." Elise wrote *Toby* on the list of outline assignments and reached for another beer. All the windows were open but no air stirred through the room; her skin felt damp, as if she'd just stepped out of the shower. "Jesus, it's hot."

"I know," Daren said. He'd been sitting a few feet away from her but scooted over like a crab. He set down his beer and touched her neck with his fingers; they felt cold, removed from his body. Chills bloomed on her arms.

"Mm," Elise said. It was the first time he'd touched her since they kissed in Madsen's parking lot; she shut her eyes, thinking vaguely of cost-benefit analysis, the cost of an affair versus whatever benefit it might confer—but ultimately he's the one with something to lose, he's the one who's married, she's just an innocent bystander drinking coffee under a window when a piano falls out on top of her.

By the beginning of July, Daren and Elise are spending almost all their time together, studying, or drinking, or in bed; he leaves her apartment at midnight, goes home to sleep, and returns around ten the next morning. Elise imagines the conversation if his wife complains: Daren, his voice low but firm— *I've got to study*—and the underlying implication: *Do you want me to stay home and fail? Then where'll we be?*

Daren arrives in the morning of Bar Day minus 3 and Elise—showered, legs shaved—lets him in the apartment and fixes coffee. She feels calm in the mornings, cheerful, hardly ever hungover though she suspects she should since they've been drinking so much.

"Get this," Daren says, stirring sugar into his coffee.

"Hm?" Elise says.

"This morning, Sally was in the kitchen before she went to work—I guess she didn't hear me when I got up and so I was right behind her before she knew I was there—"

"Yeah?"

"She was looking at a checkbook, at the balance sheet. It wasn't our checkbook—all the entries were in her writing and the balance was over five thousand dollars."

"Five thousand?" Elise says. Sally would've been dressed for her job—she was an accountant—in a blue suit, probably, her blond hair pinned against the back of her head. Or maybe Sally had an efficient short haircut. Hearing Daren, she'd shut the checkbook, slid it into her purse. "What do you think she's planning to do with it?"

"I don't know," Daren says. "Divorce me, maybe?"

Would it be better to feel hope at the word *divorce,* or anxiety? The thought of Daren being single makes Elise a little nervous. Would she actually want to date him? There's an element of silliness to his personality she finds a little distasteful. She remembers one time: Elise and Daren walked into The Mill, a coffee house frequented by beatnik writer types, not law students. While Elise ordered coffee, Daren picked up one of the mugs that lined the walls and said in a wacky, nasal voice, "Coffee, tea or me?" He glanced around, waving the mug. "Coffee, tea or me?" Everyone in the coffee shop stared disdainfully. Elise smiled, gritting her teeth.

This is what she'd have to accept if they were dating: public embarrassment, and sober.

"Don't be crazy," Elise says. "Maybe she's saving up for a car and it's a surprise."

They take their coffee into the study and spend three hours reading torts questions.

> Paulsen was eating in a diner when he began to choke on a piece of meat that had lodged in his throat. Is Peters, a physician sitting at a nearby table, obligated to render aid?

"Nope," Elise says. "No duty."

> Dave is a six-year-old boy who bullies younger children. His parents have encouraged him to be aggressive and tough. Dave, for no reason, knocked down, kicked, and severely injured Pete, a four-year-old. What is the most likely result if a claim has been asserted by Pete's parents against Dave's parents?

"Maybe they're liable for negligence?" Daren says.

"Bingo," Elise says.

By one o'clock, they're famished and feeling virtuous; in the kitchen, making lunch—turkey sandwiches and fruit—Daren says, "I think we're in pretty good shape."

"Yes," Elise says. "Another three hours this afternoon and we'll have torts under control."

"Ray sips a Low Quitter," Daren says.

"What would be in a Low Quitter?" Elise asks. "Would it be good or one of those gross drinks like an abortion?"

"Oh, it'd be good," Daren says. "Ray's not the kind of guy to drink something gross."

"We should make one," Elise says.

"All right," Daren says. "I'll make my interpretation of a Low Quitter, and you make yours. Then we'll decide which is best." They begin eating their sandwiches as they walk around the kitchen, gathering liquor and mixers.

"Dibs on the blender," Elise says. She opens a can of peaches, drops four in the blender, adds bourbon, vodka, sugar, ice.

Daren's mixing away on the bar, his back toward her. "Don't look," he says over his shoulder. "This is intellectual property."

Elise laughs. She blasts the blender, pulverizing everything together, and pours it into a tall glass. Not bad, she thinks after the first sip. "Done yet?" she asks Daren.

"Yep," he says. "It's a masterpiece."

"Let me try," she says.

"Shut your eyes," he tells her. "It's part of the test."

Obediently Elise shuts her eyes. "Here," he says. Elise drinks; it's her own version. "Now taste *this*," Daren says. The second Low Quitter is wonderful—it tastes slightly orange and slightly tart, like strawberries.

"Yum," Elise says. "I could drink that for breakfast." She opens her eyes. "What's in it?"

"Company secret," Daren says. He takes a drink. "I'll make you one."

"Okay," Elise says. They each have a Low Quitter while they finish their sandwiches, and another one for dessert. Elise begins to feel pleasantly dizzy.

"I'm too drunk to study now," Daren says. "Let's have another one."

"All right," Elise says. She lights a cigarette and leans back against the counter, idly trying to see around Daren's back to determine his Low Quitter ingredients.

"No peeking," he says.

"How could you tell?" Elise asks. "Besides, why won't you tell me?"

He turns, handing her a glass. "Just so I know something you want to."

"Now why would you want that?" Elise says.

"You're right," Daren says. "We should know the same things, so we both pass or we both fail." He walks over to her, takes the cigarette from between her fingers and taps it out. "Let's drink these in bed."

In bed Daren lies with his face between Elise's legs, pressing an ice cube from his drink against her and licking away the moisture as it melts. "Ray sips a Low Quitter," he says.

"Don't make me laugh," Elise tells him. Sweat breaks out on her face and she shuts her eyes, hears herself breathing hard in the quiet room, moves against his mouth, again, again.

Afterward, they have another Low Quitter and then Daren calls Sally, tells her he's going over to Toby's for dinner and to do some studying over there. He gives her a phone number that's two digits off in case she needs to reach him. Daren makes another batch of Low Quitters and announces they're out of vodka.

"Let's drink these," Elise says, "and then go to the store." She finds her keys, makes sure the blender's unplugged, and they walk outside.

Staggering down the street, Elise is momentarily awestruck that it's still light out, that the people in cars look through the windshields, sober, thoughtful; Elise feels like everyone's stereos should be blaring, they should be shouting, singing along.

"Jesus, I'm drunk," she says to Daren. "What'd you put in those Low Quitters, heroin?"

Daren laughs. They walk a few blocks through air scented with cut grass and gasoline. Elise sees fuzzy figures sitting on porches, hears dim snatches of conversation.

"Look out," Daren says, pulling her away from a tricycle sitting in the middle of the sidewalk. Elise trips, bumps into Daren, and he staggers a few feet. Swaying slightly, they look at the tricycle, a potential instrumentality of accident, innocent as the scale in *Palsgraf* before it fell.

"Close call," Elise says. They realign themselves and continue walking. The smell of gasoline and exhaust fills her sinuses and Elise is suddenly overcome with dizziness.

"I need to sit down," she says. She collapses onto the sidewalk, her back against the rough brick of the Towne Center Building, and shuts her eyes. They're close to one of the busiest intersections in town; she's aware of little drafts as cars drive past.

"Are you okay?" Daren says, but Elise knows he's almost as bad off as she is, there's not much he can do. "Do you want me to get you a Coke or a beer or something?"

"A beer," Elise says and begins to laugh—the idea of beer as a step in the direction of sobriety. She's laughing when a bike cop rolls up. He squeezes and releases the bicycle's brakes a couple of times before he speaks.

"What's going on?"

Elise knows she should stop laughing but she can't. "A beer!" she says.

"We're not driving, sir," Daren says.

"You know there are laws against public intoxication," the cop says.

"Of course I know there're *laws*," Elise says, struggling to her feet, scraping her elbow on the building. "We're law students, of course we know." She looks down at her elbow. "Ow."

"Elise," Daren says.

"Oh," the bike cop says. "Law students."

Cops, Elise thinks: there's an established animosity between cops and attorneys, the professor talked about it in Crim Law—cops jealous of lawyers' education, power, higher pay; cops fucking up the simplest things like making an arrest and forgetting to recite *Miranda* rights, the suspect freed to drive drunk, steal, murder. Now, of course, this particular cop is in a position to make life difficult for Elise, and she'll think later that it's a miracle, really—because there's a small part of her mind saying *Let him know what you think, he's just a stupid cop*—that she doesn't tell him off.

"I'm sorry, sir, I'm taking some allergy medication, you know you're not supposed to operate heavy machinery or anything while you're on it—"

"Elise," Daren says. He holds out his left hand toward the cop. Elise sees his wedding band and realizes what he's doing: he's trying to show the cop they're legitimate, they're married, although why marriage might be a defense to public intoxication isn't clear to her. "My wife," he says. "She's a little worried about the bar exam, you know. . . . She's not herself." He takes her elbow. "Really, there won't be any trouble," he says to the cop. "We're almost home."

They start to walk away, testing the water, since the cop hasn't officially released them—but he hasn't officially detained them, either. They move slowly, carefully, expecting the cop to yell *Stop,* but he doesn't. Elise is conscious of walking and breathing. When Daren glances back and reports that the cop has cycled off, they turn down an alley, sneak back to the liquor store, and pick up another bottle of vodka. Walking home—it's dusk now—Elise feels like a prisoner who's successfully escaped: safe, saved.

"Close call," Daren whispers, trying not to bump against her.

Close call: maybe it's a sign, Elise thinks the next morning. Two days left until the test. She and Daren study hard, spend eight hours quizzing each other, until they're both hoarse from reading questions out loud. Toby stops by, they talk about civil procedure—depositions, interrogatories, dates for filing. It's dark when Toby leaves. Elise and Daren take a quilt out to the balcony and slide out of their clothes. There's a faint touch of breeze, their arms and legs seem almost invisible. Though the comforter's thick, Elise is aware of cement underneath; it reminds her of their first night, on the living room floor, both of them sweating, carpet scraping at her elbows to reveal new skin, pink and painful when she touched it.

The room where the bar exam is held is in the University Union, and, walking in, surveying the lines of tables, coolers of water in back, Elise thinks she may have been in this room before: senior prom, silver crepe paper strung along the walls, romantic darkness, the noise of the band and conversation filling the air.

Now, the air is sterile, too bright. It's ten of eight. Groups of people cluster together, talking in low voices, cracking knuckles, gesturing. It's a little like a class reunion; Elise nods and smiles at people she hasn't seen in the two months since graduation, evaluating who's gotten tan and—the tan suggesting frivolity, leisure time—may not pass, and who looks prepared. Daren moves behind her, she hears him speaking. She wonders if anyone knows about them, or suspects: Do they stand too close together, does she smile at him too much?

By the second day of the test, Elise has other things to worry about beyond what people might or might not be thinking. She's answered two hundred multiple-choice questions; her nose is filled with the smell of lead, the start of a headache licks behind her eyes, her hands feel sticky. Now, the final afternoon, they've been answering essay questions. She raises her hand to go to the bathroom and a woman proctor walks up to where Elise sits and nods. She follows Elise down the hall and stands in the bathroom, waiting for Elise to come out of the stall. It's like being in jail, Elise thinks. At the sink, she looks in the mirror at the proctor, who's gazing up at a corner of the ceiling. Back in the room, Elise reads the last question:

> Assume that Congress in its quest to balance the budget has passed a special tax on income from the sale of wine, beer, and distilled spirits payable by any entity who derives such income. South Carolina, Iowa, and some other states have established state liquor stores as the only establishments where liquor may be purchased. The governors of these states believe that the income derived from liquor store sales should be immune from taxation. As the attorney general, you are asked by the attorneys general of the states affected to join with them as *amicus curiae* in the suit urging that taxation is improper.
>
> WHAT WOULD YOUR RESPONSE BE TO THE MERITS OF THEIR CASE? WHAT IS THE BASIS FOR YOUR RESPONSE?

Jesus, Elise thinks, and her heart begins to pound heavily: she has no idea. Be calm, she tells herself, though her brain refuses to be fooled by abstractions. She really has no clue. State-owned liquor stores? None of the liquor stores she and Daren have gone to this summer were state-owned. But that's not the issue. In the room around her, pencils scratch away, the girl in front of her gently adjusts an earplug, she hears bodies shifting. *What if I don't pass?*

Daren's a couple of rows ahead of her, and she looks at the back of his head, thinking of afternoons on damp sheets—only two days ago, she'd heard his voice: *Are you close? Do you like that?*—the two of them driven into bed as a distraction, the affair giving them something else to think about as well as an excuse—Well, if we don't pass it's because *you know*—

Elise looks down at the question again. WHAT WOULD YOUR RESPONSE BE TO THE MERITS OF THEIR CASE? The thing with Daren was a big mistake, she thinks; maybe if she'd been alone, she would've gone over the tax section more, maybe she'd be facing this question and thinking *Oh, an easy one.* She presses the pencil against her lips; she's not scared now—maybe whatever she answers might not really matter. So she places the point of the pencil on the paper and watches her hand begin to move. The first sentence she writes is "This question is somewhat taxing."

She finishes early, twenty minutes till five. There's no point in sitting, agonizing over her last, silly answer so she raises her hand; the proctor collects the blue book, nods at Elise, and she stands, picks up her pencils, candy wrappers, pushes the chair against the table, and leaves the room.

She could (should?) wait for Daren right outside the room, but she feels herself forgetting about him; he exists now in the corner of her mind, like a task completed: Oh yes, I did that. She wants to be outdoors, away from the artificial air. She walks down marble stairs, through the heavy doors, sunlight warming her face.

She sits on one of the wide stone railings that line the steps and lights a cigarette. Waiting for Daren and Toby to come outside so they can go to Cliff's to celebrate, she looks around the campus, which is quiet; late on a summer afternoon, almost everyone has found more desirable places to be.

Elise presses the fingers of her right hand into the back of her neck, into a hard knot of cramped muscle. "Ow," she says out loud. Tipping her head to one side, straightening her shoulders, she becomes aware of a monotonous tapping noise, like cracked knuckles, and sees a woman sitting in a parked car across the street. The woman holds one arm out the window and hits the side of the car with her hand. She's blond, she might be Elise's age or a little younger. Could she be Sally, here to meet Daren—a surprise—after the test?

When Elise raises the cigarette to her lips, she sees her own fingers up close, quivering. The woman tilts the rearview mirror and applies lipstick. She's wearing a T-shirt—surely it's not Sally, she's still at work. Surely.

Retribution, Elise thinks, staring at the car, the last essay question rolling through her mind. Was that last question her punishment? Will she end up failing the exam? Or will her punishment be a phone call from Sally some afternoon, Sally's voice saying *I know what you've done?*

Perhaps the retribution is knowing that she's culpable, even though Elise bites gently on her lower lip, willing herself to unlearn the way Daren is in bed, willing the act undone. The woman in the car glances at the Union, then looks toward the Figi house. Elise shuts her eyes and rubs the back of her neck again, hard enough to make goosebumps rise on her arms. *Res ipsa loquitur,* she says to herself, turning the inside joke back outside, back into what it's supposed to be: a presumption of negligence. Negligence makes her think of *Palsgraf,* though she still can't remember the holding of the case—was it something about foreseeability and causation? Against her eyelids she watches the fireworks fall, their first burst of flame, sizzling noise of explosion, gasps from the ticket takers, the scale standing upright. In that significant moment before the accident, with fireworks exploding over their heads in brilliant streamers of color, Elise wonders if the porter and the traveler looked up, awestruck— before fingers started pointing *It's your fault*—and watched as the train station filled with sulfur and light.

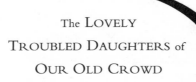

The LOVELY
TROUBLED DAUGHTERS of
OUR OLD CROWD

*John Updike*

**JOHN UPDIKE** was born in 1932 in Shillington, Pennsylvania. He graduated from Harvard College in 1954, and spent a year in England on the Knox Fellowship, at the Ruskin School of Drawing and Fine Art in Oxford. From 1955 to 1957 he was a member of the staff of *The New Yorker,* to which he has contributed poems, short stories, essays, and book reviews. His fiction has won the Pulitzer Prize, the National Book Award, the American Book Award, and the National Book Critics Circle Award. His recent books include *Golf Dreams, In the Beauty of the Lilies,* and *The Afterlife.* He has lived since 1957 in Massachusetts.

WHY DON'T THEY get married? You see them around town, getting older, little spinsters already, pedalling bicycles to their local jobs or walking up the hill by the rocks with books in their arms. Annie Langhorne, Betsey Clay, Damaris Wilcombe, Mary Jo Addison: we've known them all since they were two or three, and now they've reached their mid-twenties, back from college, back from Year Abroad, grown women but not going anywhere, not New York or San Francisco or even Boston, just hanging around here in this little town letting the seasons wash over them, walking the same streets where they grew up, hanging in the shadows of their safe old homes.

On the edge of a Wilcombe lawn party, their pale brushed heads like candles burning in the summer sunlight, a ribbon or a plastic barrette attached for the occasion—I can see them still, their sweet pastel party dresses and their feet bare in the grass, those slender little-girl feet, with bony tan toes, that you feel would leave rabbit tracks in the dew. Damaris and Annie, best friends then and now, had been coaxed into carrying hors d'oeuvres around; they carried the tray cockeyed, their wrists were so weak, the devilled eggs slipping, their big eyes with their pale-blue whites staring upward so solemnly at your grinning grown-up face as you took your devilled egg and smiled to be encouraging. We were in our late twenties then, young at being old—the best of times. The summer smells of bug spray on the lawn and fresh mint in the gin; the young wives healthy and brown in their sundresses, their skin glowing warm through the cotton; the children still small and making a flock in the uncut grass beyond the lawn, running and tumbling, their pastel dresses getting stained with green, their noise coming and going in the field as a kind of higher-pitched echo of ours, creating their own world underfoot as the liquor and the sunlight soaked in and the sky filled with love.

I can still see Betsey and my own daughter the night we first met the Clays. They had just moved to town. A cousin of Maureen's had gone to school with my wife and sent us a note. We dropped by to give them the name of our dentist and doctor and happened to hit it off. April, it must have been, or May. Cocktails dragged on into dark and Maureen brought a pickup dinner out to the patio table. The two baby girls that had never met before—not much more than two years old, they must have been—were put to sleep in the same bed. Down they came into the dark, down into the cool air outdoors, hand in hand out of this house strange to the two of them, Betsey a white ghost in her nightie, her voice so eerie and thin but distinct. "See moon?" she said. Unable to sleep, they had seen the moon from the bed. The Clays had moved from the city, where maybe the moon was not so noticeable. "See moon?": her voice thin and distinct as a distant owl's call. And of course they were right, there the moon was, lopsided and sad-faced above the trees just beginning to blur into leaf. Time (at last) to go home.

Now Betsey works at the paint-and-linoleum store on Second Street and gives guitar lessons on the side. She fell in love with her elderly married music teacher at Smith and went about as far as she could go with classical guitar, even to Spain for a year. When the Episcopal church sponsored a refugee Cuban family last winter, they called in Betsey for her Spanish. She lives with her mother, in that same house where she saw the moon, a gloomy place now that Maureen has closed off half the rooms to save on heat. The Clays broke up it must be all of ten years ago. There were some lovely times had on that patio.

Betsey sings in the Congregational choir alongside Mary Jo Addison, who after that bad spell of anorexia in her teens has gotten quite plump again. She has those dark eyebrows of her mother's, strange in a freckled fair face—shaped flat across and almost meeting in the middle. Both the Addisons have remarried and left town, but Mary Jo rents two rooms above the Rites of Passage travel agency and collects antiques and reads books of history, mostly medieval. My daughter invited her over for Christmas dinner but she said no, she'd rather just sit cozy by her own fire, surrounded by her things. "Her nice old things," was how it was reported.

Evelyn Addison liked nice things, too, but in her case they had to be modern—D.R. sofas covered in Haitian cotton, Danish end tables with rounded edges, butterfly chairs. Where are they, I wonder, all those heavy iron frames for the worn-out canvas slings of those butterfly chairs we used to sit on? A man could straddle one of the corners, but a woman just had to dump herself in, backside first, and hope that when the time came to go her husband would be around to pull her out. They had an authentic 1690 house, the Addisons, on Salem Street, and curiously enough their modern furniture fit right into those plain old rooms with the exposed beams and the walk-in fireplaces with the big wrought-iron spits and dark brick nooks the Puritans used to bake bread in. It may be that's what Mary Jo is trying to get back to with her antiques. She dresses that way, too: dusty-looking and prim, her hair pulled into a tight roll held by a tortoiseshell pin. Her mother's auburn hair, but without the spark rinsed into it. None of these girls, the daughters of our old crowd, seem to wear makeup.

The New Year's right after Fred had moved out, I remember walking Evelyn home from the Langhornes' up Salem Street just before morning, an inch of new snow on the sidewalk and everything silent except for her voice, going on and on about Fred. There had been Stingers, and she could hardly walk, and I wasn't much better. The housefronts along Salem calm as ghosts, and the new snow like mica reflecting the streetlights. We climbed her porch steps, and that living room, with its wide floorboards, her tree still up, and a pine wreath hung on an oak peg in the fireplace lintel, hit me as if we had walked smack into an old-fashioned children's book. The smell of a pine indoors or a certain glaze on wrapping paper will do that to me, or frost in the corner of a windowpane: spell Christmas. We sat together on the scratchy D.R. sofa so she could finish her tale about Fred and I could warm up for the long walk back. Day was breaking and suddenly Evelyn looked haggard; I was led to try to comfort her and right then, with Evelyn's long hair all over our faces, and her strong eyebrows right under my eyes, we heard from on high Mary Jo beginning to cough. We froze, the big old fireplace full of cold ashes sending out a little draft on our ankles and, from above, this coughing and coughing, scoopy and dry. Mary Jo, about fifteen she must have been then, and weakened by the anorexia, had caught a cold that had turned into walking pneumonia. Evelyn blamed Fred's leaving her for that, too—the pneumonia. Coughing and coughing, the child, and her mother in my arms smelling of brandy and tears and Christmas. She blamed Fred but I would have blamed him less than the environment; those old wooden houses are drafty.

Thinking of upstairs and downstairs, I think of Betsey Clay at the head of her stairs, no longer in a white nightie seeing the moon but in frilly lemon-colored pajamas, looking down at some party too loud for her to sleep through. We had come in from the patio and put on some old Twist records and there was no quiet way to play them. I was sitting on the floor somehow, with somebody, so the angle of my vision was low, and like a lesson in perspective the steps diminished up to her naked feet, too big to leave rabbit tracks now. For what seemed the longest time we looked at each other—she had her mother's hollow-eyed fragile look—until the woman I was with, and I don't think it was Maureen, felt my distraction and herself turned to look up the stairs, and Betsey scampered back toward her room.

Her room would have been like my daughter's in those years: Beatles posters, or maybe of the Monkees, and prize ribbons for horsemanship in local shows. And dolls and Steiff animals that hadn't been put away yet sharing the shelves with Signet editions of Melville and *Hard Times* and Camus assigned at day school. We were all so young, parents and children, learning it all together—how to grow up, how to deal with time—is what you realize now.

Those were the days when Harry Langhorne had got himself a motorcycle and would roar around and around the green on a Saturday night until the police came and stopped him, more or less politely. And the Wilcombes had put a hot tub on their second-story porch and had to run a steel column up for support lest we all go tumbling down naked some summer night. In winter, there was a lot of weekend skiing for the sake of the kids, and we would take over a whole lodge in New Hampshire: heaps of snowy boots and wet parkas in the corner under the moose head, over past the beat-up player piano, and rosy cheeks at dinner at the long tables, where ham with raisin sauce was always the main dish. Suddenly the girls, long-legged in their stretch pants, hair whipping around their faces as they skimmed to a stop at the lift lines, were women. At night, after the boys had crumped out or settled to Ping-Pong in the basement, the girls stayed up with us, playing Crazy Eights or Spit with the tattered decks the lodge kept on hand, taking sips from our cans of beer, until at last the weight of all that day's fresh air toppled everyone up toward bed, in reluctant bunches. The little rooms had dotted-swiss curtains and thick frost ferns on the windowpanes. The radiators dripped and sang. There was a dormitory feeling through the thin partitions, and shuffling and giggling in the hall on the way to the bathrooms, one for girls and one for boys. One big family. It was the children, really, growing unenthusiastic and resistant, who stopped the trips. That, and the divorces as they began to add up. Margaret and I are about the last marriage left; she says maybe we missed the boat, but can't mean it.

The beach picnics, and touch football, and the softball games in that big field the Wilcombes had. Such a lot of good times, and the kids growing up through them like weeds in sunshine; and now, when the daughters of people we hardly knew at all are married to stockbrokers or off in Oregon being nurses or in Mexico teaching agronomy, our daughters haunt the town as if searching for something they missed, taking classes in macramé or aerobic dancing, living with their mothers, wearing no makeup, walking up beside the rocks with books in their arms like a race of little nuns.

You can see their mothers in them—beautiful women, full of life. I saw Annie Langhorne at the train station the other morning and we had to talk for some minutes, mostly about the antique store Mary Jo wants to open up with Betsey, and apropos of the hopelessness of this venture she gave me a smile exactly like her mother's one of the times Louise and I said goodbye or faced the fact that we just weren't going to make it, she and I—pushing up the lower lip so her chin crinkled, that nice wide mouth of hers humorous but downturned at the corners as if to buckle back tears. Lou's exact same smile on little Annie, and it was like being in love again, when all the world is a hunt and the sight of the woman's car parked at a gas station or in the Stop & Shop lot makes your Saturday, makes your blood race and your palms go numb, the heart touching base.

But these girls. What are they hanging back for? What are they afraid of?

## PERMISSIONS

"Hairball" from *Wilderness Tips* by Margaret Atwood. Copyright © 1991 by O. W. Toad Limited. Used by permission of Doubleday, a division of Bantam Doubleday Dell Publishing Group, Inc. Also used by permission of the Canadian Publishers, McClelland & Stewart, Toronto.

"Adultery" from *Success Stories* by Russell Banks. Copyright © 1986 by Russell Banks. Reprinted by permission of HarperCollins Publishers, Inc.

"My Wild Life" by Abby Bardi. Copyright © *Quarterly West*. "My Wild Life" by Abby Bardi first appeared in *Quarterly West*.

"Flipflops" by Robert Boswell. Reprinted from *Dancing in the Movies* by Robert Boswell by permission of the University of Iowa Press. Copyright © 1985 by Robert Boswell.

"Ike and Nina" by T. Coraghessan Boyle. Copyright © 1982 by T. Coraghessan Boyle, from *Greasy Lake and Other Stories* by T. Coraghessan Boyle. Used by permission of Viking Penguin, a division of Penguin Books USA Inc.

"Ray Sips a Low Quitter" by Amy Knox Brown. Copyright © 1996 by Amy Knox Brown. "Ray Sips a Low Quitter" first appeared in *The Missouri Review* and is reprinted here by permission of the editors.

"The Year of Getting to Know Us" from *Emperor of the Air*. Copyright © 1988 by Ethan Canin. Reprinted by permission of Houghton Mifflin Company. All rights reserved.

"Dick York" by Max Garland. "Dick York" first appeared in *The Gettysburg Review*, volume 8, number 2, and is reprinted here by permission of the editors.

"Pie Dance" by Molly Giles. "Pie Dance" is reprinted from *Rough Translations* by Molly Giles. Copyright © by Molly Giles. Reprinted by permission of the publisher, the University of Georgia Press, Athens, Georgia.

"Secret" by Ivy Goodman. Copyright © by Ivy Goodman. First published in *Epoch,* volume 43, number 3, 1994 series. Reprinted by permission of the author.

"When Dogs Bark" by Charles W. Harvey, first printed in *Dispatches from the Front: Young Black Men on Love and Violence,* edited by Rohan Preston and Daniel Wideman, published by Viking, 1996.

"Goodness" by David Huddle. Copyright © 1996 by David Huddle. "Goodness" first appeared in *Five Points*.

"The First Snow" by Daniel Lyons. "The First Snow" is reprinted from *The Last Good Man,* by Daniel Lyons (Amherst: University of Massachusetts Press, 1993), copyright © 1993 by Daniel Lyons.

"Bitter Love" by Lynne McFall. Copyright © by Lynne McFall. First appeared in *Story,* Winter 1991.

"Spats" from *The Consolation of Nature*. Copyright © 1988 by Valerie Martin. Reprinted by permission of Houghton Mifflin Company. All rights reserved.

"Cleaning House" by Alyce Miller. Copyright © by Alyce Miller. "Cleaning House" first appeared in *Sonora Review*.

"The Middleman" from *The Middleman and Other Stories* by Bharati Mukherjee. Copyright © 1988 by Bharati Mukherjee. Used by permission of Grove/Atlantic, Inc. Also reprinted by permission of Penguin Books Canadian Limited.

"When Love in Autumn Blooms" by Gregg Palmer. Copyright © by Gregg Palmer. "When Love in Autumn Blooms" first appeared in *The Georgia Review*.

"The Wild" by Sara Powers. Copyright © by Sara Powers.

"Buoyancy" by Richard Russo. Copyright © by Richard Russo.

"A Hole in the Language" by Marly Swick. Reprinted from *A Hole in the Language* by Marly Swick by permission of the University of Iowa Press. Copyright © 1990 by Marly Swick.

"The Lovely Troubled Daughters of Our Old Crowd" from *Trust Me* by John Updike. Copyright © 1987 by John Updike. Reprinted by permission of Alfred A. Knopf, Inc.

"Silent Partners" from *Terrible Kisses*. Published by Simon and Schuster. Copyright © 1989 by Robley Wilson, Jr. Reprinted by permission of the author.

"No Pain Whatsoever" by Richard Yates. Copyright © by The Estate of Richard Yates. Reprinted by permission of the Ned Leavitt Agency.